GABRIEL

THE MURDER SERIES

FOR THE MURDER

CITY OWL
PRESS

FOR THE MURDER
The Murder, Book 1

CITY OWL PRESS
www.cityowlpress.com

Cover Design by MiblArt. All stock photos licensed appropriately.

Edited by Danielle DeVor.

For information on subsidiary rights, please contact the publisher at info@cityowlpress.com.

Print Edition ISBN: 978-1-64898-121-0

Digital Edition ISBN: 978-1-64898-122-7

Printed in the United States of America

To Stacy,
for not giving up on me.

PRAISE FOR GABRIELLE ASH

"*For the Murder* is a wonderfully creative, unique, fast-paced story about a crow shifter searching for a murder to belong to and an angel in service to a demon searching for freedom he never expected to find. Throw in some of Hell's generals, a magic blade, a boy possessed by a cat demon, and werewolves and you might get the idea of how deliciously fun this story is! The chemistry between Sasha and Diana sizzles. Sasha is the reluctant hero we all need and Diana is so beautifully portrayed as a woman abandoned over and over who finally finds a family. I think Natsu, the cat demon, is my favorite though! I'm so thankful that Gabrielle Ash provided me with an early copy of this book. Highly recommend!" – *Jess K. Hardy, author of Love in the Time of Wormholes, Missing Charlie, and The Bench*

"Delivering humor, intrigue, romance, and supernatural drama, *The Family Cross* is a wickedly original story that's impossible to put down." – *Kat Turner, author of Hex, Love, and Rock & Roll, and Blood Sugar*

"With a gift for painting vivid descriptions, a unique cast of supernatural creatures in a crowded genre, and seamlessly blending the paranormal with the real world, Gabrielle Ash hits the ground running with this gritty new urban fantasy series in *For the Murder*." – *S.L. Choi, author of Bad Girls Drink Blood*

"*The Family Cross* by Gabrielle Ash is a fun, fast-paced urban fantasy. Part detective story, part princess-meets-henchman, Ash harmoniously blends dark and light moments as the two main characters fight off monsters, maneuver corporate politics, and evade death. Fans of *Supernatural* will be delighted." – *Sarina Dahlan, author of Reset*

"*The Family Cross* is a delight. Action packed and filled with engaging characters, this story hooked me and wouldn't let go. Melding a world of diamonds and deceit with a darker underbelly of paranormal hit men and saviours, Gabrielle Ash offers us an enticing first book in what I hope will be a long series." – *Clementine Fraser, author of Dust Bound and Siren's Call*

"*The Family Cross* is an enthralling debut filled with unexpected twists and fast-paced action. A story of intrigue and vengeance and the dark side of Manhattan, it kept me hooked until the very end." – *Jessa Graythorne, author of Fireborn*

"Ash's debut is a gripping and imaginative tale into the paranormal. Readers will be taken on a thrilling ride filled with intrigue, tender moments, and unexpected twists and turns. *The Family Cross* will captivate your senses and have you screaming for more." – *J.E. McDonald, author of the Wickwood Chronicles*

ONE

DIANA

All crow shifters had the same eyes—dark brown, practically black. Unless the crow was old, anyway. Her father, despite all his mistakes, somehow still lived. His irises, once so dark they looked like caves, were now slate gray.

He leaned forward and propped his elbows on the old desk across from him. "But this knife can kill anything."

Diana Van Doren narrowed her eyes at her father lounging in a decrepit chair. Charles couldn't ignore shiny objects, especially expensive ones. But his crippling addiction aside, she didn't much care to be used in his schemes to acquire them either. "Most knives can."

"No." Charles's chest rose and fell in a steady, quiet wave. His salt-and-pepper hair had been swept back in an arc, which made the collar of his thick coat seem impossibly tall. Charles Van Doren was important, damn it, and everyone around ought to know. "It can kill...*anything*."

It took longer than she liked to admit, but when her father's true meaning sank in, it rendered her immobile.

"You're joking." The words left her mouth in a whisper so faint she almost doubted she spoke at all. Had her father actually located something with use beyond lining his pockets? "There's no way. No such thing exists."

"It does, and I found it. Forged in the fires of Hell. Very old and very powerful."

The chill that raked over her arms had nothing to do with the breeze flitting past the broken glass in the window frame and into the room. A knife that could kill any sentient being? If they got a hold of something like that, then all their problems would be solved.

"Where did you find it?" Diana dared ask. The shallow ceiling seemed to creep closer with every breath as the possibilities seeped into the wrinkles of her brain. She could be safe. Finally.

"Dallas," her mother, Amelia, spoke up from her place on the wall before taking a few strides toward her husband.

Diana had often wondered why her mother tolerated her father all these years, but she supposed Amelia had no choice. Magic made murders. Once a crow shifter was bound to a murder, they were always bound to that murder. Being kicked out of the flock didn't change that. Her mother had once described the separation from the rest of the crows as carving out half her heart and leaving it behind in a field. Diana figured staying with Charles was a way to assuage the pain.

When she said nothing, Amelia cleared her throat. "The knife is being auctioned."

Dallas. A couple hours by car, but shorter by air. She'd be able to get there quickly, but once she had the knife, it would be impossible to fly all the way back. She'd have to drive, which would keep her in the open longer.

A demonic knife that could kill anything. It would be going for thousands, if not millions, of dollars. Dollars they did not have.

Diana pulled the rest of her inky hair over her shoulder and started to braid it, an action done more out of a desire to busy her hands than a real need. "Auctioned?"

"Some anthropologist has it. He's dying though, allegedly from cancer, and he wants the funds to pay for treatment." Her father sighed and steepled his fingers as he leaned on the desk. Even though he no longer remained a leader in the murder's assembly, his arrogant demeanor followed him. "He's invited people in his immediate circle and work colleagues."

Diana froze midbraid, her fingers stiff with irritation.

"We've...arranged for you to meet with someone on the list to gain admittance tomorrow night." Amelia tucked a thick lock of hair behind her ear.

"I'm sure you have." Annoyed, Diana finished her braid with a snort.

"All you've got to do is steal the knife and bring it back. Your mother and I wouldn't survive the auction, or we'd go." Charles's voice, soft and pleading, rattled down her ear canals. Her father had always been a good liar. "We can fix this. All of it. We just need that knife."

She didn't even try to fight rolling her eyes. Everything her father stole carried promises of a new future. Except when they didn't. Which was always.

"If we don't do something soon, we will be found. Amir called and told me the demon is looking for us, and she's close. Lead Crow and the assembly will follow." Charles paused and looked down at his hands folded in his lap. She hadn't seen true remorse on his face since he got kicked out of the murder, and their exile was entirely his fault. One didn't swindle a demon and walk away unscathed. "This knife will get us back into the good graces of the murder. They'll have no choice but to allow us back. Let us fly with them again. Hell, they might even let you in officially."

Her father's voice showcased none of the seriousness such a claim deserved.

Diana reluctantly met his gaze, and her father's smirk grew. She wouldn't have taken the bait if he hadn't dangled the one thing she really wanted right before her eyes. "How do you figure? I'm sure Lead Crow and the assembly have a healthy arsenal already."

"They do." Lead Crow, the head of her parent's old flock, had always planned for the worst. "But if we don't rejoin the murder on good terms soon, we're dead...or worse. We have to try."

"Please, Diana." The desperation in Amelia's voice didn't mesh with her stern face. "We've been hiding away for years. I wish to see your sister...to go home."

She frowned. The last time her father had planned something stupid, she'd been shot through the wing. It had taken weeks to heal, and the rug she'd stolen had decidedly not been worth it. "You think I don't? I'd love to be home. To see Olivia again. But I'm not the one who landed us here, and I'm having a hard time getting excited for a heist that might end with me dead or left behind even if I succeed."

Amelia's gaze flitted to the floor, and she tugged at the thick fibers on the hem of her sweater. As frustrating as she was, her mother had lost a child to her father's mistakes. Two, if they counted the first years of Diana's life.

She bit the inside of her cheek. Olivia had been welcomed into the murder at a young age. Barely a toddler. Her magic connected with the flock in a way Diana had yet to experience. However, that bond was the only thing that kept Olivia safe. Lead Crow allowed her to stay with them since she was a child, instead of forcing her to run from a demon for five years like her.

Diana swallowed her bitterness. Or tried to, anyway. Maybe if her parents hadn't neglected her in infancy, she could've been like Olivia.

"Diana." Her father stood up again, face soft. "If you get this blade, I'm almost certain the murder would accept you...bond with you. They'd be fools not to."

A sickness swirled in the pit of her stomach. She did miss her sister. Terribly. But throwing herself into danger again when she potentially wouldn't get what she wanted in the end was hard to do.

However, she was twenty-eight, alone, and running out of options. If she hoped to finally be welcomed into the murder with open arms, she had to prove herself worthy of the murder's magic. Maybe getting this knife to fight off the demon pursuing them would do it.

Diana took a breath. A lone crow was a dead crow, and she had no intention of dying.

TWO

SASHA

Sasha Sokolov was a patient man. He'd waited years on recruits for his employer to cross his path and months for magical artifacts to drop at his feet. When one could see bits of the future, patience was often easy to come by.

But patience did not come easy tonight.

He drummed his fingers along the steering wheel of his rental car. While no stranger to the United States, he loathed the South. Loathed Texas in particular. It was too damn hot. He preferred the cooler climate of Chelyabinsk. His childhood home near the Urals was a world away from the hellish nightmare that was a Texas summer. While it was winter, Texas winters were the equivalent of Russian summers, and he found himself walking the street without his suit jacket several times in the past hour despite everyone else wearing earmuffs and gloves.

Where the hell is she? Sasha glanced at the clock on the dash. If his visions were more cooperative, he'd have a better idea of when his boss would show up.

Too bad he couldn't see everything that would happen to him. Only the dangerous parts.

The parking lot he'd found in the center of downtown Dallas was empty save for his sedan. He glanced at the clock again before pulling a cigarette from the pack in his coat pocket. Last cigarette and he'd call it. If she couldn't be bothered to show up on time—

A familiar burn in the back of his mind stopped his fingers from curling around the gear shift. Sasha swallowed and closed his eyes, fighting the urge to grimace as a wrinkled face, gray hair, and red irises flitted behind his eyelids.

Great. He'd have to tread carefully. At least she'd finally shown up.

He opened the door and swung his legs out, dress shoes scraping the asphalt as a crisp breeze sliced across his cheeks. Having been cursed from the womb with a healthy dose of angel blood, it had taken Sasha until his late teens to figure out how his visions worked. Be it from a fist, a gun, or a nasty set of teeth, his mind always warned him of the coming dangers, and seeing his demon boss, Madame, skulking about in the depths of his mind certainly didn't bode well for him. Despite his angelic lineage, he could still die if the circumstances were right, and Madame would make sure that death was painful.

He put the cigarette to his lips as he shut the car door. If Madame didn't need him so much, he'd be more worried. Sasha inhaled a drag when a familiar figure approached from a nearby alley.

"I'd hoped you were still here," Madame called out to him as she adjusted her fur coat along her neck. She tried to play human and failed miserably. Too robotic. Too stiff. Not to mention demons were walking furnaces—she didn't need the coat.

"May I ask what kept you?" Sasha kept his annoyance from his face. If Madame was angry, and his vision indicated she might be, a clear face was necessary.

"Caught wind of a pesky bird hiding close." Madame narrowed her eyes and looked up at him. "Van Doren is nearby."

Ah. Van Doren.

"And when I get him, I'm going to kill his family and tar him with their feathers for making a fool of me." Madame flexed her fingers at her sides, tremors racked her arms, and the skin along her cheekbones began to peel away from her human exterior.

If he weren't careful, she'd kill him for simply standing there. Demons had a nasty penchant for violence and didn't discriminate. The elusive crow shifter and con artist, Charles Van Doren, had no idea what he'd done when he'd swindled Madame. People didn't deceive her unless they'd already come to terms with their god and picked a cemetery plot.

"You'll get Van Doren. Crows are smart, but not that one. If he were, he wouldn't have crossed you to begin with." Sasha closed his eyes. No more visions. Good. Perhaps he would escape her wrath after all. "Am I here to find him?"

"At the present? No." Madame took a breath as the skin on her face mended and slowly stitched together again. "There's an auction in Highland Park. I'll have the details sent over. I need the big-ticket item."

"Which is?"

"A knife." Madame's jaw tightened. "The knife forged by my dead associate hundreds of years ago: Sheturath."

There was only one blade Madame would put off skinning Van Doren for, and it was that one.

"A contact claims Van Doren is going to steal it though." Madame's lips curled in the feral way only demons could do, and her pointed teeth glinted in the moonlight. "If he is as stupid as you say, you could kill him and take my knife all in one fell swoop."

Sasha flicked ash onto the ground, focusing on the feel of the cigarette between his fingers instead of the overwhelming urge to groan. He'd been doing this shit for Madame and her gang of conscripted agents for two decades. Despite only being thirty-two, he felt ancient.

It was always something.

"Get my knife. Get the crows." Madame leaned forward, fire dancing inside her irises. "If you get them both, I'll cut you loose."

He frowned as another brisk chill rolled over him and brushed his sandy-blond hair across his forehead. "Surely you don't think I'm falling for that."

"I knew you wouldn't, so I brought this." Madame reached inside her fur coat and pulled out a rolled-up *something*. Sasha stared at it longer.

Cow hide. His heartbeat quickened exponentially as his honey-gold eyes took in the leather. He knew exactly what that was.

"Bring me my knife and those goddamn birds dead or alive, and I'll sign this." Madame unrolled the hide. While only about a foot long, the sharp strokes of dark, inky blood spelled out an intimately familiar set of terms. "You'll be unemployed."

Sasha fought to breathe.

"In the meantime"—Madame rolled up the hide and gave him a sly look—"I have a new one."

He managed to take a breath. The demon watched him exhale, gaze hard and fixed on his jugular, and she put the hide back inside her coat. "I am not inclined to sign another one of those."

"This one you will. Already signed. Fresh." She pulled out another hide, unfurled it, and let it lie flat atop her hands.

The prospect of freedom proved much too strong for him to ignore. Sasha took a step closer, just enough to see Madame's jagged calligraphy.

"If you present both the knife and the Van Dorens, I'll incinerate your original pledge." Madame extended her hands out farther and gave him a glimpse of her true name etched at the bottom in an unfamiliar alphabet.

Sasha dropped his cigarette on the ground and crushed it beneath the sole of his oxford.

Years of servitude to Madame could be over. Done.

He could go back to Chelyabinsk. He could see his mother again.

His family would be freed from a monster.

"You're serious." Sasha kept his voice level, sounding uninterested by most standards, but dealing with Madame was a deadly game.

She sighed. Bored. "If you're not interested, I can find someone else."

"I'm interested." Sasha tucked a hand in his pants pocket. "I'm curious why you don't go handle it yourself."

Madame stilled. He'd made a mistake. *Tread carefully.*

"If you think we're the only ones interested in Sheturath, you aren't as smart as I thought. I lost my kingdom in Hell, and I won't risk my gains on Earth due to arrogance." A growl pushed past Madame's lips. "Several things there will possess the power to kill me, and I'd rather not be in the same room as that knife."

Sasha smirked. An opportunity to get back in her good graces. "Unless you're wielding it."

Madame's fangs twinkled as she grinned. "Exactly."

The demon slinked forward and placed the hide on the hood of his rental sedan. "Do we have a deal, Aleksandr Ivanovich Sokolov?"

Sasha swallowed, taking in the bloody text carefully as sweat collected between his shoulder blades. *I, Aleksandr Ivanovich Sokolov of Chelyabinsk, agree to procure the blade Sheturath and find the roost of Charles Van Doren in exchange for my release of service. Release will be granted when Van Doren and Sheturath are in possession of Madame, former general of Hell.*

Plain. Boring. Clear—like he wanted.

He pulled a slender blade from the holster beneath his black suit jacket and pierced the tip of his left index finger. Blood bubbled up immediately and rolled down his knuckles after a breath.

Sasha kept the apprehension from his face and pressed his bloody fingertip to the hide, writing his name in Cyrillic.

A knife. A crow.

He'd find them both, and he'd be free.

THREE

DIANA

For five years, they'd lived in exile in the hill country of central Texas, sequestered in a small, condemned, wood-framed house sandwiched between cornfields and dirt roads. The unbearable heat had finally taken its two-week hiatus as the state's short winter fell upon them like a heavy blanket. The lack of a heater made existing in the house absolutely miserable, but no one would know it given the sudden accumulation of sweat beading between her shoulder blades.

Diana cursed under her breath and sagged against her bedroom door. Her parents wanted her to steal a knife from an auction that would be packed with other supes. She needed to find Amir to verify some information since her father clearly could not be trusted, and she had no desire to die for a fool's errand.

She pulled off her clothes despite the cold, letting them fall to the dusty floor in a pile. A chill racked her body, and her teeth slammed together. How did humans stand the cold? Crow shifters by nature didn't like it, but she loathed it.

Diana closed her eyes and tugged at the pulsing core of her being, a warm ball of energy swirling in her chest, wrangling it with ease as she tucked her arms and legs close. Her skin, hot with magic, pushed feathers out along her spine and neck in a flurry of black as she shrank into a crow before flying through the broken window and into the night. Shifting, the only painless part of her being, felt like the only thing she could control anymore.

The small farming town they'd hidden in was as far from civilization as one could get in America. Acres of farmland stretched wide, intermittently dotted with homes and streetlights and bonfires. While she hadn't forgiven her father for landing them there, she was thankful to have freedom to roam, be it as human or crow. Her parents didn't have the luxury, not when they'd ironed their faces into the mind of a demon.

If Lead Crow found them again, he'd certainly kill them now after all the trouble they'd caused in their five-year leave. Casualty of her father's mistakes or no, he'd kill her too. Maybe her father was right in that regard. Maybe the knife would be enough to change Lead Crow's mind.

Diana held her wings aloft and drifted through the chilled night. A bigger city loomed in the distance, perfect for an evening roost. Cities were warm, and there was plenty of food that wasn't roadkill. More than that, Amir was there, and she needed to speak with him.

Even in the dark, her eyes were good. She closed one and focused on a tightly packed cluster of buildings, smoke billowing out of chimneys and chatter drifting in the wind. People walked around bundled in coats and hats and scarves, holding hands and carrying bags of brightly wrapped boxes. Music temporarily jarred her attention, but as she flew closer to the streetlamps, she noticed speakers poking out from behind green wreaths and holiday lights.

Have a holly, jolly Christmas, indeed.

Diana batted her wings, slowing her descent, and wrapped her talons along a power line beside a chimney. So warm. Comfortable.

As her bones warmed, she thought back to her parents. The knife. Her parents made it seem like such a simple task. Steal the knife and they're free. That's it. But she knew it would be tougher than that. Expensive things, rare things, always had more than one set of eyes on them. She'd have to be careful because the odds of her being the only supernatural being at the auction were slim to none.

"Dude, check out that bird." A guy with a cigarette pinched between his fingers nodded toward Diana, his breath white puffs swirling in the air.

She cocked her head at him, unimpressed with his scraggly beard.

"What? It's a bird." His companion, a man in a heavy, brown coat, narrowed his eyes and made to keep walking.

"No. Look at it." Cigarette Guy motioned to her. "It has three damn legs!"

Diana sat still for a moment as the two marveled. Like werewolves being bigger and stronger than their animal counterparts, she didn't look exactly like a typical crow. She, too, was larger than average. Her height and wingspan were a little over six inches longer, and her bill a bit thicker. And, more notably, she had three legs when she was a crow, like the creature that created all crow shifters thousands of years ago.

Instead of worrying about the idiots below, she left the wire to find Amir.

She flew close to the buildings, basking in their warmth. What she wouldn't do for a home again. A house with heat and plumbing and *food*. The items her father found through contacts kept them from starving, but it was far from enough. The last retrieval he sent her on, the one where she got shot, had kept her out of the air for two months. She wasn't entirely sure how they didn't die from a lack of things to eat.

Well, she did know.

Amir.

She drifted into the broken second-story window of an abandoned storefront: her usual stop. In the corner of the room behind a pile of cardboard boxes was another box with a tank top and a pair of jeans inside. It wouldn't be warm enough in this weather, but at least she wouldn't be naked.

With the same painless ease as before, Diana shifted to her human form and got dressed in a matter of seconds. She wrapped her arms around herself and trotted down the steps to the ground floor, dodging dead rats and piles of trash left behind by the previous tenants. The back door, unlocked thanks to an exceptionally strong werewolf breaking the lock off the latch, swung open with ease, and she briskly moved into the street.

Across the street was an open courtyard. A fountain sat in the center, decorated with wreaths and tinsel. Farther into the expanse was the town Christmas tree, adorned from top to bottom with ornaments and lights. The smoke from nearby chimneys assaulted her nose, but she didn't mind. It was a welcome reprieve from the shit she'd been forced to smell in their temporary abode.

On a bench in the courtyard sat Amir.

Diana jogged ahead and ignored the strange looks other pedestrians cast her way. Although, she couldn't blame them really. She was the one wearing a tank top when it was thirty degrees outside.

Diana assumed Amir knew she was coming even though his back was to her. Werewolves had an exceptionally good sense of smell, just as she had exceptionally good eyesight. He turned around, tired eyes framed with wrinkles, looking somewhat annoyed. Poor Amir. He'd risked a lot to keep her alive.

"I was hoping you'd come." Amir pat the bench beside him. A brown paper bag sat between his legs, and the second Diana's thighs hit the cold metal, he heaved a thick coat onto her lap. "Not a good time to be without."

Her heart swelled as she took in the jacket. Heavy. Canvas. She stuck her arms in the sleeves and basked in the warmth.

"It's Thursday, so I'm here." Diana exhaled a wave of hot air into her palms. "I don't think I can ever repay you for all you've done for us."

"For you, Di." Amir gave her a look as his beige skin glowed beneath the yellow light of the streetlamp. Despite looking to be somewhere in his early forties, Amir was almost one hundred. "It isn't fair to you. Your parents are not fair to you."

"I know." Diana swallowed and nudged him with her elbow. "How's Farida?"

"She's well." Amir smiled a little. So faint she might've missed it if he hadn't tried to hide it by stroking his chin. "Pregnant."

"Excuse me?" She leaned closer, eyes narrowed. "Farida is pregnant, and you're just now telling me?"

"It never came up."

"Then bring it up."

"It's...precarious." Farida was human, and if the embryo carried any of Amir's werewolf magic, she'd miscarry. Diana knew they'd lost two already, and given Amir's glassy stare, he was prepared for it to happen again.

"Hey." Diana elbowed him again as a chilled breeze brushed her cheeks. "The baby could be human this time. It happens. My father claims one of my cousins is human."

"Your father is also a liar."

"Yes, he is. Which brings me to an important question." Diana sighed and stared into the courtyard. Couples walked around the fountain, taking pictures and casting coins. Carefree. Happy. "My father said the demon woman is close. I'm not sure if he's being honest or lying to make me do something stupid."

"She's very close." Amir rubbed his hands together. "Madame is somewhere in the metroplex."

A shriek of laughter from a pair of women holding hands in front of the Christmas tree brought a wistful smile to Diana's lips. "Should we move?"

"I'm not sure." Amir watched her. Pity lingered on his face. "I'm afraid if you move, you won't escape."

"But if we continue to hide, we won't make it." Diana fell against the bench. Great. The Hell-forged knife looked more promising by the second. Sometimes she wished she'd been born a more physically formidable creature. Or changed into one like Amir.

She remembered being cornered by Amir five years ago. His keen nose sent him on her trail, and he followed her for several blocks before cornering her in an alley. After a snarl filled with sharp teeth, Diana had been sure she was going to die.

It was laughable now. Amir had simply introduced himself and invited her to his house for dinner. His pack had the unfortunate honor of being indebted to the demon hunting her family down, but he always made sure to share any information he could spare. Anything to help keep her alive.

The pair sat in silence as she reflected on their predicament. Diana shifted against the bench, stomach tied in knots, and cleared her throat. "My father said there's a knife that can kill Madame up for auction tomorrow. If I get it, we might be able to convince the murder to let my parents back in. Exchange a place in the flock for the knife."

"Your father says a lot of things, and you have no guarantee the murder will let you come with him in an exchange." Amir sighed and ran a hand through his thick mop of dark hair. "You've got to stop trusting him."

Her heart thumped against her sternum, loud and strong. Amir was right. She needed to stop.

But if she stopped, she'd have nothing. If she stopped, she'd never have a home.

"You need to find someone worthy of your trust, Di." Amir pinned her with a hard stare. "You need to stop trying to dig goodness out of someone who has nothing good to start with. Screw your father and his murder. Go find some new crows."

"There aren't any more. That I know of, anyway." Diana tried to shut out the sharp pinch in her chest. A cool breeze whipped against her cheeks, and her hair lashed across her face. "And as much as I hate to say it, I'm afraid I lost my shot at joining them."

"Why?"

"Because most crow shifters are accepted into the murder when they're young. Everyone unclaimed by the murder's magic gets kicked out to fend for themselves or killed after a while. Liabilities. I only got to stay for so long because Lead Crow felt guilty." White-hot pain tore through her at the last memory she had of the murder, left to stand alone in the middle of a crowded room. Crow shifters not welcomed by the murder's magic were something of a pariah, and the rest made their dislike no secret.

Nausea settled in the pit of her stomach. She'd never told anyone what happened to her in her formative years—the years she should've had with the murder—and Diana intended to keep it that way. If the murder found out how she'd stayed alive after falling from the family nest, there would be no hope of joining them. Not even her parents, the ones who left her behind back then, knew the truth.

Diana blew another puff of hot air into her hands. "I'm twenty-eight, and the murder is getting smaller all the time. If they were going to accept me, I'm afraid it would've happened already."

Amir didn't say anything. The speakers hanging on the nearby lampposts switched to a piano rendition of "O Holy Night," and Diana couldn't help but wonder what it must be like to spend Christmas with someone who looked at her with love.

"But I can't stop trying, so I guess I'll be stealing a knife tomorrow." When Amir didn't respond, she longed to fill the silence. She sighed and shook her head. "I think I'm broken, Amir."

The man snorted. "Your priorities are wrong, but you aren't broken."

Diana scowled.

"You need to ditch your dad and the hope the murder will one day accept you. Our pack magic isn't so selective, but it won't work unless the pack and new wolf want it to work." Amir leaned over a little and bumped her elbow. "You came to me for the truth. Here's some truth: you need to focus on what you want, and I don't think it's a knife and spending a life with people who treat you like shit."

She pulled herself deeper into the warmth of her new jacket. She didn't give a damn about the demon knife and even less about her father's clemency. But she did care about her own pardon, and the slim hope of the murder finally welcoming her into their ranks was all she had left. Even if she could just coexist with them as she had been doing for the years prior to her mother and father's—and by proxy, her own—exile, it would be better than living in a collapsed shack with her selfish parents.

If she were going to be alone forever, Diana would rather be alone in a crowded room with the murder than in no room at all.

FOUR

SASHA

Sasha sat on the edge of the bed and relished in the weight easing from the soles of his feet. His home for the night, a motel room decked in yellow wallpaper soaked in years of cigarette smoke, did little to detract from the shock and, dare he think it, *hope* coursing through his veins.

Freedom. He'd been expecting danger, perhaps even death, and Madame had offered him freedom instead.

Meeting with Madame always required an extra amount of vigilance. The ancient demon, temperamental and unable to truly relate to humans, snapped with little notice. At the moment, she needed him. That need had kept him alive over the years, but there was never a guarantee it would last. Bound to her, he always felt lucky to see the next day.

Sasha fell backward on the mattress and pressed the heels of his palms onto his eyes. His visions had promised danger, and it had never come. At least on the surface it hadn't. Madame was dangerous because she was one of the five demonic generals booted from Hell a millennium ago, which meant the danger usually coincided with the bodily harm she could inflict. Since Madame hadn't attacked him, he had to assume either the future had changed during the course of their conversation, or the danger was in the task she'd presented him.

He grimaced at the smell of burned dust billowing into the room as the heater kicked on. *Freedom.* Whatever the cost, it had to be worth it. It had to be better than continuing to live like this.

The sharp ring of his phone shook him from his thoughts.

Sasha sighed and pushed himself up. The mattress squealed beneath his thighs. Old springs. He should stay in better motels.

He reached into the pocket of his pants and pulled out a black flip phone. Old by every standard, but it was also harder to trace and easier to toss. He popped it open, and his heart dropped into the depths of his increasingly empty stomach as a familiar number blinked up at him from the tiny, pixelated screen.

Sasha swallowed and pressed the phone to his ear. "*Mama*...are you all right?"

The phone crackled on the other end, but a soft breath settled his heart rate.

"*Da.*" He could hear his mother smile. "I just needed to hear my boy."

The soothing words did the opposite of what his mother likely intended. Instead of warmth, there was pain. Remorse. The lingering swell of years away and the break in her lonely voice were obvious, and no matter how many times he heard it, his own pain at hearing it never subsided.

"Have you been eating?" she asked.

"Yes." Sasha ran a hand over his face. "Have you?"

"I've gained six pounds this month," she said, voice doused in disappointment.

"Good. You were too thin last time I saw you."

"You haven't seen me in years, Sasha boy."

He propped his elbows on his knees and closed his eyes. Guilt. Always with the guilt.

"I'm not keeping you, am I?" his mother asked next.

"From?"

"A bed." She dropped something. Something metal. Perhaps she was cooking. It was early morning in Chelyabinsk, so maybe breakfast. "A friend."

More guilt. "No. You're not."

"Are you going to let me die without grandchildren?" She tutted into the receiver. The sound of water hitting a sink basin filled the silence.

"What are you baking?"

"Cake. But that is not what we are talking about."

"Given my current employment, children are the least of my concern." Sasha stood up from the bed and looked to the ceiling. *Every time.* Like she didn't know what would happen should he get comfortable. Complacent. "The dangers of my job notwithstanding, I've also committed a few murders in my day. Most decent people aren't into that sort of baggage, which makes finding a woman to have said children with especially inconvenient. Then there's the issue of Madame, who, thanks to my contract, would steal any of my children when I inevitably die."

Unlike the past bouts of silence, this one was heavy. The kind that squeezed one's throat and crushed it shut. He was a bad man on a predetermined course, and his mother refused to see it.

"Please, Sasha. I beg you." The weak, desperate tone in his mother's voice prepared him for what came next. "Please let me take your place. Let me assume your contract. It should've been mine from the start."

His mother asked to take his contract with Madame each time they spoke. Madame's deals, constructed to keep families tied to her indefinitely, moved between family members. When the person with the contract died, Madame would pass on the contract to the next available family member. Always tethered, even in death.

While Madame and the other four generals had lost their foothold in Hell to the current Devil, they had no intention of going quietly. Since they lost their domain of hellfire and brimstone, they each sought pleasure on Earth instead, hoping to remake their legions and riches on the backs of the formidable beings that had the misfortune of crossing their paths.

He, notably, was one of those beings.

"*Nyet.*" Sasha would do many things for his own benefit, but sacrificing his mother to Madame's iron grip wasn't one of them. He heard his mother's breath stop short, which prompted him to explain more than he knew to be wise. "It will be over soon anyway."

"Over?" His mother's voice broke at the end. She assumed the worst. He should've been more purposeful in his words. "What do you mean?"

"Madame has given me a task with the guarantee of release should I complete it," he clarified, although Sasha knew it would invite more questions.

"You should know better than to trust Madame. Vile creature."

"She signed the agreement in blood under her true name." Silence echoed on the other end of the phone. Surprised, most likely.

"I still don't like it." His mother snorted at the end, and Sasha smiled. Only his wary mother always could bring his stony face out of its perpetual look of misery. No one else had managed it yet. "I don't like it, her, or your faith she'll be honest."

"I don't either. But it's the best chance I've been offered, and I'm going to take it"—Sasha paused—"or I did take it, I suppose."

"I could strangle you, Aleksandr." The phone rustled on the other end, and he grimaced. He hated being called Aleksandr. Names were important to demons, and Madame always called him that. "I hope you know what you're doing. This makes me nervous."

He swallowed. Time for the hard part. "If you do not hear from me in two weeks, I need for you to do something."

Silence answered him. Could she feel his ghost already?

"Tomorrow morning, I am going to send you a package." Sasha licked his lips, mouth dry. "Inside that package will be a key. That key goes to a safe-deposit box. There will be instructions with the key detailing where it is located."

"Sasha—"

"You will then locate the box and follow my instructions to the letter." A sharp breath rattled on the other end. "Please."

"Let me take your place—"

"I will not." As much as his tone pained him, it was necessary. "Promise me you'll do as I asked."

A sniffle answered him first. "I promise."

"I am good at planning. Please allow me to do it." He stuck his hand in his jacket pocket and pulled out his cigarettes and lighter.

"Allowing people in on your plans every once in a while might not be so bad."

"People are easier to predict when they know nothing." Sasha turned his pack of cigarettes in his hand. "Human nature is fairly easy to account for so long as you remove certain variables."

"They're even easier to predict when you can trust them." His mother paused. *Trust.* "I hate that Madame has beaten that out of you."

"I'm not so sure that was Madame. When you can see everyone trying to kill you before they even have the thought, trust is hard to come by." Sasha hated this subject and therefore decided to change it. "If I don't die in the coming days, I'll come visit."

"I'll believe that when you're in my arms, boy." His mother chuckled, although a bitter note hung inside it. "In exchange for following your safe box demands, can you make a promise to me?"

He snorted. "Depends."

"You cannot stay alone forever, Sasha. Look at what loneliness has done to me. It is no way to live." If there were a way to end the conversation then and there without hurting his mother's feelings, he would've done it. "Promise me you will find someone to remind you there is a heart inside your chest."

So much guilt. The longer he stayed away, the longer he worked for Madame, the more his mother foisted upon him. A large part of him couldn't blame her, not entirely.

Sasha inhaled slowly. At this point, one more lie wouldn't damn him. "I will try. I'll be home soon."

His mother sighed. "Good night, Sasha."

Sasha stared at the phone in his palm long after his mother hung up. He'd started his service to Madame at the tender age of eleven to keep his mother out of her grasp. Angel blood was a nice thing to have on supply, even as diluted as theirs happened to be, but their clairvoyance had been especially tantalizing to Madame then.

She'd wanted a strategist. A man with a plan. A guiltless plotter who could orchestrate her wildest schemes that could help her extend her control from continent to continent. She'd dumped years and years of training into him, and now Madame was willing to let him go? Let him walk out the proverbial door and free him to the world? All for some crows and a knife?

Despite the signed contract only waiting for him to uphold his end of the bargain, Sasha didn't like the risks involved. His mother was right to be worried. But for the first time in a long while, he decided to ignore the risks because the reward was too great.

He looked to the clock. Twenty-one hundred hours. This time tomorrow, he'd hopefully have the blade and the Van Dorens.

Then he would be free.

FIVE

DIANA

DESPITE THE CHILL WRAPPED AROUND HER ARMS AS SHE STOOD outside an enormous house in Highland Park, Diana could only find it within her to focus on the person she'd be using to get inside the auction.

"The name's Nobu, and you can stop staring at me like that." The Japanese man—*young* man—frowned. His brown hair hung in his eyes, pushed to the side in a careless manner that screamed teenager. A pair of hoops hung at the tops of both of his ears, and the reflection of the waning moon glistened on the sterling silver despite the clouds drifting above.

She ground her teeth together, still not over it. Her father had chosen a cat demon—whatever the hell that was—as her partner in crime. Or at least, a kid possessed by one. She'd felt the subtle swell of demonic darkness around him when they met, and her father verified what she'd feared. To make things more annoying, she had been expecting an adult to be her ticket into the auction. Not some kid.

She'd admit Nobu had an eye for high-rolling formal wear though. He'd brought her a dress and heels for the evening heist, and while not appropriate for the cold, it was the nicest thing she'd ever worn. Apparently, her threadbare T-shirt and ripped jeans weren't up to par for the dress code.

Unsure how to proceed and frustrated, she huffed. Her breath came out of her mouth in a white cloud thanks to the cold. "Are you even allowed to drive?"

"Yeah. I'm older than I look. I've been possessed for a while." Nobu huffed into the palm of his hands and rubbed them together. "Happened right before I was supposed to graduate."

Diana ran her palms over her arms as a brisk wind swept along them, and embarrassment tugged at the bottom of her stomach. *Possessed.* She couldn't imagine having to share her body with anything else, even with the immortality perk.

She pursed her lips as another thought crossed her mind. Was she dealing with the demon or the kid, and how would she know the difference? Not one to leave her fate in the hands of a stranger, Diana figured she'd ask. "Am I talking to Nobu, or am I talking to the asshole inside him?"

Nobu winced. "It's really me. If you weren't talking to a human... well, you'd know."

According to Amir, demons weren't good at pretending to be human, and they got their lackeys by forcing them into deals. Nobu moved human enough. Emoted. Carried appropriate inflections in his words. While she didn't trust him any farther than she could throw him, she believed Nobu when he said he was in charge.

"Diana," Nobu said, exasperated.

Oh, right. He'd asked her to stop staring. Easy enough.

"Sorry." Diana rubbed her arms again as heat blistered under her eyes. "Let's get inside."

They stood on the long driveway leading to the expansive mansion where they'd parked as close to the open wrought-iron gate as they could manage. Not only would it provide an easier escape, but close to the mansion wasn't the sort of place to park a Corolla with mismatched rims. It stuck out like a crow among canaries, and at least parked away from the luxury cars, people might assume a delivery person had stopped in with *hors d'oeuvres* instead of a pair of thieves looking to lift a knife.

Diana appraised her partner for the night. Possessed or not, Nobu looked like a child. He straightened the red tie hanging around his neck, fidgety in the three-piece suit and dwarfed by the jacket. She was a twenty-eight-year-old woman wandering around with a boy who, to all appearances, couldn't even buy cigarettes. If there were any humans at the auction, she'd be getting a shitload of stares, which wasn't conducive to stealing anything.

The entrance to the house held a pair of heavy mahogany doors surrounded by Grecian columns. A couple of pots with shriveled vines sat on either side of the door, and beyond them stood a tall man wearing a black tuxedo. While the house was large, it had been built in the middle of several acres of land, and the sprawling expanse of dead fields made it seem much smaller.

"Sphinx," Nobu muttered under his breath as they approached the bouncer. Diana, having never met a sphinx, studied him closely.

"Tanaka Nobuyuki," Nobu said to the sphinx the second his foot crossed the brick arch denoting the porch. He glanced over his shoulder at her after a moment, and she had the distinct impression Nobu was weighing the benefit of her presence. "This is Diana Jannsen."

Her brow twitched. While a surprise, the alias made sense. Using Van Doren would only make half the building's inhabitants want to kill her.

The sphinx looked at Diana over a pair of spectacles, yellow eyes taking her in. His warm golden skin like desert sand glowed beneath the lamp affixed beside the door. Most supernatural creatures could sense other magical things, and while the sphinx might not know Nobu was possessed and she was a crow, it could feel their magic. Of that, she had no doubt.

"What is cold, but sometimes warm; has a shadow, but not a form; some try to run, but cannot hide; for it comes as sure as the evening tide?"

Sphinxes wasted no time with their riddles.

"Death," Nobu said effortlessly. For being a teenager, he seemed pretty smart. Then again, he claimed his appearance didn't align with his life experience. Maybe he'd told the truth. "Might we go in now?"

Diana pulled her shoulders back when the sphinx put a hand on the knob of the right door and opened it. He took a step back and gestured for them to go inside. There would be creatures inside the house that would kill her if they figured out she was a Van Doren, yet she crossed into the foyer anyway.

How irredeemably stupid, Diana thought.

She stifled a gasp when her heeled feet hit marble floors. She'd stolen many things in the last five years, but the things inside the mansion were far grander than all of them. Vases. Portraits. Sculpted busts and tapestries. The chandelier hanging above her head held around fifty strands of crystals—it weighed at least a hundred pounds. And these were the normal, human things.

Beyond the foyer was a pair of staircases that wrapped around the back of the room, punctuated by another chandelier hanging between them. More vases and flowers lined the walls, which drew her gaze toward tall paintings stretching several feet to the ceilings. They might not be magical in the same way she was, but they were breathtaking all the same.

Diana walked behind Nobu as he led the way out of the foyer toward the room with the stairs. At a glance, she could see a few werewolves. After hanging out with Amir, she'd learned some things to watch for, but the one she readily noticed was the sharp, pointed nails present even in human form. Amir tried to keep his filed flat, but after a change, they always reverted.

A selkie stood by a flower arrangement and a painting of a Victorian woman on a chaise. While disguised as a human at the present, he had gills. They were small, but they were there. The selkie spoke to... something inhuman. The woman didn't look untoward, but the rigidity in her movements gave her away. The closer she got, the same faint darkness that Nobu exuded sent a chill down her spine.

Her heart dropped into her stomach. *Demon.* The woman was a demon. If Nobu and whoever the hell lived inside him had some sort of plan to screw her over, the night would get a lot more dangerous.

She swallowed her apprehension and made a mental map of the house. To the left of the staircase was a formal living area. Or what she supposed had been intended as a living area. Twelve-foot walls supported vaulted ceilings, lined with heavy, cream-colored curtains that billowed to the floor. A wide fireplace sat on the far wall, and her gaze immediately locked onto the fire dancing away inside it. A pianist plucking the keys of a grand piano attempted to lure her into a false sense of security with a cheery, holiday tune, and it took more effort than she'd like to admit to pay attention to the glass boxes on golden pedestals throughout the room.

Nobu led her to the first box. She'd seen displays like this before at museums, but instead of an old rock, this box held a pair of sapphire earrings. Massive gems encased in gold settings. The placard read TIDE JEWELS beneath some kanji.

"Do you know what the blade looks like?" Nobu asked her under his breath and kept his eyes on the earrings.

"No. But it shouldn't be too hard to find. It's a knife."

"You'd be surprised how many rare items are weapons." Nobu let out a puff of air and gave her a once-over with a small smile. "Or maybe you're not. You're the career criminal."

"You're here with me, so maybe keep your judgment to yourself." Diana smoothed out her dress and wrapped her arms around herself, still chilled, but the fireplace took the edge off.

Nobu dropped his eyes, smile gone. "Sorry."

"Um, it's not a big deal. Don't worry about it." Diana frowned as guilt snaked its way through her chest. While she hadn't meant to hurt his feelings, at least she knew Nobu's demon was dormant for the time being. From what Amir had said, demons didn't apologize for anything.

When some witches made their way over to the Tide Jewels, Nobu led her toward the back corner instead, right into a table of food.

"I'm curious—what did my father pay you with?" Diana's mouth watered as she looked the table over. Tiny sandwiches, macaroons, and fruit platters. An odd assembly, but she hadn't eaten a proper meal in at least a week and consequently didn't care. She picked up the tea sandwich, shoved the entire thing in her mouth, and relished in the burst of cucumber coating her tongue.

"Pay?"

Diana swallowed the sandwich but quickly replaced it with another. She ignored Nobu's wrinkled nose and talked through the mouthful of bread. "Yeah. Why did you bring me here if not for money? Because I promise you, he doesn't have any."

Nobu's eyebrows furrowed, and his gaze dropped to the table. Only for a second, but she only needed a second to come to her own conclusions.

Her father had promised him money.

She swallowed the sandwich and groaned. Fucking hell, her father was the worst. "Listen. Help me get this stupid knife, and *I'll* pay you. Okay? I'll find something. There's plenty of things here to steal."

Nobu sighed and brushed his bangs out of his eyes. He played it off better than she thought he would, although she wondered what his demon thought about all this. "Let's find your blade and get out."

She couldn't help but be thankful he wasn't leaving her to try to steal the knife alone.

They walked toward the glass cases on the far wall nestled close to the deep marble fireplace. The fire crackled and popped, and it took everything within her not to curl up on the hearth and bask in the heat. What she wouldn't give to live in a house with a functioning heater and fireplace again.

"This is nice." Nobu stopped in front of a swath of gray leather held up by silver hooks within a case. The placard said LEVIATHAN'S HIDE. "Holy hell. Super expensive too."

"I can't imagine paying three million dollars for fabric." Diana licked her lips. She would buy food. Clean water. Clothes.

"This isn't just fabric. You can make some sick armor with this." Nobu nodded toward it with a smirk she didn't much like. "Impenetrable."

"I'm not in the business of armor making." She looked around for anything vaguely knife-shaped and came up short. "I just want to get the knife and leave."

Nobu shrugged and glanced around. How he could see through the curtain of hair hanging in his face, Diana didn't know.

"I'll move around a little. See if I can find it." He rubbed the back of his neck. "Although, it might be in storage until the last second. They usually bring out the big stuff at the end."

Her eyebrows furrowed. "If this thing is so great, why did you agree to help me get it?"

"I'm looking for something else." Nobu's gaze flickered away from her face to survey the room. "I'll be back shortly. Keep an eye out."

Diana scowled at his retreating back. What could a boy possessed by a cat demon possibly want if not a knife that someone else could use to kill him? If she were him, she'd rather have it in her possession than an enemy.

She wrapped her arms tight around her torso. This is what Amir had been talking about—she put faith in people who didn't deserve it. Hadn't earned it. She trusted demon-possessed Nobu to tell her the truth, and that trust might prove to be a fatal mistake if she weren't careful. For all she knew, Nobu and his demon had other plans—plans that included screwing her over and taking the blade for themselves.

As much as she hated the thought, she didn't have a choice. For the time being, it would be best to treat everyone like a potential threat. Even Nobu.

SIX

SASHA

The house holding the auction crawled with supernatural beings. Not only had Sasha seen them lurking about in his subconscious, but the first three people he had encountered upon his arrival had been a sphinx, a werewolf, and a selkie. All three of which would pose a problem should they catch wind of his true purpose.

The knife Madame wanted would go for millions, and he had no intention of buying it.

While he hadn't seen far enough to know how the evening would end, there were definitely variables he could count on. Someone, perhaps even Charles Van Doren himself, would make an attempt to steal the blade. It would be foolish, certainly, but Van Doren wasn't known for being intelligent. The man would slip up, and that was the moment Sasha hoped he could take advantage of.

The foyer stretched several yards in either direction and broke into an open space with dual staircases. The only way out was the front door, and the flower arrangements were positioned as to funnel everyone into the adjacent room, presumably where the auction would be held. The smell of warm chocolate and peppermint hung in the air, and if the house weren't filled with dangerous beings, he'd assume it was a holiday party. The pianist playing "O Come, O Come Emmanuel" somewhere beyond the foyer didn't help that assumption either.

Sasha glanced at the watch on his wrist. Ten minutes until the auction started. He felt for the burn in his mind and closed his eyes. Threats lay in wait everywhere. It was time to figure out which ones posed the most risk.

Like a film, several werewolves immediately flashed behind his eyelids, flexing their hands and rolling their heads along their shoulders. Out of everything that he knew to be present, he liked werewolves the least. Werewolves were human enough to pass, but they were driven by instinct. Instinct was hard, if not impossible, to control, which made it almost impossible to plan for what they might do.

The future was never absolute though. He only saw what happened to be a threat at a given moment in time, but that moment could easily be changed.

After the werewolves, he saw a woman.

Sasha pulled himself out of his thoughts. The night had suddenly become much more interesting, especially if his magic thought the woman was somehow dangerous to him.

He meandered through the foyer and toward the formal living room, dodging pedestals holding brilliant red poinsettias and draped with Christmas wreaths. Glass cases were immediately visible the second he crossed under the archway, and while there were about thirty individuals viewing the merchandise that lined the room, he knew the thing everyone was there to buy or steal hadn't been brought out yet.

Sasha tucked one hand in his pants pocket and plucked a flute of champagne from a waitress's tray with the other. When Sheturath was revealed to the masses, an organized bidding wouldn't be on the table. In his vision, he'd seen several flipped tables and flashes of broken glass in his premonitions, and given his company, he was surprised there hadn't been blood. Perhaps there would be later.

Sasha pressed the cool glass to his lips and took a sip. According to his research, the seller was human, which meant he didn't understand the inner workings of monsters. Most supernatural creatures didn't see themselves as creatures bent on survival, but most of them were regardless. People had been hunting shifters of all kinds for millennia. Vampires were a particular favorite to kill, although most humans couldn't get close enough if they tried. Witches spent hundreds of years being burned at the stake or tossed into lakes with rocks bound around their ankles. Since billions of people would pay to watch them die, a blade that could kill anything in their path would be quite the thing to have. A thing most of them would kill to acquire.

A flash of black drew his gaze away from the pack of wolves situated at the front of the room. Someone caught his attention. Someone he'd seen in his visions in the foyer. A woman nestled by a fire.

The petite woman shivered despite the warmth pushed from the generous heaters and large fireplace. Long, inky hair hung to her elbows, swaying in a silky curtain as she eyed the room. A red dress clung to her body like cellophane, hardly covering her shoulders and barely reaching the top of her knees. Not the ideal outfit to wear in the winter, even as mild as Texas winters were. She was thin—too thin. Malnourished. Dark eyes. Skin so pale she was practically translucent.

Dark hair. Dark eyes. Slender limbs. Sasha flexed the fingers of his free hand. *Crow.* He'd bet she came to the auction at the behest of Charles, which begged the question of her relation to the crow he'd been tasked to find.

He switched his attention to her accomplice. To all appearances—a teenage boy. Two rings in his ears. Impractical haircut. Suit too large for his frame. However, appearances were certainly deceiving, especially when supernatural beings were involved, and the wave of something otherworldly emanating from the boy's body assured him he didn't see a typical youth.

If he didn't know any better, he'd guess a demon. Whatever entity was inside the boy certainly felt like one, and Sasha had been raised with them, so he'd know. But the kid's languid movement around the room, slinking about the cases and almost nervous glances over his shoulder, didn't speak to a demon. So either he was wrong, which he didn't want to entertain, or the demon inside the kid was incredibly lazy.

Sasha edged close to a cocktail table and set his champagne down as he appraised the rest of the room. He knew all Madame's agents, and none of them were here. But that said nothing of the other generals and their agents, and he couldn't imagine a scenario where Madame would be the only one interested.

"Excuse me," a light, feminine voice spoke up beside him. Blond. French. Vampire. "My friend suggested you might be looking for some company this evening?"

Sasha grimaced, watchful eyes still trained on the crow shifter that stood by the fire. He hated vampires. Vampires loved angelic blood—many angels had died thanks to a greedy pair of fangs, and he had more important things to do than be a vampire's dinner. "No, thank you. I've got company."

The woman's eyebrows screwed together. "Jean said you did not arrive with anyone."

"I didn't." Sasha gave her a brief glance and turned on a heel. "Good night."

The crow and the boy were going to try to steal the blade. He needed to figure out how, and more importantly, he had to figure out how to get the blade for himself without dying. The female crow would lead him to Charles if he played his cards right, and if he were especially vigilant, he could do that and get the knife at the same time. All he required were the right words.

He walked closer to the crow and the demon boy, but strategically kept a distance while he worked through the problem at hand. Given the potential buyers present, the odds of the woman and the boy getting Sheturath and surviving the heist were abysmally low. If the woman were anything like the kleptomaniacal bird Madame sought, she wouldn't have much in the way of a plan or subtlety, and crow shifters were largely harmless without their murder.

Which meant he could count on a scene after a botched attempt.

While Sasha preferred to work on the sly, a scene here would actually be beneficial to him. However, he wanted the impending chaos to be somewhat controlled. He wanted it to happen right there in the room. Not outside. Not on the road. Right there. One door in. One door out.

He felt along his side, fingers grazing the holsters strapped beneath his suit jacket. He carried two handguns with a combined total of twenty-two silver rounds between them—a Glock 19 and a Sig Sauer P226. While they wouldn't kill everything present, it would take care of the biggest threat to his plans—the werewolves.

Sasha kept his eyes on the crow and the boy as he moved past a cluster of witches ogling an eye floating in a jar within one of the cases. The lights in the room dimmed, and the scattered conversations dropped to whispers. The auction would start soon.

He looked from the door leading out to the foyer and back to the room, glancing between the werewolves, the witches, and the selkie. How could he instigate the chaos he needed to achieve his desired end result?

Much to his annoyance, a wolf let out a howl as a pair of women—also werewolves—sauntered into the room wearing stilettos. Each creature presented a different threat to him. The crow would have exceptional eyesight. The vampires would be keen to suck on his neck. The werewolves would be immeasurably strong, especially if they decided to shift, and that said nothing about their irrational instincts.

He turned his gaze to a vial of red liquid tucked within a case labeled the BLOOD OF CHRIST, but his attention was on the pair of thieves. He stared at the vial in the case, but the voices from the fireplace were the only thing he truly noticed.

"I'll move around a little. See if I can find it," the crow's companion said. "Although, it might be in storage until the last second. They usually bring out the big stuff at the end."

The demon boy came to auctions often. Interesting.

The crow said something, but she spoke too quietly. Clearly, she had more experience trying to be immemorable. She knew people were watching. Listening.

"I'm looking for something else," the boy said, attention elsewhere. "I'll be back shortly. Keep an eye out."

Sasha drummed his fingers on his thighs as the boy walked away from the crow and into the crowd. His goal wasn't to get Sheturath for himself? Right. He'd believe that right around the time he believed in God.

However, the obvious lie aside, there were several things he took away from the brief exchange. The woman and the boy probably didn't know each other well, as she hadn't known his true objective. She's also stood a polite distance from him, and her arms were crossed. Closed off.

But more importantly, it didn't sound like they had a plan.

The crow shifter didn't move, but her gaze roved the cases. According to Madame, Charles Van Doren had been ousted from his murder after he'd put them in her cross hairs. While he didn't know much about crow shifters or how they functioned within their murders, he knew that anyone seen as complicit to his dealings would've likely been exiled with Charles. Logically, that pointed to family.

The woman looked too young to be his wife. Daughter? Did Van Doren have children?

Sasha abandoned his place by the case, crow in sight as the perfect plan fell into place. There was only one thing he could say that would cause a riot in this room, and it would also answer his question as to who she was.

"Van Doren."

SEVEN

DIANA

Ice splintered in Diana's veins and shot from her heart down into her limbs.

Shit.

Diana worked to keep the fear from her face, but the once-chilled room was now entirely too hot. Her face burned, and sweat lined her palms. She hadn't even been there five minutes! Who recognized her? She was too afraid to look, but the whispers hitting her ears didn't bode well for getting out of the house unscathed. It was only a matter of time before someone really dangerous and really pissed off heard she was here.

Whoever had addressed her had a deep, masculine voice with a heavy accent. German, maybe? Russian?

She kept her gaze tacked to the fire, but the looming presence of the man became entirely too obvious and impossible to ignore. Out of the corner of her eye, she could make out the dark fabric of his suit jacket, her face level with his bicep. Whoever this was, he was tall.

Diana dared to look up at him.

He was, without question, the most beautiful person she'd ever seen.

Her heart dropped in her chest as she fervently recounted everything she'd ever taken at her father's behest. She'd stolen from a ton of people since they were exiled, but she was certain she'd never stolen from him. His face was too memorable. Angular. Serious. She knew without a doubt she'd remember seeing eyes like his: light brown... almost gold.

Her chest, right where her magic lingered in a tight mass, the place she tapped into when she needed to shift, started to burn. Diana inhaled and slowly let go of all thoughts revolving around the man's jaw and mesmerizing eyeballs. Whoever this beautiful person happened to be was doing something to her magic, and she didn't care for it.

"I was right then?" Definitely a Russian accent. The corner of the man's lips turned up, but only a little. It was so minute, Diana wasn't sure she didn't make it up, and if he noticed her pain, he didn't let on. What was this jerk doing to her magic? Being able to shift and escape this supernatural hellscape was vital to her survival if things went south. "Van Doren. Obviously not Charles, and you're too young to be his wife."

Diana continued to say nothing because saying anything would have her head separated from her shoulders faster than she could run. The werewolves in the room could definitely hear whoever this guy was if they were paying attention, and there were plenty of other creatures with impeccable hearing too.

If this guy didn't shut up, she'd be dead before she could even see the stupid knife!

"You could be from a smaller, somewhat secret murder of crow shifters, and you're simply here for work, but given how rare you lot are, I doubt it." The man shrugged and pinned her with his eyes. They really were compelling, even though she wanted to wring his neck presently. "So I'm willing to bet you're a daughter."

Diana growled and fought the urge to smash his mouth shut with her shaking hands. Getting the knife would be the least of her concerns if he didn't stop talking. She ground her teeth together as the sharp twist of pain behind her breastbone increased. What the hell was he doing to her magic?

"You seem to think you know a lot about me, but I don't know who you are." Diana swallowed and desperately wished Nobu would return with something to drink. Although, given her current company, he'd probably give them a wide berth. She couldn't blame him. "So I'm willing to bet you're...unimportant."

"Depends on who you are." His dirty-blond hair, tousled in a purposeful way, glistened in the light of the fire.

Diana observed her dirty fingernails to keep from looking at him. "You must not have anything expensive, or I'd know who you are. If you don't have expensive things, you probably don't have much money." The weight of his gaze caused warmth to creep up the back of her neck. "If you don't have money...well, you probably aren't impor-tant in a way that counts."

"That's rich coming from a homeless crow who steals for a living."

"I never claimed to be important. Not as important as this crow you're looking for seems to be anyway." Diana looked up from her nails, dismayed to find the man hadn't taken his eyes off her face. "But I'm not going to sit here and argue with someone when I have something to do."

"Something to steal, you mean?" His words kept her feet glued to the floor. "I think you can wait a bit longer. The thing you want isn't out here yet."

"I'm sorry, but how is it you know what I want?"

"You want the thing that everyone here wants." The man raised both his eyebrows and leaned forward a bit, just enough to make her uncomfortable. Goose bumps ran down her arms as he positioned his mouth beside her ear, his breath ghosting her skin. "Hell's blade: Sheturath."

While his voice was quiet, his words were not. Even the music in the background couldn't smother them. Her stomach clenched as they sank in, and the overwhelming amount of people in the room suddenly became claustrophobic.

"Don't look so shocked." The man backed away and tucked a hand in the pocket of his pants. "But if you think you have a chance of stealing it here...you're mistaken."

"Who the hell are you?" Diana asked, careful to keep her voice low. It didn't detract from the venom though, and her chest continued to quake in tight pain. "And why are you doing this? If you want my father, he isn't here."

"Sasha Sokolov." He extended a hand. No rings. No weapons. Just a watch peeking out from his sleeve. "And I know your father isn't here. That's why I want you instead."

The color drained from her face, and she dropped her gaze to his hand. He could break her wrist. Sling her into a chokehold. Grab her by the chin and snap her neck. Reaching for his hand would be stupid.

"I can't imagine why. I've never stolen anything of yours." Diana tried to hide the shake in her voice as she watched Sasha drop his hand back to his side.

"You haven't." He shrugged. "But I need your cooperation."

She put her hands on her hips. "I want the knife. Why would I help *you* get it?"

"No, no. You misunderstand." Sasha held up a hand, face chiseled into indifference. "I don't want your help to get the knife."

Diana looked him over. He seemed serious. "You don't?"

"No." Sasha glanced toward the front of the room, and she followed his gaze. A woman was pulling out a table on wheels with something bulky on top, but whatever it was had been covered in a black sheet.

"Then what do you want?"

"I want an audience with Charles Van Doren." His words made her blood run cold. Of course, he'd ask for the one thing she couldn't guarantee. Her father was everything but cooperative. "In exchange, I'll help you get your knife."

Diana closed her eyes and took a breath, trying to still her heart and the twist behind her sternum. It felt like an elephant was sitting on her chest. "If you know Charles, you know I can't guarantee anything."

"That's fine. I don't need a guarantee. Just a place to start."

"That sounds suspiciously like something my father would say. Not to mention the deal is lopsided." Diana shrugged and held her hands in front of the fire. "Sounds great on the surface, but nothing's free...especially that knife."

Sasha kept his distance uncomfortably close in an obvious attempt to intimidate her. "You're right. Nothing is free."

She swallowed and looked at him when the pain in her chest got too tight. "If you want my help, you've got to stop messing with my magic like this."

Sasha's eyebrows furrowed. "Pardon?"

"You know what I'm talking about." Diana frowned, but the man didn't relent. Perhaps he wasn't the one doing it. Although, even if Sasha were elbow deep in her magic, would he tell her the truth?

"We were wondering if one of you crows would show up," a new voice growled.

Diana stilled. The idiot had been too loud. She slowly moved to face the newcomer and unfortunately met the gaze of three werewolves with tight shoulders and curled fists.

Acting tough wouldn't save her, but she wouldn't roll over. "I don't know what you're talking about."

The one in front, presumably their pack Alpha or his second, crossed his arms over his chest. He wore a tank top and cargo shorts—a strange outfit for anyone not a werewolf in the dead of winter. Tanktop's sharp nails wouldn't have scared her on a normal day, but his eyes were a dangerous shade of green. Amir only had eyes like that close to the full moon.

He sneered at her. "I think you do...Diana Van Doren."

The room, now silent, watched them intently. Another werewolf behind the leader, a squat woman with blond hair, bared elongated teeth.

Damn you, Dad, she thought, taking a step back into Sasha.

"Your father screwed us over one too many times." Tanktop's nails stretched forward like slender knives, and a grin twisted along his stubble-coated jaw. He had a very punchable face. "I'd like to let him know exactly how I feel about it."

"Do you think he'd like her head?" the other male werewolf asked, eyes also shimmering green. His long, dark hair was pulled up in a topknot.

"Head? No." Tanktop uncrossed his arms as his canines pressed out from behind his upper lip. "Let's send him the thief's hands."

Diana weighed her options. She could try to shift and fly out, but werewolves were fast, and she didn't have a clue what Sasha could do. Then there was the problem of the fire blazing away beneath her rib cage. Something was clearly wrong, and she wasn't sure her magic would cooperate. Between the werewolves and Sasha, she couldn't see a way out of the house or the mess she found herself in. If she somehow managed to survive, she would let her father *have it*.

The wolf took a step forward, and Diana latched onto the magic within. Attempting to fly off would be her only choice. Fuck, this had to work.

"I'm going to insist you step aside." Sasha held a gun level with the werewolf's forehead. "This isn't the time or the place."

She gaped, instinctively taking a step back toward the fire. The heat blistered up the backs of her legs and neck.

"And who the fuck do you think you are?" the werewolf with the man bun asked, inching forward.

Diana moved closer to Sasha, positioning herself behind him and his gun. As much as she hated it, she hated the idea of dying a lot more.

"Her father—"

"Is not here."

She continued to move around Sasha, now cleared on the right side to run or shift if given the opportunity. No one in the silent crowd had moved to attack—yet—but she'd need to keep an eye out. Nobu still remained elusive, and given the thick pack of bodies surrounding them, rapt with curiosity, the boy would likely remain that way.

"I think we should gut you too." Man Bun growled, jaw cracking as his face began to shift. "She's trash, and if you're willing to protect trash...we've no use for you."

Several shrieks rippled from the crowd as a howl shook against the ceiling. None of the werewolves in front of her had done it, which meant there were more in the house somewhere.

She'd never escape at this rate.

"That's fine. I've no use for you either." Sasha threw his hand out to the side, gun tucked tightly in his palm, as a wolf from the crowd bounded toward them. Diana, paralyzed in fear, could do nothing but watch her death barrel toward her like a furious, frothing cannonball of fur and teeth.

Sasha didn't even turn to face him. He just pulled the trigger. Sent a bullet into the bridge of the wolf's nose without even looking.

Diana gasped as the wolf dropped to the ground in a lump of twitching flesh. Werewolves didn't go down like that unless they were shot with silver, and most people didn't keep silver bullets on hand. Who the hell was this guy?

Tanktop threw his head back and released a howl so thick it shook the ceiling. "Rip their throats out!"

Man Bun surged forward and swiped to the left as his body continued to shift into its true form. Diana leapt out of the way of the claws, but slipped on her heels and slid onto the marble.

One of the glass boxes behind her shattered despite being out of the immediate reach of the brawl. Someone was taking advantage of the distraction, and in any other circumstances, she'd join them. However, given that the fight in question centered on her beating heart, she had more important things to worry about.

She pulled on the magic aching in her chest and shifted midair, shaking free of her dress and pushing toward the ceiling the instant her arms morphed into obsidian wings. Diana held her wings aloft and coasted along the draft in the room, blood hot and heart erratic with fear. While thankful she could still utilize her magic, she wasn't sure what good it would do her without a way to escape the house.

The room had descended into chaos. Glass boxes fell to the floor, items of immeasurable value being swiped left and right from witches and fae and who knew what else. The sphinx, still human in appearance, wrapped a hand around the throat of a witch and held her there until a ruby amulet fell from her hand and struck the marble. Shortly thereafter, the selkie from the foyer tried to swipe the Tide Jewels, only to immediately be intercepted by the peeved sphinx.

Another gunshot redirected her attention back to Sasha, and she landed on a curtain rod. Man Bun lay dead on the floor, and blood pooled beneath his skull. The female werewolf had jumped between Sasha and Tanktop, fervently swiping toward her opponent as he bobbed and weaved.

Watching Sasha move was...well, Diana didn't know how to describe it. Confident where fear should've been, and he stepped and ducked with precision. She closed one of her eyes and focused on Sasha's torso. To anyone not a crow or some other creature with unnatural eyesight, it would seem like Sasha was simply well-trained. Years of fighting contributed to muscle memory, and muscle memory could definitely explain his ease with evasion.

But she was a crow, and she saw what most could not. Sasha moved milliseconds before the werewolf did. Like he knew what the werewolf was going to do and dodged accordingly. This went beyond experience. Beyond muscle memory. This was something else.

A female wolf slunk around in the back of the room and tried to come at him from behind. She had shifted before coming in, showcasing long, lean limbs, the height of a small horse, and a bushy white coat. Diana clung to the curtain rod and watched in apprehension. Sasha was no friend, of that she was certain, but he did intervene on her behalf. Should she try to warn him?

If he died, there was no way she'd get out.

Diana took to the air again and tucked her legs to her body. She couldn't believe she was purposefully diving right into a werewolf. How stupid.

The wolf's eyes moved to Diana, paws sliding on the tile to change course. She kept flying toward the wolf and hoped she wasn't making an irreversible mistake.

Sasha turned, arm slicing through the air in a sweeping arc, gun trained for the white wolf as it bounded through the room. Diana, seeing the movement in her peripheries, veered left. The recoil of the gun echoed along the marble floors and high walls.

The werewolf fell to its side, spasms racking her legs.

Staring at the dead wolf, Diana flew back to her perch on the curtain rod. Much too close for comfort.

The blond woman began to shift during Sasha's distraction and latched a partially morphed set of teeth on his left bicep. He jerked around with a grimace, pressed the barrel to the werewolf's temple, and pulled the trigger twice in quick succession. The woman, stuck in her midshift state, died in a bloody heap at his feet.

The uncomfortable thought that should've bothered her more during their conversation lingered well after Sasha held the last pair of werewolves at gunpoint. They were in human form, hands up, palms out.

What *was* Sasha?

"Are we done?" Sasha asked, voice level despite the dead were-wolves in the room and blood leaking from his arm.

If there were a time to fly out of the room, it was then. Diana knew that. But she couldn't pry her talons from the rod. This whole thing —*him*—was utterly bizarre, and she wasn't convinced he wouldn't know she left her place on the curtain and shoot her as she tried to escape.

"You're going to—"

"Pay?" Sasha interrupted Tanktop, and Diana squeezed the rod tighter.

Tanktop didn't intervene on behalf of his pack? Perhaps he wasn't the Alpha then, or even his second. Amir always spoke about his Alpha with nothing short of reverence, and this wolf didn't deserve that.

"I doubt it," Sasha finished confidently.

An eerie calm blanketed the room. No one moved save to breathe, and Diana didn't know what to do next. Leave? Find Nobu?

Was there even another exit? The only one she could see was blocked by the sphinx.

Soft clicks echoed against the marble floor, drawing everyone's attention to the woman who had wheeled out the covered table before the brawl. Her warm skin had paled considerably, and she took great care to avoid stepping in the blood pooling near her expensive stilettos.

"The auction has been canceled." The woman grimaced at the bodies bleeding out on the tile.

The sphinx stood off by the exit, which kept everyone else in place. The blood splattered along his cheeks and neck made for an ominous picture.

"It is time for you all to leave. Immediately," the woman said, voice firm.

Her hopes vanished. *The knife.* She had come for the damn knife, and she didn't even get to see it.

"Of course. Van Doren." Sasha looked up to Diana and lifted a hand. She relaxed marginally when she realized it wasn't the hand with the gun in it. He beckoned her with a quick bend of his fingers. "Come on. We have business."

After watching him shoot everyone else without even so much a glance, Diana held little hope she could escape him easily. Granted, she was a smaller target, much smaller, but the windows were all closed to the winter air, and the only way out was through the door she'd used to enter. The one guarded by the sphinx currently eating the selkie's dismembered arm.

She weighed her options, gaze intently focused on the gun as she shifted her weight on the curtain rod.

"Van Doren." Sasha's voice, tighter this time, shook along all the vertebrae in her body. "I'm not asking."

Diana relinquished her grip on the curtain rod and drifted down, dread hanging on every feather. Even though she still breathed, this single act of compliance felt entirely like a death sentence.

"Thank you," Sasha said as she landed on his shoulder. She tried to dig her talons in deep enough to poke him, but his suit jacket was too nice and thick. "You won't make it off this property alive without me, so I recommend not flying off."

Diana knew he was right, but she still hated it. She hated she the position she was in.

More than anything, she hated her father for sending her here in the first place. While she was the one who took the job, he was the reason they had no murder. He was the reason they were being chased by a demon.

And while she loathed to admit it, he was the reason she felt entirely expendable.

EIGHT

SASHA

Sasha winced as pain lanced through his arm. He hated werewolves. Their instincts completely overrode any urges to make intelligent decisions. As someone who valued plans and those who stuck to them, werewolves, naturally, weren't his favorite creatures to deal with. Given what he'd seen of her before the brawl, he had a feeling he wouldn't like working with the Van Doren woman either.

She dug her talons into his shoulder. While she was compliant for the time being, he could tell she didn't like it.

Sasha stopped walking and picked up the discarded dress and shoes. He'd need to speak to the woman eventually, and she'd likely be more amenable to his plans clothed. Boots scraping against the marble floor reached his ears, but no visions of danger graced him. Yet.

"Hey!" the werewolf with the highest rank present—the coward who let his pack mates die in his stead—hollered at his back. "We aren't done with you—"

"You are done," the woman of the house interrupted, mouth twisted in a grimace. "If you spill any more blood here tonight, Mr. Whitaker has threatened to inform your leader."

"My Alpha—"

"Not your Alpha." The woman crossed her arms.

Silence echoed along the walls, but Sasha didn't need the woman to explain. The owner of Sheturath—Whitaker—had clearly invited more than one general to the bidding war. Perhaps the owner of Sheturath was not as human as the rumors made him out to be. He needed to proceed carefully, or he'd risk starting a fight with another demon before he got his freedom.

"I haven't heard from my boss in over a year. I doubt he'll start giving a damn now," the wolf snarled, but made no moves to proceed. The other remaining werewolf, a female with flaming red hair, cowed at his side.

Sasha scowled. If the wolves weren't at the auction at the behest of the demon who bound them, then why were they there in the first place?

With no one to oppose him, the room parted. Van Doren kept her talons wedged deep into his jacket, clinging tight as he pressed through the crowd toward the door. He snorted, amused. She could try to stab him all she liked, but she needed him. The woman needed to get over it.

"Where's your friend?" he asked his unwitting companion as he stepped past the sphinx and out the front door. Van Doren cocked her head at him, which drew his attention to her animal form. He'd never seen a crow shifter up close before. Although getting a proper look at her was difficult with her perched so close to his face, one detail stood out. Three legs—interesting.

Blood continued to leak from his shoulder. Werewolves and their damned erratic instincts. He hadn't intended to let that wolf bite him, but he hadn't accounted properly for her change of course once he'd killed her pack mate. Wolves were loyal to a fault and tightly bound by magic to those in their pack. If he'd been smarter, he'd have known she would react as she did. In that respect, he probably deserved the bite.

Van Doren moved along his shoulder and angled her head to look at his wound. She opened her beak a bit, sending a wave of panic down his nerves that she planned on digging in the bloody gouges, but instead, she pinched a loose piece of fabric out of a chewed patch of skin and tossed it away.

The last thing he suspected was for her to be interested in his injury, much less care about it.

Unsurprisingly, no one tried to accost them on their way to the car. He welcomed the chilled night air that snaked around his neck and face, cooling the warmth of adrenaline. The crow shifted on his shoulder closer to his face, ruffling her feathers and tucking her beak to her chest. Given this alongside her place by the fire at the beginning of the night, Sasha gathered that crow shifters didn't care for the cold.

Despite her mouthy tendencies, the desire to learn smothered most of his dread at working with the woman. Crow shifters were relatively rare, and not much was known about them. Knowing more about them would make catching the elusive Charles Van Doren much easier, and more than that, he liked to know things others didn't.

Anticipating a need for a quick exit, he'd parked his rental car toward the back of the driveway and close to the gate. The objective to disrupt the event had been a success, and now he had less risk to contend with as long as he could shake the wolves. If he could do that, all that would stand between him and Sheturath would be whatever Whitaker kept in his house.

Sasha basked in the chilled breeze. He got a crow that could lead him to Charles Van Doren. Now all he needed to do was convince said crow to go along with the rest of his plan.

"I imagine you want to shift back?" Sasha asked and held up her clothes. While she couldn't respond, she didn't peck him, which was as good as a yes. He unlocked the car, and the crow flew inside. The second he hit the leather seat, he turned on the car and its heaters, knowing full well that the woman would be a shivering wreck when she shifted back.

He'd only just gotten his bloodied suit jacket off when he realized she was watching him. The crow held out her impressive wings, feathers ruffled and beak open. A shrill caw pierced the quiet of the car as she beat her wings around on the console.

She wanted him to get out.

Sasha huffed and glanced between the bird and his bleeding arm. He had more important things to worry about than her nakedness. They locked gazes, both stubborn for different reasons, and despite being annoyed, the desire for his plan to succeed won out. He opened the car door and stepped out into the chilled night.

If their partnership continued to be this obnoxious, perhaps he should reassess his plan.

"Hey!" A shout. Young voice. Male. "You! What the hell are you doing?"

Sasha pulled a knife from the holster along his side and cut away the bottom half of his shredded sleeve, barely paying any mind to the boy that stalked toward him. The crow's escort.

"What are you doing with her?" The boy pointed toward the car with a scowl. His shag of bangs hung in his eyes and eclipsed the true fear Sasha knew lurked within them. "You can't kidnap her or—"

"I'm not. She's coming with me." Not exactly a lie. The woman would go with him eventually. She just didn't know it yet.

He returned his knife to the holster and wrapped the loose fabric he'd taken from his sleeve around his bite. He'd had to wait to properly clean it, but he didn't want to bleed all over his rental. Trying to explain that away when he turned it in would be far more trouble than it was worth.

"Wait." The demon host held up a hand. "Why should we go with you? Everyone else is trying to kill us."

"Kill *her*. Not you. You're free to walk away." Sasha pulled the fabric taut and winced as more blood slid down his elbow and forearm.

"My name is Diana."

He turned around as she emerged from the back of his car. Fully clothed, but exhausted. Irritated. Her face was red, she'd propped her hands on her hips, and she had his bloody jacket on. Diana, indeed.

"And leave him alone. He's a kid."

Nobu scowled. "I'm not a—"

"He's a kid that is not involved in our business." Sasha finished tying off his makeshift bandage and held out a hand. "Cigarettes, please."

Diana stuck a hand in the inside pocket of his jacket and pulled out his pack of smokes and lighter. Sasha took them, not missing the way she jumped a little when his fingers grazed her palm.

Shivering, she glared at him. "Nobu is involved in my business, which means he's involved in our business."

Growing more irritated by the moment, he plucked a cigarette from the pack and stuck it between his lips. "Van Doren—get in the car. We need to leave before the wolves do. The last thing we need is to be followed."

"My name is *Diana*."

"And she's not going anywhere without me." Nobu crossed his arms. "You might be a total weirdo, but she owes me money."

Sasha took a moment to mentally regroup and light his cigarette. This endeavor would be more taxing than he planned on. "Fine. Get in the car before the wolves recover."

"Hey, you hold on!" Diana took a few steps forward, face flushed. "Why the hell do you think I would ever willingly go with you anywhere?"

"You want the knife, and I want a face-to-face with your father." Sasha ignored her attempt to instigate an argument and walked to the driver's side of the car. "Seems like a fair trade."

"Are you out of your mind?" Diana crossed her arms and scowled. She might not be a werewolf, but she was just as volatile. He didn't like that. "I watched you slaughter several werewolves, some of which weren't even in your line of sight when you shot them. Perfectly. In the head. Why in the world would I ever agree to work with you?"

All valid questions. "Because you'll never get your talons on Sheturath without my help."

Diana bit her lip and burrowed herself deeper in his coat. "What are you?"

Sasha closed his eyes and fell into the pieces of the future his subconscious decided to show him. The werewolves would be upon them if they didn't leave soon. He opened his eyes and found Diana's dark ones, surprised to see none of the venom he heard in her voice. Her gaze bounced to his bloodied arm for a moment, and the corners of her lips tipped down.

Desperate to end this ridiculous waste of time, he took a final drag, dropped his cigarette, and crushed it beneath his heel. "Get in the car, and I'll tell you."

Diana glanced at the kid a moment before heaving a sigh. "Fine. But if I change my mind, I can and *will* leave you."

Right. She could try.

Sasha popped open his door and sat in the seat. The leather had already started to warm marginally from the heaters, and Diana made it no secret that she enjoyed it when she collapsed beside him in the passenger seat. Then the door behind Diana opened, and the kid slipped inside, just as Sasha knew he would.

They barely reached the gate before Diana asked her question again. "So I'm in the car. What are you?"

He pressed his foot on the accelerator and sped up to sixty-five. The wolves would come after them soon, and they were fast and had keen noses. He needed to put as much distance between them as possible. The speed continued to climb. "In a word? A clairvoyant."

"Not in a word?"

"A man with a marginal amount of angel blood and the ability to see bits of the future." Sasha couldn't help but look at her as he whipped the sedan around a sharp corner. Diana had burrowed farther into his coat, eyes turned to her knees.

"Angel, huh?" She stuck her face close to the hot air coming out of the vent. "No wonder you shot everyone so easily. You know what everyone is going to do."

"No. The future changes, and I hardly see everything." Sasha motioned to his bleeding arm with a tilt of his head. "Clearly."

He kept his speed upwards of seventy until they got into town. They'd hit the highway and pick up speed again until they hit Dallas.

Between the distance and the smells of the city, they should be safe to stop at a motel for the night.

"You really need to take care of that."

Diana's voice drew his attention, and while he expected to see her eyes on him, he didn't expect to see her clutching at the fabric on her chest. The sweat on her brow. The shake in her hands. She slumped forward and brought her knees to her chest, shivering despite the generous heat billowing out of the vents.

How curious. She hadn't been hurt by the wolves. Had she been hit by a spell or something similar? There had been several witches present.

Sasha sighed. On second thought, finding a motel sooner rather than later might be the better choice.

NINE

DIANA

Diana hadn't wanted to stop at a motel with the sketchy sort-of angel or her demon-possessed companion. She wanted to leave both of them, slink back into the mansion, and steal the blade herself. While admittedly stupid and almost guaranteed to fail, especially because she didn't have a plan, at least she could get away. Something was making her unbearably uncomfortable, and when they parked, she couldn't get out of the car fast enough.

Her magic twisted within her chest and pulled at every nerve with enough tension to make her skin crawl. She couldn't sleep like this. She couldn't do *anything* like this. It had been bad at the house, but it only continued to get worse.

"Yo." Nobu nudged her with his elbow. She hadn't realized he got out of the car. "You okay?"

Diana inhaled and tried to will away the discomfort. Letting her potential enemies get the better of her wouldn't keep her alive. "Not really. This entire night was a disaster from the beginning."

"That's not what I mean."

"I'm fine."

Sasha had stopped at a motel right off I-35 South. It was a small, single-story beige block sitting next to dead shrubs beneath bare trees. Only two other cars were parked in the lot, thankfully. At least there wouldn't be many witnesses or ignorant victims if the werewolves found them.

"I'm going to get a room, and we'll regroup," Sasha announced as he stood from the car. He'd taken off his holsters, and blood still leaked from the fabric fastened around his bite.

Nobu cast her a sidelong glance. "We still haven't agreed to anything. There are things to discuss."

"Of course."

Diana bit her lip as she watched Sasha walk away, angry because he assumed she would agree to help him and frustrated as hell because the man had a nice ass. He disappeared behind the glass entry to the motel. The Christmas wreath hanging on the front jingled in his wake, shaking with a clang when the door slammed shut behind him. She could only imagine what the lobby receptionist would think about his bloody arm.

"He's gone." Nobu stepped in front of her, eyes narrowed. He was a few inches taller and somehow managed to be more imposing while looking down his nose at her. "What's wrong?"

"I don't know." Diana licked her lips. "My chest hurts, and I don't know why."

Nobu frowned. "Did you get hurt in the fight? I tried to watch, but a warlock almost got ahold of me."

Her stomach turned. She hadn't even thought about what Nobu might've gone through during the whole werewolf debacle, and here he was trying to take care of her. "No. Sasha handled it."

"Hm." Nobu let out of a puff of air into the cold night, and a chill racked her arms. "I don't like him. He's up to something."

That much was obvious. "You don't have to stick around."

"I'm here until I'm paid."

Diana's thoughts turned sour. If she happened to survive this whole thing, she might kill Charles herself. "But my father doesn't have any money. I told you that."

Nobu smiled in a way she could only describe as feline. "You said you'd pay me instead, remember?"

That was before everything went up in smoke, she thought wryly. Diana pulled the jacket tighter and took a deep breath. She had said it though. So stupid. "Won't your parents be worried?"

Nobu's gaze dropped to the ground. Given his youthful appearance, the question seemed appropriate. But Nobu was possessed. He could be a hundred years old for all she knew.

"No."

She deserved to be eaten by a werewolf at this rate. "I'm sorry."

"It's okay." Nobu put his hands in his pants pockets and shrugged. "What's your story then? I know your dad got kicked out of your murder, but I've never heard what you did."

Anger zipped along her nerves instantly. "I didn't do anything. I was just...easy to get rid of."

The sound of jingle bells thankfully stopped any sort of questions Nobu might've had. Sasha strolled toward them, lips pressed into a fine line. He was annoyed, and Diana didn't like that she knew that after only knowing him for an hour.

"We've got a room, but we can't stay long." Sasha walked over to the trunk and popped it open. He pulled out a black duffel bag and slung it on his shoulder before jerking his head toward the iron stairs leading to the second level.

The doors to each room had some degree of peeling paint and a holiday sign. After they drug themselves up the steps and in front of room 2G, Diana found herself face-to-face with a picture of a Santa Claus smiling beneath the peephole of their room.

While Sasha had chosen a lackluster motel for their evening accommodations, Diana hadn't stayed in anything so nice in years. The room was small and covered from top to bottom in green wallpaper that peeled up at the baseboard, accented with a worn couch and a single lamp. Carpet, two beds without dust, and—wait—a heater?

"Thank God." She shoved past Sasha, stood in front of the wall unit, and turned the knob all the way over. Warm air pushed through the vents and blanketed her skin in a cocoon.

"You act like you weren't just sitting in a heated car," Nobu said and closed the door.

Sasha dropped on the bed and set his black duffel beside him.

Diana watched Sasha peel off his makeshift bandage, uncomfortably aware of how much his injury bothered her. She returned her attention to Nobu instead. "I haven't lived in a place with proper heat and air conditioning in five years. I am going to enjoy it. Bask in it even."

"You won't have long to enjoy it," Sasha said, voice heavy. He unraveled the first layer of his bandage, and blood rolled down his arm in a thin trickle. "Staying in one place for too long will give the wolves ample time to find us."

"Yeah. Thanks to you." Nobu crossed his arms and leaned against the door. He'd pulled his tie loose and untucked his shirt, which made him seem so much younger. A boy in a man's clothes.

Sasha said nothing about the charge leveled against him. She figured he knew there was no sense in arguing about what all of them knew to be true. "We won't have to hide long. Tomorrow is a full moon, and all of them will return to their Alpha."

"That one jackass will have a lot to answer for." Diana clenched her teeth. The wolf who caused the trouble survived, but she didn't think he would much longer. Werewolves weren't known for letting cowards live long. "Hopefully, he gets his throat torn out."

"Whatever that guy has coming to him, he deserves." Nobu pushed his bangs out of his eyes to get a better look at Sasha, only for them to fall right back in the way. "I'm more interested in what *you* have in terms of a deal. I know you're up to something."

"I think we're all up to something." Sasha pinned Nobu with a pointed glare before turning to Diana. She swallowed as their eyes met, but she couldn't look away. "But it doesn't matter. There's a way for all of us to get what we want."

Diana turned her back on the heater, tired of watching her

companions through her peripheries. The hot air baked the backs of her legs. She really needed an outfit with better coverage. "Which is?"

"You want Sheturath." Sasha pressed his ripped sleeve to his bite, rust brown dried along his nail beds. "Now that the auction was canceled, we won't have to contend with as many risks. We will only have to deal with whatever Whitaker has inside his house when we steal it. After we get the knife, I'm sure you can work something out with our resident demon host in terms of the payment your father promised him. You take me to your father afterward."

"Diana and I could cut you out of the deal completely," Nobu said, the ghost of a smirk on his lips. If he weren't careful, Diana feared Sasha might do to him what he did to those wolves. "We're both discreet and can blend. No one would suspect us. We don't need you."

"*Humans* wouldn't suspect you. After tonight, I'm sure Sheturath is under constant surveillance, and I'm not sure the owner, Whitaker, is as human as we believed. And there are other creatures in his home that can figure you out...especially if they know what to look for. I knew the second I saw you both."

Diana dug her fingers into the fabric of Sasha's bloody jacket and winced as the pain surged in her chest. She hadn't ever stood a chance tonight. Had her father known of the risks?

She scoffed. Of course he knew. He just didn't care.

"You think you know what I am, but you don't." Nobu shifted his weight to his other foot. "And I fail to see what benefit you bring to the table. Seeing the future won't help us sneak into a mansion."

"I'm not keen on divulging my secrets, much like I'm sure you both have your own stories to tell." Sasha pulled back the ripped fabric and dropped it on the bed. The bleeding had slowed somewhat. "However, my plan for getting the knife can't be achieved without the two of you, and without the knife, I can't speak to Van Doren's father. That alone should assure you of my dedication to our task."

She bit back a retort. *My name is Diana, for fuck's sake!*

The room fell silent again. None of them trusted each other, that much was clear. However, Diana knew she couldn't return home without the knife. The demon hunting them was much too close, Amir had confirmed that the night before, and the knife was the only chance they had to appease the murder. As nice as flying off to some place warm and safe sounded, safety would never be a reality for her. Not alone, anyway.

"What's your plan?" Diana swallowed and tried to ignore the ache as her magic twisted behind her sternum. "You want to talk to my father? Fine. But I'm with the kid. What do you bring to the table?"

"Aside from being a clairvoyant and expert marksman?" The way Sasha looked at her made her face hot. "I can speak to the owner of the house. Distract him while you take the knife."

"Why do you think he'll give you the time of day? You ruined his auction."

"Unlike you, I was issued an invitation." Sasha cursed when more blood seeped from his wound. "Whitaker made contact with my boss in hopes he could sell us some of his artifacts. I'm sure he'll spare some time, ruined auction or no."

Diana groaned, frustrated with how little she truly knew about Sasha or Nobu. How could she trust either of them?

Lack of trust aside, she knew she had no choice but to go along with Sasha's suggestion that they work together. Not only did she not have a worthwhile plan of her own, but she desperately needed help. If Sasha proved to be dishonest, she'd take the knife and leave him. She wouldn't feel bad about not completing her side of the deal anyway. Not when a place with the murder was on the line.

"Quite frankly, if I don't get the knife, I'm dead." Diana laughed bitterly. "I'll take all the help I can get."

Nobu pushed off the door with a groan and watched Sasha. "Fine. But I don't trust you."

"Duly noted." Sasha reached over to his bag. "We'll leave here in four hours."

"All right." Nobu grabbed the doorknob. Where did he think he was going? "I'll be back then. I gotta let the cat out for a while, or we'll pay for it."

Diana licked her lips again, desperately searching for moisture. *Let the cat out.* What did Nobu mean, exactly? What did cat demons even look like?

However, the boy didn't explain. Sasha tossed him an extra key card. He gave the man a nod, pulled open the door, and left, leaving her alone with the man who could quite possibly know her every move.

TEN

SASHA

The pain rippling across Sasha's skin and deep into the tissues of his bicep stole his attention when the door clicked shut behind the boy. He'd gone an uncomfortably long time without addressing the bleeding, and if he didn't take care of it soon, his companions would start asking questions. While the angel blood coursing through his veins gave him the ability to heal his injuries, it wasn't something he liked to advertise. Having someone on hand that could heal wounds at the expense of their own safety was nice to have, but something people also tended to abuse.

It also came at a cost. A cost he wasn't keen to pay with unknown variants around.

He dug inside the duffel bag beside his leg as he loosened his tie. Gauze. Tape. Ointment. He'd probably have to suture some of the wound too. Sasha glanced at Diana, unsurprised when she wouldn't meet his eyes. "What kind of demon does the boy harbor?"

Diana's shoulders jerked. She swallowed and looked to the door. "Um. A cat demon? Whatever that means. That's what my father said."

Sasha paused, fingers stilling against a package of gauze. He had a feeling given the cat comment, but having it confirmed didn't make him feel much better.

"What did Nobu mean about letting the cat out?" Diana's voice, quiet against the rattling of the heater, barely reached him. She put on a good front, he'd admit, but she was scared...of him, in particular.

"I'm not sure. Cat demons are notoriously hard to control. They use their hosts for maybe a month and then leave them empty." Sasha stared at the door, almost hoping the boy didn't return. Christ. How did he manage to get stuck with Van Doren's daughter and the host of a cat demon at the same time? The odds were astronomical. "Perhaps they have a deal on how to share the body."

Diana grimaced. "You've met one before?"

More blood spilled from a deep puncture. Definitely needed stitches. Or privacy. "No. I've only ever heard of them. They don't make it a habit to get caught."

One of the exiled generals was a cat demon, but he'd never met it. All he knew were Madame's complaints regarding its somewhat flippant behavior.

Diana stared at his arm, lips pursed. "Do you want some help with that?"

Sasha rummaged through his bag for sutures. He really wished Diana would leave the room so he could heal his injuries. If he went into the bathroom and reappeared without a bloody arm, it would raise questions he did not want to answer. The last thing he needed was for her to know his weaknesses, and his ability to heal certainly came with one. "That's unnecessary."

She snorted and walked toward the bag. "I'm right here and not doing anything. If you're going to help us tomorrow, I'd rather you not half-ass your wound care."

Sasha assessed his reluctant companion. She still had a hand pressed to her chest and clenched the fabric of her dress. Given the woman's occupation the last several years, her aversion to blood surprised him. "Why does it bother you? You don't know me, and from what I can tell, you don't like me."

Diana ground her teeth together. "Honestly? I have no idea because I shouldn't care about your stupid arm. But you're taking forever to fix it, and it's driving me crazy, so let me help."

While he knew very little about the intricacies of crow shifters, he knew that much like werewolves, their inner animal drove a lot of their decision-making. However, he didn't figure them to be especially squeamish. When he didn't move to give her permission, she reached for a clump of gauze and the bottle of peroxide and dabbed the edges of his bite.

Her dark hair hung along her skin in a curtain and skimmed her jaw. Soot-colored lashes hid her eyes as she gently wiped the blood away, and something told him she liked it that way. After hiding from almost everyone since her father got kicked out of the murder, it probably felt more like home.

Sasha continued to study her. If he had to guess, he'd say Diana was somewhere in her late twenties. Despite being improperly fed, she really was quite beautiful, and that wasn't a compliment he doled out often.

The thought bothered him the longer he dwelled on it. How did a crow shifter in her prime, a *female* one no less, get booted from her murder when their species continued down the slope to extinction? Crows weren't formidable fighters, which was why Madame never attempted to recruit them into her ranks to begin with, and their habit of dying prematurely in attempts to survive was no secret.

Sasha decided to ask. "What did you do?"

"What do you mean?" She paused in cleaning his wound, her face somehow even more pallid than it had been at the auction.

"What did you do to get ousted from your murder?"

"Why do you ask?"

"Just curious." Sasha angled his head to get a better look at her, but Diana kept her eyes averted and hidden beneath her lashes. She resumed cleaning along the longest of the lacerations. "From what I understand, crows are social creatures dependent on the safety of their murder. I can't imagine what could've compelled you to leave that for your dreg of a father."

"I didn't exactly get a choice," Diana bit out and pressed some gauze against the deepest puncture. He ground his teeth together with the increase in pressure, not missing how she appeared somewhat remorseful as blood continued to leak down his arm. She finally looked at him. "It won't stop bleeding."

If he didn't care about arousing suspicion, Sasha would've forced her to leave the room then. But since revealing his latent healing abilities was out of the question, he decided to resort to the more human remedy. "Suture it."

She frowned and picked up a suturing kit he'd tossed on top of the bed. "I have no idea how to do this."

"I'll do it. Just keep the blood off the bed." He put the kit in his mouth and tore the package with his teeth. "What happened with your murder?"

"God. You're so nosy. Is this really the time for these questions?" The pressure of her fingers against his skin grew as she caught the errant blood with the gauze. "Besides, it's personal."

Interesting.

"How far can you see?" she asked, changing the subject.

"Wondering if I see your deception, Van Doren?"

Diana gritted her teeth and glared. "No. I'm worried about those wolves coming to eat me. I didn't know if you'd see them coming."

"Moments. Sometimes hours. No more than that." Sasha threaded his suture and pressed the needle into his skin. Diana closed her eyes a moment but opened them again to keep the blood off the bed with the gauze as he asked. The sharp bite of the needle point drew a grunt from his chest.

"Are you okay?" Her eyebrows knit together, and she stared at him wide-eyed.

Sasha paused, the needle resting against his flesh. Something about the way she looked at him made him distinctly uncomfortable. It had been a long while since anyone had watched him with concern, and seeing that emotion on her face shifted something inside him that he hadn't felt in quite some time.

Then, as if remembering who he was, Diana dropped her gaze to the blood leaking down his skin. "I mean, if you turn into a werewolf, I'm not sticking around."

"I'm fine." While werewolf bites could change the average human, thankfully he was not average. Life bound to a ball in the sky and unreasonable instincts would be his personal hell. He returned to the suture. "If this bothers you, rest assured I can do it myself."

She wiped up more blood. "Hurry up."

Sasha continued sewing his skin back together in silence. While Diana was quiet, her presence was not. Uncomfortably aware of her, he tried to focus on his task. He didn't want to think about what his mother would say about his plan to betray her in the end.

Sasha swallowed and steeled his resolve. The situation, no matter how distasteful, warranted the payoff. He'd weighed the risks accordingly. He'd planned for several outcomes, and so far, his precognition hadn't reared its head, which meant all was, presumably, well. No more bloodshed for the time being. Everything had started to fall into place as he planned that they would, and that was all that mattered.

Or at least that's what he told himself. Diana still hadn't looked at him again, and for some reason or another, it bothered him. Before Madame stole his childhood, he hadn't been an unreasonable bastard, yet now it occurred to him with astounding clarity that he was.

"Thank you for your help."

Diana kept her eyes down. "No problem."

After placing the sutures, they'd wrapped up his arm in a copious amount of gauze and tape. As Sasha watched, Diana secured the last bit, the shake in her fingers reminded him that while she was a magical being, part of her was also very human. The human part of her struggled to keep up in a world diametrically opposed to the one her crow desperately wanted. A life on the run alone was not a happy one for a social bird, and she'd been living it for years.

She tossed the remainder of the tape roll back in the duffel and pulled his ruined suit jacket close. Her eyes still didn't meet his, and she said nothing as she turned to the door. "Where are you going?"

"If you think I'm going to sleep in here and drop my guard around you, you're not as smart as you think you are." Diana turned slightly. "Too many people want to kill me, and I wouldn't put it past you either."

"Why would I kill you?" he challenged, surprised at the vague notion of insult nestled in his stomach. Of course this woman would feel threatened by him, only an idiot wouldn't be, but he hadn't actually done anything to warrant this suspicion. Yet. "I need you alive if I hope to speak to your father."

She shrugged. "You could be lying."

"I could be, I suppose. But if I wanted to kill you, I've had ample opportunity. Opportunity I, notably, haven't taken." This also bothered him, although it was true. He was lying to her in the grand scheme of things. "I won't kill you. You have my word."

"And how good is your word?"

Both of them fell silent.

Once upon a time, his word had meant something. In some instances, Sasha supposed it still did. He'd promised his mother he would come home. That he would break his ties to Madame and end her control over their bloodline forever. He had also promised Madame in the form of a blood-bound signature that he would retrieve Sheturath and the Van Dorens, and he intended to keep that promise lest he wished himself very dead.

Sasha traced Diana's face. Her charcoal brows. Her sharp nose. While quite pretty, that wasn't the part about her the stuck out to him the most. A familiar glaze in her eyes, one that spoke to years of loneliness and exhaustion, reminded him entirely too much of the eyes he saw each time he looked in a mirror. It was the look his mother somehow knew about despite being across the globe.

"I'm not going to kill you, Van Doren." Sasha stood and zipped up his duffel. His clothes were in the trunk of his rental car. He could switch out the bags. "You said yourself that you haven't slept in a heated room or a proper bed in years. Take advantage of it while you can."

The woman eyed the other queen-size bed, clearly torn.

"I understand your apprehension," Sasha continued, eyeing the door. "A lone crow in the wild is a dead crow, yet I can assure you our interests tonight align far more than any deal you've made with your father."

"You assume I trust my father. I don't." Diana smiled bitterly. "Don't be offended by my hesitation. I haven't truly slept in years."

He could only imagine what his face looked like. He, Sasha Sokolov, *offended*? By her, no less? Absolutely not. The implication was almost laughable.

She walked away from the door toward the bed closest to the bathroom. "I'll stay. But know if you kill me, you'll probably never find my father, and I know for a fact he won't come out of hiding to come look for me either. And if you do anything else, I'll kill you. Knife or no."

Sasha gripped the doorknob, unsure how to proceed. However, after several beats of silence, he decided against responding at all. The woman wouldn't be comforted by his half-truths even if he uttered them, and continuing to spin them only offered up moments to screw up. He jerked open the door and strolled out into the December night, thankful for the brisk wind. The sky, clear and bright with stars, painted a peaceful backdrop to their dangerous evening.

When he returned to the room, Diana lay curled on top of the comforter on the far side of her bed. She'd drawn her knees up to her chest and draped his bloody jacket on top of her arms and legs, shivering despite her place closest to the heat and the blanket under her legs.

Sasha made a face. How inefficient. There was a perfectly good comforter right beneath her.

But hours later, long after he'd changed and tried to close his own eyes, it occurred to him that Diana hadn't been inefficient at all. She had kept distance between them and didn't risk the potential restraint of a blanket. She'd plotted as he did—make a move, but always plan for a quick exit.

Diana Van Doren had lived in fear for years, and she still did. This time she feared him, and she took steps to escape if she needed them.

For some reason, as he watched her form rise and fall in shaking breaths, shame crept inside his chest like an insidious disease. A disease so malignant and infectious, every horrible thing he'd ever done played inside his mind like a film reel.

His mother hoped for him to find someone, anyone, to help him keep his humanity. She knew what he'd been tasked to do over the years for Madame. Yet for some inexplicable reason, she never once doubted or thought ill of him for it. Hell, some part of her thought he deserved peace. What a novel thought.

Sasha rolled his head along the pillow and watched the tight form of Diana quake in the light of the moon spilling in through the window.

His poor mother would be disappointed in him, but perhaps she'd forgive him when he was finally free.

ELEVEN

DIANA

Diana woke up to something batting at her nose. Once. Twice. Three times. She swatted at whatever it was and opened her eyes, hazy vision greeted by something undeniably inhuman and furry. Was that a tail?

She almost careened right off the edge of the bed and into the slim gap between it and the wall. Her heart beat furiously in her throat, and the urge to vomit grew with each passing second. Her magic, inflamed in both fear and confusion, arose completely from her crow instincts. *Not safe. Not safe. Not safe.*

"It's fine, crow."

The unfamiliar voice focused her eyes on the green wallpaper as panic welled inside her stomach. Had Sasha betrayed her? Had he offered her up to the wolves in exchange for the pack's forgiveness? The thought pulled at her stomach, but it also brought attention to the feeling, or lack of feeling, in her chest.

Whatever made her uncomfortable the night before had stopped. On the contrary, she felt warm. Different.

"Yo. Crow lady."

Diana swallowed and redirected her attention where it should've been all along—the voice.

A voice that belonged to a black cat. One that, aside from the voice, appeared to be completely ordinary. She narrowed her eyes at his ears. The fur coming out of them curled toward the center of his head, which made them look like horns.

Sasha's description of cat demons came back in a rush. She leaned forward a bit, nose scrunched. "Nobu? Is that you?"

"The kid's not here right now," the cat said.

She sat up and appraised the beast. "I expected you to look more...malevolent."

The cat's tail whipped around. "And after listening to the kid's inner monologue about you all damn night, I expected you to be a little less rude."

Diana frowned. This demon was a world away from Nobu. "How long have you been here?"

"Awhile. You've been asleep too long, and the Russian is awake."

Diana bit her lip and focused on her surroundings. Sasha's bed was empty, but she could hear the shower running on the other side of the wall behind her. The sky outside the window was still dark, so she hadn't slept for more than a few hours. Sasha had said four hours until they moved again to keep distance from any wolves should they be hunting them. Maybe they were about to leave.

The thought sank in deeper. She'd slept in the same room as a clear threat, and she'd slept peacefully. What the hell was wrong with her? She didn't wake up once.

Diana ran a hand through her hair, and her fingers tangled in several knots. What she wouldn't give for a brush. "Do you have a name, cat?"

"Natsu." The cat stretched and flexed its claws against the comforter. "The kid got you some stuff. There's a few bags on the floor."

Diana's eyebrows inched up her forehead in surprise. Nobu got her something? She crawled to the opposite edge of the bed and peered down, shocked to find several things.

"Why did he do this?" She reached down and snagged a plastic bag between her fingertips. Jeans. "I figured he was desperate for money since he agreed to work with my father."

"He said we'd stick with you until you paid him. I guess he didn't want to walk around with someone who looked like they lived in a dumpster." Natsu hopped down to the carpet and swatted at another bag. A couple of T-shirts and socks tumbled out. "I tried to talk him into leaving the both of you idiots, but he didn't want to. Can't imagine why. Nasty bird."

Diana scowled. "You're one to talk, *demon*."

"I let him do his thing. I'm not that bad."

She rolled her eyes, unconvinced. The rest of the bags had all sorts of random things—even boots. How long had Nobu been out to get all this?

"Did Nobu get to sleep at all?" Diana asked, guilt twisting inside her stomach.

"He doesn't need to sleep. Not with me."

Nobu never had to let his guard down. "Huh. That must be nice."

"We're going to be working together to get this knife." Natsu cocked his head at her, tail whipping around behind him.

She hadn't considered that. But Natsu would likely be more helpful in a heist. No one would suspect a cat.

"If you're nice, I won't eat you."

"You could try, but I could always peck your eyes out."

The cat appraised her. "I think we'll get along fine. Besides, the kid likes you. I won't eat the first person to pay him any attention in months."

Diana frowned and sifted through all the clothes. She hadn't even been particularly kind to Nobu. Poor kid must've been as lonely as she was if his demon made a point to mention it.

Something else about Natsu's comment bugged her though.

"Months?" Diana asked. Didn't Sasha say cat demons only

possessed their hosts long enough to leave them a dead husk after the fact? "How long have you possessed Nobu?"

"About a year."

"A year?" Nobu really was still a kid then. She pulled a shirt from the bag. A flannel. "He told me he'd been possessed for a while."

"You know how kids are. No concept of time."

Diana felt along the flannel. Nobu had gotten her sizes right and everything. Thoughtful kid. Her heart sank. "Why did you possess him?"

The lingering *he didn't deserve it* hung in the air.

"Not my story to tell." Natsu walked over to her pillow and pushed around on the cushion with his paws. "You need to be careful."

The cat's abrupt command made her heart rate climb. "I know that. Obviously."

Natsu blinked. "No. I don't think you do."

She made to retort, but the door to the bathroom swung open. Diana clung to the flannel in her hands, fearful all over again for reasons she couldn't explain.

Sasha glanced at her as he walked back into the room. He had on a crisp white dress shirt free of blood and a tie slung around his neck. His sandy hair, still damp from his shower, clung to his forehead in tousled disarray. She hopped to her feet and busied herself with putting together an outfit, but even after that, Sasha still stared.

"What?" she asked, making sure to weave a healthy amount of bite into her words. However, the effect was ruined by her sudden desire to hyperfocus on him. On everything about him. The way his hair shimmered *just so* in the light of the lamp.

Sasha lifted a hand and motioned to her mess of hair with a lazy bat of his hand. A drop of water rolled down his neck and slipped beneath the collar of his shirt. "What did you do to your hair?"

The humiliating realization that she'd been staring set her body on fire. How embarrassing. "It's called sleep, asshole."

Sasha glared at her hard. He clearly didn't like that nickname, and suddenly calling him an asshole seemed like a colossal mistake.

"Sorry," Diana said, despite not being the least bit sorry. She absently ran a hand through her hair. It didn't feel any different than usual. A knotted, dirty mess like it had been prone to being the past five years. The lack of accessibility to a shower certainly hadn't helped her in having exceptional personal hygiene or a fashionable style.

Her gaze slid to the open bathroom door. Some time under the hot water would be nice. Her last shower at a campsite was cold as shit, and maybe she wouldn't look like roadkill anymore.

Heat blistered under her eyes. God—why was she embarrassed? She didn't care what anyone in the room thought of her morning hair.

Or at least she shouldn't have cared.

Sasha was still staring, and her heart dropped. "Why are you staring at me?"

He rubbed both of his eyes with a forefinger and thumb. "I apologize. My eyes are...well, I'm not sure what they're doing."

Diana squeezed the flannel to her chest and glanced at his bandaged arm. Was he sick? Maybe he'd gotten some weird werewolf infection or something. "What do you mean?"

Sasha inhaled and shook his head. "I'm sure it's nothing."

She propped her hands on her hips with the flannel clenched in her fist. "Are you turning into a werewolf? Did that bite change you?"

"That isn't possible."

Diana didn't know if it were possible or not, but she wasn't happy with such a vague response. "Then what do you mean? What's wrong with your eyes?"

The two stared at each other in silence.

"I bet there's nothing wrong with your eyes." Natsu's voice broke their battle of wills. Sasha didn't seem pleased with Natsu being in the room. His lips flattened into a tight line as he took the cat in. "In fact, I think you're seeing the best you ever have in your life."

Diana swallowed, uneasy for some reason. She looked at Sasha expectantly. "Is that true?"

The man sighed, annoyed. He walked away from them both and headed for his suitcase. "Yes."

Did he have to be difficult? She cleared her throat. "I'm confused. Why is your eyesight suddenly good?"

"It was never bad." Sasha looked up from his suitcase as he latched it shut. "I'm just seeing things in more detail. Crisp."

"I bet that's hard for you to understand, crow." Natsu turned around in a circle and curled up on the pillow, tail waving. "You've always had impeccable vision."

Her uneasiness increased. "How did you even know he could see better?"

"Just a feeling I got." Natsu closed his eyes and wrapped his tail around his body.

Seriously? That's all the cat had to say?

Diana snorted and dug out some jeans from the bags Nobu brought and silently assembled her outfit. Too many strange things had happened since she woke up, the demon cat notwithstanding. She'd slept peacefully. Her chest didn't hurt anymore. Sasha, for whatever reason, could see better than he had the day before.

Cold crawled up her neck.

Sasha could *see*.

She collected her clothes, bolted to the bathroom, and slammed the door behind her in a flurry. There was no way. Surely not.

Diana tossed her clothes on the laminate counter and held up her fingers, ticking them off as she mentally listed all the suspect phenomena. All the signs were there. But again, surely not.

The pain in her chest. The uncomfortable surge of magic as she watched Sasha and his stupidly handsome face by the fire at the auction. The fact she'd felt safe enough to sleep with him only feet away. Sasha waking up with enhanced vision.

No. It wasn't possible.

She couldn't have bonded with Sasha.

Diana sank to the linoleum floor and sat against the wall to pick apart her theory.

Bonding: the foundation of murders. The magical connection that linked each and every crow welcomed into the flock.

All the crows shared magic, and that's what made murders the safe harbors they were. They could pool their magic together in times of hardship and funnel it to Lead Crow to protect them or teleport them away from danger. It was the only reason their species had survived as long as it had. Alone they were weak. Together they could survive.

A more distressing thought pierced her brain, much like the bullet she'd taken in the wing, a thought she used to find comfort in: the murder bond was forever.

"I swear to God." Diana tilted her head back and hit the wall with a thud. If her fucked-up magic had bonded with that infuriating man instead of the crows...

She growled as another thought weaseled its way into her mind. Maybe she was wrong.

Yes—she had to be wrong.

She'd never heard of a crow shifter bonding with anything other than a crow before, and the more she thought about it, the more asinine it seemed. Humans—angels—couldn't be murder. They weren't safe. They weren't family.

Sasha must be turning into a werewolf. Or maybe he got nailed by a rogue spell in the turmoil at the auction.

But that wouldn't explain why the pain in her chest was gone...

Diana shook her head and pushed herself to her feet. She must've gotten too much sleep. That was the only explanation for a thought as stupid as that one had been.

TWELVE

SASHA

Sasha didn't know what to think about Diana's strange mood from earlier that morning. He hadn't been in the company of others much in recent years, and while he could study them, he oftentimes couldn't relate to them. Living with demons for years would do that to a person. He supposed this was one of those times.

Although, his new and improved eyesight couldn't be ignored.

Sasha stared down at his coffee and watched the ripples as he lightly moved the mug. While his vision hadn't been terrible, it had been nothing like this. Clear. Damn near perfect.

Hopefully, he hadn't been wrong about the werewolf bite.

They'd left the motel before sunrise, hoping to keep their distance from the werewolves that were undoubtedly hunting them down. However, getting the knife later that night would require all the concentration and energy they could muster, so they stopped at a run-down diner in a Dallas suburb for some breakfast. Much to his consternation, the coffee was terrible, and he'd seen two cockroaches brushed under the hostess stand. However, his two companions didn't seem to mind.

"He likes you. Swear." The demon cat had relinquished control of

Nobu, and the boy was himself once more. He sat across from him in the booth, currently attempting to smother a grin. Nobu had smiled more in the last hour than Sasha remembered witnessing from a single person. It was unsettling.

"Your demon needs to watch his mouth. Threatening to eat me and whatnot," Diana said with a mouthful of eggs, with more dangling from her fork. She'd already eaten two plates.

"Natsu isn't so bad." Nobu's nose crinkled as he appraised a fleck of egg stuck to her chin. He leaned into the window beside him. "You eat like an—"

"Animal?" Diana shrugged. "I haven't had a full meal in months. I'm literally starving."

Sasha's grip on his coffee mug increased. What he knew of Charles Van Doren he didn't care for, and Diana's comment certainly didn't help.

The boy grimaced and pushed his side of pancakes over to her. "Sorry."

"It's fine." She gave him some side-eye. "Natsu told me you've been possessed for a year. That's a little less time than you implied last night."

Nobu blushed and looked at the table. "I'm still not a kid."

"Unless you're over the age of twenty, you are a kid to me."

Sasha tightened his fingers around his mug again as he tore his gaze away from the waves in his coffee. The demon had stayed with Nobu for a year? Unheard of. "I'm surprised he didn't leave you for dead months ago."

Nobu shrugged. At some point during the night, the kid had gotten himself and Diana clothes. He looked much more at home in the long-sleeved T-shirt than he had in the oversize suit. "Like I said, he's not so bad."

"Will he cooperate in our heist? I imagine he'll be the one doing the heavy lifting," Sasha asked. The last thing he needed was a volatile demon on top of a volatile crow.

"Yeah."

Sasha took a drink of his coffee and savored the warmth sliding down his throat despite the taste of burned grounds. "Van Doren—can you work with the demon long enough to get Sheturath?"

Diana slumped against the booth and wiped her mouth with the back of her hand. A long, dark braid hung over her shoulder. Between it and her red flannel, she looked like a lumberjack. Or so he told himself.

"Of course I can." Diana sighed. She'd never given him an explanation for her sudden bolt to the bathroom that morning. Not that it really mattered. They wouldn't be working together long anyway. But it was curious. "I would really appreciate you using my name. Like I've asked several times."

"Van Doren is your name."

She pulled her shoulders back, drawing his attention to the slope of her neck. A tiny scar lingered beneath her jaw, and he wondered how she got it. "My name is Diana."

"Anyway," Nobu interjected with a wary glance between them. Soft holiday music played in the background, but it wouldn't be loud enough to drown out a potential argument. Perhaps the boy had a more level head than he thought. "What's the plan?"

Diana pointed at Nobu with her fork, eyes narrowed. "Why are you asking him?"

"Because he can see the future. Makes sense, don't you think?" Nobu pushed her fork out of his personal space with a finger.

While clearly miffed, Diana said nothing.

"As I said last night, I can't see everything, and the future is always changing." No need to tell them he could only see when *he* was in danger. That would only give them more reason to distrust him, as if they didn't have enough. "However, what pieces I have seen held the sphinx and Whitaker, so we'll need to be mindful of both of them."

Diana's eyebrows knit together. "Whitaker?"

"Edward Whitaker. The owner of Sheturath."

"No. I know that." She swatted a hand around, dismissing him. She used so much emotion even when she said nothing. It was irritating. "My father said the guy who owned the knife was human."

"Human as he might be, that doesn't mean he didn't stumble into something he should've kept buried." Sasha thought back to the woman in the heels from the night before. Whitaker knew about the generals, which meant they needed to proceed with extreme caution. Normal humans didn't know about them. Hell, most supernatural creatures didn't either. "At any rate, we need to be careful."

"Did you see Whitaker last night?" Diana turned to look at Nobu, eliciting a whine from the booth's red vinyl.

"If I did, I didn't know it. Natsu and I got cornered by that warlock, remember? He tried to bind us." Nobu spun his glass of orange juice between his palms. "He wanted Natsu, but I'm not sure how he knew about him in the first place."

Diana frowned at what remained of her eggs. Sasha hadn't known the cat dealt with a warlock, and he sincerely hoped said warlock wouldn't be at the house today. Humans willing to sacrifice their souls to use malignant magic were hard to predict since they didn't abide by logic. Clearly.

"If you know what a demon feels like and how they act inside their host, it's easier to pinpoint them," Sasha offered, although the cogs in his brain continued to turn. He didn't like the uncertainty of a warlock purposefully seeking the cat demon hiding within the boy. There was no telling how far the warlock would go to get him, and they already had enough to worry about with the werewolves.

"No. He wanted Natsu specifically. Knew what he was and everything." Nobu pushed his bangs out of his eyes. "And I don't tell people about him. The only reason I told Diana's dad was because he could feel Natsu in me when we met. He wanted to make sure I wasn't carrying around a demon named Madame."

Sasha hoped the surprise in his chest didn't show on his face.

"Yeah. That bitch has been trying to kill us for a while." Diana polished off her eggs and moved on to Nobu's pancakes.

"I asked Natsu if he knew Madame. For what it's worth, he also called her that."

Sasha drummed his fingers along the side of his mug. He'd have to be careful around the cat, especially if he knew Madame. The last thing he needed was for his plans to be spoiled because of a lazy demon.

Although if Natsu knew who he worked for, wouldn't he have mentioned it that morning?

A shadow moved over the table, and the conversation stopped. While it was only the waitress, she didn't need to hear about them stealing a knife, or the creatures they might or might not encounter. Humans didn't tend to react well to talk of the supernatural variety.

"Can I get you anything?" she asked. Blond hair, piled high on her head in a knot, framed a tanned face and blue eyes. The waitress looked at him and smiled a little, bright-red lips curling along her jaw.

Sasha lifted his coffee and nodded. "We're fine."

"I like your accent." She dropped a hand on his shoulder, and irritation zipped down his back. "Where are you from?"

"Russia."

She smiled wider and leaned forward a little. Her hand still lingered on his shoulder. "What brings you to Texas? Business...or pleasure?"

"Business," Diana ground out from her place across from them, gaze hard. She held her fork like a prisoner would a shiv, and a part of him wondered if she'd stab the waitress with it. "Which we are trying to take care of...if you don't mind."

Nobu winced, possibly embarrassed. "We'll let you know if we need anything else."

The woman blinked and looked between all of them, her gaze remaining on Sasha the longest. "Of course. I'll come by again later."

Sasha drummed his fingers on the table. Shifters and their instincts. He'd have to do something to keep the crow in check. Diana could spoil everything if she didn't keep her emotions under control, although he didn't know what got her riled up to begin with.

Doing work for Madame alone was much easier. Dealing with erratic emotions? Entirely too taxing. "She wouldn't have harmed us."

"That's not the point." Diana shook her head and pushed the plate with the remainder of the pancakes toward the center of the table. "We ready?"

The boy stood up, looked at him, and shrugged. "Sure. We can go over specifics in the car. Right?"

Sasha nodded and drank the rest of his nasty coffee in a single gulp. The waitress made to come to the table and see them off, but he didn't plan on waiting or potentially causing a scene. He dropped a fifty-dollar bill on the table, which more than covered their expenses, and stalked to the door. His mother would be terribly displeased with his manners.

The wind jerked the door out of his hand when he opened it, causing it to crash into the wall behind it. A cold front must be coming, and given the drape of clouds hanging in the distance, Sasha figured rain would come too. Or snow, if the temperature dropped a little. It didn't snow much in Texas, but it might be enough to frost the roads. If that happened, they'd have to avoid the highways. People in the southern states had no idea how to drive on ice, and since they were bound to travel by road, planning for adverse weather made sense.

Diana's shivering form stole his attention from the horizon. Thanks to his new eyes, every dark strand of hair tied back in her braid was known to him. The dirt beneath her fingernails. The red at the tops of her ears. Another scar at the base of her neck.

Utterly fascinating.

He cleared his throat. "Why'd you do that?"

Diana turned around to face him and pushed her shoulders back. "Excuse me?"

She waited until he caught up to her before walking again. Sasha tucked his hands into the pockets of his pants. "The waitress. I thought you might stab her, and I would like to know what provoked your behavior."

She sighed and stopped walking. "Instinct, I guess." Her shoulders hunched over as she squeezed herself tighter. "I don't know. I could tell you were uncomfortable when she touched your shoulder, so I said something."

He blinked and thought on his next words carefully. "You could tell I was uncomfortable?"

Diana brushed a stray hair out of her face, but she couldn't hide the red along her cheeks. "You did this thing with your eyebrows—I don't know. You were uncomfortable."

Sasha could only imagine what his face looked like. They'd known each other for less than twenty-four hours, and after years of keeping his true feelings from the world, Diana had somehow managed to discern that he didn't like being touched. He knew he'd been somewhat ill-equipped to decipher most emotions given his childhood in relative seclusion and living among demons, but *Christ*. She'd gotten that from eyebrows?

Diana turned on a booted heel and walked toward the car, arms wrapped around her stomach. Like the rest of her outfit, the coat Nobu had stolen for her was a little too big. It didn't help that she might've only weighed one hundred pounds.

Sasha drummed his fingers against his thighs in contemplation before walking to the car, checking his eyebrows in the rearview mirror once inside. His eyebrows didn't say anything. They simply existed. There was nothing special about his eyebrows, and they certainly didn't tell Diana anything.

He thought back to her defense. *Instinct*. He hated that word.

They drove around for a while after that, making sure to take several turns and stick to highways to throw off any potential were-wolves tailing them. However, for the first time in recent memory, Sasha found himself completely befuddled. He couldn't focus on the plan, the knife, or even the potential of encountering a warlock. All he could think of was Diana's words, her red face, and how she somehow got a read on him.

He'd have to keep his new and improved eyes on her. Diana Van Doren wasn't as simple as her father, and the last thing he needed was for her to ruin his plans.

THIRTEEN

DIANA

D<small>IANA HAD NEVER BEEN MORE THANKFUL FOR SUNSET IN HER</small> entire life. In the dark, no one could see the lingering blush on her face or the all-consuming humiliation that had coated her from head to toe since breakfast.

She'd basically threatened that waitress. For Sasha. Like an idiot.

Truthfully, she hadn't even thought about it. Aesthetically, Sasha was attractive, so it was no surprise the waitress flirted with him. Had it ended at flirting, she wouldn't have said anything. She had a pair of eyes, really good ones actually, so she'd known the moment the woman had taken her flirting a step too far. The second he flinched. But the waitress kept going, and for whatever reason, it pissed her off.

She glowered. She shouldn't have cared. Yesterday, she probably wouldn't have. But between now and then, she'd apparently come to the conclusion that the clairvoyant angel person who'd invaded her life was, indeed, deserving of protection. However hopeless and inconsequential hers happened to be. Except, much like her desire to tear the head off the waitress, she didn't understand why she suddenly cared about his comfort. By all rights, she shouldn't. If it came down to protecting Sasha or getting the knife, she would choose the knife.

Her chest tightened as the thought she'd had that morning crept into her brain. Could it have happened? Could her magic have—

"No." Diana squashed that line of thought. "Absolutely not."

"What's wrong, Diana?" Nobu asked. He leaned against Sasha's car, hands tucked into his jacket.

"Nothing." She'd rather die than tell him the truth. Thankfully, Nobu dropped it.

They'd parked the car on the main road and off the inordinately long driveway leading to Whitaker's house. Now they waited for Sasha to assemble his weaponry. As it turned out, he had quite the arsenal in his truck.

"Why do you have all of this?" Diana asked, voice tight as her gaze roved over the guns, knives, and bullets hidden inside. She'd almost died on Whitaker's property yesterday. She needed to know why Sasha had a mobile arsenal now and verify that he had no plans to use it on her later.

Sasha reached down and picked up a short knife and placed it in the tactical holster slung on his lower back. He'd taken off his suit jacket in the car, which left him standing in the cold in a dress shirt with rolled-up sleeves. How was he not freezing to death? "The obvious answer is usually the answer."

Diana narrowed her eyes. Ass.

Night had taken over the sky quickly as it tended to do in the winter. The full moon hung high in the clouds and blanketed the stretch of dead field between them and Whitaker's house in a white light. Anyone could see them coming if they stayed parked on the road and walked. Nothing lay between them and the house to hide behind. However, the plan presently had them parking right at the front door, so it didn't much matter unless they were forced to run.

"I'll go in through the front door." Sasha ignored her curious stare into his trunk. What was his day job again? "You two need to find another way in."

"Chimney," she said. Much to her consternation, she'd gone

through several chimneys in recent years. "As long as there isn't a fire going."

"Obviously," Sasha said, unhelpfully.

Diana glared. If he kept it up, she'd tear off his head and boot it across Whitaker's expansive field, or she'd try at least.

"And if there is a fire going?" Nobu asked.

"I'll figure it out." Diana turned her attention from Sasha's armory to the house sitting all alone in the field.

"You have no plan?" Sasha's question sent a wave of irritation down her back.

"I have a plan…generally speaking." Diana kept her face toward the house as heat collected on her cheeks. She absolutely did not have a plan, but she usually never did, and things worked out. "There's usually some sort of access into the attic that humans don't notice. Mice will likely have taken care of that for us."

Nobu snorted. "If you say so."

Her focus remained on the house. It seemed so much larger now that the ocean of cars from the auction had gone away. No one would know it held magical artifacts, a sphinx, and who knew what else. If they died in there, no one would be the wiser.

Diana chewed on the inside of her cheek. Was getting this knife worth the risk?

The wisp of *what if* continued to fester and grow, gracing her with memories of flying high in the sky with the murder. Of eating dinner alongside her sister and being surrounded by other crow shifters as they traveled from sea to shining sea. Good lord, she missed it! She missed feeling some sort of hope that perhaps her life wouldn't always be this terrible ache of loneliness day in and day out. While none of them were family by bond, they were crow. They were familiar.

She stole another glance at Sasha and watched him intently as he pulled on his suit jacket. She didn't know his true intention or end game. She knew nothing about him, really. Would he really help her get the knife, or would he stab her, quite literally, in the back? Diana bit down on her tongue, trying to ignore the unexpected tinge of betrayal the idea invoked.

Moreover, why did she care about him being loyal in the first place?

Sasha closed the trunk, shaking Diana from her thoughts. "I'll try to distract him for half an hour. Don't go over that amount of time."

"What makes you think you can get him to talk that long?" Nobu asked, skeptical. It was a good point, she conceded. What could Sasha possibly have to talk about with Whitaker that could keep him contained for thirty minutes?

"Work." Sasha walked toward the driver's door.

Diana frowned. "And what, exactly, do you do?"

"That doesn't pertain to our objective here today. All that matters is that I can keep him occupied."

She clenched her fists and fought everything inside that told her to pop him in the nose. Not that she actually could. He'd see it coming. "How you are able to distract Whitaker does matter when you could be walking in there to sell us out."

The crickets singing around them had somehow gotten impossibly loud.

"I'm not going to sell you out in there, Van Doren." His refusal to call her by her first name only made her more frustrated. She defended him this morning, only to be completely disrespected. Jerk. "I need to talk to your father. I can't do that if you're dead."

"Why do you need to talk to him so bad?" Diana hated how her voice sounded. Like he'd hurt her feelings even when he hadn't. "Are you going to kill him?"

Sasha stared at her, not indicating how he felt one way or the other. "No. I'm not going to kill him."

Her throat, dry with fear and thirst, made swallowing impossible. So she glared at him instead, dismayed to find that the irritation in her died when she met his eyes. It was like a wave of calm had doused her from head to toe.

Magic curled and rippled in her chest. It didn't hurt, but it was different. Like she'd fallen in a lake and washed out all the anger in her heart.

What the hell was wrong with her?

"Are you done?" Sasha asked. The wind picked up the longer pieces of his hair and pulled them along his forehead, but the chill didn't seem to bother him. In fact, he looked downright comfortable in the cold. Comfortable *and* extremely good-looking, much to her consternation. When she didn't answer, he adjusted his suit jacket—a new one free of werewolf bites—and turned away.

They all piled into the car and rolled down the driveway toward the house.

Diana seethed in silence. There were too many variables. Too much risk. Not for the first time, she wondered how her father could send her to do this. Was he desperate, or did he truly care so little for her well-being? Sure, he wanted to go back to the murder. They all did. But would it be worth it to him to be welcomed back into the murder even if he lost one of his daughters along the way?

She withered. Of course it would.

Sasha rolled to a stop in front of the door. Unlike the night before, the sphinx was nowhere to be seen. She didn't see any smoke curling out of the chimney either. While being covered in soot wasn't her favorite thing, it would be much easier to get in that way.

"Remember." Sasha shifted the car into park and turned to look at her. "Half an hour. Get the knife and get out."

He didn't wait for them to say anything. Sasha popped open the door and swung out a leg, and in that paralyzing moment, Diana felt the familiar thrum of fear beneath her skin.

"Wait." She bit her lip. What was she doing? He didn't care about her, much less her anxiety. "Be careful, okay?"

Sasha didn't look at her, and sick anticipation coiled in the pit of her stomach. He faced the dark night, hiding whatever expression he had on his face from view.

"I don't feel good about this," Diana continued, chest tight. "Any of it."

Sasha's shoulders heaved beneath a deep breath. "I don't either."

Diana fell back into her seat when Sasha shut the door. The once steady beat of her heart continued to escalate as she watched his back, silently willing him to get back in the car. She'd never cared about another person's fate viscerally before. Not like this. Not like her own life hung in the balance.

"How very curious."

She glanced in the rearview mirror. Natsu had already taken Nobu's place. A pile of clothes on the seat was all that remained of the teenager.

"I don't know what you're talking about." Diana shrugged off her jacket and tried to ignore how infantile her protest sounded.

"You do." Natsu hopped into the driver's seat, black tail swaying behind him like a banner in the wind. She didn't like that Natsu knew so much as they'd only talked once. "Even if you won't admit it to yourself."

Diana leaned over the console to open the window beside him. Shifting without a way out of the car would be stupid. "Have you stolen anything before? Well, aside from Nobu's body."

"That's unfair." A burst of cold shot through the open glass. Natsu, unbothered, continued to sit there expectantly.

"I'm sure the kid feels the same way about carting you around."

Natsu stretched and sharpened his claws on the leather. "I think you're taking out your own insecurities on me."

"And I think you're an asshole," Diana growled and stared at the house. Sasha still stood in front of the door. Was anyone even home? "So have you stolen anything before?"

"Yes." The cat stood on his hind legs and propped its paws against the door. "How do you plan on getting the knife out of the house?"

Diana bent down and unlaced her boots. "If it's not too long, I plan on flying out of the chimney with it. My legs are pretty strong, and I have three of them. I won't be able to fly far, but I should be able to get out of the house and back to the car."

"I've been around awhile, and I always forget you crow shifters have three legs. Hard to blend in with normal crows thanks to that perk, huh?" He continued to look outside but gave her no hint as to what he was looking for. "I'll be able to feel if the sphinx is around." Natsu turned his head to look at her. "Or any living thing that might be in the house, for that matter."

"And if we get caught?"

"I'll eat them."

Her hand faltered, and she dropped the shoelace. "How can you feel them?"

"At our core, all demons live to consume other life-forces. Naturally, that means I will feel them near."

Diana continued unlacing her boots and pulled them off. "Why don't you go in alone and eat everyone then? Save me the trouble."

"The form that would facilitate such a thing would tear the kid's body apart. I can't use it for very long without risking irreparable damage to him." Natsu's words made her heart sink. "That is something I would like to avoid."

Her eyes widened, and she made to speak, but Natsu jumped from the car window, leaving her alone. She wouldn't pretend to understand demons, but Natsu's concern for his human host didn't mesh with Amir's descriptions of the heartless monsters. Hopefully, it wasn't all a ruse that would get her killed.

FOURTEEN

SASHA

Sasha had been ready for their evening heist. He'd planned his conversation with Whitaker down to the detail, and if things went from bad to worse, he'd put a bullet between his eyes. The easier, less risky option would be to get Sheturath without a fight, but given the circumstances, he wasn't opposed to killing him either. At any rate, Sasha hadn't been worried when he stepped out of the car.

Until Diana opened her mouth.

He drew in a sharp breath. She cursed him one second and then expressed worry for him the next. It made no sense, and he hated it. Or at least he thought he did.

Sasha ran his tongue over his teeth as he approached the front door to Whitaker's home. The way she'd looked at him—wide-eyed and panicked—spoke to true concern. Her voice had wavered. She'd bitten her lip.

Why?

He shook his head. Here he was—thinking about Diana instead of the danger beyond the door. How foolish.

Sasha banished all thoughts of Diana's worry and pressed the doorbell. He had other things to be concerned with. Knife. Sphinx. Possible warlock.

The door opened, and a very new concern presented itself. A concern he hadn't thought to be worried about, but now regretted it.

A demon.

"You're the dude that shot all those wolves," the demon said with a grin. This demon had possessed a blond woman with a teased head of hair, low-slung jeans, and a crop top. While the outfit would likely garner several stares being it was December, the demon wouldn't mind.

"And you're a demon." Sasha fought the urge to groan. "What are you doing Earth-side?"

The demon's face fell. "Got bound by the asshole who owns this dump."

Although the home was not synonymous with the word *dump*, the demon most certainly meant Whitaker. It wasn't the best news to hear, but he could see hope. The demon didn't seem happy to be in Whitaker's service. Perhaps he'd share some intel.

"Why did he summon you?" Sasha asked.

"He wanted to learn the secrets of the dead because he's dying," the demon snarled and clenched its fist. "Problem was he knew my real name. Stuffed me in this body."

The demon held out its hand. A seal, a *W* in a circle, had been branded on the palm.

"How'd he come to know your name?"

"Followed my story on the news, I guess. I haven't been doing this long. I got the death penalty like a year ago." The demon's admission gave Sasha pause. Most souls that found their way to Hell were eternally damned, but not bad enough to get the so-called promotion to demon. Whoever this demon had been in life must've been truly wicked. The demon opened the door, revealing the familiar foyer. "C'mon in. If you wanna kill him and set me free, I'd be sure to return the favor."

Sasha said nothing. Demons never pledged loyalty to anyone, and he had no intention of agreeing to any more demon deals. Even lesser demons were dangerous.

The house was the same as it had been the night before, but dark, and the smell of the chocolate fountains had yet to dissipate. None of the lights were on. The temperature was chilled, even by his standards, and the loudness of the complete and utter silence rattled him.

Things in this house were not as they seemed.

"This way." The demon took him through the foyer and into the room with the twin staircases. Instead of going to the living area where the auction had been slated to occur or up the steps, the demon ushered him to the double doors beneath the stairs, ones that had been closed the night prior. "He's in his study."

Sasha said nothing and continued walking behind the demon. No visions plagued him yet. Not for the first time, he wished his angelic blood blessed him with the ability to see more than his demise. Something more reliable.

The doors led to a short hall and into another living area. The only thing giving any impression that someone was in the home at all was the sliver of light beneath the lone door beside the entertainment center.

"He's in here." The demon took a left through another living area and stopped at the door. "Again, if you kill him, I'll return the favor...by like not killing your friends, for example."

Apprehension shot down his back. He'd hoped the demon had been inexperienced enough to miss Diana and Nobu, but apparently that wasn't the case. Sasha, unwilling to commit, continued to stay silent. The demon smirked and pushed open the door.

Given the darkness of the house, the dimmed lighting in the study was much more violent on his newly sensitive eyes than he anticipated. Bookcases lined the walls, featuring an odd mix of both modern literature and occult. The desk, piled high with loose pages and pens and scrolls, spoke to a studious owner. The jars of body parts beside the scrolls, however, spoke to a studious *warlock*.

Whitaker, the owner of Sheturath, sat in the center of the room in a high-backed chair. The floral pattern in the upholstery of his seat better suited an old woman with a basket of yarn and knitting needles. Not a demon summoner.

"Aleksandr Ivanovich Sokolov, the man who ruined my auction." Whitaker closed the book propped on his knees—*Your Small Business and You*—and stood. He was a clean-shaven man in his late sixties. Whitaker's appearance said demon summoner even less than the fabric on his chair. He wore a sweater, khaki pants, and loafers with tassels. The whites of his eyes were yellowed, and small bruises lingered along his jaw. He extended a hand, skin mottled. "Edward Whitaker."

Sasha fought a grimace as his palm met Whitaker's. Sweaty. "I'm here at the behest of Madame."

Whitaker stilled. "Madame?"

"Yes."

"Now I know who to contact about those wolves." Whitaker motioned to the other chair sitting across from him—a shorter one with green fabric and scuffed legs. "Have a seat."

"Those wolves broke your trust by attacking someone inside your home. That's not our business, and I can guarantee that Madame does not care about them."

"Fair enough. What brings you to my home, Mr. Sokolov?" Whitaker picked up a crystal decanter and a pair of glasses from the center of the table between the two chairs and poured: bourbon. The liquor swirled around in the bottom of the glass, a deep bronze beneath the brilliant chandelier above them. He sat the decanter back on the table. "I figure it must be important if Madame sent you out here."

"You sent Madame the invitation to your auction. I think you know why I'm here." Sasha eyed the glass Whitaker handed out to him. Reluctantly, he accepted.

Whitaker shrugged and plucked his own glass from the table. "Never hurts to verify, yes?"

In any other situation, Sasha would've been peeved the man dared to waste his time. However, given that his objective was to do just that, he let it go. "It's reasonable."

"You want Sheturath." The older man settled back in his chair. The demon stood off by the bookcase, mouth pulled into a taut line. How long would the demon wait before informing Whitaker about Diana and Nobu?

"Madame wants Sheturath." Sasha swirled the bourbon around in his glass. As parched as he was, there was no guarantee it wasn't poisoned or cursed. "I'm here on her behalf."

"In either case, it's too late, Mr. Sokolov. Sheturath was purchased last night."

Sasha kept his face neutral, but inside, every single muscle tightened. "If I recall, you canceled the auction."

"If you recall, you also shot several werewolves in my house, chasing off almost all my potential buyers." Whitaker slumped farther into his chair and brought his glass to his lips but didn't drink. "I was met with an offer I couldn't refuse. Since your conflict with the wolves ruined my auction, I didn't dare turn my nose up at the only reasonable offer I'd likely get from someone other than a general."

Sasha tightened his grip on the cool glass. "A general didn't get it?"

"No."

The former generals of Hell had one goal in mind: build the strongest army powered by the strongest weapons to build their own kingdom on Earth. Since they lost Hell, they wanted the next best thing —and they had no intention of sharing with each other. They would not rest until the demon-killer, Sheturath, was secured. Whoever dared purchase Sheturath was either a fool with a target on their back or powerful enough to keep themselves out of the control of a general.

Neither of those options looked good for him or his freedom.

"I'm surprised you'd sell Sheturath at all." Sasha decided not to mention the obvious. He glanced at the watch on his wrist: just under twenty minutes before Diana and Natsu would be out of the house. Hopefully they would stick to the plan and leave when time ran out instead of looking for a knife that was no longer there. "Nice thing to have when you're surrounded by valuable merchandise."

"The only thing that scared me were demons." Whitaker pressed his glass to his lips and tossed it back. He sat his empty glass down on the table with a loud *thunk*. Sasha eyed the man's hands—the ends of his fingers were charred, like he's stuck them in the fireplace. "I've got my own way around them now."

Sasha glanced at the demon in the woman's body. Its face, twisted into a snarl, was nothing short of murderous. "Controlling demons isn't an easy feat...and comes with a certain amount of risk. Makes one wonder what your end game is."

"Makes one wonder, or makes Madame wonder?" Whitaker leaned forward and steepled his fingers over his stomach. "Tell you what—if you answer my next question, I'll tell you who bought Sheturath. You can go...negotiate with 'em."

Promising.

"What is your question?"

"Cat demons." Whitaker gave him a pointed look. Sasha's mind went to Nobu, but he continued to school his expressions into relative disinterest. "What do you know about 'em?"

A betting man would say that Edward Whitaker was the warlock who'd attempted to bind Nobu and Natsu during the auction. Since he didn't bet—too much risk—he instead relied on decades of practice in reconnaissance.

"They're hard to bind and even harder to locate." Sasha recalled the diner and Nobu's grimace. "If you're more specific, I might have better information to share."

Whitaker picked up the decanter and refilled his glass. "I've been following the story of a boy that I'm certain is really the host of a cat demon. You can find a lot of creatures by simply keeping up with the news. Although I'm sure you know that."

"Hm." Sasha did know that. That's how Madame found his mother. "Why do you think the boy in mind is a cat demon's host?"

"You might remember him from last night. Japanese kid wearing a suit too big for his frame?" Whitaker kept his eyes on the bourbon sloshing into his glass. "He only knew about my auction because I put the event in his path and hoped he'd take the bait."

Sasha kept quiet. This was an attempt by Whitaker to showcase how clever he was, and Sasha didn't want to entertain him. However, he was curious what the man could've baited Nobu with in the first place and why he wanted the boy at all.

"I caught wind of his story on the Internet. He'd moved from Japan when his mother married a senator. They lived in Oklahoma." Whitaker frowned at his glass. "They lived there happily until an angry constituent broke into their home and started shooting."

Sasha glanced at his watch. Ten minutes left. He closed his eyes, hoping to see if Whitaker presented any threat. A vision pulsed in his mind, and he acknowledged it, feeling for the burn of magic inside his head. His fingers itched to grab the Glock strapped to his side.

Except it wasn't his eyes he saw from.

Sasha tried to hide his shock from Whitaker, but if the man had any experience at all analyzing facial expressions, it would be clear that something was amiss. His heart rate climbed, and there wasn't a muscle in his body not bound by shock.

For the first time in his life, Sasha hadn't seen his future. He hadn't seen the dangers coming his way or watched his mangled corpse take its last breaths.

Instead, he'd seen Diana's future.

More importantly, he'd seen Diana die.

FIFTEEN

THE CHIMNEY HADN'T BEEN CLEANED IN AN AGE, AND DIANA WAS tempted to attack Whitaker out of spite for it. A dark plume of soot exploded around her as she fell from out of the flue and landed in a feathery heap on the ground.

She would've growled had she been human and not trying to commit a theft. Instead, she settled for flopping onto Whitaker's corduroy couch and rolling all over it, smearing black dust into the taupe fabric. Satisfied with her mess, she shook her head and flew over to a window. Natsu waited on the ledge on the other side.

While there were several other things she'd rather do than shift back to a naked human in the ice-cold house, Diana didn't have a choice. Despite having three legs, she couldn't open the window as a crow.

Natsu bounded in and trotted to the fireplace. "You're covered in soot."

Diana scowled and shifted back before she popped off. No sense in arguing over the obvious.

Now empty and devoid of the throng of supernatural creatures from the night before, the mansion wasn't as beautiful. All the lights were off, including the lamps in front of the massive portraits, and even though Whitaker must've had a ton of money to afford such an expansive property, the heater wasn't on. Easily below sixty degrees.

Natsu stopped at the foot of the left staircase beside a pedestal of poinsettias. "Something is amiss, bird. Do you feel it?"

While Diana couldn't respond, she landed beside him and dipped her head. She didn't know what it was she felt, but she felt something. And it wasn't good. If her demon compatriot felt bad about whatever it was, their future likely held something unpleasant, and encountering either Whitaker or the sphinx wouldn't end well.

The thought of the future reminded her of Sasha. She hoped that he was fine with Whitaker, although being worried about a relative stranger made no sense whatsoever. His lovely face be damned.

Natsu glanced around the room. "I'm not sure where he'd keep his prizes. Perhaps a basement?"

She shook her head. Houses in Texas largely didn't have basements. The ground was made of clay and sandy loam, so it shifted too much.

"Attic, then? Or top floor?" Natsu hopped onto the first step. "More difficult for thieves to escape from the top."

Diana dipped her head in agreement, took to the air, and flew to the landing. She stopped on the banister and hooked her talons along the oak as she observed the second floor. The hall in front of her dripped in shadows and chilled her bones, but unlike the foyer, had absolutely no decoration. No paintings. No vases. No poinsettias.

Natsu reached the top of the stairs and hissed. "Something malicious is here." She couldn't help but appreciate the irony of a demon calling something else malicious. "I imagine we'll run into some interference with the sphinx."

Her grip on the banister tightened. Interference. What could she do against an insane monster in her current state, peck him to death? There was a reason crows stuck together, and survival was one of them. Alone she was nothing, and if she weren't careful, she'd die that way.

Diana chided herself and closed her eyes. The house was utterly silent—one of those quiets that rang in one's ears if they listened too long. If Sasha were truly visiting with Whitaker and distracting him, wouldn't she hear them talking? Arguing...something?

Or maybe she'd been right to be worried out by the road. Maybe Sasha had other motives and had no intention of upholding his end of their bargain.

"Bird." Natsu trotted down the hall. "Come on."

The hallway, equally bare and impersonal as the landing, darkened the farther they traveled down it. Diana kept to a slow coast, and Natsu trotted below her. The light soon dwindled to almost nothing. Not even her aloft wings cast a shadow along the wood floor.

Four doors lined the walls. Natsu stopped, paw held up midstride. Could demons feel other demonic auras, or were they limited to beings they could possess? His tail hovered close to the ground. His ears twitched.

"Death is here. A lot of it." Diana's wings dipped at Natsu's words. "I think Whitaker is the warlock that tried to trick us last night, and he has been up to some nasty magic."

She'd just have to trust Natsu on that. Death was sort of a demon thing, like stealing was hers.

After a few more moments standing in the silence, Natsu continued to putter down the hall. His steps were slower now. Measured. If a demon were worried about what Whitaker had behind the walls, Diana ought to be worried too.

He kept moving and almost reached the end of the hall before stopping in front of the last door on the left.

"Here." Natsu looked at her. Her stomach knotted up. "Something malevolent is in that room."

Probably the sphinx. Which meant that the weapon they sought would likely be there too, since the odds of Sheturath sitting out unguarded were abysmal.

Diana shifted into her human form and suppressed a shiver. The house was so cold. Did Whitaker's evil magic require a chill that rivaled the north pole?

"You can handle the sphinx if he's in there?" Diana asked.

"I can distract him if that's what you mean. Are you certain you can pick up the knife and fly out with it?" Natsu asked.

Diana nodded. Unless it was a really big knife, closer to a sword in size, she should be able to get out as a crow. That's why she'd been so successful in her father's unsavory business. As a crow shifter, she could get into houses through unconventional means. She blended well in the dark, could fly out of harm's way, and had strong, supernaturally powered legs with which to hold things for short distances.

Auction aside, she'd only been caught one time—the night she'd been shot stealing that goddamn rug for her father.

She turned the knob slowly and pushed the door open. The plan for the sphinx was to let Natsu distract it while she searched, and since she didn't want to fight with the thing, she had no complaints. Once Natsu slipped through the crack, she shifted back and took to the air.

Diana landed atop an armoire. Like the other rooms in the house, it was dark. The only light came from the full moon shining through window and coating the floor. Natsu had slunk out of sight.

Unlike the neat assemblies from the auction, the room had been filled with wooden crates. All of them, stacked high and disorganized, sent a wave of fear billowing down each feather. It would take forever to search every box, and they only had thirty minutes. Probably closer to ten or fifteen now.

Diana drifted down to a crate and peered between the slats to get a glimpse of the contents. Or tried to. Too many packing peanuts. She stuck her beak closer, tilting her head until she saw a glimmer. Diamonds. Not the knife.

Unsure what to do, she cocked her head to the side and tried to find Natsu. If she shifted back to search, she'd be easier to spot if Whitaker or the sphinx showed up and would present a larger target should they try to kill her. And while she'd like to think Natsu was more useful than Nobu, she didn't know what Natsu could do as a ten-pound feline either.

Hopefully, Sasha would keep Whitaker busy.

Diana flitted to another stack of crates filled with jars and wood chips. No knife. She looked for Natsu again. Where the hell did the cat go?

As her gaze traced along the floor, movement caught in her peripheries.

Natsu?

Her stomach clenched, and she kept still. A low growl shook against the floor, and a hulking figure left its home from behind some crates to stalk in front of the window. Even in the poor light, Diana could see the cracked bones of the creature's spine pressing beneath the skin in the white light of the moon.

"Intruders." Its voice creaked like an old chair.

Her eyes focused, and the urge to flee escalated. But flying away wasn't the plan. Natsu better be able to handle the sphinx. Her job was to find the knife. While she didn't want him—and consequently Nobu —to get hurt, she had to find the blade.

The bouncer from the night before had dropped his human visage. His golden face remained, but the rest of him had morphed into a true sphinx with a human face attached. The head connected to a lion's body, its neck a twisted array of bones beneath thin skin and sparse fur. A scaled tail whipped around against the floor, coiling like the snake it was.

"Visitors. Not intruders," Natsu's voice replied. Diana still couldn't see him but didn't dare move.

"Intruders." The sphinx lifted a paw and pointed into the dark with a jagged claw while its serpentine tail slammed against the floor. Once. Twice. Three times. Diana's heart rate quickened. Was it signaling someone? Something? "You are not welcome here."

"Are you bound to serve Whitaker?" Natsu asked.

"By bind or will, does it matter?" The sphinx opened its human maw, revealing rows of lion's teeth. "I feel you, demon. An old soul, you are. Edward Whitaker would love to have you in his collection."

"I don't much care to be collected, thanks," Natsu said, although his voice was quiet.

Where was he hiding?

The sphinx unfolded the eagle's wings from its back, and the feathers brushed the wall on either side of it—a wingspan she could never hope to match—knocking some crates to the ground.

"You came seeking treasures." The sphinx's talons dug into the wood. "All you will find is death."

SIXTEEN

SASHA

Sasha recounted his vision carefully, shocked at what he'd seen. If Whitaker had noticed his lapse in attention, he didn't say. On the contrary, he continued his inquiry about cat demons and explaining why he believed Nobu to be the host of one.

"After the man shot the senator and his family, police arrived on scene. The boy's mom was dead. His stepfather, the senator, was dead. The man who killed them? Ripped to pieces." Whitaker finally met his gaze. "The boy was missing."

While he didn't know Nobu's story, Sasha knew Whitaker had pinned the boy for what he was. However, he had no intention of verifying it. "That doesn't necessarily mean it was a cat demon, Mr. Whitaker."

"The police found a dead cat on the scene. Feet away from the attacker's corpse." Whitaker shrugged.

Sasha could see why the warlock put the pieces together as he had. Cat demons were, allegedly, the corrupted souls of cats. While he'd never dealt with one aside from Natsu, one of the more popular theories as to how they were made was extensive abuse. Perhaps the murderer had harmed the cat, and it became a demon. Possessed

Nobu's body to exact his revenge. However, since Sasha didn't know for certain, he kept quiet. Better to remain silent instead of advertising his ignorance.

Whitaker stared at him when he said nothing. "I think the demon possessed the boy, killed the shooter, and then ran."

Sasha thought back to Natsu. He didn't have much interaction with the cat beyond their chat that morning, but it was odd that the demon could've potentially outed himself for a human's sake. "That's too much speculation for my taste."

"Regardless, I want him. I want to know what you know about them."

He swallowed and tightened his grip on his glass of bourbon. Distracting Whitaker was no longer imperative anymore, especially since Sheturath wasn't on the property. If he didn't move soon, Diana would die, and the mystery of why he saw her future would die with her.

It bothered him that he didn't know which death was more disappointing.

Sasha opened his mouth to speak, but a loud slam on the ceiling killed the words before he uttered them. The chandelier ahead shook beneath the sound, crystal strands clanking together. Then again, and again. Particles of dust billowed from the crystals in small plumes, hanging in the air a moment before disappearing from sight.

They'd been found out.

The familiar burn of danger crawled into his mind, and he dared to indulge. His stomach clenched when he saw Diana die again. Crushed by the sphinx.

"Looks like you didn't come alone, Sokolov." Whitaker leaned forward and sat his glass of bourbon on the table. His eyes, almost swallowed by folds of loose skin, narrowed a bit. "I don't take kindly to people breaking into my home to steal from me."

Sasha pressed his lips together. He needed to hurry. "You bind souls. You steal what doesn't belong to you all the time. At least the object we seek is inanimate."

"I'm not going to be lectured by Madame's right-hand man. I can only imagine the atrocities you've committed in her name."

He watched Diana die again in his mind and bile shot into his mouth. *Enough of this.* He reached into his jacket, pulled out his Glock, and squeezed the grip tight. "Your imagination alone wouldn't paint as full a picture."

The *thump-thump* against the ceiling punctuated the silence hanging around them, his pulse beating in tandem with the steady sound.

Whitaker sat unbothered by both Sasha and his gun. "So what do you plan to do, Sokolov? You need me if you want Sheturath. If you shoot me now, you might never find out where it went. Not to mention my associate over there will tear you to pieces. All he needs is my command."

Sasha's eyes flickered over to the demon standing by the door. The demon shrugged in response, seeming to say *I'll help you if you help me.*

If he were the type to sigh, he would've. Sasha indulged the burn in his mind once more and leaned forward a bit in his chair, fixing his grip on his Glock. "Unfortunately, I'm going to have to take that chance."

He squeezed the trigger, and the bullet pierced the bridge of Whitaker's nose before the warlock could lift a hand.

Sasha inhaled. Whitaker, now slumped in his seat with his head lolled against the wing of his chair, sat in a lifeless heap. The blood from the hole in his nasal bone trickled alongside his nose and down his cheek.

The thumps along the ceiling ceased and morphed into fevered scampering. His normally steady pulse continued to escalate, and Sasha turned to the demon. Its eyes bled crimson as it took in the brand on its palm.

"What the—?" The demon hissed and whipped its head toward him. "He's dead! Why am I still in this body?"

"I can get you out of that body." Sasha holstered his Glock. No gun could kill a demon anyway. "But I need to know where Sheturath is."

The demon's nose crinkled. "Who says I know where it is?"

"The creature that has my knife would've likely been too big of a risk for Whitaker to meet alone. His sphinx is upstairs guarding his treasures, which leaves you." The last bit had been a guess, but when the demon rolled its eyes, Sasha knew he'd guessed correctly. "Do you want to be free of your host or not? I don't have much time."

The demon glowered but relented. "I'll tell you, but we're square after this."

"Of course." A loud crash overhead shook Sasha's attention. If he didn't get upstairs soon, Diana would die. His pulse beat in his ears at the thought. If she died, he'd never know why he saw her in his visions, and not knowing why his magic suddenly changed was unacceptable. Or he told himself that was the reason. "Where is Sheturath?"

"He sold it to some old ass vampire. Jacques something or another." Sasha's blood ran cold. "He lives in some farming town outside Philadelphia."

"Do you know the town?"

"No." The demon shook its head. "He talked about the cornfields around his house. Kept saying no one bothered him out in the middle of nowhere."

Sasha reached for the knife strapped to his side and motioned to the coffee table. "Hand on the table, seal up."

The demon dropped its hand on the mahogany. "That sphinx is strong. Better hurry or your friends are dead."

"I'm aware." Sasha gripped the knife and plunged it through the demon's palm, point in the center of the seal. "Enjoy Hell."

The demon never replied. The creature slipped from the woman's body in a thick shade that oozed through the wooden slats beneath the woman's feet. The body teetered and then crumpled to the floor.

WHILE SASHA HAD NO IDEA WHERE DIANA AND NOBU HAD ENDED up in the house, all he had to do was follow the noise.

He licked his lips and watched visions flicker, his feet moving on autopilot up the stairs. Diana kept dying. Over and over and over again. Her every move in the dark room gave him a new vision. A new premonition of her demise.

How was he seeing her future? More importantly, *why?*

His visions had only ever told him his future. They'd only whispered secrets to him about him—the dangers lurking around every corner. Why did he see the danger coming for Diana now too?

Sasha reached the landing and drew his Glock, the pistol loaded with silver rounds. He'd never fought a sphinx before. They were pretty easy to avoid or appease, but Whitaker likely bound it to his needs, and if he did, the sphinx would fight for whatever that need might be. He'd have to shoot it first and hope for the best. Silver worked on werewolves. Maybe he'd get lucky.

He picked up the pace and pressed down the hall. The wood floors shook beneath his feet. A screech ripped through the air, rattling around in his ear canals enough to make him wince. His new vision offered an excellent view in the dark, and now he couldn't imagine having survived this long in the shadows without it.

Sasha swallowed and allowed himself a moment to regret. If he died in Whitaker's house, his mother would inherit his contract from Madame. Was saving Diana and Nobu worth that possibility?

He got eyes on the open door as a wooden crate shot past the frame and crashed into the hall. Wood splintered, and the contents of the box shattered within the crate, scattering glass crystals along the floor.

While he'd seen sphinxes before, he never could shake the eerie nature of their being. The neck especially. The thin vertebrae one twist away from pressing through the skin always sent a wave of nausea curling in his gut.

"Death! Your death is all you'll find!" The sphinx threw back its head and screeched as its tail whipped along the wood floor.

A black shape darted along the ceiling. Diana.

"Another thief," the sphinx said, voice cracking in its throat as it noticed him.

Sasha squeezed the grip of his Glock.

"You'll never get what you seek," the creature said.

"What we seek isn't here." Sasha glanced at Diana, perched on a tower of crates. The reach of the sphinx would catch her if she tried to fly out of the open door. "And Whitaker is dead."

The sphinx growled. "I feel him in my veins. He is not dead."

"That is your seal." Sasha aimed at the sphinx and braced his wrist. "I can free you, if you'll let me."

"I will free you from your weak body." The sphinx bared its teeth. "Then I'll eat the remains."

The sphinx barreled forward and swiped. Sasha stepped to the right, eyes wide at the talons flexing toward his face, and fired. A bullet lodged into its fur-covered shoulder. It reared back on its hind legs and stumbled into the drywall, leaving a hole and crumbling plaster beneath it.

Sasha dodged the flailing body of the sphinx and ran into the room, surrounded by haphazardly stacked crates filled with magical artifacts. The sphinx readjusted, seemingly unfazed by the shot, and no blood dotted his fur. He now blocked the one exit, and since the bullet didn't seem to slow him down any, Sasha had no idea how to subdue the creature.

Another black shape crept along the wall. Natsu.

"Any idea how to kill a sphinx, demon?" he asked, watching the sphinx shake free of debris.

"Tear it apart," Natsu said.

Sasha's lips thinned. He could do many things, but ripping a sphinx limb from limb wasn't one of them. "Sheturath isn't here. We need to leave."

Natsu didn't get a chance to respond as the sphinx hurtled forward, claws extended. A bullet didn't do much except piss him off, might as well try a blade. Sasha holstered his Glock and ripped the knife from the holster slung on his lower back. The blood from the demon's host downstairs glistened along the edge in the moonlight let in from the window.

He dodged behind a tower of crates. The sphinx batted the boxes down with a wide arc of his foreleg, slinging the wood and shredded packing paper into the air and floor.

The cold of the house had been replaced with heat of adrenaline, and the more he bobbed and weaved, Sasha found himself at a loss for what to do. Perhaps a strategic escape would be best. Diana couldn't fight, and Natsu likely wouldn't risk ascending to his true form to kill the sphinx.

The sphinx leapt forward. "I'll lick your skull clean once I tear it from your neck." Sasha moved according to his visions, but at the last moment, the sphinx changed course. His left claw, not his right, reached for his eyes.

His stomach clenched, and his grip on the knife tightened. Sasha brought his forearms up to protect his face.

The pain never came, but an otherworldly shriek rattled the room.

Sasha dropped his arms and was greeted by the sight of Diana digging her talons into the sphinx's eyes. Thick blood ran down the sphinx's human face.

"You're small, but I need a snack." The sphinx reached up and snatched Diana within its grip. Sasha had never heard a crow cry out in pain before, shifter or otherwise, but the guttural squawk that shook the room hit him in the chest in a way nothing else had managed to do.

Gripping his knife harder, he shot forward. He twisted away from the sphinx's strike, aiming the point of his blade beneath its ribs. The sphinx recoiled in pain as he wedged the sliver of steel in its skin.

The sphinx's grip on Diana loosened, and she fell to the ground. Limp.

Lifeless.

The word inspired several emotions. Anger, at the idea of his plan falling apart, and remorse, for a reason he couldn't explain. Regardless, both emotions prompted him to move toward the sphinx in an attempt to salvage what was left of their plan.

The sphinx staggered back on its hind legs and thrashed around to shake the blade free. Sasha reached forward and picked up Diana, holding her close to his stomach before running toward the door. If they were going to escape, now was the time.

"Sokolov."

He'd been so focused on the sphinx and Diana that he'd forgotten about Natsu.

The cat demon, now much larger than he had been, stared at him with orange eyes. Sasha had never seen a cat demon ascend to their true form before, but he'd heard about it. The lower demons that had surrounded him in his youth were in awe of them, and now he knew why.

Natsu somehow managed to be more frightening than anything he'd ever seen, and he'd seen a lot.

The demon cocked his large head to the side and stretched his jaw, showcasing a set of slender, elongated teeth. Natsu's hind legs, now long and thin with inverted joints, held him up on two feet, his head almost scraping the ceiling. Forelegs—now arms—hung at his sides, serrated claws dragging on the floor.

"I can't stay this way long without killing the boy." Natsu snarled at the sphinx before looking back to him. "Get her out."

SEVENTEEN

SASHA

Natsu didn't wait for a reply, and Sasha was simply too shaken to offer him one.

As the cat demon charged toward the sphinx, Sasha took the exit. He sprinted into the hallway and down the stairs, trying his best to ignore the house shaking around him as the two creatures fought tooth and claw.

He would've kept running to the car if the relatively weightless crow didn't shift back into a very cold, very naked human in his arms. Sasha stumbled into the foyer thanks to the sudden change of weight and collapsed to his knees. Diana's body shook in his arms and blood slipped between his fingers.

She opened her eyes. Dark like pits.

"Why did you do that? That was dangerous. Irresponsible," he asked and held her chin steady. Diana tried to focus on him, but her eyes rolled. Desperation gripped him. If she died, he would never find Charles Van Doren. He would never be free. "Van Doren...*Diana.*"

Her eyes snapped open, instantly tacked to his. Blood trickled down the side of her nose from a laceration on her forehead. "Instinct."

She went limp in his arms. He lightly shook her, but she didn't move. Blood smeared along the white of his shirt and hands, yet he could see nothing but her face pressed against his chest, skin pallid. "Diana."

Her eyes opened again.

Sasha knew what he needed to do, but he didn't want to. "Do you trust me?"

Given her state, he hadn't expected to see any sort of emotion aside from unrelenting pain. He was well-versed in pain, and with his years of expertise in both receiving and inflicting it, Sasha knew he didn't see pain on her face then.

It was something else, and it made him uncomfortable.

"I want to," Diana said, voice hoarse. She licked her lips and swallowed.

His chest tightened. The idea of her dying caused him more emotional duress than he expected.

"Sasha." She tucked her head against him again, eyes closed. "If you can't help me, just kill me. Don't leave me to die with that thing upstairs or for the wolves to find."

By all accounts, Diana's words shouldn't have bothered him.

But they did. And he hated it.

SASHA DIDN'T REMEMBER FINDING A BED. HE DIDN'T REMEMBER stumbling through Whitaker's dark house as he hoped to find some place far enough from the fight so he could do something for the woman struggling to survive in his arms. All he did was move and ignore his visions. He'd simply grown tired of watching her die.

If Whitaker had other creatures in the house, he and Diana were in trouble, but he'd have to deal with those issues as they presented themselves.

He found a room—a guest room by the looks of things. Plain and ordinary, with a bed and a desk. Sasha jerked the top sheet loose and settled Diana on the bed. The house was frigid, and she was shivering.

He wrapped her up tight from her breasts down, leaving the wounds to her chest and neck visible, alongside the blood dumping down her collarbones from deep gouges at the base of her neck.

His heart rate picked up at the sight. Why had she done something so reckless? So foolish? She could've—no, *should've*—let him take the hit. She should've let him die instead.

"Sokolov."

Sasha looked to the door. The enormous, hulking body of Natsu eclipsed the frame.

"Sphinx?"

"Dead." Natsu glanced at Diana, blood matted in his fur. "Fix her."

Sasha narrowed his eyes. He didn't like that Natsu somehow knew his one secret.

"I can tell you're going to be a stubborn idiot. Diana and the kid might be easy to dupe, but I'm old as fuck. I've met many an angel in my time," Natsu snarled, exposing bloody teeth. "And every single one had a talent in common. I think you know what that is, yeah?"

When Sasha said nothing, Natsu took another step closer. The demon could reach forward and crush his larynx if he wanted.

"I've got my own secrets, and trust me, I understand the value in keeping some of them. But don't let your pride damn her." Natsu looked at Diana. "She risked her neck for you. Honor that."

Sasha hesitated. He grew up around enough demons to know not to trust one. "You're a demon. What do you know of honor?"

"Everything has a code."

He put a hand to Diana's neck. Weak pulse. "Is honor how you ended up sharing that body? I know you want to take the kid's form for yourself."

"You don't know what I want, Sokolov. Don't pretend otherwise." Natsu paused, as if listening. But the room was like a graveyard: quiet and filled with monsters. "Don't let your fear get in the way. Out of everyone on this godforsaken planet, she is probably the last I'd suspect of betraying you."

Sasha's eyebrows knit together. "Why? Why her?"

The demon didn't respond. Instead, he lumbered out, heavy tail dragging on the ground.

Sasha kept his hand on her neck. Too many questions and not enough time. "Diana."

Nothing.

Blood slid from the wide gouges beneath her collarbones. While he was peeved beyond a shadow of a doubt, Natsu was right. Diana had saved his life, and she was also unconscious. She'd never know his secrets. Sure, she would wake up with questions. But he wasn't bound to answer them.

Sasha took off his jacket and rolled up his shirt sleeves, walked over to the desk chair, and yanked it from its designated place before slamming it on the floor beside the bed. Diana didn't move. Didn't stir. She was basically dead already.

Years under the heel of Madame bore down on him like the sky and landed square on his shoulders. He could, presumably, let Diana continue as she was for a moment more. Natsu wouldn't know if she'd died from a lack of intervention or not. Then he wouldn't have to incapacitate himself—an unwise move with werewolves searching for them.

An uncharacteristic growl shook the back of his throat, and Sasha dropped in the chair. He might not like using his talents or putting himself at risk to heal her, but Diana dying was inexcusable.

Sasha pressed his hands back onto her neck, fingers slipping in the wet red. So much warm blood, yet she was cold, and the stark contrast brought forth the skill he'd always smothered, especially in the presence of others.

Where demons could manipulate, angels had an innate ability to heal. As diluted as his blood was, he couldn't perform miracles, but he could heal most things if he had enough time. However, given the amount of blood Diana had already lost, it might not be enough to keep her from the great divide.

Sasha closed his eyes and pulled the magic forth from where it lay inside his chest, a constant warmth that soaked him to the bone and coiled through every vein. Heat pulsed from his fingertips and pressed into Diana's skin, and once pain started to ripple across his body, he focused.

All magic had a price. Werewolves were bound by the moon. Vampires couldn't feel the sun. Demons needed hosts to wander the Earth.

He had to harm himself to help others.

Sasha shook his head. Time to concentrate.

As seconds passed to minutes, he distracted himself with questions. How had he seen Diana's future? He'd never seen a future aside from his own, and the thought that she'd somehow weaseled her way past that weakness alarmed him. Had she done something to him? Did crows have other abilities aside from the obvious?

The door opened behind him, but he didn't turn. He could smell Natsu. No—the footfalls were too quiet. Nobu. The demon must've surrendered control.

Sasha's breathing, now heavy and labored, could no longer be ignored. He sagged in his chair, weak with fatigue. He hated that his power sucked the life out of him, rendering him completely useless for hours while his enemies plotted and pursued, and that said nothing of his tentative alliance with Natsu—something the demon could end at any time. But a debt was a debt, and until Diana was off the Reaper's doorstep, he'd continue.

He forced his eyes open. The smaller lacerations had melted back together, leaving nothing more than jagged pink lines on her skin. The deepest one along her chest stopped bleeding but remained open like a crater. He grimaced and pulled his hands back, dizzy and weak, and looked to the floor.

Nobu had gotten his duffel of medical supplies from the car. The boy, now dressed, sat slumped against the wall, covered in blood. The vessels in his eyes had ruptured. Blood dumped out of his nose and mouth and ears. Using Natsu's true form might have killed him.

Still might, Sasha thought, the room swaying. He couldn't let a kid die just feet away from him—

"No. I have Natsu." Nobu shook his head and coughed. Blood shot into the air. "She has you."

The boy's eyes closed. A heavy breath shook his chest. Hopefully the cat was doing some major reconstruction inside him.

Sasha grabbed his duffel bag, vision blurring as he reached inside and felt around for gauze. His fingers grazed something soft, and he latched on, hoping to take care of the bleeding before he passed out. He bit his lip and focused long enough to pack the deep gouge with the gauze and secure it.

He watched her bare shoulders shake with uneven breaths. Diana fought to stay alive, but unless he used a little more magic, she'd die. The deepest gash had already started to bleed again, soaking the fresh gauze.

Sasha pushed himself to his feet and knocked the chair back with his legs. It clattered to the floor. Instead of picking it up, he maneuvered around the bed, holding himself up through sheer willpower alone.

With every step, he cursed. He cursed Diana for somehow bullying her way into his psyche. He cursed Madame for sending him on this mission, and his mother for birthing him in the first place.

After what felt like an eternity later, Sasha collapsed on the other side of the bed. He would pass out if he continued to heal her, but he didn't have a choice. Darkness had already started creeping into his vision, and Diana needed him.

He rolled onto his stomach and threw his right hand on Diana's neck. The familiar pain of magic leaving his body momentarily snapped him awake, and in those moments, he focused on Nobu's words.

She has you.

EIGHTEEN

DIANA

Diana had never been in so much pain. Every nerve in her body ran tight and hot like telephone wires did in summer. She didn't want to move. She didn't want to breathe. Right at that moment, she wasn't sure if she even wanted to be alive.

Alive. The last thing she'd remembered saying had been something along the lines of telling Sasha to kill her. Clearly, he hadn't followed her instructions, and he'd somehow brought her back from the brink of a very cold and lonely demise.

The thought of Sasha caring enough to not put a bullet through her skull prompted Diana to open her eyes. The room, thankfully dark, didn't hurt them. She could see well in the dark, at least enough to know that she was alone.

Heaviness settled in the back of her throat as she took in the empty room. Great. They'd left her...wherever she was. Of course they had.

She bit her lip and pushed herself up, arms barely able to support her weight. What had happened? The only form of cover she had was a thin sheet, and the second it slid down her bare body, a shiver rolled down her limbs. Not only was she weak and unable to shift, but she was naked. Her blood would undoubtedly be everywhere, and any werewolves around would smell it. If the werewolves found her now...

"Get dressed," Diana told herself and swung her legs off the bed. She winced when the bottoms of her feet pressed against the cool wood. So sore. "Get off your ass, Diana."

The thought of being ripped apart by werewolves got her off the mattress. She held the bloody sheet against her body and looked around, standing on shaking legs. Where had they left her?

Sickness crept into her stomach. The wood floor here was the same as the wood in Whitaker's house. Did they leave her with the warlock?

"Wait," Diana whispered to herself and slapped a hand against her neck, feeling around what seemed to be intact skin. Where were the gashes? Panic continued to mount as the familiar cold of Whitaker's mansion crept up her back.

After a few quick breaths, she noticed a light in the back of the room. Light—maybe a bathroom? She held the sheet close and slowly crept toward the door outlined in gold. Her skin chafed and burned despite touching nothing, and every inch of her was torn between staying naked to avoid more pain or getting dressed to escape.

"Clothes, clothes, clothes..." Diana swallowed and tried to ignore the pang of loneliness and panic gripping her as she looked around the bedroom. "Hopefully they didn't leave me here with *nothing—*"

Diana threw open the door and narrowed her eyes in the light. Shower. Toilet. Sink.

Her clothes. She scrambled for the clothes haphazardly hanging in the basin on the counter. She wrapped her fingers around the flannel and made to jerk it over her head.

Then she saw her face. Then her chest. Her back. Stomach.

"I'm a walking bruise." Diana leaned forward and grimaced at the blood caked along her collarbones. However, all her wounds had been closed, leaving behind only the faintest of scars.

Whatever. She'd have to worry about it later. Werewolves had probably picked up her trail, she might have been abandoned with the warlock, and she was alone. Again.

Like always.

Despite pain shaking every fiber in her body, Diana got fully clothed in less than sixty seconds. After a quick drink of water from the faucet, she jerked on her coat and staggered from the bedroom.

Unfortunately, they had left her at Whitaker's house, and the jerks hadn't even thought to turn on the heater before taking off. Her pace quickened.

Diana frowned and opened the front door, freedom in sight. She had to somehow get a ride back to her parent's temporary home. She was in no condition to fly the entire way—

"Going somewhere?"

She stilled at the familiar voice and the sight of Sasha Sokolov leaning on the wall beside the door. Surprised, she hesitated a moment before scowling and descending the steps leading to the driveway.

Sasha hadn't left her at all. He looked like absolute shit, but he hadn't left. The thought brought warmth where cold had been. "Uh. I thought you guys left me."

He didn't say anything. Sasha kept his gaze on the moon and brought a cigarette to his lips with a shaking hand.

"How long was I out?" Diana pulled her coat close, suddenly all too aware of her broken body. While less broken due to...whatever Sasha or Natsu did to save her, it was still covered in blood. Bruised. Ugly. Not that she should've cared.

"Two days." Sasha's eyes had lost some of the brightness she'd come to enjoy since meeting him. "The boy and his demon have been protecting us. I only just woke up myself."

Ugh. She'd been out cold and naked with relative strangers for two days.

"What happened?" The thing she should've thought about immediately invaded her brain with startling fervor. "Did we get it? The knife?"

Sasha dropped his cigarette and crushed it beneath his oxford. "No. Whitaker sold it. Sheturath is somewhere in Pennsylvania with an exceptionally old vampire. I don't know the name or exact location. That was all the information I was able to get."

Her heart sank to her ankles. If she had been alone, Diana might have found it in her to cry in frustration. Instead, she ran a hand down her face, disgusted at the feel of dried blood cracking beneath her fingertips. "Shit."

"Indeed." Sasha kept his gaze to the sky. "I shot Whitaker, and the cat killed the sphinx. The only things we have to worry about now are the werewolves and getting Sheturath."

She coughed and stared into the dark night. They'd lost two days, and the knife wasn't even in Whitaker's house anymore. "What are we supposed to do if we don't know exactly where the knife is?"

"Go to Pennsylvania. I have contacts, and I'll make some calls." Sasha swayed a little and caught himself with a hand on the brick. "Although, I think our more immediate concern is leaving the house. If a wolf from the auction gets ahold of your scent—"

"I think our more immediate concern is that you're dead on your feet." Diana took a few steps closer. Sasha narrowed his eyes at her, although she wasn't sure why. "What happened to you?"

Shaking his head, he let go of the wall. One step toward the front door, and he propped himself on the wall again. "You saved my life. I saved yours. We're square."

She stepped closer to him in case he fell. The sudden tension in his shoulders and neck wasn't lost on her, and Diana tried to shove the hurt away. She looked gross, but she only wanted to help him. It was only right after he saved her life.

"I'm not sure what you did..." Diana watched him while he only had eyes for the moon. "But I'm thankful."

Sasha still didn't look at her, which only made the question of *how did you save me?* all the more heavy.

"Why did you do it?" he asked.

"Do what?" She pulled her coat closer.

While his nose burned red from the chill, his cheeks were pale, and the hand at his side still trembled a bit. What had he done to keep her alive? It certainly came at a cost.

"Why did you save my life?" he asked. "Why didn't you assume I could see the sphinx's attack coming?"

"I don't know." Diana tucked some hair behind her ear as the wind picked up. The lack of an answer made her heart rate pick up.

The fight in Whitaker's house was more or less a blur. She remembered the sounds her bones made when the sphinx crushed her. The way its talons dug into her flesh.

A sharp breath got stuck in her chest as the vivid image of Sasha getting his throat ripped out invaded her psyche.

Diana shook her head. No. That wasn't possible. How could she have seen that if Sasha stood intact beside her?

If Sasha noticed the panic erupting across her face, he didn't mention it. Instead, he rubbed his eyes and yawned. "You're a better person than me."

Diana focused on a steady inhale and exhale. Now that she'd had time to think about it, she knew she'd seen Sasha die. Blood had been everywhere. So much blood. The sphinx had torn his throat out with one exceptionally large paw.

Yet Sasha stood on his two feet. Whole. Breathing. It was like she'd seen a version of the future and prevented it.

Cold caressed her face and hands, but it had nothing to do with the wind.

"You saved me, and you certainly didn't have to." Sasha closed his eyes and relaxed against the wall. How he continued to stand was a miracle. He looked like a dead man walking. In fact, according to the vivid memory, he should be a dead man walking.

Her theory from the motel crept into her brain. It couldn't be—

"Yo." She jumped at Nobu's voice. He emerged from the house with a platter of sandwiches—the same tea sandwiches from the auction. After observing her, Nobu held them out. "You look awful. You *both* look awful."

"Thanks a lot." Diana picked up a sandwich and stuffed her

worries back into her brain where they belonged. While her appetite had been sufficiently destroyed, she knew she needed to eat. Especially if they had to go steal from a vampire. "You are surprisingly clean for surviving a sphinx fight."

"I took a shower. Whitaker has a sick setup in the master bathroom. There's a TV in it and everything." Nobu turned his attention to Sasha. "You guys want to get cleaned up?"

"No." Sasha shook his head and inhaled deep. His tight jaw didn't go unnoticed. Whatever he'd done to save her, she imagined he regretted it right about now. For some reason, the idea he might regret it made her chest ache. "We need to leave. I'm surprised the wolves haven't found us already."

"I wiped up Diana's blood in the hall with some towels." Nobu's voice was small, like he was afraid. The sandwiches suddenly became very interesting to him. "Then I drove around—sorry, Sokolov, I had to borrow the car—and tossed them in the fields about twenty minutes away in the opposite direction. Wolves have probably been following that trail instead."

Diana's eyebrows crept up her forehead. Smart kid. Even Sasha, who didn't emote much beyond his default of relative disinterest, managed to appear surprised.

"Hm." He nodded toward Nobu. Approval.

"Good job, kid." Diana elbowed Nobu. He fought a smile and failed. "Your idea? Or did Natsu tell you to do that?"

"Mine." Nobu pulled his shoulders back and plucked a sandwich off the tray. "I actually haven't heard from Natsu much. He's been almost dormant. Said he had to focus on fixing me."

"Shifting to his true form did a number on you." Sasha dug in his pants pocket and pulled out the keys to the rental. It was the first time she noticed all the blood on his clothes, and the embarrassment that overcame her in a wave was swift and unmerciful. Good lord. He'd literally cradled her bleeding, broken body.

"That's what he said." Nobu took a bite of his sandwich. "I made him do it. He was really mad at me afterward. He ignored me for at least four hours, and that's hard when he literally lives inside me."

Diana bit her lip as Sasha and Nobu moved back into the house, presumably to get their things. Her heart, while unbearably heavy with fear, also felt full of something she'd never experienced before and couldn't quite name.

Sasha had severely debilitated himself in order to do whatever he did to keep her alive. Nobu had, quite literally, risked his life to kill the sphinx so Sasha could take care of her.

The wind pulled through her hair and rolled along her cheeks, but instead of being violently cold, she was confused. Two strangers had given up more for her than her parents ever had.

Troubled, Diana followed behind them and disappeared into the house. If they were willing to risk so much to keep her alive, the least she could do was help them get ready to run.

NINETEEN

DIANA

Diana pushed the eggs on her plate around in lazy circles. Despite a shower and the food being on Sasha's dime, she couldn't force herself to eat. All she could think about was how close she'd been to death and the sacrifices of her companions. Of how Nobu kept the werewolves away from her with bloody towels. The recurring memory of Sasha's death—the death she had prevented.

"You okay, Diana?"

She made a deliberate effort to soften her face before answering Nobu. She wasn't okay, but it wasn't the kid's fault. "I'm fine. Just tired."

"Maybe you can sleep on the plane."

Diana shrugged. She'd never been on a plane before simply because she could fly on her own. Since Sasha and Nobu could not, however, they needed to take a flight to get the knife. "Maybe. How long will it take to get to Pennsylvania?"

"A little under three hours," Sasha said and took a drink of his coffee. He'd thankfully changed into an outfit free of her blood. The clothes were tossed into a dumpster, along with Nobu's. There was no way to salvage any of it after the sphinx. "Plenty of time to rest."

She continued to push her eggs around on her plate. Rest. While she knew she needed it, Diana didn't know if she'd be able to sleep. Her mind was too full—too *busy*—and the implications of her thoughts made a normal resting heart rate impossible.

Diana sneaked a glance at the man consuming her thoughts. Did he always take his coffee black? Maybe if he used a couple of sugar packets, he'd stop grimacing at it so much.

She had no doubts that she'd seen Sasha die. Yet here he was, scowling at his coffee so thoroughly, it was a wonder the expression hadn't become permanent. She tapped her plate with her fork. Had she truly experienced one of his visions? If so, how?

Glaring at her plate, she dropped her fork. Nothing else could explain what she saw, and continuing to deny the obvious wouldn't change anything.

"Diana?" Nobu glanced between her and her discarded fork.

"I'll be right back." She pushed her chair back and dropped her napkin on the table.

Nobu stilled, his glass of orange juice frozen inches from his lips. He sat it down with a clank. "Are you sure you're okay? Should we wait to—"

"I'm fine, Nobu." Diana offered a small smile. "I have to make a phone call."

"A phone call?" Sasha appraised her in veiled suspicion. Really? She'd saved his life, and he still didn't trust her intentions.

"You want to see Charles when this is done, right?" Diana didn't wait on him to answer, if he even intended to. She didn't look at him before walking off toward the hostess stand.

Like the diner from the day before, there were hardly any people inside. According to the advent calendar on the hostess stand, there were somehow only five days until Christmas. Everyone was probably shopping or hanging out with their families.

"While I'm planning to steal a knife. How merry," Diana muttered under her breath, although the idea of enjoying Christmas was a novel one. She'd never had the opportunity.

The hostess, an old woman with a holiday brooch pinned to her chest, smiled as she approached.

"Can I borrow a phone?"

The woman smiled, pushing wrinkles up her cheeks. Diana could only imagine what she thought of her bruised appearance, not to mention the fact she didn't own a cell phone. "We don't have a public phone, dear."

"I know. But it's an emergency." Diana hoped the hostess would change her mind. She didn't want to ask Sasha to borrow his cell phone. He had hardly spoken to her at all that morning. "Please. I have to call my father."

The old woman adjusted her glasses and pursed her lips. After a moment of thought, she spoke again. "I suppose you can borrow our landline in the back. Are...are you all right? Do I need to call the police?"

She shook her head. "No. I'm fine. I just need to call my father."

"Are you sure?" The hostess looked toward the table a moment before leaning in. "Is that man hurting you?"

"No! He isn't. He...helped me get out of a bad situation. But I need to let my father know I'm okay." Diana's face reddened. Oh, if this poor, unassuming woman only knew. She circled her face with her finger. "This happened in an accident."

An accident involving her getting crushed by a sphinx, but whatever.

The woman didn't look convinced but relented. "The phone's for pickup orders, so it'll have to be quick."

"I understand. It'll be fast."

The hostess led her to the back of the restaurant and through a pair of silver doors. The smell of bacon grease and maple syrup invaded her nostrils, and if she weren't about to make an unpleasant phone call, she might've stopped to bask in it. She'd been relatively full for the first time in years thanks to Sasha buying their meals, and the thought of eventually going back to digging in trash cans for food didn't make her already small appetite that morning any better.

"Here." The old lady stopped at a metal table with a white, cordless phone and a notepad. She picked the phone up from the cradle and handed it over. "I'm not sure what happened to you, but if this is an emergency—"

"I'm fine."

The hostess took in a slow breath and gave her a final once-over before, thankfully, leaving her in peace without another word. The only other people around were chefs and servers, but even they were several yards away. Diana sighed and dialed.

Her father had two phones. One was a permanent number only a few people knew, she and Amir being among those people. The other phone changed weekly—burners he'd toss after jobs finished. Hopefully, he'd still answer even though he wouldn't know the diner's number.

"Hello?" Diana breathed a sigh of relief when her father picked up. She hated his stupid voice, but damn it, she actually needed him for once.

"It's me."

"I thought you'd been killed, Diana." Charles's voice, tight and high, didn't carry the air of relief she'd hoped to hear. He sounded frustrated. Maybe even angry. "We haven't heard from you or Nobu in days."

She swallowed and drummed her fingers on the notepad. She still had blood in her nail beds. "I almost did die, actually. I've been unconscious."

"Did you get the knife? Did you get Sheturath?"

Her heart sank. Of course, he'd only care about the knife. "No. But we know where it is."

"We?" A pause. "You and the boy, right?"

"Nobu and I were...forced to partner up with someone else." A heavy silence hung on the other side. Diana could almost picture him stalking around the dirty, dilapidated house in the middle of nowhere, fighting everything in him to cuss up a storm.

"You foolish girl!" Diana recoiled and pulled the phone away from her ear. "You think someone is helping you get Sheturath to be nice? They'll use you to steal the blade, and then they'll take it."

She hesitantly put the phone back to her ear. "Actually, they're helping me get the knife if I take them to *you* after we steal it."

Another heavy silence lingered between them.

"Who is it?" her father eventually asked, voice edged in suspicion.

"His name is Sasha Sokolov." One of the servers came over to the desk and swiped the notepad. Diana smiled meekly.

"I don't recall having business with a Sokolov. What is he?"

"Mostly human but has enough angel in him to be useful, I guess." Diana really hoped none of the humans around could hear her. "You must've screwed him over at some point. His only condition was speaking to you after we get Sheturath."

"And you agreed to this?"

Anger simmered under her eyes and coated her entire body down to her toes. Everything inside her ached, and all he could do was insult her and chastise her like a hatchling? "Listen. I almost fucking *died* getting this for you. So yes—I agreed. Speaking to him is worth it, don't you think?"

"Has it occurred to you that he might kill me instead?"

"He won't." A weak protest if she ever heard one. "I asked. He said he wouldn't kill you. If he does anything shady, I'll ditch him."

"And you believe him? I raised you to be smarter than that."

"You didn't raise me at all."

Since they both knew she was right, her father didn't snap back. "It's no matter. Say I'll speak to him long enough to get the blade, and when it comes time to meet...I'll have a plan."

"You mean you want to cheat him."

"Cheat him, kill him. Whatever I need to do. Once we have Sheturath, we can go back to the murder. We won't need to run like this anymore anyway." Her stomach turned at her father's words. "Whoever this Sasha Sokolov is can feed the rats."

She dropped her forehead in her free hand. As rude and

unpleasant as Sasha had been, she still didn't want him to die. "Can you guarantee they'll accept me?"

"What?"

"After I get Sheturath...can you guarantee the murder will accept me?"

"I can't force anyone to *accept* you, like you mean." For the first time in their conversation, Diana actually felt Charles was sorry.

She bit her lip and inhaled as a waitress walked by with a stack of blueberry pancakes. "What's it like?"

The other end of the phone crackled. "What? What's what like?"

"How does it feel to be one of the murder?" In any other circumstance, she'd rather crucify herself than ask her father this question. But seeing as the concept of *murder* mattered to her now more than ever, Diana had to ignore her worn pride. "Like...how do you know the murder's magic accepts you?"

"You just do, Diana. You just know." Charles sighed. Annoyed. "Your magic becomes theirs, and theirs becomes yours. You are one, but you hold the magic of hundreds. It's impossible to not know when that happens."

Her throat dried. "Does it hurt?"

"It's uncomfortable for a while, but not long. The pain is worth the comfort that comes after."

Diana's mind went back to the morning after the auction and her sound sleep. The first peace she'd known in years.

"But the pain you feel without them...that's the real anguish. I'm ready to be rid of it. Once the murder takes me back, I'll be whole again."

Diana licked her lips. "You mean *we*. You and Mom...and me."

Even though she sat in the middle of a bustling kitchen, Diana didn't hear anything but her father's breathing. His silence was more telling than anything he could ever say. "Get Sheturath. Then we'll meet. All right?"

She sat with the phone pressed to her ear long after Charles hung up, fighting a burn behind her eyes. Her father, unbeknownst to him, had confirmed what she'd been trying to deny since the morning after the auction.

The fact she'd been comfortable enough to sleep. The worry when Sasha walked into Whitaker's house. The painfully obvious—undeniable—reason that they'd started to acquire each other's skills.

Her magic had bonded with Sasha.

Sasha Sokolov, the grouchy asshole without a single feather to his name, was now her murder.

TWENTY

SASHA

I<small>F</small> S<small>ASHA</small> <small>HAD</small> <small>KNOWN</small> D<small>IANA</small> <small>WOULD</small> <small>BE</small> <small>SO</small> <small>DIFFICULT</small> <small>AFTER</small> saving her life, he might've let her die instead.

He drummed his fingers on the steering wheel. No. He wouldn't have let her die, but she made it really hard to feel good about what he'd done. All she'd done since was mope. Even the kid couldn't get her to crack a smile, and Diana was usually pretty good at responding to his attempts.

Sasha risked a glance at her as he turned through the gate leading to a private airfield. She didn't look half as bad now that she'd showered, but nothing could overcome the bruising along her nasal bone and neck. Her chest and arms probably looked worse, but they were buried under layers of fabric. Perhaps she was upset about her appearance.

Although Diana hadn't seemed to care much about how she looked in their time together. Her focus had always, sensibly, been on basic necessities like food and shelter. But despite the bruises, he could only see unwavering selflessness, and there was nothing to be ashamed of in that. In fact, it was one of the most intriguing things about her.

Diana caught him staring and dropped her eyes. "I know I look awful. You don't have to stare at me."

Sasha tightened his grip on the steering wheel. "I was just making sure you're all right."

"I'm fine."

He caught Nobu's wide-eyed gaze in the rearview mirror that communicated the same warning that flashed in his mind.

Diana was not fine.

He tried to focus on the feel of the leather beneath his fingers and keeping the car on a steady path to the airfield, but his attention continued to stray. Perhaps she was angry about losing the knife.

Regardless, if she were mad at him, she wouldn't talk to him, which was a problem if he ever hoped to figure out why he'd started seeing her future alongside his. Sasha couldn't very well ask her about it if she wanted to hurl him into the sun.

He cut her a look. "You're lying."

Pulling her loose hair over both her shoulders, Diana failed to hide the flush that colored her cheeks. She'd tried hiding behind it all day, which didn't make him feel much better. "Well, it's none of your business."

Curious. "If you're wanting me to apologize for saving your life, I won't."

"I don't." A growl shook Diana's throat. "I need some—"

"Some?"

"Ugh. I don't know!" She threw up her hands. "My face hurts and—" She paused abruptly and fell back in her seat. "I have a lot on my mind."

Nobu leaned forward from the back seat and poked his head between them. "How do you have a private jet, Sokolov?"

Sasha took a deep breath, thankful for Nobu's interference. "I don't. It belongs to my employer."

"And who is that again?" Nobu asked.

"As it doesn't affect getting the blade, that is none of your concern."

With a scowl, Nobu slumped in his seat. Diana said nothing at all.

The hangar sat back from the road, amid dead grass and cracked runways. They'd left Dallas behind the same night Diana woke up. One thing he'd learned early in life was supernatural creatures had networks, and ones looking for revenge made generous use of it. They hadn't been caught leaving Whitaker's house, but someone had undoubtedly gone by to investigate by now. Nobu's deception could only stall the bloodthirsty wolves for so long.

Sasha parked the rental car beside one of the hangars. A metal garage door had been rolled open, revealing the small luxury plane—property of Madame.

"Stay here." He didn't wait for his company to protest before stepping out of the car.

He made it three steps from the rental before a blond woman popped out from behind the metal building. While most would assume her to be harmless given her slight build and furry boots, Sasha knew better.

"Sokolov." She smacked her gum and slipped her hands into her coat pockets. Her job as a pilot for Madame meant a lot of time spent doing nothing except waiting on passengers. "Whatcha doing here? I haven't heard from—"

"Hello, Tess. Surprise trip," he interrupted. While Nobu and Diana were in the car, he didn't want to risk them figuring out who he worked for. "Can you take us to Philadelphia?"

"Philadelphia?" Tess scrunched her nose. "They got nailed by a snowstorm yesterday. Gonna be cold."

Great. Diana would hate it. "Which doesn't bother you, so you shouldn't mind."

Tess smiled and stood on her toes, craning her neck to peek behind him. Her braid fell over her shoulder. "Who's in the car?"

"Business associates."

"I ain't never seen them before."

"You haven't seen a lot of people before." Sasha straightened his suit jacket. "How soon until we leave?"

Tess pursed her lips and cast a cursory glance toward the plane. "Gimme 'bout thirty minutes, all right?"

A snow-plagued state, an old vampire, and an angry crow who hated the cold. This trip was getting better all the time.

Diana looked deflated but got out of the car without comment. Nobu carried two backpacks filled with things he'd stolen for the two of them, looking somewhere between concerned and smug.

"What is she?" Nobu asked.

"A pilot."

"Not what I meant."

Sasha adjusted his bags in his grip. "A water nymph."

Diana remained quiet. She wouldn't even look at him, and why should he care? He rolled his tight shoulders and scowled.

As they walked to the plane, his mind wandered. He'd done something that made her utterly uninterested in him or anything he had to say, and he wasn't sure what that something was. Keeping someone alive usually instilled some sort of gratitude, yet if she had any, she'd stuffed it so far down Sasha wasn't sure he'd ever see it.

They settled inside the plane to wait on Tess. Diana made a beeline for a seat by a window and buried herself inside her coat. Nobu paused by the mini refrigerator while he stowed his suitcase beneath one of the tables situated to the side of the cabin.

"No alcohol," Diana quipped from her seat, eyebrows pinched together.

"What are you, my mom?" Nobu rolled his eyes, but notably didn't grab the liquor. He brushed the tiny bottles aside and latched onto a water bottle instead.

Sasha risked a glance at Diana when she didn't immediately say anything. For reasons unknown to him, the grip on his bag faltered when he noticed she'd already completely divested herself from the conversation. Her coat was pulled up around her cheeks, and she stared out the window into the hangar.

Nobu must've noticed too because the boy was staring at him.

Tess's footsteps echoed into the cabin as she walked inside. The blonde smiled at him and popped her gum. "I think I can get us in the air in about fifteen minutes. That okay?"

Sasha nodded, and Tess turned to Nobu.

"There are movies on the TV. Just gotta search the library." She waved to a small television mounted in front of a seat. The sides of the private plane were lined with single leather chairs, all with personal televisions and tables, and Nobu's eyes twinkled in delight at her words. The boy dropped into one of the seats, water bottle in hand, and immediately started searching for something to watch. "Is there anything I can get y'all before we're wheels up?"

"I think we can manage." Sasha took his own seat and relished in the weight lifted from his soles.

With a smile, Tess nodded. "See y'all in a bit."

Giving only a grunt in response, Sasha didn't watch Tess go as his mind had gone back to Diana's interesting mood. While he didn't really understand her mercurial responses, something told him her demeanor stemmed from an emotion far more burdensome than irritation or anger. He drummed his fingers on the tops of his thighs and watched Diana's reflection in a bit of chrome trim. She hadn't moved at all except to retreat farther behind her hair and jacket.

Body moving of its own accord, Sasha stood and walked over to the first woman who'd ever caused him a great deal of emotional duress—aside from his mother. Between this uncharacteristic worry and seeing the woman's future, perhaps Diana doing something otherworldly to him wasn't too far off base.

"Van Doren." He didn't miss the suspicion on her face. Not that he blamed her.

She pulled her coat closer. "Will you *please* call me Diana?"

Sasha blinked, unsure if the crack he heard in the back of her throat actually happened or if he imagined it.

"Diana." At the sound of her name, she finally turned to face him. He motioned to the long couch on the opposite side of the cabin. They'd be in the air soon, and he couldn't imagine sitting for three some-odd hours wondering what the hell had happened to her. No. He would settle this now. "Lie down."

Diana raised an eyebrow smothered in a deep-purple bruise. "Excuse me?"

Sasha paused and took a moment to inventory his thoughts. If he wanted to fix her mood and figure out why he could see her future, he had to put forth a genuine effort to make amends for whatever it was he'd done. "I would like to heal your face if you'll let me."

Gaze hard and guarded, Diana sat still a moment before she stood and moseyed to the couch. Whether it was shock at his words or a desire to rid herself of the pain that got her to listen, he couldn't know. "Heal?"

"It takes a lot out of me to do, so I focused on your life-threatening injuries the other night." His throat, now impossibly dry, made talking difficult. He'd never shared his skill with anyone lest they decide to abuse him, and telling Diana about it made his limbs heavy. "I would like to help you again...if you'll let me."

Suspicion remained in her eyes, but Diana eased herself down on the cushions and crossed her feet at the ankles.

Sasha sat by her head, wondering where the sick apprehension that blossomed in his gut had come from, and settled his hands on her temples. She jumped beneath his fingers, although that might've been from the coat of figurative ice along his palms. He ignored it and pressed his magic out and into the blood collecting beneath her skin. The hum bit away at his core. A familiar pain he hated, but desperately needed all the same.

Diana stilled. He watched her carefully, almost unsure if what he witnessed was real. Ever so slowly, she relaxed completely beneath his hands. Her eyes were closed, inky lashes fanned against her cheek-bones. Her breathing was even and remained that way for several minutes as he stared in wonder.

She wasn't scared of him. At all.

Sasha ignored the pain slicing away beneath his rib cage and contemplated. The only person he knew to be completely unafraid of him was his mother. Everyone else had a healthy fear of him and his powers, even old acquaintances and bedmates. All of them had thought of killing him at one point out of fear, and he'd seen those instances play out in his mind so often he wasn't surprised by them when they cropped up.

But not Diana. The thought prompted him to lightly brush her brow with his thumbs, and warmth invaded the perpetual darkness clinging to his ribs.

"Where are you from?" she asked, voice relaxed.

He blinked and focused on the woman beneath his fingers. He'd been so entranced by her peace that her question caught him off guard. "Russia."

She snorted. "Well, I know that. But where in Russia?"

"Why do you want to know?"

"I..." Diana's lips turned down a little. "Never mind."

Sasha's gaze was on the receding bruise around Diana's nose, but his focus was elsewhere. Why did she want to talk to him so much? Was she trying to make him comfortable to facilitate an easier kill later?

No. That couldn't be right. She'd almost killed herself to save him.

The bruise along her nasal bone faded, and he slipped his fingers to her jaw. Her lips still hadn't gone back to neutral, and something about it made him...uncomfortable. Diana had been somewhat peaceful with him, something he'd never known another human being to feel in his presence, and he'd spoiled it.

"I'm from Chelyabinsk." Diana's eyes opened. Dark pools of obsidian tacked to his. "It's a city near the Urals."

Eyebrows lifted, she asked, "Are those mountains?"

Sasha nodded, and the bruise along her jaw began to fade. "Yes."

She smiled a little and closed her eyes again. "That's why you like the cold."

Not for the first time, Sasha was confused. Diana always seemed to know things about him he'd never commented on. Not once. "I don't remember telling you I liked the cold."

"You didn't. I can just tell."

"How?"

"Because I have eyeballs?" Diana opened her eyes again to give him a look—one that said she was making fun of him. "Of course, it would be easier if you talked every once in a while."

"It is unnecessary most of the time."

"Unnecessary?" Diana sat up and twisted her torso around, sticking her face only inches away from his. Her eyes weren't completely black up close, he noticed. Just a really dark brown. Her lips were also very inviting, and he imagined they'd be pillow-soft should he dare kiss them. Not that he would. "You don't talk to people simply because it's necessary."

Her breath was hot on his nose, but he didn't pull away. "In my line of work, you do."

Diana's eyebrows crept up her forehead. "Which is?"

This hadn't been where he'd wanted the conversation to go. Yet for some inexplicable reason, he answered. "Acquisitions."

"Acquisition of?"

"Anything my employer desires."

She cocked her head to the side, sending all her dark hair over her shoulder like a curtain. "I'm not sure why that would mean you're not allowed to make friends. That has to be lonely."

Something about that stole his breath. He swallowed and regained composure, although with eyes as good as Diana's, he knew she noticed. "It is."

She pursed her lips and dropped her gaze to the beige couch beneath them. "I need to tell you something."

Oh, thank Christ. Maybe now he'd know what the hell he'd done. Or better yet, maybe she'd tell him why he was suddenly seeing her die in his visions. "Yes?"

"Um." Diana made a face—a displeased one. Like she'd eaten road-kill. "Well..."

"Yes, Diana?"

Her lips parted in obvious surprise. She stared at him, unblinking, and then turned away, easing her body back down on the couch. "It's nothing. I just think you should get a new job."

Sasha smiled bitterly, tracing the lines of her face with his gaze. He placed his hands on her temples. "I intend to."

TWENTY-ONE

DIANA

Diana wanted to vomit.

She focused on moving one foot in front of the other and followed Sasha to a car parked right outside the hangar on wobbly legs. She'd never been in an airplane, and if she had her say, she never would again. Bile shot into her mouth, and a chill ran up her back. Thank God she was a crow.

Much to her dismay, central Pennsylvania had been buried under two feet of snow. The dead cornfields were mounds of rotten stalks and ice, and the temperature sat uncomfortably close to the negatives. Despite only having been there for less than ten minutes, Diana unabashedly hated Pennsylvania.

The pilot, Tess, had gotten them to a small airfield outside Phil-adelphia in good time—less than three hours. Landing had taken a bit thanks to the snow, but once they were safely out of the tin can with wings and back on land, she could breathe.

She opened the passenger door to the car and collapsed inside, quite certain she'd never be warm again. Shivers racked her body, which made it impossible to form a single coherent thought.

"What's the plan?" Nobu poked his head between the front seats, head angled toward Sasha. She was glad he had the wherewithal to speak because she sure didn't, thanks to her chattering teeth.

"I need to make some calls to get a location on our vampire friend. In the meantime, let's find a hotel and get something to eat," Sasha said.

He threw the car in drive and easily maneuvered along the icy asphalt. Used to it, she supposed.

After a glance her way, Sasha turned up the car's heater. "We'll need some time to case Jacques's property before a proper heist can proceed."

Snow-covered trees taunted her beyond the window, and she huffed in annoyance. Unsurprisingly, her breath came out in a thick, white cloud. It was too damn cold. "Do we need to be afraid of Jacques?"

"Yes."

Her stomach turned. Great. She'd never gone toe-to-toe with a vampire before. Even her father had limits, and sending her to trick vampires had been one of them.

Nobu reached between the front seats and tossed his jacket in her lap. "What could a vampire want with that knife?"

Diana burrowed underneath the jacket and cast him a thankful glance.

The boy gave her a slight smile before going on. "I'd think the old ones are more than capable of keeping themselves safe. Not to mention simply having it would draw people to his sleeping place."

"It is interesting. Not the smartest move," Sasha said, voice tight.

Diana watched Sasha focus on the stretch of road before them with a clenched jaw, hard stare, and white knuckles.

He was nervous.

It hadn't been that long since he'd shown her the most care she'd known in years, so to see Sasha this tense gave her whiplash. He'd taken his time on her bruises, erasing each and every one from her face. Her cheeks flushed at the memory of his skin on hers, calluses gently caressing her jaw and neck. For someone who'd otherwise shown himself to be cold, he was actually very warm. So warm, in fact, that the idea of his hands skimming down her arms and back invaded her thoughts all too easily.

Diana buried herself into the jacket in shame. It was *not* a good time to think about that. She had enough to worry about since she would be tied to Sasha for life. She didn't need to set the bar for their relationship at unattainable heights.

No. She needed to focus on getting him to like her at the most basic, fundamental level. If this new partnership were going to work, Sasha, at the very least, needed to find her tolerable.

Jacques the vampire wasn't brought up again during their drive. The rest of the trip in the rental passed in silence, and during her valiant attempts at distancing herself from thoughts of Sasha's adept hands, they'd somehow ended up at a motel as the sun fell below the horizon. It was the nicest one they'd passed, and it had a continental breakfast according to the sign.

"I'm going to let Natsu out until dinner. He's been weird since Whitaker's place." Nobu pressed a palm to his chin and popped his neck as Sasha opened the door to their newest accommodations: an older version of the first motel, bearing blue wallpaper instead of green. "I'll be back in an hour or so."

The boy didn't wait for an answer. He watched them go into the room and left, pace just short of a run.

Diana bit her lip. "Do...do you know Nobu's story?"

Sasha's face remained unchanged, but he eventually nodded. His sandy hair hung in his eyes, but she'd never not see the gold shining in them. "I know parts. Although it's not my place to say. His relationship with Natsu is one of the better arrangements I've ever seen between a human and a demon, so I imagine he has to keep to a strict schedule to keep it that way."

"Hm." How curious. But the curiosity didn't keep her heart from sinking into her stomach. "Poor kid."

"You assume bad circumstances?"

She snorted. "I don't think anyone would allow themselves to be possessed for fun."

The corner of his mouth lifted, but it was so slight and brief it might've been her imagination. He tossed his suitcase on his bed.

Diana padded over to the edge of her bed. Still cold, she kept her arms tightly wrapped around her torso. Sasha had been so *different* on the plane. Emotive. Somewhat vulnerable. Like maybe he'd seen her a bit. Like maybe he saw her as more than business as she lay beneath his palms.

She considered using that momentum to help their relationship. Or like the little voice in her head kept saying, she could tell him the truth. Get it out in the open.

Ha. Right. Doing that would go over terribly. Her gaze darted to Sasha and back to the tops of her legs, and a heavy weight settled in her stomach. Perhaps she could tell him a different truth. One that was almost as important.

"You asked me the other night what I did to get kicked out of the murder." She swallowed and tried to ignore the sudden scratchiness of her throat. "Do you still want to know?"

While Sasha's expression didn't change, his attention shifted squarely on her face. Were angels always so...cagey?

After allowing herself a few moments to worry about it, Diana decided she didn't care what he wanted to know. If she hoped to build something between them because of her crow's stupid decision to latch onto his magic, Sasha needed to know. He needed to know where she came from. "I was never a part of the murder to begin with."

"You've never had a murder?" His eyebrows screwed together. "I thought all crows were born into one."

She shook her head. "Most crows are accepted by the murder's magic when they're young, but not all of them. Definitely not me."

Diana licked her lips. She'd never told anyone this. But if she ever hoped to have anything worth having with the man, it had to be done as much as she hated it. Murders were forever—and she wanted her forever to be built better than whatever she had with her parents.

She took a deep breath. "When I was a hatchling, I fell from my nest because my parents left me alone. Allegedly, something dangerous approached the murder, and Lead Crow whisked them away with his magic, teleporting them to safety. Whatever the case, they all left me there." The words came out faster than she expected. Like vomit. "Crows generally spend part of the year as birds. Not long...a few weeks. Enough time for kids to hopefully imprint on the murder and be accepted by their magic. The farmer who owned the land during that time found me squawking in the grass. He could've left me there or whatever, but he didn't. He picked me up and took me into his house." She closed her eyes. It was hard to tell a story never told. "And while inordinately generous of him, if humans aren't careful rescuing birds...the birds imprint on them instead of their own kind."

A heavy silence hung between them. Sasha was intelligent. Surely he could fill in the blanks. She dared a glance at him.

"You imprinted on a human?" he asked, voice neutral.

"Yep. Which is typically a death sentence." Diana turned her gaze to the threadbare comforter beneath her thighs to keep from looking at him. "So I changed into a human and stayed that way. Anyway, he raised me until I was eight or so. He couldn't send me to school or anything because he didn't know if I was...safe for others."

She was lightheaded at the thought of what Sasha might be thinking. Now that he was her murder, she cared about his opinion of her. She knew she'd been nothing but trouble the past week, and she hoped she could salvage it. "But he taught me how to tend a farm, and I helped him until my murder came back to the field to roost again eventually. Lead Crow recognized me for what I was...and I was tentatively brought back in and reunited with my parents."

She would likely never use the word expressive to describe Sasha, but he managed to look somewhat confused. "Tentatively?"

"Crow shifters are weird. Murders aren't simply a matter of flying together. You have to be accepted into the murder by the magic that *makes* a murder. Like werewolves and their packs. The magic that makes a murder is founded in safety, and I guess they felt I was a liability." Diana thought of Sasha unwittingly taking the opportunity from her to join the crows, and it quickly changed to the feel of his hands on her face.

Get a grip, Diana!

She eased out a shaky breath. "Anyway, I was brought back in out of guilt. Allowed a chance. But I still had to wait to for that acceptance. If they found me worthy, I'd be welcomed in by the magic that makes them a family, and I would be bound to the murder for life. Never alone. Never left to die again. Safe."

Her voice cracked at the end. She sneaked a glance at him, unsurprised that his face remained the same variant of indifferent as always. "Fifteen years come and go, and they haven't let me in. I follow them around and keep trying." Sasha kept his eyes on her, staring so intently her cheeks caught fire. "Then, one day, Charles ruined everything."

"What happened?" He popped his suitcase open. His folded shirts and slacks were visible from her place across the room.

Diana pulled all her hair over her shoulder and ran her fingers through it. "Five years ago, my father screwed over some demon. Put the whole murder at risk. They kicked him out, which meant my mother got booted too, and since I wasn't a part of the murder officially, kicking me to the curb was a pretty easy thing to do. They finally had their excuse."

When he didn't say anything, Diana couldn't help but look at him. His hands, completely still against the clothes in his suitcase, matched the rest of him. Sasha didn't move. Didn't breathe. Didn't blink. "They kept my younger sister though, who had been welcomed into the murder almost immediately after her birth. So at least she's safe."

He still didn't speak, and her heart dropped. Great. He probably thought she would get him killed or something.

Sasha finally moved to pick up a shirt from the top of the suitcase. He cleared his throat. "Is that why Sheturath is so important to you?"

Diana shrugged. "We can't survive like we have the past five years. Charles thinks if we bring them the knife, we can join them again."

"Will they accept you into the murder even if you bring them the blade?"

Diana shook her head. They definitely wouldn't now—they couldn't. "No, but they might let me fly alongside them like before."

Sasha rubbed the back of his neck. "You don't think you'll ever properly join their murder?"

Oh, the irony. "I know I won't."

"Why?"

The truth bubbled in the back of her throat. If she told him now, maybe she could start building something with him. Lay the foundation of their partnership.

Figure out if he even wanted it.

Her heart bashed against her sternum as the words formed on her tongue. Telling him the truth, that she'd bonded with him and there was absolutely nothing she could do about it, would change so much. It would change everything.

But when her gaze locked onto his, guilt killed the words in her mouth. Sasha didn't ask for it. Hell, she didn't ask for it either. Putting him on the spot like some petulant brat wasn't fair.

"That stupid wolf from the auction had one thing right: I'm trash, Sasha." The words left her mouth all too easily. "My parents didn't want me. No one else will either."

Diana pushed herself to her feet, grabbed the backpack of stolen clothes on her bed, and retreated to the bathroom, leaving Sasha no opportunity to respond. She wanted to earn his friendship. She wanted him to wake up every morning and see her as she was coming to see him. As a safety net. A rock. The one constant in a sea of variables.

Forcing him to like her wouldn't cut it, and she had no intention of trying. If there had been one thing she'd learned over the years of trying to force her way into the murder, it was that she could never make anyone accept her. To want her. To like her, even.

She had never been given a choice, and she had no intention of taking Sasha's away.

TWENTY-TWO

SASHA

Sasha hadn't known what to do with Diana after hearing her origin story. It wasn't every day someone dredged up their darkest secrets for his sake, and he remembered why he hated those sorts of conversations moments after she disappeared into the bathroom.

He forced himself to breathe as her words continued to haunt him well after her departure. *I'm trash, Sasha.*

How could the very people she lived and breathed for make her hate herself so much?

Diana had been treated terribly from the onset. Abandoned. Forgotten. Yet she still worked hard to appease her parents. She was loyal to a murder that didn't want her and to parents that used her. Loyalty like that didn't happen often, and Sasha wondered why she bothered. He wouldn't have.

The question troubled Sasha well after Nobu came back to the hotel and they left to find dinner, lingering in the back of his mind as he drummed his fingers along the steering wheel. Having been raised by Madame, her fellow demons, and other supernatural creatures with no conscience, Sasha didn't know what it was like to feel that level of loyalty to another person. The only person he'd ever felt that strongly for had been his mother, but even then, he hadn't gone to see her in years.

So after everything she'd been through, how did Diana have anything left to give for those who cared so little? If safety made murders, would her magic even recognize crow shifters as *safe* when they'd done nothing but leave her behind?

Sasha stared at the steering wheel after he parked despite Diana and Nobu getting out, fighting the irritation thrumming beneath his skin. Everything Diana did made no sense, and trying to parse out the logic in her decisions was a waste of time.

The pub they'd decided to eat at that evening had been built inside the basement of an old house. The original wood floors creaked beneath his feet when they walked in, and he had to hunch his shoulders a bit to get around thanks to the short ceilings. However, the smell of steak and gravy made him realize how long it had been since he'd eaten, and the ceiling height became less of an issue.

Diana and Nobu sat across from him in a booth as they had been prone to do since they started working together. The former caught his gaze, smiled a bit, and dropped her eyes.

Perhaps he'd fixed whatever had happened with Diana on the plane. The thought that he'd helped her, that maybe he'd done some good for a change, made him feel some sort of way. Since meeting Diana, he'd known nothing but discomfort and confusion, but he doubted discomfort and confusion would cause the warmth radiating behind his breastbone.

Whatever the emotion involved, he hoped he could get to the bottom of his newfound connection with her and figure out why the hell he saw her die in Whitaker's house.

"Good evening." A woman with warm skin greeted them at the table. Her copper hair was cut short, which revealed a trail of flower tattoos from her ear to her collarbone. She held out some menus. "Can I get you some drinks?"

Sasha muttered something about a water when a distinctly super-natural individual caught his eye behind the bar.

The waitress's voice echoed in his subconscious, but his gaze was elsewhere. The woman slinging drinks at the bar wasn't simply a woman. The distinct brand, a magical burn, on her collarbone saw to that.

"Sasha."

The hard voice of Diana broke him from his intent stare. She followed his gaze to the bar and quirked an eyebrow. The waitress had left.

"Little old for you, Sokolov," Nobu quipped.

He pressed his lips together in a fine line and nodded toward the bartender. "She's a witch."

Nobu sat up a little straighter and held up his menu to hide most of his face as he observed. Not entirely discreet.

"Really? How can you tell?" Diana scowled and watched the witch saunter over to a booth with a pair of glass mugs. "They normally have those amulets on."

It figured she'd notice that of all things. *Crow.*

"Witches and warlocks use a distinct, self-made brand when carrying out certain types of magic," Sasha said.

Diana's eyebrows lifted. "So that swirly burn thing on her chest is a brand?"

"Yes." The way she stared at him told him to elaborate. "For exam-ple, when we were in Whitaker's house, I found a demon he'd bound to Earth. He'd channeled his magic into a brand on the demon's palm to keep the demon in its host body."

"Excuse me?" Diana frowned and leaned over the table. "Whitaker had a demon in his house? What happened to it?"

"It was a minor demon. Relatively new." He hadn't realized he'd kept that detail from them. "In exchange for information on Sheturath, I freed it. Broke Whitaker's brand."

Nobu dropped his menu on the table. "You know an awful lot about supernatural creatures."

"If you recall, I am one."

"So are we, but we aren't walking encyclopedias." Nobu looked him up and down.

Sasha ignored him.

The waitress returned, dropped off their drinks, and took their orders—Diana's amounting to two plates. Sasha had a sneaking suspicion that Diana had gained a few much-needed pounds the past few days on Madame's dime. If her father was going to keep using her for his own ends, he really needed to do a better job of keeping her fed.

"So this vampire. Jacques," Diana said, name laced with a faux accent. "Why is he so dangerous?"

"He's old." Sasha adjusted his suit jacket. The basement pub, warm and somewhat humid, brought him close to taking it off. "Old vampires are strong. Their ability to blend with humans is also much better than their younger counterparts."

"By strong, do you mean physically?"

"Among other things." Sasha glanced between Diana and Nobu. "What do you know about vampires?"

"They suck out your blood. They don't die." Nobu held up two fingers and raised a third. "They sleep in coffins."

"Actually, vampires can die. Everything can die, but some things are harder to kill than others. That is where the value in Sheturath lies." Sasha tapped his fingers on his thighs as he thought about the pertinent information. "Vampires must be staked and decapitated."

"Is that all?" Diana crossed her arms and snorted. "Did you happen to pack some pointy sticks in your suitcase between your ties and wool socks?"

"I grabbed some from my trunk before we boarded the plane." If he were the sort to laugh, he would've laughed at Diana's blush. "Do you know what the true danger of a vampire is?"

"The fact that it wants to tear out your jugular for dinner?" Nobu pressed his lips to his frosted glass.

"Vampires have neurotoxic venom in their bite." The teenager's face, despite the dimmed lighting, grew notably pallid. "The venom is a biological feature that more or less aids new vampires in subduing more obstinate prey. It operates similarly to that of a viper's venom: drowsiness, paralysis, and eventually death."

"Is there a cure for this venom?" Diana's face had also gone pale.

"There is, but it comes at a cost—a steep cost—and is difficult to find. We best focus on not being bitten to begin with," Sasha said as Nobu slid down in the booth and covered his face with both hands, defeated. "If one of us needs to get bitten, Natsu would be able to fight it off. Demons are immune and protect their host bodies."

"Wow. Thanks a lot." Nobu glared between his fingers. "Way to keep yourself off the chopping block."

"I would be the next best option given my lineage. I could probably stay alive long enough for either of you to find an antivenom should you decide I am deserving of one." Sasha tried not to think about how much vampires loved angel blood, or how easy it would be for his companions to leave him to die. They didn't owe him anything. In fact, the one he still felt indebted to stood to lose the most in the vampire's den. One bite would end her in a heartbeat.

His appetite inconveniently soured at the thought. "Diana, you need to stay away from Jacques. No more...selflessness."

She nodded and ran a hand on the back of her neck. "I'll try—"

"You will stay away."

Diana recoiled and met his stare, yet she didn't look afraid. The longer they locked eyes, the more her face softened, and he would've paid quite a bit of money to know what she was thinking.

"Okay." Diana smiled a little but broke their connection in favor of the witch behind the bar once more. "I'll stay away."

"In case she can't help herself"—Nobu elbowed Diana and nodded toward him—"I'd like to know where I could find this elusive, expensive antivenom...unless you can heal that too."

"It would require more than I have to give. Much more. If I had to guess, in order to heal a vampire's bite, I'd have to be a Nephilim at least." Sasha didn't like how easily the words left his mouth. He'd only shared his secret with Diana, and consequently Nobu, that afternoon, and now he was telling them everything about his lineage.

"So?" Nobu shook his head, sending his mess of hair into his eyes. The boy really needed a proper haircut. "Where's the antivenom?"

"Most witches can make it." Sasha didn't miss Nobu's glance at the woman behind the bar. "Not all of them. But most can. From my understanding, it takes several expensive ingredients to brew, so the cost is usually high."

"I bet that witch working here, so close to Jacques's house, isn't a coincidence then." Diana pursed her lips and massaged her temples. "She might enjoy having the business."

"If there is one witch in the area, there are several witches in the area. Covens are tight-knit. Almost like you crows and your murders." While he'd never admit it, he was impressed with Diana's deductive reasoning, and he was hardly ever impressed with anything. "I'm sure their being here isn't a coincidence at all."

"Could they have a partnership with Jacques?" Nobu asked.

"Perhaps."

The table fell silent. Diana, the very definition of a people watcher, continued to analyze the witch behind the bar. Nobu had his gaze somewhere different entirely. It wasn't until the sound of a cue ball breaking a game of pool hit his ears that either he or Diana bothered to take notice of what the boy had been watching.

"Go play. She looks nice." Diana jerked her head toward the pool table tucked in the back of the pub. Sasha hadn't noticed a girl at first, but she was there all the same. A thin girl with ochre skin and a ponytail.

"But—"

"No buts." She motioned to the pool table with her thumb and got out of the booth to allow him out. "Your life was stolen by a demon. Go make a friend or whatever."

"Fine." Nobu sighed and slid out of the booth. "But Natsu didn't steal my life. He saved it."

Diana's mouth dropped open, poised to question further, but Nobu walked away. She didn't sit down until he picked up a pool cue, and when she sat, she instantly found Sasha's eyes. He knew curiosity ate her alive, but Nobu's story wasn't his to tell. Besides, Whitaker could've been wrong.

He needed to change the subject.

"Is wandering into Jacques's den worth it, Diana?" Sasha watched her intently. "Do the benefits outweigh the risks?"

She tucked her lip between her teeth. "If I get the knife, my family—"

"No." He leaned forward over the table and looked at her from beneath the loose strands of hair hanging in his eyes. "Do the benefits outweigh the risks *for you?*"

Diana ran a hand down her face. "Probably not."

The waitress graced the edge of their table with a pair of baskets: one with mozzarella sticks and another with fries. Diana wasted no time in picking up the fried cheese and cramming it in her mouth. Madame had forced him to commit many unsavory acts over the years, but turning over Charles Van Doren to the demon would almost be a reward.

Meanwhile, Sasha couldn't find anything to say in response. Diana knew she stood to gain nothing but an early grave for her trouble, yet she fought to get Sheturath anyway? She was willing to lose the one life she had to help people who didn't deserve her attention, much less her sacrifice.

It was asinine. Illogical. Foolish in every conceivable way.

Yet Sasha couldn't help but wonder what it would be like to have someone like that in his corner. Someone who fought for him on the days he didn't deserve it. Someone who saw good when there wasn't any.

He dared himself to think what he'd been purposefully ignoring.

What would it be like to have someone like Diana?

As he tried to banish the thought, another one he loathed more invaded his psyche: did he still want to betray Diana and join the leagues of people who've always used her? The ones who'd made her incapable of seeing how good she was?

I'm trash, Sasha.

Sasha bit the inside of his cheek, partially to keep from scowling and partially because he deserved the pain.

TWENTY-THREE

DIANA

After days of reconnaissance and driving around, they finally found Jacques's house in a farming community about an hour outside Philadelphia. Diana wasn't impressed. For someone with enough money to buy Sheturath, the vampire didn't seem to care about taking care of his house. His windows probably hadn't been cleaned since they were installed, and the paint had started to peel from the siding. While the home was surrounded by oceans of cornfields, the two-story building could still be seen from the road.

They'd also run into several witches during their search. As Sasha predicted, the witch from the bar hadn't been the last of them. After he questioned her about Jacques, she directed them north. Her information led them to a young witch, probably no older than Nobu, and she pointed them to another witch who ran a general store.

Now they sat parked a mile down the road from the vampire's den beside a mess of dead corn.

Diana climbed into the car and rubbed her arms before sticking her red nose to the heater. They were on day three of casing the place. She'd been flying around the property all morning looking for ways in and out, and it was too damn cold for it. Not the way she imagined spending Christmas this year. Although, spending it with her parents wasn't great either.

"Has anything changed?" Sasha asked, drumming his fingers on the steering wheel. He did that a lot, she noticed.

"No." Diana shook her head. "Nothing went in or out. No movement in the windows, but they all have curtains."

"Feel anything?" Natsu had already taken Nobu's place and hopped onto the console. The cat hadn't spoken to them much since they started observing Jacques's farm. A complete one-eighty from the morning Diana met him. He was probably still peeved about their botched foray into Whitaker's mansion.

Diana huffed into her hands. So. Cold. "No. But I imagine you'll have an easier time."

"While we've seen no change in the exterior of the home, it does tell us some things about what is likely inside." Sasha kept his gaze forward and fingers tapping. "Since Jacques hasn't left the property, we can assume he has some form of sustenance."

"Ew. Like people?" Diana grimaced as her stomach turned. She did *not* want to run into any corpses.

"That is likely." Sasha didn't seem to feel any particular way about the possible bodies. "While he is old and can survive without fresh blood for a time, he just returned from Texas. His routine and regular food supply wouldn't have been readily available to him for at least twenty-four hours. He's probably trying to recoup."

"We should watch the house again tonight to be certain." Natsu turned and smacked her in the face with a flick of his tail.

"We need to wait and go inside during the day though." Diana shrugged and watched the sun. "Going in while Jacques is awake would be stupid."

"Jacques is old. He is not bound by the sun." Sasha paused and rubbed the back of his neck. "Well, he's not bound like his younger counterparts would be. He can survive indoors outside his coffin during the daylight hours. Stand in the shade. He could probably survive in broad daylight for a few moments if he had no choice. That means we can't rely on the sun to save us."

"So he'll always be around." Diana frowned and held her stiff fingers in front of the heater instead.

"He'll have to leave to go find more blood eventually." Sasha kept his eyes from Natsu. He apparently still didn't trust the demon. "Perhaps waiting until that moment would be best."

Diana groaned. "It's so freaking cold. I'm tired of flying around."

"If we don't plan this carefully, you'll be dead." Sasha gave her a look. "It's worth the extra time in the air."

"Coming from the guy without wings."

Sasha shrugged. "We each have our own uses. Yours happens to be the most beneficial to our goal at this time."

"Whatever." Diana cast a glance toward the back of the car. "If we're going to keep this up, I need a nap."

After a look from Natsu, she opened the door and let him out. The cat hopped onto the dead grass and narrowly missed a patch of ice left behind from the snowstorm. Did demons feel cold? If not, she should make Natsu do all the reconnaissance.

"Thank you." The words flew out of her mouth before she could stop them. She'd been wanting to thank Natsu since Whitaker's house, but he'd been so elusive she never had the chance.

The demon turned around. How did he feel about her gratitude? Reading a cat's face for cues was impossible. "I'm not going to risk the kid like that again."

Diana nodded. "I don't want you to."

Natsu dipped his head a moment before bounding off toward Jacques's farmhouse.

As she retreated into the back seat of the car, Natsu's words hung in her mind. Did the cat care about Nobu, or did he care about Nobu's body? While she hoped for the former, Diana also knew not to expect much from demons. She'd never met a nice one. Not that she'd met many in the first place.

Diana settled in the center of the back seat, positioned behind the console. Sasha watched her in the rearview mirror. Why? She didn't have a clue. But the sudden creep of heat settling beneath her eyes certainly didn't help anything.

Trying to will the scorch on her face away, Diana cleared her throat. It didn't work. "If Natsu is immune to Jacques's bite and can protect Nobu, why do we need to go in at all?"

Her voice broke Sasha's concentration on the mirror. Instead, he relaxed in his seat and closed his eyes. He looked peaceful. Not at all concerned about trying to dupe an old, powerful vampire. "Natsu can protect Nobu from the venom. He cannot keep Jacques from tearing off the kid's head."

Her stomach flipped. "Did you have to say it like that?"

Sasha's eyes remained closed. "It is accurate. To say it any other way would be inefficient."

Inefficient. A complete antithesis of the man if she ever heard one. Diana huffed and peeled off her jacket. It would make a fine pillow. Better than the buckle of the seat belt anyway.

A phone rang. Sasha's phone.

Sasha opened his eyes and glanced at the screen. She watched him stare at it, unmoving. Who was it, and why wouldn't he answer? Diana sat up a little and peeked over his shoulder.

The damn screen was in Cyrillic.

Her mind went in several directions. She still didn't know who Sasha worked for. He was a gunslinging clairvoyant who could get a thirty minute face-to-face with Whitaker due to whoever it was that employed him. The possibility that someone dangerous could be on the other end made her palms sweat despite her recent foray in the chill outside.

But the longer she stared at him, the idea of someone loathsome calling Sasha ebbed. His face softened as he looked at the text on his screen. Something—maybe relief—flooded his eyes. It struck her with an astounding amount of force that whoever it happened to be, Sasha cared about them.

The robot had a heart in his chest somewhere.

Diana waited until the phone stopped ringing to speak. "Who was that?"

Sasha dropped the phone in the cupholder, gaze hard again. "No one."

Right.

"Sister?" Diana took a breath. "Wife?"

As selfish as it was, she hoped it wasn't a wife. Another woman probably wouldn't like Diana's magic staking a claim on her husband.

Sasha glanced over his shoulder. "Mother."

The muscles in her shoulders relaxed a bit. "You miss her."

"I do." His answer, firm and unquestionable like everything else, sounded strange coming from his mouth given his general lack of compassion.

Diana leaned onto the console. "When was the last time you saw her?"

"Twenty years ago."

Her eyebrows lifted. "Why haven't you gone back?" She hated the lingering dread that wrapped itself around her neck. If he'd gone twenty years without seeing his own mom, whom he clearly cared for, why would he allow her to tag along if she told him that her magic bonded with his? The answer came all too easily: he probably wouldn't. "Whoever you work for obviously pays well, so I imagine money isn't the issue."

"It isn't."

Diana closed her eyes and took a measured breath. Was he always this difficult?

"Can't be convenience. Your boss flew us here on a private plane." Diana leaned farther over the center console and propped herself on her forearms.

With an uncharacteristic sigh, Sasha finally looked at her. He didn't seem annoyed, but then again, he never seemed any which way. "Convenience has nothing to do with it."

"Then what is it?"

His gaze never left her face. She'd leaned close enough to feel his body heat without touching him, and the thought made her increasingly aware of her heartbeat. Sasha's gaze raked over her face. "Why does this matter to you?"

Diana flinched at his tone. She'd never heard so much irritation in Sasha's voice. She didn't move from her place on the console though, which was undeniably reckless. Instead, she cocked her head to the side, putting her temple much closer to his arm than necessary. "Because it's sad. I can tell you miss her. So—go see her. I'm sure she misses you too."

Sasha turned away and faced the windshield, which left her feeling lonely despite him not actually going anywhere.

Diana fell back into her seat again, both embarrassed and confused. If Sasha missed his mother, and his mother missed him, their continued separation didn't make sense. He had the money and the means to get back to Russia. Given the inordinate amount of time he'd spent thus far on getting her knife, the hours in the day weren't the problem either.

Maybe he was just stubborn.

"If someone missed me, I'd go to them in a heartbeat," she said, voice heavy. "If I die during this vampire thing, you know who would care? No one. Literally *no one* would give a shit." Diana made sure to keep her eyes elsewhere, but she could feel Sasha looking at her. "You have someone that cares, and you're wasting it."

He said nothing, and she was glad. Stubborn butthole.

"I'm going to take a nap." Diana stared at the back of Sasha's head. His gaze was on the steering wheel now. "You should call your mom back."

Sasha didn't answer her, which wasn't terribly surprising. Diana slumped down onto the seat and smashed her jacket under her head for a makeshift pillow. She wrapped her arms over her chest and brought her knees closer to her stomach. Taking advantage of her time to sleep would be the only way she'd survive another night of surveilling Jacques.

As a chill racked her body, something warm fell over her arms. Diana opened her eyes, surprised to see Sasha turned around in his seat, leaning over the console and draping his suit jacket over her torso. His eyes, carefully diverted from hers, focused on the fabric as it fell against her arms and neck.

He pulled his hands away all too soon and plucked his cell phone from the cupholder. Diana tugged the jacket closer to her face and burrowed in the warmth and comfort of his scent. She didn't know what it was he smelled like, something woodsy and warm mixed with a hint of cigarettes, but something about it calmed her.

"Merry Christmas, Sasha."

Hand faltering on the door handle, he paused but didn't say anything. After a moment, he opened the door and stepped out.

Diana, despite his silence, smiled against the fabric of his suit jacket. Maybe Sasha wouldn't make a bad murder after all.

TWENTY-FOUR

SASHA

Dusk had fallen upon them, and Sasha desperately hoped Jacques would finally leave the confines of his home to hunt. It had been four days since they'd made the plan in the car—which meant seven agonizing days of staring at Jacques's farmhouse—and he was ready for it to be over. The vampire would have to come out eventually to eat, or he'd starve. It was just a matter of when.

He turned in his seat and glanced at the bunched-up body passed out in a heap. Diana had been asleep for almost three hours now, soft snores pressing past her lips as she burrowed farther into her makeshift cocoon. Being in close proximity for a week had done something to him. Something that Sasha was pretty sure he liked but couldn't put a finger on.

He'd given her his jacket again. She'd never asked him for it, but after the first instance four days ago, he kept peeling it off and draping it on her sleeping body. He didn't think she noticed at first, but he'd always later see her bringing it close, tucking it below her nose.

For the first time in his life, he'd brought someone comfort instead of pain.

Sasha forced himself to look away. Too much thought into something that ultimately didn't matter wouldn't get him what he wanted.

In the dark, beyond the road and from the ocean of dead corn, Natsu emerged, bounding toward the car. Normally, the cat lazily walked back to them, sometimes stopping to stretch his legs.

It must be time.

Sasha opened the door and met Natsu along the side of the car. A brisk wind wrapped him up tight, but adrenaline had already started to replace the relative boredom the past week of surveillance had brought him. Once they got the knife out of Jacques's house, his freedom would be all but won.

His heart lurched, and he cast a glance toward the car where Diana slept.

As much as he hated to think it, getting his freedom no longer presented itself so easily.

"He's gone. Watched him take off into the field." Natsu walked up to him, keeping a careful distance. "Since vampires are technically dead, I won't be able to feel him come back if we're still inside. If we're going to steal it, we need to go now."

"Agreed." Sasha walked to the back of the car and popped the truck. If the vampire returned, he'd need stakes. He'd brought two with him—one for him and one for Diana.

Natsu followed him to the truck. "I've already told the crow, but I'm going to tell you too. I won't risk the kid again."

"I'm surprised you did the first time. In my experience, demons don't tend to risk mutilating their hosts beyond repair."

"And pray tell, what is your experience?"

Sasha slammed the trunk shut. "I grew up with demons, and I'll be honest—your end game...I can't see it."

"This may come as a surprise to you, but not all demons are the same."

"They have been in my experience."

"Perhaps your experience is narrow." Natsu turned toward the house and flicked his tail. "Get the crow. We need to hurry."

Sasha didn't much care to be bossed around by the demon cat, but Natsu was right. Their window of opportunity was slim. He opened the back seat, expecting Diana to be up and ready.

She wasn't.

"Van Doren," he said. She didn't move. On the contrary, she snored. "Van Doren."

She still didn't move. The days of monitoring had taken more out of her than he thought.

The longer he stared, the more powerful her sleeping form became. The first night they'd met, she'd positioned herself as far from him as she could manage. She hadn't trusted him to not kill her, much less keep her safe. Now she slept so deep she didn't move despite him asking her to.

Then, in a move Sasha didn't plan on or really understand, he bent down, one hand against the seat, and leaned over, lightly shaking her bicep.

Diana bolted up, grabbing his hand and watching him wide-eyed. Her hair pulled across his skin, draping over his fingers, and she jerked her head left and right. Panicked.

"Diana." He tried to ignore the softness of her skin. The way she tightened her fingers around his at the sound of her name. She focused on his face once more, sleep leaving her eyes. "It's time to go."

She yawned and shook her head, her hair waving against his wrist. Diana looked down at her hand wrapped around his and dropped it like a piece of hot coal.

"Right." She looked anywhere that wasn't his face. "Let's go steal this thing. And not die."

Sasha stepped back and allowed Diana out of the car, absentmindedly passing her a stake as she stood. Something had moved in his heart. A wall previously erected had fallen. A fissure had shaken a part of him loose that he'd thought long dead.

His freedom was close. At his fingertips.

But so was something else, and he wasn't sure which one he wanted more.

———

JACQUES'S FARMHOUSE SAT COMPLETELY DARK AGAINST THE dimming horizon. No light pressed from beneath the drawn curtains or the doorway. All was quiet, and it was in the quiet, Sasha had found, where the most risk typically lurked.

As far as vampires went, he didn't know too many of them. Given how they were forced to live, they didn't venture out of their dens much, and the ones Madame had succeeded in cornering up worked alone or alongside creatures that didn't possess blood. Since he had a lot of blood—angelic blood, for that matter—he always gave the things a wide berth.

"He went north. Cut through the field toward town." Natsu bounded ahead, paws smacking the dead, cracking grass. "We need to hurry. He's fast."

"Vampires are." Sasha readjusted his grip on his stake. "Most homes in this area have basements. I don't believe this one will be any different. I imagine both his coffin and Sheturath are in the basement, but we can't be sure. We need to split up and search the house to maximize our chance of success."

Diana's face paled. All signs of sleep had left her.

"I'll go in the basement." Natsu hopped up onto the wooden porch surrounding the house. "If he gets home before we're done, I'd stand a better chance of escape than either of you."

"Diana." Sasha walked up to the front door and gripped the knob. "Search upstairs. If he comes home, throw open a window and fly out."

"But—"

"Don't be selfless today." He stared at her and hoped the woman understood how much danger she was in. She'd got lucky at Whitaker's house. Jacques's bite would kill her in moments, and the thought of holding her broken body again made him nauseated.

Sasha's grip on the knob faltered. He never used to get too invested in his feelings. What had changed?

"I understand." Diana nodded. "Let's get the knife."

He opened the door, unsurprised at the long whine of the old hinge as it swung into the wall. The front door opened into a foyer, and a thick rug stretched out from the threshold into another room. A set of stairs sat beyond it. Sasha looked behind him, both pleased and surprised to find Diana right on his heels. He motioned toward the stairs. The faster she got up there, the farther away from the danger she'd be. Diana stepped around him, one foot in front of the other, up on the balls of her feet.

Her shifting abilities aside, Sasha hadn't known what benefits her human form might have in regard to theft. She had good eyes, of course, but that was all. At least, that was what he believed until right then.

He hadn't known how Diana could move in the dark.

A ghost. That was the first thing to come to mind as she moved, marching forward on light feet. Exceptional balance. Perfect, if such a thing truly existed. No floorboards squealed. The house didn't creak. If she ever got wise to his deal with Madame, he'd never be able to sleep again. Diana would be able to sneak up on him easily if he weren't actively searching the future for his next enemy.

Diana looked back at him a moment, and the hand holding the stake dipped. What was she thinking? However, whatever it was must've not been important. She turned away and ascended the stairs as a specter. Even if a werewolf were in the room, he doubted they'd hear her move.

Natsu danced around his feet. He needed to find the access to the basement, not stare at Diana.

Thanks to his new vision, something he'd still been unable to figure out, he didn't need much light to maneuver around the home. A little light managed to pour in from around the curtains, enough to guide his steps. Natsu pattered into the next room. Sasha squinted. The cat had gone into the kitchen.

"Smell that?" Natsu's voice seemed too loud in the quiet.

Sasha inhaled and swallowed the consequent bile rising in his esophagus. "Death."

"Death, indeed." The cat demon stopped in front of a door. "It's coming from here."

"I suppose he keeps his victims in the basement until he drains them."

"There's a pigpen behind the barn." Natsu must've seen it during his surveillance. "I imagine that's where the corpses go once their blood is gone."

Sasha gripped the doorknob and turned. After a moment, he pulled. Unlike the front door, it opened quietly. Stairs led from the kitchen into a dark pit.

The heavy scent of illness, of life almost gone from its host, enveloped his being. He closed his eyes and focused on breathing from his mouth. People were dying in the basement. Several, given the intensity of the smell. "How fortunate. Demons thrive in both death and the dark."

"You're too quick to paint everyone with the same broad brush." Natsu flicked his tail and said nothing else. Instead, he meandered down the steps and disappeared into the expansive black.

Sasha frowned and stepped away from the door. The demon knew nothing but torment. *All* they knew was torment. Natsu was no different. If he were, he'd let the boy have his body back.

Sheturath wasn't in the living area, the kitchen, or the foyer. There was only one other room on the bottom floor, and while he would do his due diligence, Sasha already knew the knife wouldn't be there. The ground floor was the most illogical place to put the knife. It was the least secure floor of the house.

As he crossed back through the living area, a sudden burst of moonlight poured along the wood, highlighting every groove and grain. Sasha had closed that door. His heart stopped at the realization of what that meant.

Sasha looked for the future, but he saw none.

He listened to the dark and squeezed the wooden stake. Nothing. He heard nothing, but the irrefutable fact remained that the front door waved in the wind.

If Jacques had come home already, that meant he didn't think his home was secure. But how could he have come to that conclusion? Furthermore, if he didn't think Sheturath was safe, why would he leave the house at all?

His gaze flickered toward the ceiling. Vampires were fast. Had he gone straight upstairs?

Had he gone for Diana?

Dread crawled up his arms. He'd seen visions of Diana dying a thousand times in Whitaker's house—perhaps he could do so again. Sasha felt for the familiar burn in his mind, teasing a bit of the future out.

Jacques's mouth pressed against Diana's throat. Sharp teeth ripping away at the flesh. Blood running into her shirt.

Cold sank into his skin.

Being quiet was no longer an option. He climbed the stairs two steps at a time, breaking past the landing and making a sharp right. He ran into something soft, warm—Diana. Sasha reached forward and grabbed her arms, forcing his heart rate to slow.

"Sasha?" A frown pulled at the corners of her mouth, and she lightly gripped his jacket. She stood in the doorframe of a small room. A room lined with bookshelves that housed a thick oak desk.

The wood behind him creaked, and her grip on him tightened. He sought the future again, just in time to tighten his hold on Diana's biceps and shove her back into the room.

Sasha tried to adjust and duck from the sweeping arm of the vampire behind him, but his time spent on Diana had taken any edge his ability might have granted him to escape. A crushing grip seized his arm and slammed him into the wall.

"I'll assume you're here for Sheturath," the vampire said, voice crisp and enunciated. Inflected with the barest hint of a French accent. Jacques's cold hand pressed him into the wall, sharp fingernails slicing into his throat and the flesh of his wrist.

The vampire nuzzled his neck and pulled in a long, slow drag through his nostrils. Sasha tensed when Jacques's breath hit his skin, the smell of death and rot snaking its way into his nose. He could try to move—should try to move—and fight for his own life. But he hadn't heard a window open, and Diana needed to get out.

The hand on his wrist moved down to his fingers, prying the stake away and dropping it to the ground. "I thought Whitaker knew better than to break confidentiality agreements with his clients."

"Whitaker can no longer honor his agreements," Sasha said, voice strangled. He looked to the future. His stomach clenched when his death played for him much like Diana's had facing the sphinx.

Jacques's grip tightened. "Dead?"

"Dead."

"Old fool." Jacques sighed. Bored. "Perhaps I'll pay his home a visit and relieve his descendants of his immense collection. I doubt they'd appreciate any of it."

Sasha closed his eyes. He had yet to hear any sign of Diana trying to escape.

Jacques wrapped his free hand under Sasha's arm and pressed his palm to his chest. "I'm not sure why you and your woman decided to risk it all for Sheturath, but I'm sure you're aware I cannot let this go unanswered."

You and your woman. Jacques didn't seem to know about Natsu yet.

"Fucking hell. Angel blood. I haven't had that in an *age*." Sasha grimaced as Jacques pulled him close, breath hot on his neck.

"I've smelled your blood for days." He could hear the vampire smile. "I just needed to lure you in. I knew you were an angel, but I didn't know who your friends were. Too much risk in the open." Jacques pressed his nose to Sasha's throat and inhaled.

As sharp, hot pain entered his neck, Sasha could only find it in himself to feel grateful for the strange happenstance that connected him to Diana. Without it, he wouldn't have known to find her.

He was going to die, but she would live, provided she did as she promised she would: find a window.

And while he would die, in his death, he would be free.

TWENTY-FIVE

DIANA

Diana had never felt so many emotions all at once. Fear. Rage.

A broken heart.

While the bond between her and Sasha's magic was likely the culprit behind the immeasurable wave of grief coating her from head to toe, no one had ever sacrificed any bit of themselves for her sake, and there was no guarantee that alone wasn't what tore all the optimism from her chest like a soul being split from its body.

Diana growled and pushed herself up, failing to temper the tremors of rage rattling down both of her arms. She stood and advanced toward Jacques, gaze pinned to the back of the vampire's head.

She'd told Sasha she'd leave if things got bad. She promised she would find a window and fly away. But Diana wasn't especially good at doing things for her benefit, and she had no intention of leaving her murder of one to die alone.

"Let go of him, you glorified corpse!" Diana surged forward, latched onto Jacques's shoulders, and yanked him back. Or tried to.

He didn't budge.

Jacques pulled away from Sasha's neck and turned, peering at her over his shoulder, blood running over his chin. Her heart leapt into her mouth when they locked eyes, his pupils constricted to fine points. All he had to do was lean in a little. One bite would end her, and he knew it.

"I've been around for a very long time. You crows aren't fighters." Jacques made a show of running his tongue along one of his bloodied fangs, his breath hot on her face. Dark hair fell in his eyes as he cocked his head and smirked. "I'm going to finish this delectable blood, and then I'll take yours. Even though it smells like bloated rats."

Diana didn't even have time to breathe before Jacques moved.

He held Sasha against the wall with his right hand and threw his left elbow back. Air shot from her mouth when his elbow hit her in the stomach, and she lost her grip on the fabric of his shirt. Pain exploded from her abdomen into her chest as she fought to breathe, and she staggered back.

Doubled over, she didn't see his next hit coming. The back of his hand smacked against her cheek, and pain splintered along her jaw. The sharp burn radiated into her eye and ear, and in her disoriented staggering, she collided into the wall and fell to the ground, collapsing feet away from the stairs.

Diana gasped for air, vision swimming as she tried to piece together a plan—anything—to save Sasha. But nothing came. As her vision focused, all she could see was Sasha's sagging form hanging limp in Jacques's grasp and drops of his blood on the floor by his feet.

This entire fucking thing had been a trap, and now he was going to kill them both.

She pushed herself up on her palms, and a wave of nausea bubbled in her stomach. Diana collapsed again, too exhausted. Exhausted and hurt and scared. She was a crow. A worthless crow without a hope in hell of killing a vampire.

Something brushed against her arm.

Diana rolled her head over, fighting the ache in her jaw, shocked beyond measure at what greeted her eyes.

Natsu held a blade with a length somewhere between a knife and sword between his teeth.

Diana kept still and watched the demon carefully set the knife by her hand. He'd said before that he wouldn't risk Nobu for them again, and now that she and Sasha would both likely die, she wanted the demon to keep his promise. He was only a step or two away from the stairs, and if he hurried, he could get away.

"Go," she mouthed and reached for the knife.

The demon dipped his head and slipped back down the stairs. Hopefully, he'd actually leave. The thought of the kid being killed—

No. She couldn't think about that.

Afraid but desperate, Diana inhaled quietly and squeezed the handle of the knife. The fabled Sheturath. Perfectly balanced. Never had anything felt so right between her fingers.

She stood on shaky legs, her attention on Jacques. With a silent prayer to whoever would listen, Diana took a step—

"I wouldn't do that, girl."

Her heart stopped. Jacques had pulled his teeth out of Sasha, blood dripping out of the corners of his mouth and slathered along his chin. His grip on Sasha lessened, and the man she'd quickly come to see as terribly important to her slid from the vampire's hands and collapsed on the ground in a heap.

With a deep breath, Diana readjusted her grip on the knife. The sight of Sasha so still forced a hot current of hellfire to shoot through her veins. "I'm going to carve your heart out with this."

Jacques shrugged and licked his lips. "Sheturath or no, the only thing here that can kill me is that demon I felt slinking around, and it left you to die."

Diana swallowed and tried to ignore Jacques's prodding. She might be a useless crow, but she was a useless crow with an angel for a murder.

Sasha could see the future. She didn't know exactly how, but she'd somehow channeled that ability before. She really needed to do it again.

Jacques moved. Except when he moved, he moved like fog. Not even her eyes could keep up. She held her breath and focused.

On instinct, or maybe something else, Diana swung Sheturath diagonally, right to left. Jacques dodged and swiped his hand through the air, dragging his long nails across her eye and cheek. Fire blistered along her skin, but she swung again, readjusting her feet as Jacques lunged.

Her head burned. No—her brain burned, and it burned deep. She squeezed the handle and fell into a swath of something, a lake of the unknown, now pooling along the surface of her mind.

Diana licked her lips, flipped the blade handle up, and lunged to the right as Jacques reached for her throat.

Long fingernails raked the air where she'd been.

She stepped out wide, bracing the blade along her forearm, and followed her elbow as she spun toward Jacques's back. The blade pushed through his shirt. Then his dead skin. Through muscle and bone.

And then he froze.

Jacques didn't move. He didn't jerk around or try to rip her jugular out. He simply stood there, shoulders hunched and breathing labored.

"I've been alive for over three hundred years." Jacques's voice came out in a whisper. Pained. If she hadn't watched him suck the life out of Sasha, she might have felt bad. "And this is how I die? Being stabbed by a godforsaken crow?"

"Yeah, and you can choke on it." Diana jerked Sheturath from Jacques's back, and he fell to his knees. She didn't bother waiting on him to face-plant.

"Sasha." She ran to his side, dropping Sheturath to the ground beside her without another thought.

He was still. So, so still.

"Sasha, no." Diana rolled him over and felt along his neck, blood smearing between her fingers. Pulse. Faint, but there. "Wake up!"

His eyes opened a bit, enough to see his eyeballs rolling around. She held his face between her hands and put her own close enough to touch his nose with hers. "Sasha. Why did you do that? You always know when things happen. You should've seen it coming!"

His eyes opened once more, unfocused. Slurred whispers slid from his mouth, but she couldn't make them out. Too hushed.

She held her ear close to his lips. Sasha slid a lazy hand up to the back of her neck. His breath sent a chill down her spine.

"I-I...would miss you."

Sasha's hand fell and smacked the ground. Diana pulled back, heart lodged in her esophagus. His eyes were closed, but there were still breaths. Faint ones. Small ones. But breaths.

"Sasha." Diana closed her eyes and focused on the night at the bar. What had he said about vampire bites? Venom. Their bites used venom that caused drowsiness and immobilization.

And eventual death.

"Antivenom. He needs an antivenom." Diana stood and wrapped her hands under his arms. "Jesus. You're so heavy."

She pulled. He slid a few inches.

Pulled again. A few more.

"Sasha, you idiot, you have to help me!" Diana closed her eyes and felt for the burn again. Looked for Sasha. Saw him dead. "Wake up!"

Hurried breaths pressed from her lungs and past her lips in short bursts. Dead, dead, dead. If she kept trying this path, he'd die, and he'd die soon. A strangled scream tore from her throat, and she pulled on him again, nausea returning when Sasha's body hardly moved.

Footsteps in the bottom floor of the house sent her heart from its place in her throat into her mouth instead. If they were anyone aside from Nobu, she was screwed. She'd never abandon Sasha there. The footsteps took to the stairs and shook the farmhouse with a fervent *clomp-clomp*. Diana turned and put herself between whoever the hell was coming and Sasha, only then becoming aware of the blood leaking off her own face.

"Holy shit." Nobu emerged on the landing, cramming his arms through the sleeves of his shirt.

"I know." Diana tried to keep her breaths even and focused on Sasha. "Help me get him to the car."

"Diana." Nobu looked between her and Sasha, face ashen. "I tried to get Natsu to help—"

"Stop." She tried to steady both her voice and her heart. "Your life matters. Natsu wanted to protect it. Do not fault him for that."

Nobu's gaze dropped to Sasha's neck. His throat bobbed as he motioned to Sasha. "Give him to me."

"He's heavy—"

"Natsu will help with this."

Diana quickly moved, and Nobu took Sasha under his arms, hoisting him easily into a shoulder carry with his demon-enhanced strength. Without wasting anymore time, the pair ran toward the stairs.

"Where's the knife?" Nobu asked as he began his descent. He carried Sasha effortlessly along his shoulders.

She'd completely forgotten about Sheturath. "Go to the car. I'll get it."

"Then what?"

"Antivenom," Diana called out over her shoulder as she turned back to the hallway. Her heart had never beat so furiously, she was sure of it. "We need to find a witch."

TWENTY-SIX

DIANA

The closest witch to Jacques's farm was half an hour away. In a situation where every second counted more than ever, Diana couldn't will the car to move fast enough. But from the sound of the engine, she was pretty sure Nobu had it floored already.

She cradled Sasha's head to her stomach, fingers tangled in his hair. Blood leaked from the extra shirt she'd pressed to the vampire's bite, staining her pants and running into the white collar of his dress shirt. His breathing had slowed, but he still breathed. His heart still beat. She hoped it would hold out.

Diana ran her thumb along Sasha's jaw. Hope. The only thing that kept her together.

"How's he doing?" Nobu asked from the driver's seat.

"Um." Diana hated how her voice sounded. Heavy and broken. "He's still alive."

Nobu took a sharp right, and she struggled to hold Sasha steady as she was slung into the car door. The dark of the night pressed into the car, only offering brief light when they passed beneath a light pole. "Have you tried healing him?"

Diana licked her lips. "What?"

"Natsu suggested it."

Several things immediately came to mind with Nobu's question. She inhaled and pressed her fingers to Sasha's throat. Still had a pulse. "You know?"

"Natsu suspected your weird crow magic might've latched on him the night of the auction." Nobu kept his eyes on the road. "He didn't mention it to me until today, and he only did because I was worried Sokolov would leave you in the vampire's house defenseless."

Her heart sank with guilt. The kid worried about her still.

"He doesn't know." Diana traced Sasha's face and memorized every detail. Wanting more than anything to see the golden depths of his eyes. "I never told him."

Nobu drifted right and took the exit. The first one for miles. "Natsu thinks you might be able to heal him."

Her heart rate increased. "I don't know how it works. I don't know how to do it."

"Do you remember Sokolov saying anything about it? Anything that might give you a clue?"

"No. I mean, I figured out how to use his visions, sort of. I did it on accident at Whitaker's house. I used it fighting Jacques." Diana's voice grew heavy again. Failure. Sasha suffering like this could have all been avoided if she told him the truth to begin with. Even if he didn't like what she had to say, she'd at least know how to use his skills in case he was harmed. Should've, could've, would've. "Healing a person has to use more purposeful skill than that."

"Maybe." Lights from the town ahead reached her eyes. "You should try. We'll be to the witch's store in about five minutes. Buy him some time until we get there."

Diana pulled the shirt from his wound and winced as blood trickled from the puncture marks on his neck. Black pooled beneath the surface of his skin. Like a bruise, but darker. More insidious.

Venom.

She slid her fingers over his clammy skin and held her palm over

Jacques's bite. How did Sasha heal her after the sphinx? Would he access it like she did with her crow's magic?

Diana readjusted her hand on Sasha's neck, his body completely limp against her legs. Sasha had mentioned on the plane that healing took a lot out of him. She remembered him grimace as he fixed her face. She remembered his hands jerk against her skin, like perhaps he'd pulled too much magic at once. Whatever he did to heal, it hurt him.

To use his visions, she focused on seeing. She had focused on Sasha and on her fear that the sphinx and the vampire might hurt him.

She followed her train of thought and pictured her fingers mending his skin. In her mind, she pulled the venom from his veins drop by drop, siphoning it from his blood and sending it out into the great unknown.

Diana bit her lip. She never needed anything as badly as she needed him. She had to fix this!

Her arched fingertips trembled against his neck until she flattened them. Fire burned behind her eyelids, sinking deep into her skull and filling her mouth with helpless dread.

"I can't do it." Her voice cracked. Damn her and her fear! If she had told him the truth, he might've told her how to use it. "I tried. I can't."

The car shook as the tires took on a busted slip of road, bobbing and dipping along the potholes.

"It's okay." Nobu's voice was soft. Sincere. "We're almost there. The witch will know what to do."

THE GENERAL STORE WHERE THEY'D FOUND THE LAST WITCH during their search for Jacques was dark when they pulled up. Not a single light shined beyond the window or beneath the door. The sight of it plunged Diana's heart into the pit of her stomach.

"Maybe she's in the back," Nobu suggested, car door already open.

"The store's closed. The sign says as much." Her voice had taken a sharper edge, somehow both aggrieved and angry all at once. "She was the closest witch, and Sasha won't survive a drive to the others."

Sasha's slowing breaths were all the more dismal now.

The boy paused, hand lingering on the car door. "Natsu says that witches usually cast wards around their places of business."

He didn't wait for her to respond. Nobu ran through the gravel parking lot to the building and gripped the metal handle of the door, shaking it hard enough for her to hear from the back seat.

"Hey!" Nobu continued shaking the door handle. "You've got business. Big business!"

The boy backed away from the door and looked up toward the roof. Whatever Natsu was telling him to do better work.

"There was a ward. I felt it. Hopefully, she'll come," Nobu said as he trotted back over. He slid his hands under Sasha and lifted him from her legs. "C'mon. When she gets here, we need all the time we can get."

Diana felt empty when Sasha was taken from her arms. When she stood, her wet shirt peeled from her stomach. Blood. So much of it. What if it was too late? What if they weren't fast enough?

"Diana."

She stuffed her anxiety as far down as she could and looked to Nobu. His gaze was tacked to the shop door—to the woman standing beyond the glass.

The witch looked the same as she had last week. Short. Somewhere in her thirties. Platinum-blond hair and tanned skin. She wore jeans but with a green sweater instead of blue. She had a seal on the top of her left hand and an amulet around her neck.

"You're back." The woman opened the door and appraised them, annoyed. She ran her fingernails along her scalp, tucking some loose white hairs into her bun. "I've been wondering when you'd drag someone here. Messing with Jacques only means death."

Diana tried to still the tremor in her hands. "Can you help?"

"Perhaps." The woman held open the door to her shop, bell jingling overhead.

It took everything in her not to sprint inside. "We need to hurry, or he's going to—"

"Die?" The witch shut and locked the door when Diana's foot passed the threshold. "I've been at this awhile. I know what death looks like."

"Awhile? You're not much older than they are." Nobu jerked his head toward Diana, holding Sasha awkwardly in another shoulder carry.

"I'm far older than I appear, boy." The witch gave Nobu a once-over. "Although I suspect you're also not as you seem."

"Touché."

The witch led them past the shelves of candy and chips to a white door in the back. A sign reading EMPLOYEES ONLY hung in the center. Someone had drawn a smiley face beside it.

"My name is Marion." The witch rolled up the thick sleeves of her sweater to her elbows.

"I'm Diana. The kid is Nobu." Diana swallowed and motioned to the limp body draped on Nobu's shoulder. "That's Sasha."

"How long ago was he bitten?"

"Thirty, forty-five minutes ago." Diana wrapped her arms around herself, chilled.

Marion frowned and motioned to a plastic table set up in the back. "He's not dead yet?"

Her stomach turned. "Not yet."

"What is he?"

Diana wasn't sure if Sasha wanted his ancestry out in the open or not, but since Marion was the only thing keeping him on the mortal coil, Diana thought it worth the risk. "Mostly human. A little angel."

"Angel." Marion's eyebrows crept up her forehead. She knocked the stray notebooks on top of the plastic table onto the floor. "I haven't seen an angel in a long time. They don't like us."

"Yeah, I imagine they don't." Nobu cleared his throat before heaving Sasha on the table.

Diana fought to keep her fingers from pressing along Sasha's neck.

Did he have a pulse still? She curled her fingers into her palms and relied on her vision and closed one of her eyes to better focus. Sasha's chest still moved.

Marion grabbed Sasha's chin and turned his head, exposing his bite to the blinding fluorescents above. The blood had started to leak out of the punctures again and rolled onto the table. "His angelic heritage is the only reason he isn't dead yet, but I'm afraid it won't last much longer."

"Then what do we do?" Diana stepped close to the table and dropped a hand on Sasha's chest. "As long as he breathes, there has to be something we can try."

Marion raised her eyebrows. "Oh, there are things you can try. I'm just not sure you'll be willing to pay."

"I think you might be surprised."

The witch smirked and dropped her gaze onto Diana's hand splayed on Sasha's chest.

"I'll take a finger." Marion cocked her head to the side and lightly tapped each finger on Diana's left hand. She tapped her ring finger twice. "That one."

Diana frowned. "A finger? What do you need a finger for?"

She shrugged and turned her back on them, making her way toward a cabinet on the far wall. "I can take an eye instead. You decide."

Diana stared at her ring finger as Marion puttered off. The man who found her after she fell and raised her had a ring on his left hand. She'd asked after it once because he'd shined it, and the crow in her liked shiny things. He'd said that he'd been married once, but his wife had died. He wore his ring because, no matter where her soul might be, he loved his wife and always would.

Despite not being human, a part of her wanted to be. A part of her actually thought she was for years. A part of her wanted a ring on her finger someday.

Diana closed her eyes and steeled herself against the inevitable. Sasha dying wasn't an option, and her eyes were the only useful thing about her. "Take a finger."

"Diana." Nobu took a few steps toward her, wide-eyed.

She ignored him.

Marion turned from the cabinet with a couple of jars in her hands. She looked between Diana and Sasha. "He might be too far gone."

"No. He isn't," Diana said, voice cracking at the end. She slammed her hand on the table beside Sasha's head. He didn't move. "Give me a goddamn knife."

"You could be making this sacrifice for nothing."

She gave Marion a pointed glare. "Give me a knife. Now."

Marion popped open a drawer in the cabinet, withdrawing a cleaver and a blue rag. Diana tried not to think about how many body parts people had amputated with the knife. The woman, still holding her jars in the other hand, handed her the cleaver.

"A bit of advice, dear." The witch set the jars on the table and tossed her the rag. "Bite the towel."

The cleaver felt heavier than it ought to, but Sasha's looming death was heavier. She moved her hand to the edge of the table, resting only her ring finger on the surface and curling the rest to her palm.

"Do you want me to do it?" Marion offered. "Might be easier."

Fat chance. She'd probably take the whole hand. "Thanks, but no."

"Suit yourself."

Diana crammed the microfiber towel in her mouth and adjusted her grip.

Then she swung the cleaver down.

TWENTY-SEVEN

SASHA

He shouldn't be alive.

Every inch of his skin burned. Fire. Vampire venom was liquid fire. He burrowed into the blankets. Somehow both hot and cold, his body quaked with chills. Every blanket fiber seared into his skin. Christ. Maybe he should've just died.

Wait—blankets? Sasha swallowed, throat dry like sandpaper. He dared to open his eyes.

No—too bright.

He pressed the heels of his hands onto his eyes as memories of the farmhouse came rushing back to him. Vampire. Jacques. He'd been in bad scrapes before, but he'd never felt like he did right then. Every part of him felt dead. Decayed.

He better not turn into a vampire.

Unwilling to think on vampirism a moment more, Sasha squinted a moment and then opened his eyes again. It was night. The dark pressed through the window alongside the faint wisp of light from the waning moon. Not a sound hit his ears. His shirt was gone. He shivered and pulled the blankets close, surprised to find they did not come easily.

Diana lay beside him, hair spilling around her shoulders and sticking to her skin. Dark lashes lay against her cheekbones as soft breaths pushed past her lips, blowing some of the loose strands across her nose. Four long, deep gashes had scabbed over on her face.

Sasha frowned and continued to look her over. Her hand wrapped in bloody bandages caught his attention next. He rubbed his fingers over his eyes again to try to clear the fog. What had happened to her? Moreover, how did they survive Jacques's attack at all?

He stared at her as more implications sank in. Diana had saved him. She'd deliberately broken her promise to him and somehow pulled him off the Reaper's doorstep.

A cough rattled the back of his throat, and Diana's eyes flew open. She pushed herself up to sitting, revealing the baggy T-shirt draped over her thin frame.

"Oh my God. You're not dead." She leaned over to look at him and felt along his neck.

The chill he'd desperately hated moments before was gone and replaced by a deceptive warmth at her touch. Sasha tried to breathe but couldn't with her hand caressing him like that. Like a lover. Or at least someone closer than they happened to be.

"It worked." Diana smiled, looking, dare he think it, relieved. She pulled back and turned on the bedside lamp. "That witch said it would, but she was shady—"

"Witch?" he interrupted, voice a tight rasp. His heartbeat grew inordinately loud as her words repeated in his mind. *Witch. Witch. Witch.* Witches took their payments in flesh.

With a nod, Diana started tugging at the bandage on his neck. The scent of her peppermint soap drifted into his nose as he looked her over, wondering what the witch required as payment for saving his life. "We went to that one with the store about thirty minutes from Jacques's house. Remember that witch? Light hair?"

Sasha's answer got stuck in his throat when she moved closer and her long hair dragged along the bare skin of his arm.

Diana had saved his life for a presumably steep price, and she didn't appear to regret it. His heart swelled with something. Something he couldn't identify.

"Nobu and I got a salve from the witch two nights ago. I was afraid she lied and the antivenom wouldn't work, but...it apparently worked." The adhesive of the bandage gave a bit, but all he could really feel were her fingers. "I sent Nobu out for some things to get us by while you're recovering. Pain medicine. Food...stuff like that. I had to borrow some money from your wallet."

If he weren't somewhere close to death, he might've laughed at the look of regret on her face. However, Sasha Sokolov didn't laugh often, and he certainly didn't laugh after being bitten by a vampire.

Diana grabbed a small jar on the nightstand, struggling a moment to open it given the state of her left hand. She grimaced when the lid popped off the jar and paused to take in a slow breath. He narrowed his eyes at the thick clump of bandages.

"What happened to you?"

Diana shrugged. "Jacques scratched my face. No big deal."

Sasha ground his teeth together. "Not that. What happened to your hand?"

With her lower lip between her teeth, she smoothed the ointment over his bite. "My finger got cut off."

For a moment, Sasha forgot how to breathe. Surely, she didn't—

"Who cut it off, Diana?"

She winced, reluctantly looking at him as she pressed a fresh bandage on his neck. "I did. Witch's price."

Rage and regret and—goddamn it—*shame* crept over every cell in his body.

He needed to get away from her. Sasha pulled away from Diana and sat up, ripping the new bandage from his skin and leaving it pinched between her fingers.

"Wait. What are you—"

The muscles in his stomach and shoulders ached, but Sasha didn't allow himself to think about it. He swung his heavy legs over the side of the bed, hardly feeling the smashed, old carpet against the soles of his feet. His poisoned body struggled to support him, and if he hadn't been trained from childhood to move quickly and efficiently, he would've face-planted on the ground. Instead, he held himself up with both palms against the mattress, preparing to stand and go anywhere she wasn't.

"Sasha, you idiot!" Diana leapt off the bed and propped herself in front of him in moments, hands on her hips. Despite being sick, he couldn't help but feel a bit insulted she could impede him so quickly. "What are you doing? Lie down—"

"Why would you do that?" His chest shook beneath his labored breaths. He really wanted to stand up and get the hell away from her suffocating generosity, but his legs wouldn't cooperate. People didn't do things like this for him, and the one person that did was someone he had to betray.

Diana snorted. "I wasn't going to let you die."

Damn that vampire and damn his weak body. Sasha gave her a pointed look, surprised yet again to see compassion staring back at him. "You should've."

"You don't mean that." Diana stepped closer, their legs mere inches apart. "Sasha, you were dying. I couldn't sit there and wait for it."

"You could have, and that's exactly what you should've done." Sasha tried to focus on the shake in his arms, on anything that wasn't Diana. But he was uncomfortably aware of her keeping him alive at his most vulnerable. Anyone else would've used the opportunity to send a knife under his ribs, and he wouldn't blame them. "You don't know me, Diana. You don't know me well enough to make a sacrifice like that."

"It's a finger. I have nine more." She held up her bandaged hand and shrugged. "You only have one life. Hardly seems equal."

In an effort to keep from dwelling on her kindness, he focused on his breathing, but he failed. Miserably. He had to stop thinking about Diana treating him this way. Like she cared. Like she truly and deeply cared. "Did you think about our deal? If you had let me die, you wouldn't have to take me to Charles."

Diana's eyes shimmered, and a sharp intake of air stopped any words from coming out of her mouth. She hadn't thought about their deal at all, he realized. The feeling that he was, in fact, the absolute bastard he figured himself to be overcame him in a wave.

"Diana." Her name came off his tongue far too easily. He heaved himself forward, propping his elbows on his knees as his arms continued to shake. "If you only knew the extent of what I've done, you would've let me die. You would've let me die and said good riddance after the fact."

She bent at the waist and situated her face so close to his that her breath hit his nose. "I might say a lot of things, but I'll never say that." Her voice was tight. Firm. He couldn't tell if she was angry or hurt. "Do you think *I* should die?"

He frowned. "This isn't about you."

"No. It's about you feeling guilty. I suspect it's the same damn reason you won't go see your mom. But guess what? I've done some bad things in the past five years to stay alive. I killed Jacques after I broke into *his* house and stole *his* knife." Diana cocked her head to the side and stared at him, the ends of her hair dragging across his knee. Without thinking, he turned his left hand palm up, allowing it to fall against his fingers instead. If she noticed, she didn't say. "So—do you think I should die too?"

Sasha shook his head. How she could always see through him with the same ease as a window was a mystery to him. "It's not the same."

"It is the same."

He closed his eyes and took a breath, concentrating on the feeling of her hair tickling his hand instead of the disbelief welling in his chest. This infuriating woman. They weren't the same. Their situations were nothing alike. Would she be saying these things if she knew who he worked for?

"Get in bed." Diana's hard tone made him open his eyes. She glared pointedly at the pillow. "Now."

Sasha wasn't used to being ordered around by anyone that wasn't Madame, particularly someone who had his well-being in mind. He fell back on the bed and collapsed on his pillow, nevertheless. Diana threw the comforter over him, and while he wanted to blame the consequent shiver on the venom and not her hands tucking the blanket around his torso, he knew it would be a lie and therefore illogical.

Instead, he allowed himself to enjoy it for a moment. He hadn't been taken care of in...well, a couple decades. Not many dared to get this close to him on purpose—unless they were trying to kill him.

Sasha pulled the blanket around his arms tighter. He'd been eleven years old the last time anyone had bothered with him. An eleven-year-old, starry-eyed boy who had no idea the horrible future he volunteered to take in place of his mother. And now, after twenty years of being alone and committing unspeakable atrocities, someone did bother with him...and he couldn't decide if he hated it or not.

Diana didn't say anything else as she situated herself on the other side of the bed and resumed his wound care. She smeared on more salve before unpacking a new bandage and sticking it on. "How do you heal, Sasha?"

He almost didn't hear her over the sound of his plans falling apart inside his head. "I'm too weak to do it now."

"I know." Diana folded her legs underneath her and wrung her hands. "But I'm curious."

Sasha studied her. There was something she wasn't telling him, and if he didn't feel so abhorrent, he'd spend more time wheedling it out of her. "I'm not sure what you're asking."

"Like when I want to be a crow, I think about being a crow." Her cheeks reddened, and he fought against the overwhelming urge to touch her. To do something. To see if her lips were as soft as they looked. "I guess I'm wondering what you think about."

This was an oddly specific request.

"Never mind." Diana batted her hands around and shook her head, flustered. She got flustered so easily. Something he once thought so ridiculous had turned into something endearing, and he couldn't figure out quite when that happened.

Unaware of the turmoil thrumming in his chest, Diana started to make herself comfortable on the other side of the bed.

"You don't have to stay. You've done enough," he said, voice rough. Agonizingly rough. It had been a long time since he'd slept with anyone, and while he and Diana would only be sleeping in the strictest sense, the stirrings of desire made the act not so benign.

"I want to stay, just in case." Diana curled up on the other pillow. For whatever reason, she was comfortable with him, and while the thought should've bothered him, it didn't. "You were bitten by a vampire, and the witch was very specific about putting the salve on."

His body quaked under the pressure of the vampire's venom, chills shooting down his limbs. Between that and the warring emotions fighting for purchase in his gut, he almost wished for death. Logically, it made sense that Diana stayed here since she was taking care of him.

However...

"Do you want me to leave?" She lifted her head a bit, a flash of something darting through her eyes. Fear. But the fear, strangely enough, wasn't of physical harm, Sasha realized the longer he stared at her.

She was afraid he would tell her to leave.

Sasha stared, unable to tear his gaze from her fathomless eyes. Did he want her to leave?

An unfamiliar warmth twisted in his stomach—he should tell her to leave.

Whatever he said now would change things. It would change everything. From the way he breathed to the inexplicable urge to reach out and touch the hair hanging beside her face. It could drive her away, or it could make him want to leave everything he thought he wanted in a plume of dust just to figure out what exactly Diana had done to him. To discover why he saw her future. To find out what she saw in him that compelled her to sacrifice for him again and again. Uttering *stay* could do so many horrible, terrible things to him and his plans, and he really should put more thought into it before saying such a thing.

But he was weak, and he was tired. Sasha wanted to rest.

And he wanted her there.

"No." The word fell from his lips almost as easy as her name. "I don't."

Diana smiled a little. Not a smile that ripped the sun from the sky, but a small one—a smile just for him.

She leaned over the edge of the bed and turned off the lamp before settling down on the pillow. Diana even slept like a bird—all tucked in a ball. Her chin drawn to her chest. Knees pulled to her stomach.

"Hope."

The moonlight from the window reflected in her eyes the moment she opened them. "What?"

"When I look for the future, I use fear." He turned on his side and faced her. "When I want to heal, I use hope."

Diana smiled again, this time averting her eyes. He could only imagine where her mind had gone. It hadn't been that long ago since he'd healed her, and Sasha remembered exactly what he'd been marveling at. She had been at peace with him then, and as she burrowed into the sheets, she seemed to be at peace with him now.

Perhaps hope for his soul was not lost.

"How did you kill the vampire?" he asked, tracing the shadows of the gashes on her face.

Diana gripped the comforter and grimaced. "Can we talk about it tomorrow?"

They stared at each other in silence. While he wanted to know the answer, he didn't want to make her uncomfortable. Especially after everything she'd done for him and everything she'd sacrificed.

"Very well." He heard her exhale. "Thank you, Diana."

A pause. "You're welcome."

As Sasha allowed himself to relax and drift, Diana's soft, warm hand pressed against his. Whatever Diana saw in him, it must be better than what he saw in the mirror each morning, and the thought brought him a promise of peace he hadn't known existed. So without giving it another thought, he wrapped his fingers around hers too.

It didn't occur to him until right before he succumbed to sleep that he hadn't thought about Sheturath, and even when he did, he didn't care enough to ask about it.

TWENTY-EIGHT

DIANA

One day had passed since Sasha woke up and asked her to stay. He hadn't woken up again. The only thing that gave Diana any sort of reassurance was his steady breathing, but the constant fever and sweating did little to assuage her doubts. If that witch made him some phony cure-all, she'd fly over there and do to Marion what she did to Jacques.

Diana scowled and drummed her fingers on her knees. When did she get so morbid?

She glanced over at Sasha from her place on the edge of the bed. It was early morning—still dark out—but the sweat on his brow glistened in the lamplight. His neck was the only thing that looked better, and that was after several sessions of healing.

Diana turned her palms up and stared at her fingers. Never in a million years did she believe she could be good at anything except stealing, and now she could heal.

Sasha hadn't lied. It hurt—bad. Since she hadn't really known what she was doing, she could only manage to hold the magic for a few moments. It had taken short spurts over twenty-four hours to close the wounds on his neck. Nevertheless, the murder bond was turning out to be a pretty interesting thing.

"If only Sasha knew about it." Diana turned her attention to the phone. Her father was likely waiting for an update, and she'd been putting it off. What would Charles say if he knew Sasha had become her murder?

Her face warmed at the thought of Sasha's rough skin caressing her hand. She hadn't expected him to reciprocate her feelings. Her desire to be close. While she didn't know if he'd held her hand out of genuine desire or sick delirium, Diana had never slept so soundly in all her life. She'd never felt so safe. So wanted.

So cared for.

Diana shook her head and willed the feeling away. Sasha was sick, and it all could've meant nothing. In every other instance where she'd gotten her hopes up, reality came along and crushed them shortly thereafter. Getting too wrapped up in interpreting Sasha's actions would likely lead to a very similar disappointment.

Gaze going to the bedside phone, she took a deep breath. She leaned over and plucked the plastic brick from the cradle, careful not to tangle the curly cord, and dialed a familiar set of numbers.

Charles answered almost immediately. "Do you have it?" her father asked, voice slipping up an octave. "Do you have the knife?"

"Yes." Diana rubbed the back of her neck. She shouldn't have been surprised by his immediate worry for the knife instead of her well-being. "I have it."

"B-Bring it back immediately." Charles's words ran together. Panicked, or excited? Perhaps both. "I'll call upon Lead Crow. Make him the offer."

"I can't leave right now." She winced at the growl on the other end. Impatient jerk. "I'm thinking it'll be a few days before we can get to the airport."

"You can't fly back now?" Charles sighed. "You have wings, Diana. Or have you forgotten?"

"No, I haven't. For one thing, the knife's too heavy for me to fly across the country. Not to mention it's dangerous. Above all those things, I'm tired." Heat blistered under her eyes when her father cursed. "Shut up! I've risked my life three times now for this knife while you've sat on your ass. You can wait."

For the first time since the conversation began, silence echoed on the other end. Her father shifted the phone, and Amelia's voice drifted in through the background. Did her mother hear the things her husband said to her? Did she even care?

"Is that Sokolov man with you?" Charles asked.

Diana smiled. Oh, was he ever. "Yes."

"Try to ditch him. If not, I'll have the murder with me when we meet again. I have no doubt they'll help us subdue him once they see Sheturath in your grasp."

Diana looked down at the bandages wound around her left hand. Her father would be pissed if he knew what she'd done.

Charles hummed on the other end. "Or you could take care of him."

She growled. "If you're asking me to kill him, the answer is no. You better not lay a talon on him. All he wants is to talk."

"No one ever just wants to talk."

"I swear, if you touch him—"

"Are you serious, Diana?" Her father's voice hardened considerably. "Do you even know who the man is? I've spoken with your mother and gone through my past transactions. I've never, not once, done business with a Sokolov."

Her throat dried considerably, and she licked her lips. Her father was a liar. She couldn't trust a word coming out of his mouth.

"Why would someone I've never met or done business with need to speak with me?" Charles laughed incredulously. "Why would he risk life and limb to help you get Sheturath to meet with someone he's never met?"

"I'm not sure. You tell me." Diana ran a finger through the cord and tangled it in the coil. "You're the one always screwing everyone over."

"Which means we can't trust a soul. For all we know, he could be working for someone out for our necks."

Her blood ran hot. "If that were true, he could've made me take him to you the night of the auction. Why risk everything to help me get this demon knife if all he wants is your head?"

Diana glanced at the still unconscious Sasha. How her hollering hadn't stirred him, she had no idea.

"You trust too easily, Diana," her father said. How ironic. "Three nights. In three nights, we'll meet. Bring the blade."

Then much like he had the last time they spoke, Charles Van Doren hung up without another word.

THE PHONE CALL WITH HER FATHER HUNG ALONG HER SHOULDERS long after it ended and followed her to the diner where she met Nobu for breakfast. Diana tried to hide how much Charles's accusations hurt her, but the fact remained her father was right.

She didn't know much about Sasha. He had a mom in Russia he hadn't seen in decades. He could see the future and heal people. He had exceptional aim and a trunk full of weapons. Considering they were now bonded for life, that wasn't a whole hell of a lot of information.

He asked you to stay.

Diana gnawed on the inside of her cheek. Sasha, regardless of the rest, was her murder now. He hadn't asked for it and neither had she, but it happened. And without even knowing that, he'd asked her to stay with him in bed.

He wanted her near him. On purpose.

But what if her father was right? What if it was all some elaborate ruse to corner Charles and chop his head off with Sheturath?

"You have to tell him, Diana."

The sudden sound of Nobu's voice scared her so bad she dropped her fork. The metal struck her porcelain plate, which caused half the establishment to turn and stare at her.

Her checks burned as she glowered at Nobu and picked up her rogue silverware. "No. I can't. Not yet."

Nobu brushed his bangs out of his face and cut into his omelet. "He's a smart guy. If he hasn't figured out that something happened, he will soon."

"He might not. You only know because Natsu told you."

"I'm not sure if you noticed, but Sokolov knows a lot about supernatural creatures. In fact, he knows so much it's kind of weird." Nobu pointed at her with his fork. "You need to tell him...for both of your sakes."

"But it's not fair. He's not—"

"What? A crow?" Nobu shoveled a forkful of egg and spinach into his mouth. "What does it matter?"

Diana stabbed at her own omelet. "It matters to me."

"Why?"

She sighed and set her fork down, appetite gone. The waitress came by and refilled their coffees, and she waited until the woman moved to the next table before she continued. "Because Sasha had no choice. He walked into this—into *me*—without a clue, and it's so profoundly unfair I can't imagine making the man feel like he has to let me hang around the rest of my life."

Nobu shrugged and scooped up some spinach. "Maybe he'd like it."

"Like what?"

"Having you around."

"Right. I doubt it. Sasha hasn't seen his own mother in twenty years. He doesn't want to be stuck with me." Diana dropped her face into the palms of her hands. Such a fucking mess. She pulled her head back up to look at Nobu. "I can stick with my original plan and go back to the murder. Where I belong—with crows."

"You mean crows that treat you like shit?" Nobu's face softened. "Look. I know you have a picture of what your life should look like. I know that picture doesn't include what happened with Sokolov. I get it."

Nobu looked between her and his plate, fork wavering above his omelet. After a long sigh, he set his fork down too and folded his hands in his lap. "A year ago, I had a very different picture for my life. I was about to graduate high school. I had a month left. A scholarship to Oklahoma State. I was human, and I had human wants."

Diana shook her head. "Nobu, you don't have to dig anything up."

"Nah. It's okay. I haven't actually told anyone what happened. Probably good for me to get it off my chest." He took another deep breath.

Despite being past the holidays, a piano rendition of "We Wish You a Merry Christmas" played overhead. Had Nobu cut off his family after getting possessed? It would explain why he was with them over Christmas instead.

"My dad died ten years ago. A few years later, my mom met an American politician. They got married, and we moved to Oklahoma."

She wrapped her arms around herself and relaxed against the booth cushion. "Politician?"

"Yeah. A senator."

"Hm." Diana didn't have an opinion one way or the other. Human government was more or less not her problem.

"A guy got pissed about some legislation. It had something to do with farms. I don't know. Anyway, this guy got really mad and broke into our house." Nobu rubbed the back of his neck, keeping his gaze on the tabletop. "He shot my stepfather in the head. Point-blank. He shot my mom and me after that—got me right in the chest."

Diana wanted to breathe but couldn't find the ability.

"Natsu showed up at our house one day before my dad died. He actually came to the States with us from Japan. I thought he was just a cat." Nobu laughed, like a fond memory somehow found a place among the bad. "After I got shot, Natsu walked up to me, looked me dead in the eye, and said 'I'm sorry.' I thought I was going crazy because I was bleeding to death, but...Natsu possessed me and saved my life. Killed my shooter. Then after I figured out my parents couldn't be saved, we ran away."

There was so much she could comment on, but she had the distinct feeling Nobu didn't want to talk about his parents being executed any more than he had to. "You just happened to have Natsu as a pet?"

Nobu relaxed. "Yeah. Natsu had been hiding."

"From?"

"That demon after your family? There's more of them. Natsu decided to hide with us." The boy smiled and picked his fork back up. "I know he's a demon and all. But he's not bad."

Diana met his grin. "Saved your life."

"Yeah. Saved my life."

She smirked and crossed her arms over her chest. "You wanted the knife too, didn't you?"

Nobu dropped his gaze and blushed. "The original plan was to help you get it and then take it from you to protect Natsu...but—"

"I get it," she said, genuinely. If there was one thing she understood, it was being alone. "Natsu is all you have left."

"Yeah."

Diana reached over to the backpack sitting on the bench beside her. She hadn't felt comfortable leaving the demon knife without a conscious guard, so she brought it along. Well, that and something else. She unzipped the bag and stuck her hand inside, shoving aside Sheturath and stopping only when her fingers grazed something cool. "Here."

She held out her palm to Nobu. The boy's eyebrows crawled up his forehead.

"What's that?"

"What do you think? A ring." Diana held up the ring. Gold. Massive ruby. Magic. "I found it in Jacques's desk before the fight upstairs."

Since Nobu didn't make a move to take it from her, she sat it on the table in front of him.

"But I lied to you." Nobu swallowed. "Why are you—"

"Regardless, you got me into the auction." She pushed the ring closer to him with a finger. "I think this ring more than covers whatever my lying father promised."

He snorted and picked up the ring. "What does it do?"

Diana shrugged. "I don't know."

Nobu barked a laugh and pocketed the ring before finishing off his omelet. But as she watched him, something unexpected weaseled into her psyche. What would happen to Nobu when this was all over?

As she cut into her omelet, the past weeks played through her mind like a movie, and with a heavy heart, Diana realized that she wasn't ready for her days with Sasha and Nobu to end.

TWENTY-NINE

SASHA

Sasha woke up to an empty room.

He ran a hand over his head, displeased at the greasiness of his hair. According to his watch, it had been three days since the vampire sucked him dry. Three days since he'd had a shower, and he could only imagine how terrible he smelled. How Diana could stand to be in the same room with him for so long, he could never guess.

Speaking of Diana, where had she gone? His suitcase and two backpacks were piled in the single chair on the far wall. Thanks to his improved eyesight, Sasha was unable to ignore the piles of dust that had gathered in the corners of the room. The bathroom door was cracked, but the light was off.

No Diana. He couldn't ignore the flash of disappointment in the moment he'd realized she was gone.

Sasha swung his feet over the side of the bed. His body still ached a bit, but waiting any longer for a shower was nonnegotiable. After a deep breath and a few choice words, he stood, keeping a hand on the bed as he maneuvered toward the bathroom. A cluster of water bottles on Diana's nightstand caught his eye, and he snagged one, chugging the contents before continuing his journey to his suitcase.

After an agonizing trip across the room, Sasha brushed his teeth and heaved his ailing body in the shower. His hand stilled on his scalp when it occurred to him that he hadn't once been worried about Diana taking Sheturath and leaving him behind in the ten minutes he'd been awake. Instead, he'd thought intently on the feel of her hand in his. The warmth of her skin. Her unyielding generosity.

"Losing your touch, Sokolov," he said and felt along his neck, carefully scrubbing away the dried blood and thick layer of congealed salve. It made sense he didn't worry about Diana leaving though, didn't it? The woman had sacrificed her finger for him and stayed at his side while he flirted with Death. Why would she leave now? Moreover, why did the thought strike him as wildly unacceptable?

He separated himself from the memory of Diana's fingers on his neck when something hit him. Or rather, the absence of something.

He traced the skin behind his ear down to his collarbone. Where were the punctures?

Sasha reached forward and turned off the water as thoughts pooled together. In moments, moving somewhat on autopilot, he was out and in front of the mirror, wiping through the condensation with his hand.

He narrowed his eyes and leaned in, eyebrows furrowed. Christ.

The punctures were gone.

"Sasha?" Diana's voice on the other side of the door hit him much like the vampire had. His pulse increased and beat within his ears. What had she done to him? "I brought you some breakfast in case you woke up."

Sasha leaned closer to the mirror and felt along his skin. Not even a scar. Perfect.

Like he'd healed it himself.

But he *hadn't*.

"Hello?" Diana sounded worried instead of annoyed. "Are you okay?"

His mind moved through the past weeks, every conversation with Diana under scrutiny. His blood ran cold as a thought crept into his brain. Something that shouldn't make sense, but strangely...did.

Sasha blinked and stared at his flawless throat, reminded him again of his new eyesight. When had that started again? The night after the auction. The same day he also had a vision of Diana dying.

How do you heal? Surely, she hadn't—

A loud bang shook the thin bathroom door. "Sasha!"

He'd planned on shaving after his shower, but he had some things to discuss with Diana. Things that, unfortunately, he could no longer wait to hear. "I'll be out in second."

Sasha pulled on his clothes, mind in a fog. Truthfully, he didn't know much about crow shifters. He knew the obvious things. They were social, lived together in close communities, and spent part of the year as birds. But in the weeks he'd spent with Diana, he'd learned they also had damn near perfect vision. Could move like apparitions in the dark. These discoveries only meant one thing: there might be more to Diana than he thought.

He jerked open the bathroom door, unsurprised to see Diana standing beyond it wearing a scowl and a black-and-white flannel. When he'd first seen her the night of the auction, he'd reduced her to her appearance. Her long, dark hair and too-thin body. He'd seen her and wondered how she was dangerous and why he'd seen her in his visions, and then he used her like a step in a too-long staircase.

Now all he could see was her resilience, and it was beautiful to him.

She looked him up and down, eyebrows raised. "Wow. You own normal clothes. Little cold for the shorts though." It didn't occur to him that she'd never seen him in a T-shirt. She smiled at first, but it quickly morphed into concern. Her lips pursed and eyebrows drew together. "What's wrong?"

Sasha didn't know how else to proceed except to ask the question that might solve the strange mystery that was Diana Van Doren. "How did you kill Jacques?"

Diana paled and ran a hand along the back of her neck. "I stabbed him with that evil knife."

"I figured that much." Sasha walked toward the edge of the bed and sat down as his heart furiously beat against his breastbone. He motioned for her to sit with a wave of his shaking hand. "Where's the kid?"

"The gas station." Diana didn't smile, but she did sit beside him.

As she continued to avoid his gaze, he stared at her left hand. Her missing finger. If the woman only knew who he was. She wouldn't have dared to make a sacrifice like that.

Or perhaps she would've, and that's what he intended to find out.

"Diana." Sasha grabbed her hand and ran his thumb over the top. He sent magic into the pores of her skin and to the stump that remained of her ring finger. She didn't fight it. But his magic confirmed what he'd suspected—most of the damage was healed already. "I asked you why you made this sacrifice, and I'd like to know the truth this time."

When silence answered him, Sasha looked to her face. Diana's eyes, wide in terror, almost made him regret asking. However, he'd started coming to his own conclusions about Diana. Those conclusions deserved answers.

A shaky breath pressed past her lips. She hadn't been frightened of him since the morning after the auction, and now she trembled.

"You're afraid of me," he said, voice heavy. Sasha searched her face, surprised when her mouth dropped open.

"No. I'm not afraid of you." Diana shook her head, sending dark tendrils of hair across her cheeks. "I'm afraid of how you'll react."

His mouth grew dry. "Exactly. Afraid of me."

"No, I'm not!"

"Then explain." Sasha stopped sending magic into her hand and instead held it. Her fingers continued to shake.

"Explain what?" Diana's voice, quiet and small, told him she knew exactly what he meant.

However, instead of getting angry, he placed his other hand on top of her wounded one, holding it between his palms in the gentlest way he knew how. Because he didn't want to hurt her. Not any more than he already had. Or perhaps would.

"I lied to you and Nobu. I told you that I could see the future. In truth, I can only see my future. Furthermore, I can only see when I'm in danger." A sharp breath shook Diana's chest, but she didn't pull away. "At least, I *could* only see my future. Now, for a reason unknown to me, I have begun to see yours."

Diana didn't say anything. She stared at the bathroom door as it lightly waved from the air shooting out of the heater.

When she still didn't say anything, he kept going. "I saw you die in Whitaker's house. I also saw you die in Jacques's house, which is why I intervened when I did. And despite you trying to keep it from me, I know you healed me." Sasha continued to watch her, adrenaline surging through every fiber of his being. Answers. He would finally get answers. "Given that, I have come to the conclusion that something has bound us together in a way I can't understand. However, I have a feeling you might know what happened, and I'd like for you to tell me."

She still wouldn't look at him.

"Diana." Sasha pressed his fingers under her chin and tipped her head up. A tear rolled out of her eye and trickled down her cheek as they locked eyes. "Please."

She exhaled a heavy breath. "Remember when I told you I knew I would never be a part of the murder?" Another tear rolled out of her eyes. "I knew I could never join them because my magic bound to you instead."

He sat perfectly still, fingertips still beneath her chin. He waited for anger to burst to life in his chest. For aggravation. Panic. Anything.

Strangely, he didn't feel any of those things.

Instead, he wondered how Diana felt about it. If maybe there were a part of her that didn't hate the idea of being bound to him. "Why didn't you tell me?"

Diana shook her head free of his touch and jerked her hand away. "Because it isn't fair. You didn't get a choice."

"You didn't either."

"But I'm a crow, and this is who I am. This is what we do." Diana laughed bitterly and wiped under her eyes with the backs of her hands.

"I didn't tell you because if you never see me again after this, you won't feel any different. You'd just get to enjoy your new eyes until that demon killed me."

Sasha watched her. Waited. She finally met his stare and shrugged.

"My parents didn't want me, Sasha. They left me to die in a field. They left me behind like trash. I didn't want to tell you because I knew you'd leave me behind too."

There hadn't been many instances where he'd felt insulted to the point of feeling remorse. He must've done something to give Diana this impression, yet he didn't know what that something was. Regardless, the feeling that came with knowing that he made her feel insignificant wasn't something he enjoyed. "Do you truly think so little of me?"

She raised her eyebrows and gave him a pointed stare. "I know you haven't gone to see your mom in twenty years. If you haven't gone to see her, why would you want me around?"

Sasha drummed his fingers along his knees. When she put it like that, Diana had every reason not to tell him. "I have my reasons for not seeing her."

A shaky breath rattled from her, and she wore a bitter smile on her face. "I figured."

"Let me finish." Sasha held up a hand, hopeful she'd stay to listen. He had so much to say, but what could truly tell her? What could he say that wouldn't end with her leaving or slitting his throat with Sheturath while he slept? "You said I wouldn't feel any different if I never saw you again. Are you implying the reverse for yourself?"

Her face contorted, and in a matter of seconds, her ease had collapsed into remorse. "My mom talks about the pain of being away from the murder every day. It hurts her so bad she stays with Charles to make it hurt less."

"You were willing to suffer that pain to allow me a choice?"

She dropped her gaze and shrugged. "I guess."

Sasha relegated his attention to the dust lining the baseboards in an effort to focus his thoughts. This woman was willing to suffer every single day for the rest of her life for *him*. For someone who'd intended to throw her whole damn family into Madame's clutches.

"I'm sorry you're bound to me and not someone in the murder. I'm not a good man, and you deserve a better family than me." Sasha took a long, slow breath. "And while I haven't seen my mother in a long time, everything I have ever done has been for her benefit. I do take family seriously, and the only person I have, I care about very much. Even if I'm not the best at showing it."

The thought of Madame confronting Charles Van Doren sent him reaching for Diana's hands again. He gripped them both gently, the remnants of her tears slick on his skin as he rubbed his thumbs along her knuckles.

For the first time in his life, Sasha had no plan. He'd never been in this kind of situation before—at a loss. He couldn't know what the future held, despite being able to see it. But what he did know was that he'd never wanted so many things at once that he stood to lose.

His mother's safety. A life unbound by a demon.

But as he watched Diana come completely undone for his sake, willing to sacrifice for him as he'd sacrificed for his mother for years, he found he wanted Diana's trust too. While he certainly didn't deserve it, he wanted it. And it was that want—that selfish, burning want—that compelled the next words from his mouth. "I cannot promise to be the person you want or deserve. But I can promise to try."

Diana stopped breathing, bloodshot eyes tacked to his.

"However, in the coming days, I'm going to need you to trust me." Sasha almost didn't want to ask his next question. So many things could go wrong. "Can you do that?"

Diana choked down a sob and surged forward, colliding with his chest. She tucked her head into the crook of his neck, damp face pressed against his jugular, and wrapped her arms around his torso. The last time he'd held someone like this, she'd planned on stabbing him, and muscle memory forced him to delve into his subconscious. But no visions of danger emerged. Tears aside, he decided he rather liked her against him. She was warm. Fit perfectly. Every ounce of fatigue left him in a rush as he took her in, watching as she found comfort in him.

She pulled back and looked up at him, tear tracks glistening in the sunlight let in by the window. "Having me around is dangerous. I don't want that demon to hurt you."

If Sasha hadn't been so mesmerized by her, he'd have felt worse about Diana's words. No one had ever looked at him like Diana did. Thankful to see him. Happy to hear him and hold him and have him near. Having been raised by demons, her wide eyes sparkled with something he would likely never understand. But he did know she was very beautiful to him, and he liked being looked at that way.

Like he mattered.

"Make no mistake. You are incredibly dangerous to me." Sasha cupped the side of her face with a callused hand and dropped the other on her waist. A sharp breath shook her chest. This could be a huge mistake. All of it. But he couldn't stop himself now. "Just not in the way you think."

He watched her. Waited. Diana did the same, searching his face. But after a moment, she leaned forward and dropped her gaze to his lips. Hopeful, he met her halfway, pressing his mouth to hers.

While he'd certainly been intimate with women before, it was the first time he'd gotten the opportunity without having to worry said woman would kill him after the fact. Diana started slow, nervous if he had to guess, but when he responded, her hesitation fell away. Sasha deepened the kiss and pulled her onto his lap.

Diana pushed, encouraging him to fall back on the bed, but never once broke away from the gentle caress of their mouths. As she brought her hands to his neck, he didn't wince. He didn't pull away. No visions of murder or betrayal graced him, and even as she brushed her thumb along his carotid, Sasha didn't stop pulling her closer. He knew Diana wouldn't hurt him, and while he'd never dream of raising a hand to her, he also knew that pain would come should he not move so very carefully.

Sasha ran a hand along her waist and pushed his fingers beneath the hem of her shirt to skim her sides. He could stop this now. He could tell her how it all started. His affiliation with Madame. He could explain how everything changed course the second she risked her life for him in the bowels of Whitaker's home. But if he told her, would she believe him when he said things were different, or would he join the ranks of everyone else who'd betrayed her trust?

Sasha slipped his hand along her chin, and Diana pulled away from him, watching him through her full lashes. He rubbed her jaw with his thumb, mind rife with possibilities. Get his freedom. Save his bloodline. Keep Diana.

They could fly back to Texas, and after he spoke to Charles, he could call Madame and inform her of his location. Diana likely wouldn't keep tabs on her father after the fact, and given Charles's history, wouldn't question if he never spoke to her again. Diana never had to know about his involvement at all, and he had absolutely no remorse sacrificing her selfish parents to make it happen.

They stared at each other, breaths heavy. This better work. He'd never needed a plan to fall together more perfectly than this one. "I need you to promise that you'll trust me."

Diana smiled and nodded, sending some hair to fall over her shoulder and graze the side of his face. She hadn't answered him before, and he wanted to hear her answer. Needed to hear her answer.

"I promise."

THIRTY

DIANA

Diana let out a long-held breath when the plane stopped inside the hangar on the private airfield in Texas. She'd come to thoroughly hate airplanes. There was something unsettling about trusting a metal tube with flimsy wings to carry you so high, especially when she could fly on her own.

Sasha sat next to her and slipped bullets into the magazine of his gun. His eyes flickered up to meet hers, yet despite the lack of sight on his weapon, his fingers continued to move like a well-oiled machine.

Her cheeks warmed. Last night, those same skillful hands had held her close and crushed her to his chest. Never in her life had she felt so safe, so wanted. While they hadn't gone further than a kiss, she felt Sasha's promise in his touch, and it was the closest thing to a guarantee that she'd ever experienced.

Sasha might be her murder, but he wasn't crow. He didn't have to be there if he didn't want to be. The man was raised with demons, had the emotional awareness of a brick, and clearly had his own trust issues to work through. But he'd promised to try to be the murder she deserved, and she believed him.

As she continued to watch Sasha put his gun back together, her father's threat to have the murder hurt—maybe even kill—Sasha if she brought him along to deliver the knife gave Diana a healthy dose of apprehension. She didn't want him to die, and she certainly didn't trust her father to listen to her plight.

She sighed and twisted her hands together in her lap. "When I talked to my father the other day, he mentioned killing you. I don't think he could because you'd like *see it* or whatever, but I wanted you to know."

Sasha stared at her, but she couldn't tell if how he felt about her revelation. "I appreciate your concern."

Her palms started to sweat despite the chill in the air. "Are you going to kill him? Charles?"

Sasha continued to stare at her. His beautiful eyes, golden irises surrounded by a similarly colored halo of lashes, revealed nothing. He'd said he only wanted to talk to Charles, but the way he was holding his gun didn't bolster that claim in the slightest. "Would you like me to?"

Diana shook her head. How could he ask her something like that with a straight face? "No, no. I mean, I know he sucks, but I'd rather you not."

With a shrug, he tucked his gun back into his holster. "I'll just talk to him then."

Nobu had already stood and collected his bag, and Sasha followed suit. As Sasha moved to the front of the plane with her on his heels, panic gripped Diana's heart in that strangulating sort of way that fear tended to do. From here, they'd drive to her father. To the murder. There was no telling how that would turn out, and the thought of not knowing what her next step would be twisted her stomach into knots.

Diana reached forward and lightly gripped the sleeve of Sasha's suit jacket. "After you talk to Charles, what do you plan on doing?"

"I am going home to see my mother." Sasha looked her over, face unchanging.

Her heart sank. He planned on leaving. Leaving her. She knew she should be happy for him, but the selfish part of her wasn't.

"Oh." Diana cleared her throat. "Well, um, she'd probably like that."

Sasha brought a hand to her chin and directed her eyes to his. His fingers lingered there gently, and the memories of the night before came back in a deluge. The warmth she'd felt with him, the peace with his promise. He'd been distant that morning for some reason, like he was so deep in thought he operated on autopilot, but his desire to be cared for had been obvious the past night. At least to her.

"She would like to meet you." He moved his hand to her ear and tucked a rogue lock behind it. It was the most affectionate thing he'd ever done to her in public, and the thought made her knees weak. "However, it will require a much longer trip on a much bigger plane. If you're up to it."

Diana smiled. Afraid, but hopeful. Afraid it was too good to be true. Hopeful she was wrong. "I am."

"Very well." Sasha let his hand linger on the side of her face.

She let out a breath. Thankful. "Can Nobu come?"

He stared at her. Sasha had claimed to know some of the boy's story, but even if he didn't know the whole thing, she didn't doubt he could tell Nobu had no one else. Well, no one except Natsu. "If he desires to."

"Thank you." Diana worked her lip between her teeth and memorized the feel of his callused hand on her jaw. "For everything."

"I told you I couldn't be the person you deserved, but I promised to try." Sasha dropped his hand and walked toward the front of the plane, leaving her to stand there and gape at his back.

The night he saved her ass at the auction, she asked him what his word was worth. He'd never answered, but she had woken up the next morning. He'd kept his promise then, and she hoped he would now. Despite wanting to believe him, she'd been given many promises her whole life, and most of them had amounted to nothing. They'd either been broken or were lies at the start.

Diana's nerves calmed. Sasha was different. He was *murder*. She would have to trust him. They were forever linked, and it would not do to doubt the power of that bond.

"Diana." The way he said her name banished the temporary solace she'd found with his promise.

Sasha sat his suitcases on the ground and removed a gun from his side. The muscles in his neck were tight. Every trace of ease was gone, and she couldn't help but feel like it was a sign of things to come. An omen. A moment of comfort soon replaced by the same wrenching uncertainty she'd always known. Like he'd changed his mind about her and their bond in a matter of ten footsteps.

Thirty seconds or so passed in which he tilted his head as if listening to someone she couldn't hear. "Do you remember what I asked of you the other night?"

Her heart beat inside her ears. What could've possibly happened in so short a time to make him so tense? "Yes."

Promise you'll trust me.

Sasha inhaled and looked between her and Nobu. "We are about to be cornered by some werewolves."

"What?" Nobu dropped his backpack on the ground with a *thunk.*

"I didn't see blood. Not yet. But their intent..." Sasha kept his expression even and voice low, which meant the wolves were likely close enough to hear them. "Diana—you need to shift and fly off once you're out of the plane. Understand?"

Diana gritted her teeth. How could they have forgotten about the stupid wolves? They'd been in Pennsylvania for a while, but werewolves out for revenge wouldn't stop looking for their target. "No. I'm not leaving you both alone with those wolves when this all started because of me in the first place."

"Please, Diana, I asked you to trust me." Sasha gave her no opportunity to argue and turned to Nobu. "The wolves have no issue with you. I recommend staying human, and they'll likely let you walk away."

Nobu nodded, though obviously uneasy.

"Diana." Sasha walked to her, leaned forward, and dropped his mouth by her ear. A chill rolled down her back when his breath hit her skin. He whispered, "Fight everything in you to stay, and please leave me to deal with them."

He turned away abruptly and cocked his gun. All that was left was leaving the plane.

She didn't bother grabbing her backpack and stripped off her jacket instead. The bite of cold only put her more on edge, but she had to be ready.

"Come out, friends." An unfamiliar voice with a thick, southern twang echoed inside the plane from the open door. "Van Doren—I recommend staying human. If you don't, I'll be forced to retaliate against your buddies."

Panic surged in her gut as Diana followed Sasha to the cabin exit, Nobu on her heels. The boy's face had gone white, and he muttered to himself. Was he talking to Natsu or panicking?

The hangar looked as it had when they left for Philadelphia, with the notable exception of the body face down on the concrete. Tess lay still, a pool of red surrounding her limp form. Her mouth hung open. Eyes, light like snow glistening in the sun, stared at them without moving. Glazed. Lifeless.

Beyond Tess's corpse were the ones responsible for killing her, and a steering wheel—one she had a sneaking suspicion belonged to Sasha's rental car they'd left there. So much for a hasty escape.

The one closest to Tess's body she recognized from the auction. Tanktop. Fear seized her heart. They hadn't killed him.

If the gathering of the over twenty werewolves in the hangar meant anything, someone else was in charge today though. The werewolves stood in a cluster as humans, but the one in the front had Alpha all but written on him. The man crossed his arms, both forearms lined with scars. While Diana couldn't possibly know how old he was, the werewolf was old. Really old. The animal in her could feel it.

"We've been waitin' on y'all to come back." The Alpha took a step forward, cowboy boots scuffing the concrete. Given his assumed age and the comfortable accent in his voice, Diana thought he might actually be a cowboy from the early days of the American frontier. His eyes, a bright green, were natural. Not the scary, about-to-shift kind. "I don't much like waitin' either."

Diana felt Nobu move closer, and she hoped he kept Natsu under wraps. While the demon could heal his host from things like poison and gunshot wounds, there wasn't much Natsu could do to reattach a severed head. The boy's dark eyes met hers, and she saw legitimate fear.

"I would apologize for the delay, but I don't apologize often." Sasha's voice remained level. Calm. Everything she didn't feel in her heart. "I certainly do not apologize to those who threaten me or my associates."

"Now, now." The Alpha raised his hands placatingly in front of his chest, an easy smile on his face. "I just want to straighten something out. I can't have you going back to your boss with lies before we can settle what happened at the auction."

Sasha huffed. "Lies?"

"My pack had no qualms with you." He pointed at Diana and shook his head. "That woman and her family, however, do owe us something."

"Who are you?" Diana asked, throat tight. "I would remember if I stole from you."

She knew she would because, aside from Amir, she avoided werewolves at all costs.

"Bartholomew Evans. You can call me Bart." He tipped the nonexistent hat on his head. "And you did steal from me. You stole a very expensive rug. I'm under the impression that Miguel's mate shot you. I'd thought you were dead until I heard about the auction."

Her heart sank. The person who caught, and shot, her had been human. It never occurred to her that the fucking rug belonged to werewolves.

Sasha glanced down at her. She inhaled and tried to find comfort in him. The warmth. The safety. But she didn't find it. Not this time. Not when death lingered so close, their souls all but lost already.

"Enough. I am going to save all of us some time." Sasha turned his attention back to Bart. If there were a time to shift and fly away, it would be now. But if she left, the Alpha would hurt Sasha and Nobu. He'd said as much when she got off the plane. "I have no inclination to let you do anything to this woman."

"We have no intention of starting a fight with you or your boss," Bart said.

Diana swallowed. Somehow Bart knew who Sasha worked for, and it didn't sound like he liked whoever that person was.

"We want to get our rug back from her daddy. That's all."

Sasha straightened his suit jacket. "While it might not be your intention, if you harm her, a fight is what you'll get. I don't believe I need to remind you what happened the last time I crossed paths with your friends."

"Attacking you was a mistake my pack mate made out of ignorance." Bart laughed, but it was insincere. Sarcastic, even. "Why the hell would he knowingly attack Madame's renowned architect with so few? It is—*was*—suicide, and the last thing we need is that demon breathing down our necks while our boss is MIA."

The moisture in her throat vanished and left behind the dry, papery texture of panic and grief. Her body ran cold, but not from the wind or lack of heat. Her lungs burned, and there wasn't a single part of Diana that didn't want to die as a horrifying realization settled in her brain.

Madame.

Sasha worked for the demon hunting her family.

THIRTY-ONE

SASHA

Sasha felt Diana's fear despite standing a good three inches away, and it hurt to know the fear wasn't born from the wolves.

She was scared of him. *Madame's architect.*

He'd hoped she would've done as he asked—fly away and leave the wolves to him. But the Alpha's threats had kept her human, and now Diana knew the truth. As much as he wanted to cling to slim chance that perhaps Diana would give him an opportunity to explain, Sasha wasn't an idiot.

No. There would be no way of keeping her trust—keeping her alive was the best he could do at this point.

Sasha's gaze flickered to Tess's body. Another dead in pursuit of Sheturath. Madame would be upset about losing Tess. She wasn't important enough for the demon to expend resources, but nymphs were hard to come by.

"Your pack mate attacked me out of ignorance." He pushed his apprehension aside and fell back into the familiar: plotting. There were still some moves left that didn't end with them dead, and if he maneuvered correctly, he might still get Diana and Nobu out safely. "Did your pack mate also watch his comrades die and do nothing out of ignorance?"

Bart stilled and cocked his head. "What?"

"That man there ordered your wolves, his subordinates, to attack." Sasha motioned to the wolf in charge at the auction.

The tension in the hangar escalated dramatically, complete with soft growls shaking against the floor. Despite it, he longed to look at Diana instead. To hold her face in his hands and explain, to beg her to *trust him*. But he couldn't, not with their lives on the line. He couldn't break focus.

"He then stood by and watched me shoot them."

Bart shook his head, but Sasha had seen that look before. Significant doubt had taken root. It lingered in the corners of his mouth. "No. That ain't right because Joey came home beaten up."

Sasha smirked and mentally cataloged the horror riddled on Joey's face. "Then I imagine he also returned alone instead of with the female wolf I also left alive."

One of the men toward the back of the cluster growled and began to shift, bones cracking and twisting as fur pressed from his skin. Bart glanced behind him, but Sasha had a feeling it was more to appraise Joey than the simmering rage taking over the hangar in a blanket.

Bart looked at him again. "How do I know you ain't lying?"

"I shot your deceased friends in the head with silver rounds, which I figure you know to be true. Unless Whitaker's sphinx ate them, I know you've collected your dead by now."

Another wolf, a woman with tawny beige skin standing less than a foot away from Joey, began to change. Her bones snapped and contorted like another being writhed within her.

Sasha calculated the rest of his plan. The words he used had to be purposeful. Deliberate. "If Joey came to you with wounds aside from that, there's your proof. I'll also assume you're short a body—the female I left alive with him. The one he killed to save his own skin."

One by one, the wolves in the pack started shifting. Howls shook the corrugated metal along the walls and roof, echoing louder and louder until the only thing he could think about was shooting all of them to make it stop.

"You've put me in a bad place, Sokolov." Bart growled and bared teeth. While still human, he almost wasn't.

Sasha shrugged. "I've already told you how I feel about apologies."

Bart cursed under his breath.

Regretful, he allowed himself the briefest glance at Diana. It seemed like she'd retreated from the room entirely. Locked away inside her head. He tried to shake the guilt nestled in the back of his throat and inventoried the weapons on his person. He had the Glock and the Sig—only one with silver rounds—hardly enough to take out the entire pack. Sheturath.

"Out of curiosity"—Bart took a slow breath—"did you kill Whitaker?"

"Yes." Sasha licked his lips. "But I assume you knew that. Our scent would have been all over his house."

Bart growled, the canine fighting to get out. He had to be old to have that sort of control when his pack had none. "And that knife? Did you steal it from him?"

Sasha squeezed the grip on his Glock and waited for the burn in his mind to show him the danger. No bloodshed yet, but more wordplay was necessary. "We did not take Sheturath from Whitaker. He sold it."

"And you somehow recruited the crows to help you find it?" Bart laughed and looked at Diana. He kept his eyes on her, eyebrows furrowing. "I'm surprised she took the risk given who you work for."

He took a step toward her, but Diana didn't move. She kept her gaze on the ground, hands shaking at her sides. His heart lurched, cracking beneath the force of regret and shame, but he had to ignore it. He had to focus.

Bart stopped walking and turned his nose up to sniff the air. He shook his head, like the wolf in him didn't like whatever he smelled.

"Or maybe she didn't know the risks because she didn't know who you are. Maybe you're a bastard." Bart's face softened. What did he see when he looked at her? "You don't know how pack magic works, do you?"

He ground his teeth together. "She's not a dog."

"No. But she's an animal that thrives on companionship. Shifters like us find strength in our families. We're only as strong as our weakest link." Bart took another step toward Diana, and she still did not move. "When we're betrayed by our pack, we break."

Sasha knew these things, of course. As Madame's right hand, he'd forcibly recruited many creatures, and there was substantial risk in recruiting wolves to work for the demon. While they were formidable, the pack dynamic directly conflicted with signing contracts with demons. One could only recruit them if they successfully blackmailed the Alpha because the Alpha had the most pull in the magic that connected all the werewolves together. The strongest of the links in the proverbial chain.

"I will give you a five-minute head start while I deal with Joey. Pack comes first." Bart's eyes now flashed a dangerous green. He turned around when the growls grew too loud to ignore. Sasha knew the old wolf didn't want to do what the pack would demand. Bart glanced over his shoulder. "And since you refuse to hand the girl over, I'm coming for you next."

As Bart turned his back to them, Sasha looked to Diana. Her gaze had remained fixed on the same spot on the floor for several minutes. It was like she'd left her body there inanimate, a soulless husk she'd abandoned in search of greener pastures.

Betrayed. Broken.

His chest went numb, and the focus he'd cultivated slipped.

He'd done that.

THIRTY-TWO

DIANA

The first time Diana had felt heartbreak had been the day she'd been forced from her sister, Olivia. The day the murder had sent her parents away with her on their heels. She'd been lost, confused, completely and utterly destroyed from the inside out, and she hadn't been sure what to do afterward. Her chances of being family with the murder, of being welcomed into their ranks by their magic, had effectively been reduced to zero.

The pain she felt that day had nothing on the loss sinking its talons into her now. Even watching Sasha die had been a wisp compared to her current hellscape.

Tremors racked her hands as fervent breaths pressed from her lungs. Sasha and Bart's voices echoed in her ears, somehow unimportant despite their lives hinging on whatever it was they said.

Her magic had bonded with a traitor. The person that was supposed to be her family worked for the demon who sought to kill her parents, and Sasha's request to see her father in exchange for his help in stealing the stupid knife made perfect sense.

He wanted to know where her father was so he could turn them over to Madame. Hell, he probably planned on taking Sheturath afterward too. His promise on the plane to let Charles live? An obvious lie.

Sasha had used her from the beginning.

Diana wrapped herself around the magic inside her chest. She gripped it, wanting to retreat to her baser instincts. To find her wings and leave. To smother herself inside and let her crow handle living.

If her life was always going to be one shitshow after another—one betrayal after another—maybe ending it now would be easier. Maybe offering herself up to the wolves—

Warmth against her right hand broke her from the dangerous snarls of ideation. Diana swallowed and slid her eyes over, unsure of what she'd see.

Nobu stood there.

His hand trembled against hers and broke any sort of hold she had on being an easy or sacrificial kill. She couldn't leave Nobu there alone. She couldn't trust Sasha not to kill him. Not after this. If he could do this to her without a second thought—

Another howl brought her back to reality. The wolves had all shifted save for Bart and Joey, although the former struggled to keep his composure. Growls shook the floor of the hangar, and if she weren't swallowed with other emotions, Diana would've been more frightened.

"Diana."

Sasha's voice made her heart stop. It sounded no different than it had before this mess. Measured. Unbothered. Did he even care what he'd done to her?

"Shut up."

"Diana." Sasha's voice hardened this time. "Run."

A chill zipped down her back. She didn't want to listen to anything the jackass had to say, but Sasha had seen something. If his tone and lies were anything to go by, he didn't care if she lived. But the fact he mentioned it at all made her wonder.

She'd barely lifted her foot off the ground when the howls began anew.

Diana grabbed Nobu's arm and pulled him as she ran toward the back of the hangar. The front, completely blocked by the wolves, wouldn't work. The best they could do was run out the back, which wasn't great considering werewolves were much faster.

"Run, Nobu!"

The boy picked up the pace and veered right. "Door!"

He reached it first and held it open as she passed under the doorframe and into the winter air. Dead fields stretched around the small airport in every direction. Getting out of there alive would take a miracle.

"Natsu won't come out." Nobu's face had turned red, but from the wind or the running she didn't know. "I asked him to, but he won't. He said they'll kill me—"

"Nobu, I get it." Diana zipped around a parked biplane, hoping to put as much distance between them and the wolves as possible. She heard Sasha running on the other side of her, but she couldn't look at him. Didn't want to.

Nobu cursed but kept running. His breath came out in harsh pants. "Diana. Shift."

"No."

"If you shift, you can—"

"No," Diana said, unsurprised by the hurt in her voice. There was no way she'd leave Nobu. Not alone. Not with him.

Regardless, if she didn't get a grip, she and Nobu were both dead. Sasha too. Although, by all rights, she shouldn't care about his fate.

Her lungs burned, struggling for air as she plowed ahead. She could only imagine what her companions were thinking about the shitstorm brewing behind them, although she couldn't help but wonder if Sasha felt any guilt.

"This is your fault, Sokolov." Nobu kept pace, but Diana turned her attention to the horizon.

"Keep running." He took a deep breath. "I don't have enough silver bullets for the whole pack."

Sasha was close now. She felt him move up beside her without turning her head an inch.

"Diana. I asked you to trust me." Sasha's voice was soft. Broken.

A liar's voice.

A glance back revealed that the werewolves hadn't left the hangar yet, but their howling continued to fill her ears. "Shut up!" Her magic swallowed her whole, insidiously creeping into her vision and mouth. It hurt. Everything hurt. Diana stopped running, lungs burning, and let out a feral scream. God, she hated him. She hated everything. "You're a liar! A filthy fucking liar just like my father."

"At first, yes, I had every intention of betraying you. But not anymore. Not for a while," Sasha said as he stopped beside her, gaze never leaving her face despite the continued howls shaking the hangar across the tarmac. "But there are things you don't understand."

Diana stuck her finger in his face. The odds of escaping the wolves were slim to none anyway, and she wanted to give him a piece of her mind before she got ripped to pieces. "You had a chance to be honest with me, and you weren't."

"I know." Sasha held up his hands placatingly.

She focused on his hands. All ten of his fingers. She'd given up one of her fingers for this bastard, and he had every intention of screwing her over. "Because I'm trash. Easy to throw away when it's convenient."

If she didn't know any better, legitimate regret graced his features. Sasha's eyes widened. His eyebrows furrowed. His breath hitched. "That's not true."

"You either think I'm trash and easy to betray, or you didn't trust me with the truth. You didn't trust me to understand whatever rationale you pieced together to justify working for that demon." Diana turned away and ran.

The howls changed. No longer were they fervent and angry. The growls and snarls had ceased entirely, and now, despite being crow, she could tell the wolves mourned.

"Guys!" Nobu pointed toward another hangar several yards ahead. "There's a truck parked over there. I think I can start it."

Diana followed behind Nobu, anger propelling her every step. She should've known Sasha hadn't really wanted her. That he didn't care.

She would never know love. She would never have a murder.

She would never have anything.

For the first time in her life, Diana cursed the man who raised her. He should've let her die in that field.

THIRTY-THREE

SASHA

They had about two minutes, maybe three, before the wolves came after them. Sasha slammed the butt of his Glock into the driver's window of the truck. The glass crumbled from the frame. Nobu stuck his arm inside and unlocked the door, dragging his bicep along the shards as he hurriedly worked to get in. The boy hissed in pain, and Diana was at his side, concern pulling at the corners of her mouth. His heart sank at the sight.

Diana stood at Nobu's back as he pried the wires out from underneath the steering wheel. Blood dotted his shirt sleeves. Watching the kid's fingers sift through the wires somehow slowed down time for Sasha. He knew so painfully little about the boy. He'd never bothered to ask Nobu who he was. Where he'd been. If Whitaker's story had even been true.

"Nobu, hurry." Diana scowled and positioned herself between him and the boy. Sasha's heart somehow managed to sink farther, and he didn't know how he stood beneath the weight of it.

Nobu cursed. "I'm trying!"

As wolves bounded from the hangar, the truck roared to life. Nobu leapt over the console and into the back.

"I'll drive." Sasha jumped in the front seat, and small pebble-sized pieces of glass ground into his thighs. Behind him, heavy breaths shook the kid's chest, and despite everything they'd been through and being possessed by a demon, this was the first time Sasha had seen him so terrified.

The second Diana shut the passenger door, Sasha set his Glock loaded with silver rounds on the console and stomped on the gas.

He glanced in the rearview mirror. The wolves, an orchestrated mass running toward their tailgate, covered the tarmac in a blink. The wide expanse that was the airport had little in the way of obstacles, which meant the wolves would have no trouble catching up to them.

He pressed down on the accelerator, and they shot toward a landing strip. Even if they got caught, he owed it to Diana to try.

"Sokolov, they're gaining!" Nobu peered out the back glass. "What do we do?"

Sasha inhaled and tried to push through the visions of being ripped to pieces by several angry werewolf maws. "Kid, can you shoot?"

"Sorta."

He picked up the Glock resting on the console and held it out to Nobu. "Sixteen silver rounds. One's in the chamber. Make them count."

Nobu took the Glock and opened the back glass. His shaky breaths didn't bode well for a steady hand. Sasha reached for his Sig. While it only carried lead, it was better than nothing at all. He set it on the console and kept his eyes forward.

Sasha gripped the steering wheel tight and continued to tear down the landing strip. "Diana."

She grabbed the Sig from the console and kept her eyes on the side-view mirror. "Shut up."

"I should have trusted you with the truth."

Diana closed her eyes and inhaled through her nostrils. "I should've known better than to trust you at all."

"Sokolov, they're almost on us." Nobu's voice did little to soften the blow of Diana's words.

"Kid, breathe through your nose and out of your mouth." Sasha held the wheel steady and continued to consult his visions.

In real time, a truck emerged from the other side of the hangar, dust flying behind the wheels as it headed toward them. "White wolf on the left. Shoot that one first. A headshot will kill it. Anywhere else will just slow it down."

"Right." Three seconds later, the familiar sound of a bullet leaving the barrel of his Glock shook the car. The wolf stumbled and collapsed to the ground, but the rest of the pack continued to chase them down.

Nobu said something in Japanese, a curse maybe. "Not the head."

"It's fine." Asking more of the kid was unfair, even by his standards. "Red wolf coming up the center."

Another *pop*.

"There's too many." Nobu's voice broke. "I can't do this. I don't want to do this!"

Sasha glanced over at Diana. She'd turned completely away from him, focused on the back window now. "Do what you're willing to do, Nobu."

He drove off the tarmac and into the open field stretching beyond the airport. A chain link fence would cut them off eventually. Turning and giving the wolves a smaller margin between them was inevitable if he hoped to get to the exit. If he started turning toward the gate now, he could maximize the distance.

"One is gaining, and that truck is getting close," Nobu said. A shot echoed in the otherwise quiet car. "Wolf!"

The truck bounced under the force of a large wolf jumping into the bed. The wolf put its forelegs on the top of the truck. Thanks to a vision, he knew the wolf planned to reach in the driver window and tear his throat out. His chest tightened at the image, and he jerked the wheel to the left, shaking the wolf from the roof and onto the hard ground. A loud whine hit his ears, but a quick glance in the rearview showed the wolf back on his feet.

"Diana." Sasha licked his lips. It didn't take a clairvoyant to know how this would likely end, and his time to explain was coming to a close. "My bloodline is bound by contract to serve Madame. I was offered freedom for myself and my mother in exchange for your father and Sheturath."

Diana whipped her head around, Sig in hand with a snarl on her face. For the first time since knowing her, he worried she'd actually try to kill him. Although, since his visions kept focusing on the wolves, maybe not. "If you're looking for sympathy—"

"I'm not." Sasha gripped the wheel tighter. "That is the last thing I deserve."

Another wolf landed in the bed, and the truck chasing them had almost caught up with the pack.

"But I had a plan—thought I had a plan—that could set me free without—"

"Without telling me the truth."

"Yes." Sasha tried to ignore the visions of werewolves gaining on them and tearing into the truck. "I saved my mother the torment of serving Madame, and I can't even make myself face her out of shame. So telling you—the first person to ever find any sort of peace in my presence—that I've done horrible things while serving a demon wasn't in my plan."

Face red, Diana growled. A third wolf jumped in the truck bed. She screamed in frustration and slammed a fist against the door.

"They want me, and they won't stop until they have me." She turned around and watched Nobu, the boy holding a weapon who didn't have the heart to kill with it. "Get Nobu out of here."

Diana opened the passenger door, arms shaking as she fought against the wind. He instinctively pulled off the gas as his heart lodged in his mouth. "Diana—"

Without another word, she jumped, sidearm in hand.

Sasha slammed on the brakes and turned the wheel as her body hit the hard ground, careful to avoid the direction in which she'd rolled.

"Holy shit!" Nobu cried out and clung to the seat as the truck swung in a quick arc, dead grass and dirt spraying up where rubber met the field.

As the truck rocked to a stop, Sasha's heart slammed in his chest. Nothing the woman did made any sense. Every move she made and breath she took defied logic. There was no pattern, no reason, no *nothing* when it came to Diana Van Doren, and it hit him with astounding clarity that trying to plan with someone like her couldn't be achieved by his usual means.

But now it was too late.

"Gun." He held out an open hand to Nobu, and the boy dropped the Glock in his palm. Thirteen silver bullets left. He'd counted every shot Nobu took.

"What are we going to do?"

"I'm not sure yet." Sasha opened his door and swung out, swallowed by a wave of visions.

Diana lay in a crumpled heap on the ground. Her back heaved, and despite the blood peppering the grass, his heart lightened. She moved. Not dead.

She staggered to her feet as the wolves crept up.

The truck that had been following them slowed down behind the pack, and Bart emerged, arms aloft. Blood coated his mouth and arms. It didn't take a clairvoyant to know what had happened to Joey. "An interesting end game we have here."

"Let them go." Diana stumbled a couple feet to her left and grabbed the Sig from its place in the grass. She cocked the gun and placed the point of the barrel under her chin. "Or you'll never find my father."

Bart held up his hands as if to steady her and nodded toward Sasha, still taking slow steps forward. "Surely you don't expect for me to let him go unscathed after turning down my attempt at diplomacy?"

"If you want my father, and I think you do, you don't have a choice." Blood dripped off her chin from her busted nose. Abrasions peeked out from the torn fabric of her flannel and jeans. "You don't want them. You never did. Let them go, and I'll take you to him."

Sasha watched Diana, the woman broken in form and spirit. How had he managed to destroy someone so wholly without the intent?

"None of your wolves died by Sasha's hand today. They'll heal, and they'll survive." Diana sniffed and wiped some blood from her nose with the back of her hand, careful to keep the Sig tucked beneath her chin. He really wanted to jerk the gun away. Shake her. Tell her how irredeemably stupid she was to even threaten such a thing. "You'll get me. No more fighting."

Frowning, the Alpha appraised her. Bart crossed his arms in front of his chest, clearly torn. After all the trouble he'd caused, Sasha knew the wolf wasn't keen to let him walk away. At this point, Madame might even hesitate to retaliate on his behalf if something were to happen to him, and the demon didn't care much about her tentative cease-fires with the other generals to begin with.

"Do you honestly think I believe you'll waste your life to protect theirs?" Bart scoffed. "I've been around the block before, missy."

"I don't give a shit what block you've been on. I've got *nothing* to lose." Diana's voice climbed, nearing a scream with every passing moment. "So if you don't believe me, fine. You only get to make the mistake once."

Sasha didn't dare look to his visions. He couldn't bear it if she meant it.

"I won't touch them. You have my word." Bart dropped his hands. "But Sokolov must empty his weapon."

Diana kept the Sig positioned against her chin and slid her eyes over to him. "Do it."

Sasha took a breath and released the magazine. Even if it might mean his own death, it would be worth it after everything he'd done. One by one, he popped the silver rounds from the magazine and ejected the last one from the chamber.

"The thirteen that remain." Sasha turned his hand over, and the bullets fell to the ground. He held up his Glock and magazine and slowly bent his knees. "I'm putting down the gun."

He set the pistol and magazine in the grass and stood back up, palms out.

"All right." Bart motioned to Diana. "Your turn. Hand it over."

"And give up my leverage?" Diana gave the Alpha a look that said something along the lines of *yeah right*.

Bart sighed. "Fine. At least get it out from under your chin."

She reluctantly—almost too reluctantly—pulled the weapon from under her jaw and held it at her side. Over twenty wolves prowled around them, growling. Watching. "Now let them go. Don't chase them. Don't even look at them."

"In a minute," Bart said.

Diana clenched her teeth. "What?"

"I've got something they need to hear." Bart held up his hands and positioned himself behind her, eyes on Sasha. "Sokolov, I've got a theory."

Sasha had never felt so useless. Watching Diana, bleeding and broken, get swallowed up by Bart's muscular arms sent a wave of self-loathing through his body. The Alpha grabbed her left shoulder, paying the Sig in her right hand little mind.

He tried to still his trembling hands. "I'm not sure I'm interested in hearing it."

"Here's what I think." Bart positioned himself behind Diana and grabbed her bicep. "I think you care about this woman's well-being, be it for yourself or for Madame, as you would not have pulled the shit you just pulled if her life meant nothing to you. So I need you to listen very carefully."

Sasha curled his fingers into his palms. "I'm listening."

Bart moved his hand from Diana's shoulder to her scapula and yanked her bicep to the side with a quick jerk.

A scream tore into the still air. Nobu gasped beside him, and Sasha grabbed the boy by the arm and held him firm. A hard, choked sob racked Diana's body as she staggered into Bart, holding her arm close to her stomach with her hand. It hung limp, disjointed from the socket.

"Can't have you shifting and flying off, Van Doren." Bart kept a hand on her bicep, and she wailed. "I do apologize, ma'am, but your father has a reputation. One I'm not so sure you didn't pick up along the way."

Diana's body shook beneath the pain.

Bart stared at Sasha pointedly. "Are you listening to this, Sokolov?"

Sasha kept his grip on Nobu, if for no other reason than to ground himself. "Yes."

"I'm going to let you and that boy get in your truck and drive away." Bart motioned toward the truck with a nod. "But if you try to interfere any more with my business concerning the Van Dorens, I will crush her head like a watermelon. Do you understand?"

Sasha stared at Diana, unwilling to condemn her to anymore pain but also unwilling to abandon her. His heart stuttered, bringing him precariously close to the despair he felt the night he agreed to Madame's contract in his mother's stead.

Diana looked at him with tears shimmering along her lash line. "If you meant anything you said, you let them take me and keep Nobu safe. Don't make him pay for our mistakes." Jumping from the truck hadn't been kind to her. The blood leaking from her nostrils pooled on her upper lip and ran down the side of her mouth, and just when he thought she'd cuss him, her gaze softened. "If what you said was true, you can't die. Not here. You damned me...don't damn your mom too."

Every ounce of air left Sasha's lungs.

He had never wanted to kill someone as badly as he wanted to kill Bart. Heat crawled up his back, somehow so hot it felt cold. The only thing that kept him still were Diana's words.

Don't damn your mom too.

"Get out of here, Sokolov." Bart pointed toward the truck.

"Are we really going to leave her with them?" Nobu asked under his breath.

Sasha took a step back, and his shoe slid along the yellowed grass. "Yes."

Nobu jerked his arm away from him, but he made no move to charge Bart or go to Diana. He rubbed the bicep he'd sliced on the window glass and cursed.

Sasha memorized Diana's face before he turned around. The beauty beneath all the blood. The loyalty even now.

"Van Doren, you gotta take us to your murder now." Bart's voice echoed in the dead field. Sasha tried to ignore it as he gripped the handle on the truck door.

"My murder? Those crows aren't mine." A sardonic laugh nipped at his ears. "I've wanted a murder my whole life. What a waste of time."

Sasha bit the inside of his cheek to keep from saying anything and climbed into the truck, feeling heavy the second he slammed the door closed. His body, seeming to move of its own accord, gripped the gear shift and pressed on the gas, heading nowhere but driving all the same.

He had Sheturath. He knew where Charles Van Doren would be waiting.

Yet even with his freedom—his mother's freedom—being so close, he'd never felt more despair.

THIRTY-FOUR

SASHA

Sasha had predicted to feel much lighter the moment his freedom sat assured in his grasp. Sheturath was strapped to his side, and he had the location of Charles Van Doren. He could pluck his phone from his pocket and call Madame. His contract could be incinerated in less than an hour if he only *moved*.

Yet he couldn't.

Instead of basking in the first ounce of liberty he'd known since childhood, Sasha mindlessly turned the steering wheel, veering onto a side street with no particular goal in mind. His face pulsed in tandem with his heart and reminded him of his mother's plea not so long ago.

Promise me you will find someone to remind you there is a heart inside your chest.

His task had seemed black and white at the time. Secure Sheturath. Find Charles Van Doren. All he had to do was use Diana to get both. She was a thief. A vagrant. Leaving her at the end should've been the easiest part.

Never had a plan gone so spectacularly wrong.

Irritation tightened the muscles in his shoulders, and he pressed harder on the gas. The wind whipped around his face as it funneled into the broken window, sending his jacket and tie to flutter in the breeze. He moved his fogged gaze from the horizon to the empty passenger seat. Such a monumental failure on all fronts.

"What do we do now?"

Sasha looked in the rearview mirror at Nobu. The boy had his gaze on the empty seat too, eyes wide and red. He could've sat in the front now that she was gone but hadn't. Maybe *couldn't*.

At a loss for what to do, Sasha decided to change the subject to keep from talking about it. Nobu had said something interesting to Diana as they ran from the wolves.

He pushed an air vent toward his face. The heat brushed against his chilled nose, but it couldn't compete with the winter air coming through the shattered window. "You wanted Sheturath to protect yourself from the generals, didn't you?"

After his third glance between the mirror and the road, Nobu broke his stare on the seat and looked at him instead. "What?"

"You were originally going to take the knife from Diana to keep yourself safe from the generals." Sasha turned onto another street. To where? He hadn't a clue.

"You think I did what I did for myself?" Nobu's tone did little to banish the haze his brain was in.

"Yes."

"For someone so smart, you're a fucking idiot."

Sasha truly focused for the first time since leaving Diana at the airport. Brain clear. Fog gone. "What?"

"When I made a deal with Charles, I knew there was a good chance he wouldn't pay me. Natsu told me he was a liar, but I also knew I couldn't steal the knife by myself. I thought Diana would suck too, ya know?" Nobu grimaced. "She didn't, so I couldn't steal it from her either. Diana already knows about it all. It's not a secret."

Knowing that Nobu had been brave enough to tell Diana his original intentions didn't make Sasha feel any better about what he'd done. "Diana knowing you wanted the knife to keep yourself safe from Natsu does not negate the fact that was your intention."

"Keep *me* safe. Right." Nobu threw his hands in the air and laughed. The most sarcastic, teenage laugh Sasha had ever heard. Complete with an eye roll. "I wanted the knife to protect Natsu. Not me."

Sasha scoffed. "He's a demon."

"He may be a demon, but he gave up his body for mine." Nobu dropped his gaze to his knees. His hands were clenched into tight fists on his thighs.

"He lied to you then because demons possess bodies—they don't have their own. Only the five exiled generals and the Devil himself are capable of manifesting a body for themselves." Sasha expected to feel smug after having his doubts confirmed about Natsu, but it only added more insult to injury. Such a hollow victory now that—

"Four." Nobu took a breath. "There are *four* generals now."

Sasha blinked and slowly lifted his foot off the gas. The truck rolled to a stop as he directed it to a curb and nestled close to a dead lawn in front of a stop sign. Stunned silent, Sasha moved on autopilot and reached behind the steering wheel to shift the car into park, mind a fog once more.

Natsu was a *general?*

Sasha shook his head and stared out of the windshield. Had this entire endeavor been summarily fucked from the beginning? Had there ever been any hope of success?

He dropped his hands from the steering wheel and collapsed against his seat, unable to come to terms with the boy's declaration.

Nobu carried a general of Hell inside him. Christ.

Sasha slid his gaze to the passenger side once more, pained at the empty seat. It was disconcerting how easily Diana had weaseled into his life. So much so that the truck felt empty without her in it. Or maybe, just maybe, it was disconcerting that he had fought so hard against it.

"Natsu started coming around my house back when I was a kid," Nobu said once it became clear Sasha had nothing in him to say. "He moved to the States with us after my dad died."

Sasha pinched the bridge of his nose. "You're telling me that you adopted one of the former generals of Hell as a pet?"

"On accident." The boy shrugged. "Um...he would come and go at first. I didn't know what he did while he was gone. But Natsu would always come back, and then he'd stay longer. I thought it was normal cat behavior."

Sasha glanced in the rearview and stared at Nobu. Would he have put this together had he deigned to pay any attention whatsoever to Nobu? Had his complete and utter hatred for demons, and consequently Natsu, blinded him?

Unable to cope with the swell of regret and shame creeping up his esophagus, Sasha closed his eyes. He'd shoved his head so far up his own ass he hadn't seen what Nobu had known about Diana—that she was unfailingly loyal and quick to forgive. He hadn't seen all the signs that pointed to Natsu being a general because he'd been blinded by a lifetime of disgust.

Nobu, unaware of the mental beating he was giving himself, continued speaking, but Sasha didn't hear any of it. Not really. Every word added insult to injury and highlighted his own ignorance in a blinding shade of neon. How could he be so foolish? So—

"That's when I realized that Natsu wasn't a cat." The words hit him in the chest and brought him out from his pit of self-loathing. "When I was dying, Natsu possessed me to keep me alive."

Sasha took in a sharp breath. While not bound in a blood signature, that was a deal with a demon if he'd ever heard one.

Nobu rubbed his neck and averted his gaze. "Natsu left his own body behind to save mine, and I've been hiding him ever since. He said that others would come for him eventually. I've been trying to prepare for that moment."

Sasha thought back to Whitaker's story. He'd mentioned that there had been a dead cat at the scene of Nobu's house. At the time, Sasha had thought perhaps that the rumors were true. That cat demons were made from abuse and the spirit of a corrupted cat had left its earthly body and possessed Nobu's instead.

In actuality, a *demonic general from Hell,* not a house cat, left its body—the one thing that made it greater than the rest of Hell's rabble—for a human.

Sasha shook his head, still unconvinced. There must've been something to compel Natsu to make that sacrifice. Something he missed. "You risked your life for a demon? That's foolish."

"He gave up everything for me!"

"Do you think demons do things because they're kind?" Sasha fought to smother the rage in his chest. "Demons aren't kind. They aren't benevolent beings. You can't trust them."

"I don't trust *them.* I trust Natsu." Nobu scowled. "I don't know why I'm bothering to talk to you about it. You couldn't even trust Diana, and she almost died trying to save your life."

Nobu fell back against the seat and crossed his arms. The hair hanging in his eyes did little to hide the rage blistering across his skin.

Sasha's own rage slipped away from him. The boy was right. Nobu had placed all his trust in a demon and thought nothing of it.

He had, through no fault of his own, been blessed with a life companion. One bound to him and his well-being, and he couldn't even find it within himself to trust her with the truth.

Too many years in Madame's service. Too many betrayals. Too much baggage.

"What?" Nobu's sharp tone pulled Sasha from his self-loathing. The boy squeezed his head between his hands. "Can't it wait?"

Labored breaths shook Nobu's shoulders. "Sokolov, Natsu wants to talk."

Great. The last thing he needed was more so-called advice from a demon. He'd had enough of that to last him a lifetime.

Sasha reached forward and shifted the car into drive. Whatever the demon had to say, he didn't care enough to listen. He'd spent twenty years listening to Madame and doing everything she wanted—he wasn't about to do the same for a demon he didn't have a blood-bound contract with.

However, when the hairs on the back of his neck raised, he knew Natsu had revealed himself anyway.

"Hello, again, my angelic friend." Nobu's body seemed much more threatening with Natsu's voice. His eyes had changed too. Nobu's dark, *human* eyes were gone, replaced by elliptical pupils and a solidly orange eyeball. "I expected you to screw up eventually. I just didn't realize it would be something of this magnitude."

Sasha continued to drive without purpose. "If you're here to rub my nose in it, you can save your time. I am already aware of my error."

The pupils of Nobu's—Natsu's—eyes were difficult to look at. They belonged in a cat, not a human skull. "I don't think you are."

Sasha slammed his hands on the steering wheel. "Then what do you suppose is going through my brain right now if not my failure?"

"I think you're trying to figure out your missing variable. The part you got wrong." Natsu leaned onto the console and propped his chin in his hands. His catlike smile sent a wave of irritation along every pore of his skin. "I don't think you realize why your plan was doomed from the start."

Sasha tried to ignore the demon getting entirely too close to his person. "If you think I'm going to take life lessons from you, you're mistaken."

"That's a pity because I've lived more lifetimes than you can fathom." Natsu climbed over the console and bumped into his arm. Sasha's grip on the steering wheel tightened to the point it should've crumbled beneath his fingers. The cat demon settled into the passenger seat, moving much like Madame. Stiff. "I suppose I can't blame you. Being the servant of a demon destroys your ability to trust. And conversely, no one trusts *you*, and ultimately, you have to worry about everyone that tries to get close because they always, inevitably, try to kill you. Am I close?"

"Can't blame me?" Sasha felt the reins on his temper snapping free. "You goddamn demons have ruined my life. My mother's life. I couldn't even look at Diana without wondering when her trust would end. She gave me no reasons to doubt her—none—yet I couldn't find it in myself to—"

He stopped and inhaled. Exhaled. Losing his head wouldn't solve anything. Diana would be just as gone.

"Yep." Natsu yawned and rolled his shoulder. "That woman would've gone through the gates of Hell for you. Your plan failed because you did not account for your shame."

Sasha tried to ignore the twist in his gut. Everything he'd ever done had been in service to his contract. To being free. It didn't matter who he hurt, killed, or stepped on...survive. He had to survive to keep his mother safe. If he survived Madame, he could survive anything. But survival came with a price. A heavy one. The unbelievable weight of every soul he'd damned or destroyed. Why would Diana want anything to do with such a monster?

Hands trembling, he pulled a cigarette out of his pocket and stuck it between his lips. It took several flicks of his lighter to catch a flame.

"Are you Bart's missing boss?" Sasha asked and dropped the lighter in the cupholder. While a guess, it was an educated one. The wolves at the auction had mentioned their boss being absent, and Bart had said something similar at the hangar.

"I am." Natsu reclined the passenger seat and stuck his feet on the dash.

Sasha released a stream of smoke from his mouth. "Why did you abandon your body?"

Natsu folded his hands over his stomach and closed his eyes. "I don't want to fight the other generals for more space on Earth anymore. I'm tired. The whole 'make a kingdom on Earth' thing is an exhausting enterprise, let me tell you. Even for me. No...I'll just relax until their big battle and the consequent apocalypse."

The demon had been alive since the dawn of time. Perhaps his answer wasn't as farfetched as it sounded.

"Tired." Sasha put his cigarette between his lips and felt in his pocket for his phone. Madame would be expecting a call, and he had the information to give her. All he had to do was press one button, and his contract would be delivered. "That I can understand."

The second he plucked his phone from his jacket, a plan took root.

While he couldn't account for how the crows or wolves would react, he could account for himself, Madame, and Nobu.

And if he made another deal, he could account for Natsu.

Reinvigorated, Sasha rolled down the window and tossed his cigarette. "Do you have enough energy for a final task?"

"I guess. As long as the kid isn't put at risk." Natsu kept his eyes closed. "But we'll need something in return."

Sasha flipped open his phone. If he screwed this up, everything they'd done meant nothing.

However, if he—no, *they*—succeeded, they could all walk away alive and free.

Without bothering to look at the demon or clarify his demands, Sasha dialed Madame's number for what he hoped to be the final time. It rang once.

"Madame." Sasha inhaled. "I've got Sheturath and the location of Van Doren's roost."

THIRTY-FIVE

DIANA

For the first time in her life, Diana didn't feel fear creeping down her back. The looming dread of being alone. The terror of a life spent running—always running—never stopping in hopes of finally finding the life she somehow missed. Instead, she felt like the biggest idiot to ever grace the surface of the planet, and she hoped to be relieved of that feeling soon.

Leaving the airport had been a relatively boring affair. Now that everyone was finished posturing, they'd all retreated inside themselves as they drove to meet her father. Even Bart, for all his bluster, had gone quiet.

She stared out of the window to keep from crying the longer she thought about the past hour. God. She was such a fucking moron. To believe for one second that someone actually, truly wanted her. That someone valued her.

Diana withered as she remembered Sasha kissing her. Holding her. Tucking her hair behind her ear. It'd been so easy for him to make a place in her heart. As much as she'd like to blame the bird in her, Diana knew her magic couldn't be at fault. She'd wanted him to like her, and she would've wanted him to despite being what she was.

She rolled her head to the side and dropped her forehead against the truck window with a *thunk*. Two werewolves, still shifted and furry, panted in the back seat. She glanced at them, dismayed to find both of them watching her intently, and redirected her gaze to the window.

A couple in a sleek, black sedan drove beside them, laughing. Their clasped hands rested on the console.

Diana turned away. Her arm had gone numb with pain. There wasn't a single part of her that didn't want to give up, and it didn't appear that she'd be able to get out of this mess without someone dying. It didn't help that the people dying were likely to be her and her parents either.

Diana glowered. That stupid rug—

"Here." Bart dug in his pocket and pulled out a phone. He tossed it on the console. "Call your daddy. Make sure he's home."

Diana made no move to grab the phone. The wolves behind her growled.

"I can send the pack after your friends," Bart said none too politely. "I can give 'em a call."

She glared at him, but the fact of the matter was she had no clue if Bart would really do it or not. The last thing she wanted to do was for Nobu to get hurt.

Sasha was another story entirely.

Diana picked up the phone with her good hand and winced at the pain zipping into her shoulder. The phone rang once before her father picked up.

"Diana?" Charles's voice was high and not entirely sane sounding. He must've been waiting by his phone since the last time they spoke.

"It's me." Her voice, weak and cracked, made her stomach turn. She sounded so broken...over a man. A stupidly attractive man that had been able to dupe her with ease. How embarrassing.

"Where are you? Do you have it?"

Diana frowned at the phone. Surely Charles could hear her pain. Bart cocked his head and gave her a look. One that said something along the lines of *get on with it.*

Did the wolf know they had Sheturath?

Unsure, she decided to be vague. "If I don't know where you are, I can't very well deliver it."

A lengthy pause. "Same house. Lead Crow and the assembly will be here shortly. Hurry up."

She wanted to be surprised when her father hung up, but she wasn't. Diana dropped the phone on the console. "Keep on this highway. I'll tell you when to exit."

Bart drummed his fingers on the steering wheel like Sasha always did. Her heart cracked a little more. She turned and looked out the window instead, the passing trees a dead, brown blur in her unfocused haze.

"I have questions," Bart said, calm for someone escorting a wounded person and two werewolves on the cusp of bloodlust. He drove the speed limit. Chewed on a toothpick. Paid no mind to the blood all over his face. "If you answer 'em, I'll let you live."

"Who says I want to live?" Diana rolled her head to look at him, unable to fight the grimace as the muscles in her shoulder sent a wave of pain into her neck.

Bart pursed his lips, clearly unimpressed with her manufactured bravado. He pulled the toothpick out of his mouth. "What were you trying to steal at the auction?"

She raised her eyebrows. "A demon-killing knife."

The Alpha turned to look at her, baring teeth. The dried blood around his mouth cracked.

Diana couldn't breathe. The jarring switch in his demeanor brought fear back to the forefront of her mind. The only thing that reassured her was the fact Bart needed her to find Charles.

"We had the money!" Bart slammed a fist on the steering wheel, and she jumped. She doubled over and grabbed her shoulder as a sharp burn lanced through her chest and bicep. "We had the money to buy that knife. Since our boss went MIA, we got the invitation to the auction on his behalf. Everyone in the pack chipped in. We sold our homes. We took out loans. We did *everything* and still couldn't get it."

The muscles in her neck tightened the greener Bart's eyes got. She pushed her back against the seat and practiced steady breaths. If she'd done one thing right, clearly it was keeping their possession of Sheturath a secret. There was no telling what Bart and his wolves would do if they knew Sasha had it with him.

"I sent the money with Joey and gave him explicit instructions to keep his nose clean. All he had to do was get the knife." Bart's too-green eyes flashed.

"It's not my fault that asshole didn't listen," she said under her breath.

A snarl from the back seat reminded Diana of the precarious position she was in. Two angry wolves at her back, and they had been forced to execute their own pack mate because of her. Tensions were high, and Bart had more wolves on speed dial. If she didn't cooperate, Nobu or the murder might get hurt, and none of them deserved to die for her and Sasha's mistakes.

Bart took in a long, slow breath. "No. It isn't." He shook his head, tone softer. "Being bound to a general..." His heavy voice sent her heart right in her throat. "It's tough. You get angry. It makes you so goddamn angry that you ruin everything good you get your hands on. Joey was angry."

Diana sat up a little straighter. She didn't know who the generals were. She remembered Sasha saying his bloodline had been bound to Madame, but given they were running away from the wolves at the time, she hadn't asked him how that happened.

Bart kept his eyes on the road and merged. "When your entire life is controlled by the whims of a demon, it destroys your life. Despite Sokolov killing some of the pack, I understand why he did what he did. Survival. I've done the same."

"You can't make me feel sorry for him." *Or you*, Diana added mentally. She licked her lips and gagged at the taste of dried blood. Considering how she felt, she had to look just as awful. "Sasha said he was bound by a contract...which means he willingly signed his life away."

Bart laughed. A deep, chest-rumbling laugh. "Those of us that work for demons don't willingly do anything."

"That doesn't make a damn bit of sense." Diana glared at the back of the Prius driving in front of them. Even though Sasha betrayed her, she could technically still use his healing magic, but the thought tightened her throat. She didn't want to need him for anything. That and her shoulder was still dislocated, and magic couldn't fix it unless she knew how to pop it back in. "You made the deal."

"The generals need creatures to work for them. The general with the most formidable creatures has the most control of Earth." He smiled bitterly and deigned her with a sidelong glance. "You don't get a say in joining 'em. Not really. They find a weakness, and they exploit it."

Diana thought back to their trip to Pennsylvania and Sasha's face when his mother called him. He'd mentioned his mother in the truck, right before she jumped out.

His weakness.

"The general I was forced to sign a contract with is the scariest thing I've ever seen. I don't know if you've ever seen a cat demon before, but they are horrifying to look at." Bart shivered, but Diana's mind already started drifting to the only cat demon she knew. She'd never seen Natsu in his true form, but the demon had managed to kill the sphinx. Maybe it was best she never saw it. "So when I was given the choice to either sign my pack away or let my wife sign her bloodline away—our *children* away—signing the pack up to spare my children was my choice."

An uncomfortable pull in her stomach kept Diana's mouth closed. Things were starting to come together in a way she didn't much like, and the fact she could do absolutely nothing about the inevitable train wreck to come didn't make things any easier to dwell on.

Bart, as the leader of the pack, had condemned all of them to servitude. If Madame got a hold of Lead Crow, she'd probably do the same thing to the murder. As different as wolves and crows were, the magic binding them together wasn't all that dissimilar. All the crows, including her sister, would be bound to Madame.

"I thought my choice would at least keep everyone alive. But I hate myself for it," Bart said. The wolves whined in the back seat again. She didn't know if they did it for Bart or themselves. "Even though we haven't heard from our boss in over a year, we sit around and wait for him to show up and tear everything apart again."

The anger that simmered in her chest fizzled out as she tried to imagine a life controlled by a demon. Diana used to think any life, demon or no, couldn't be worse than hers. But maybe theirs was.

Bart smiled bitterly at her. Like he could read her mind and see her connecting all the dots. "Did y'all find it?"

Diana blinked. "Find what?"

"Sheturath."

"No." Guilt gnawed on her insides. She glanced down at the bandaged remains of her missing finger. "We didn't find it."

I killed for it.

If Bart didn't believe her, she couldn't tell. He shrugged and turned down the air conditioner. Thank God. Werewolf or not, it was too damn cold for that thing. "We had it all planned out. After we got Sheturath, we were going to kill him. Our boss. Free ourselves. Free everyone that demon bound with a contract. And even though Sokolov ruined that, I still can't blame him for what happened at the auction."

Diana looked to the tops of her thighs, unsure what to say.

Bart cleared his throat before continuing. "The moment Sokolov knew we worked for a general, he could've walked out, you know. Left you there alone."

She expected to feel a spike of rage, but she didn't. "Maybe he should've."

The man actually managed to look sympathetic. "I mean it. He knew we wouldn't draw first blood because it would start a fight between our boss and his. Since our boss is gone right now, Madame could come kill all of us without breaking a sweat...so he knew we wouldn't fight him unless he refused our demands."

Diana concentrated on the steady, tingling pain winding through her left arm. Sasha was a liar. Nothing Bart said would change that.

After catching a glimpse of some signage, she was glad to have a distraction. "Take the next exit."

Bart steered the car with one hand with his other braced against the door and merged into the far right lane. "He fought for you until you wouldn't let him fight anymore."

She clenched her only good fist and scowled. Sure, Sasha had excuses. But that's all they were—excuses. She didn't want to talk about him anymore. "Why are you telling me this? Sasha murdered your pack mates."

"Like I said, I can't really blame him for doing what he did." Bart shrugged. "Living like this...it sucks. And I don't blame you either."

A sharp breath rattled her chest, and she focused on Bart again. "Don't blame me for what?"

"I don't blame you for stealing for your daddy. You didn't have much of a choice." The old wolf rubbed the back of his neck with his free hand, lazily weaving through the cars.

She kept quiet, afraid to interrupt what was clearly his attempt at rationalizing his feelings, both toward her and Sasha. Bart turned on his blinker and drifted toward the green exit sign surrounded by dead cornstalks.

Almost home. Though referring to the run-down old farmhouse her family squatted in as home was being overly generous.

"Your father is worse than the demons," he said suddenly.

Diana stared at the weave of her denim instead of the werewolf. It wasn't until a stretch of silence that she looked up. "Why do you say that?" She noticed the upcoming intersection. "Turn right up here."

"Abusing family the way he does..." Bart shook his head and turned right at a stop sign, both sides of the road now surrounded by damp, yellow foliage. "You don't do what he does to family. You just don't."

Diana fell against the seat and tried her best to ignore the burn in her arm and behind her eyes. Between Sasha, Bart, and her father, she didn't know who she hated more at the moment. But she also didn't hate them either. Once she truly thought about it, the four of them were not that different. For them, the end had justified the means. Now they all had to reap what they'd sown.

"While I don't blame Sokolov for trying to survive, I can blame your daddy for the wrongs he's committed. For the people he's hurt. Swindled." Bart's eyes glowed green once more, and a growl shook the cab of the truck. "I am going to kill your father, Diana. It's his fault that members of my pack are dead. And I will not feel bad about it."

She expected to feel some need to defend her father, anything to remind her she wasn't, in fact, dead in both body and soul. But she felt nothing, and after a moment to think about it, she decided she didn't care that much at all.

Bart didn't talk anymore, and she was glad. Diana continued to hold her arm close, thinking again on Sasha's healing magic. Even if she wanted to use it, all the hope in her had gone, and it didn't look like she'd be getting it back anytime soon.

But as the truck tumbled along the road, Bart's words continued to beat down the walls she'd raised in her brain.

He fought for you until you wouldn't let him fight anymore.

THIRTY-SIX

DIANA

When Bart's truck rolled to a stop in the dirt driveway in front of her house, Diana forced herself to look out the passenger window. The abandoned house her family had squatted in for five years somehow managed to look worse now despite not having changed at all. The roof—still caved in. The windows—shattered. Even though the motels she'd stayed in over the weeks with Sasha and Nobu hadn't been great, they still felt more like home than this. The thought stole her breath.

Bart got out of the truck and opened the back door. The pair of wolves in the back seat hopped out and looked to him for their directives. The yellow-haired wolf seemed to hold the higher rank of the two, but she didn't know enough about how packs worked to be sure.

Diana ran her tongue over her teeth. What did Bart hope to accomplish here? Did he really want his rug back, or did he simply want to remove her father's head from his neck?

"Stay out here. Hide in the brush. The others will come at dark," Bart said to the wolves and motioned to the field across the road, the sun setting behind it. It stretched for miles back toward the highway. In the summer, it was full of corn. Now? All dead. "Listen for me."

The wolf with a burnished bronze coat yipped, and the pair slinked off into the grass.

Bart shut the car doors and meandered over to her side, taking his sweet time to get to the passenger side. With every passing moment, her nerves tightened, and more pain lanced through her arm and shoulder.

Her fingers itched to use some of Sasha's healing magic. He might be a lying, two-faced butthole, but that didn't mean the bond broke. And maybe he didn't mean to hurt her like he did—

Bart opened the door, which made up Diana's mind for her. He motioned to the house with a thrust of his chin. "You live here?"

Diana cradled her arm close and carefully slid from the seat until her feet touched the ground. "Home sweet home."

"It's terrible."

"Hey, I didn't make you come here." Diana took a step forward, a wave of nausea overtaking her along with a jolt of pain traveling from her shoulder through her chest. Her vision blurred, and spots colored her eyes. Bart's firm grip on the bicep of her good arm was all that kept her from a face-plant.

"You're almost there. Keep it together." The unsaid *or I'll split your skull open* was not lost on her.

If she had two working arms to defend herself, she would've told Bart exactly where he could shove his comments, but since she didn't, Diana kept her mouth shut as they made for the entrance. The wooden steps to the front door creaked with each step. Bart, thankfully, took it upon himself to turn the doorknob.

The smell outside had nothing on the inside. Her mother had always tried to make it clean, but there was only so much polishing you could do when you had nothing to work with. Being a crow in this instance made the living situation more bearable. They could, and did, eat roadkill, so the rat carcasses in the walls did little to bother her.

The same could not be said for her werewolf captor and his above-average sense of smell.

Bart slapped a hand over his nose. "No wonder you're okay with dying. If I lived in this shithole, I would be too."

Diana shrugged. "You can leave if you want." She had some more choice words for him, but clamoring from the back room killed any would-be insults before she could utter them.

Her mother and father also managed to look worse than how she left them. Thinner. Dark circles around their eyes. Dull hair. Amelia Van Doren was a wrong day away from the grave, and Charles...well, he appeared borderline manic.

"Who's this?" her father asked and motioned to Bart. His hair still looked ridiculous, swept back in an arc to match the self-important jacket with the high collar. "Who the fuck is this? I told you to kill that Sokolov person."

"I ain't Sokolov." Bart smiled, eyes twinkling.

"W-Werewolf," Charles stammered, taking a step back. Her mother covered her mouth with both hands, eyes wide. "You brought him here? He'll kill us!"

"Just you, old man," Bart corrected, taking another step.

Charles changed his attention to Diana, his jacket whipping around his thighs. "How could you do this? You ungrateful brat."

"What was I supposed to do?" Diana swallowed, somehow strangely detached from the situation unfolding in front of her. "Have you looked at me at all? I'm injured. I've almost died—"

"I know. You keep repeating it like it's supposed to mean something." Charles held out his hands, eyes on Bart. The wolf stopped midstride, like maybe the words hurt him too.

Diana's mouth went bone dry. For her parents to treat her this way in private was painful enough. Acting like this in front of someone else, even someone she didn't like, was a whole other level of pain.

"One life means nothing in the face of hundreds." Her father's voice climbed in volume, shaking against the wooden walls. "Everything we do, Diana, is for the murder. Not out of selfishness. Your selfishness is going to get everyone killed."

Her face grew hot, and she ached to drive her talons into his eyeballs as she had the sphinx. "You're the reason the murder is being hunted by Madame. You're the reason that everyone is going to die!"

"All I'm guilty of is trying to help them." Charles threw up his hands. "We're a dying breed. Our species can't survive against demons or werewolves or whatever else as we are. All we can do is hide, and I was sick of it. I *am* sick of it."

A loud crack shook the room. Diana jumped, letting out a cry when she jostled her arm.

Bart pulled his foot out of the now-broken floor, wood slats splintering through the pier and beam. Unnecessary, but effective. "I hate to interrupt your diatribe, but I'm gonna need my rug back."

"Y-Your what?" her father asked. He licked his chapped lips. "Your *rug?*"

"Yeah. My goddamn rug." Bart stepped forward and jabbed a finger toward him. "You sent her to steal it from me, and I'd like it back."

Charles snorted and adjusted the collar of his jacket. "I sold it."

Diana took a step away from Bart. His fingernails had started to grow into slender points, and she had no interest in being close should the old wolf shift.

Bart's eyes changed from the calm, natural green to the scary kind. "Then I want the money you sold it for and the name of the person who has it."

"I wouldn't dare betray the confidentiality of my customers."

Diana took another step back, heels hitting the baseboard behind her. Bart rolled his head along his shoulders, and his nails continued to grow.

Her father was a hopeless idiot.

The pressure of the air in the room shifted, and Diana tensed. Like the feeling of flying higher into the clouds, her ears popped and cracked. Her lungs squeezed tight, and no matter how hard she tried, she couldn't get enough air.

Damn her bond with Sasha, but she couldn't hold out anymore. Diana firmly gripped her arm and tried to push magic into the twisted muscles with a deep inhale. She needed hope, and she needed a lot of it.

But her hope had disappeared along with Sasha's promises, and no magic came to her aide.

Her ears ached as the pressure increased. Her father fell to his knees, and her mother shortly after. The room had been swallowed by magic, and it wasn't from Bart's impending shift. Only she and Bart were able to remain standing. Bart shot her a look of wide-eyed surprise, like he knew what was coming. She most certainly did. This was a magic she had felt almost all her life, yet never truly been touched by.

The murder.

"They're here." Charles fell onto his hands, propped up like a table. He glanced toward the front door. Shadows moved beneath it.

In times like this, Diana was happy not to be bound by this magic. It was absolutely stifling.

The front door flew open and slammed into the dust-covered wall behind it. Glass stuck in the old window frames clattered to the floor around her feet.

"Charles Van Doren, I hope you spoke the truth." The first person to cross the threshold was a familiar one—Lead Crow. His old, wrinkled face hadn't changed much, but his eyes had faded to more white than gray. The old asshole would die soon.

Diana swallowed as more people followed him: the assembly. One by one, the group filed in, taking their place along the walls with billowing obsidian robes. There were six of them in total. The hand of the murder, the ones entrusted with most of the murder's magic.

Every ounce of air left her lungs when her sister, Olivia, strolled inside.

She hadn't seen Oliva in five years, but she'd grown into a beautiful woman. Raven tresses hung to her shoulders in soft waves and framed a full face with a healthy glow. At least they'd taken care of Olivia in her parent's absence.

If Diana hadn't been screwed over by almost every single person to cross her path, and thus very observant to those that might do her harm, she might've missed her sister's tight jaw and the fact she walked in with the assembly with an identical robe. It appeared her sister had made her own moves to survive, and it didn't look like Olivia would show her or her parents any clemency either despite the calmness in her face.

Lead Crow, by contrast, had turned into a fuming mess. "What's this, Charles?" His face reddened by the second. "You failed to mention that Diana's accomplice was a werewolf!"

Diana froze.

Lead Crow didn't dare walk any closer given Bart's proximity, but she could tell he wanted to so he could snap her neck. He probably regretted allowing her to fly alongside them for so long. For finding her the summer after her eighth birthday.

"If your objective was to show us that we were right to remove you from our ranks, Charles, you've accomplished it." An older woman with hair cropped close to her scalp put her hands on her hips, robes billowing around her ankles.

Bart growled, silencing the room.

"Listen, I give zero fucks about your bird business." Bart held up his hands in surrender, but judging by his teeth and claws, he had no such thought on his mind. "But Van Doren has caused me a lot of problems. Problems that ended with members of my pack dead."

"Charles is no longer a member of our murder for a similar reason." Lead Crow shrugged and held his hands behind his back. "What happens to him or his is no longer our concern or responsibility."

"So I can tear off his head with no repercussions?"

"Precisely. His family too, if it suits you." Lead Crow ignored her mother's gasp. He turned to the members of the assembly. "It's been made clear to me that the only reason Charles invited us here was not to make amends, but to use us to save his own skin."

Her father gaped. "No! That's not true. I'm trying to help you. I've always been trying to help the murder."

"Then where is this fabled blade?" Lead Crow gave a sardonic laugh. "Where is this demon-killer, Sheturath?"

Charles staggered to his feet, no longer overwhelmed by the murder's magic. He motioned to Diana. "She has it."

Diana gripped her arm and wanted to disappear. Anyone that took longer than five seconds to look at her would know she didn't carry the blade. Tight jeans and a tucked-in flannel couldn't hide much.

All the crows in the room watched her with bated breath. Lead Crow raised his eyebrows, jowls jiggling. "You're a liar like your father, aren't you?"

Diana grimaced. She was *not* like Charles. "I had the knife at one point."

Bart growled but mercifully remained still. It didn't stop her heart from skipping though because now the wolf knew she'd lied. Maybe Lead Crow was right. Maybe she was more like her father than she realized.

"Then where is it?" Lead Crow asked.

Teeth grinding together with a scowl, she stared at Lead Crow. "Not here."

He cocked his head to the side. "You won't tell us? Your family?"

She wouldn't lead them to Nobu. Or Sasha, if she were really honest with herself. While he'd hurt her enough to make her question everything, Bart had been right. Sasha could've avoided a lot of trouble if he'd surrendered her easily.

He fought for you until you wouldn't let him fight anymore.

Magic pulsed from her fingers and wrapped her arm in a caress of warmth. She smothered the surprise with a glower.

"Family?" Diana shook her head and winced as the healing magic burned inside her fingers. "You're not my family. You never wanted me."

Silence echoed in the house. No one moved, breathed, nothing. Diana took long, slow breaths and continued to focus on the steady flow of magic into her arm.

This would only end one way, and she needed the pain to subside for at least a brief moment. Anything to help give her the strength to get one good swing at whoever would soon attack.

"I suppose if you truly feel that way, then I've found you guilty of endangering the murder." Lead Crow held up his hand, the light catching the wrinkles along his knobby fingers. Two members of the assembly—males—stepped forward, cloaks billowing around their ankles. "The punishment for such a crime—"

"Come on and get it over with!" Diana slowly lowered her arm to her side and squatted to the ground, wrapping the fingers of her good hand around a sliver of broken glass from the window behind her. She bit back a whine as her dislocated arm hung limp. The cuff of her flannel kept the glass from digging in deep, but the rest of her hurt so bad she wouldn't have felt the pain anyway. "Come on, kill me. You've wanted to for years!"

Her mother stepped forward and moved into her peripheries. "Diana, please—"

"Shut up," Diana seethed. "You let me fall out of our goddamn nest, and you didn't even bother to look for me."

She whipped her head around the room. Lead Crow. Charles. Amelia. The assembly. Her sister. All watching her without an ounce of remorse.

The only one who looked at her with sympathy was Bart, and maybe that shouldn't have been so surprising after their trip. If he thought Charles abused her, his family, then he probably didn't think too highly of anyone else in the room either.

"I hate all of you." Diana held up the glass and pointed at Lead Crow. She pointedly ignored Olivia. The loathing in her sister's eyes was too much to stomach. "Come on. Let's get this over with."

Lead Crow, hand still hanging in the air, sighed. "Very well."

He dropped his hand, and the assembly moved.

THIRTY-SEVEN

SASHA

In astounding contrast to every other moment in his life, Sasha itched to do something. Anything. Fuck plans—his plans in particular.

Yet despite the itch, he remained calm. Detached. If he hoped to help Diana, he had to focus. He had to act as the stalwart agent Madame made him. Anything less wouldn't achieve his ends.

He swallowed. *Their* ends. If Diana would have him.

Sasha turned to appraise his demonic ally. Despite narrowing his catlike eyeballs at the shoddy homes and wet fields, he seemed otherwise unbothered. He also kept forgetting to blink, something odd to see on Nobu's usually expressive face. "Are you certain it will work?"

"Yep," Natsu said.

Without another word, Sasha turned at a stop sign and continued to drive toward Diana's home. Thankfully, he'd asked in advance where her father had been hiding out. Otherwise it would've taken more time than he would've liked to find her. Time that might've killed her.

She might still die anyway.

Sasha gritted his teeth and focused on the road.

After seeing the town the Van Dorens had chosen to hide in, their successful evasion from Madame for years made more sense. There wasn't much there except dead crops, old homes, and a surplus of cows. Much to his consternation, the way in and out seemed to comprise a single road traveling in either direction, which left little room for error during an escape.

Sasha started to think on their escape and how to accomplish it when things at the house inevitably soured. What variables were there to consider? The constant in the equation was the single road. If they survived Madame, the werewolves, and, presumably, the murder, the odds of needing to escape quickly and efficiently were high. Especially if his plan didn't work, and he had to fight all of them.

His gaze darted along the fields as they drove, calculating. It was winter, so it was doubtful any of the farmers would take their plows and tractors out onto the road for any reason. However, there had been an inordinate number of animals, some of which hadn't been put in pens. He'd almost hit a herd of goats coming around a particularly sharp corner—

"Chill out."

Sasha turned his head and scowled at the smirking Natsu. "No."

He veered right at a single traffic light slung on a low-hanging wire. The road, lined with dilapidated homes and rusted cars, appeared to be a dead end.

"Here." Natsu motioned to a street on the right. "I see it."

Against everything his experience taught him about trusting demons, Sasha followed Natsu's instructions.

The street had homes on one side and acres upon acres of farmland on the other. The houses weren't in much better shape than the other ones he'd seen, although one did have a barn and a large tractor. He kept driving until a familiar truck caught his eye.

"Got it." Sasha pressed the brake and evaluated the escape route. It would make more sense to turn the truck around and face the way they came.

Bart's truck looked exactly as it had at the airport with the notable exception of missing the wolves inside and Diana.

The sun, on its way down, hung just above the horizon and licked the treetops. At dark, Sasha knew more wolves would appear. Running in the open during daylight hours would be difficult to do without being seen or shot, especially in rural Texas. No such limitations would exist at night.

"Park farther down," Natsu said, gaze on the brush lining the other side of the road. "I bet there are wolves in that grass."

"Why?"

"Bartholomew Armistead Evans has been bound to me for a long time. I know how he operates." Natsu shrugged, like it was the most natural thing in the world to say. "If Bartholomew is in that house, his wolves aren't far behind. I'd rather take care of them now."

Sasha's grip on the steering wheel tightened. "Since you're no longer monitoring those you bound by contract, why don't you set Bart adrift?"

"Because if he's mine, no one else can force Bartholomew and his pack into a deal." Natsu met his gaze, and for the first time since knowing him, Sasha didn't feel completely repulsed. "I feel that being bound to me and not having to work might be better than the alternative."

"Hm." Sasha slowed to a stop two houses past Bart's vehicle. "You accused me of using a broad brush once."

Natsu raised his eyebrows and pinned him with elliptical pupils. "I did."

Sasha grabbed the handle of the door and pushed it open. "Perhaps you were right."

His skin had long since acclimated to the chill thanks to the truck's shattered window, but the quiet of the outside somehow managed to cool his blood anyway. He reached inside his jacket and drew the Glock from his right side. He'd had some silver rounds left in the trunk of the car he'd parked at the airport, but not many. Better than nothing.

"Come on out." Natsu held out his arms to the brush once outside the truck. "I know you're here."

The grass moved in the wind, slowly waving. The only sound to hit his ears was the roar of an old truck driving nearby and gentle swish of the reeds.

"There's two of you here. I feel your souls." Natsu continued toward the grass and held his hands up defensively. While Sasha wasn't sure what his end game was, he did know the demon wouldn't risk Nobu. Whatever he had planned, Natsu must be sure he'd win.

The crunch of grass brought his Glock up.

It was entirely unnecessary.

Natsu dipped low and punched forward into the air as a werewolf leapt toward him from the ocean of swaying stalks. His fist connected with the wolf's chest, and a long whine squeezed from its throat.

Then it fell to the ground in a lifeless mass.

"Another one is coming. They won't recognize me in this form. Once I summon Bartholomew, they'll stop." Natsu held out his hand and crouched by the wolf. He'd never put much thought into what exactly happened after Alphas signed contracts with the generals. But Sasha supposed what Natsu said made sense. The contract would only bind Bart to him. The pack magic would ensure the others listened...as long as Bart was there to make them. "Knife."

Sasha dug in the holster on his waist and handed Natsu his tactical knife, deciding to keep Sheturath close.

"The other wolf is getting closer. More are approaching, thirteen actually, but they'll likely be a few minutes," Natsu said over his shoulder.

Sasha kept his gaze on the sea of grass. "Why didn't you warn us of the wolves in the hangar when we landed if you can feel them?"

Natsu didn't lose focus. He placed the tip of the blade against the wolf's throat, and with one clean swipe, blood spilled upon the ground. The wolf would heal from it eventually, but he'd be in a lot of pain for a while.

"When I am dormant inside the boy, I truly give him full control of his body. Giving him control means I am reduced to nothing more than a voice inside his head and a battery to keep his blood pumping." Natsu wiped the blood on his knife along his thigh and handed it back before sticking his hand in the warm blood pouring from the wolf's throat. "The boy can't be poisoned. He's marginally stronger and doesn't need sleep. But most of the benefit of carrying me is lost when I surrender control."

Despite years of living with demons, he'd never heard of this before. Perhaps demons didn't like to admit it, or maybe demons, inherently selfish beings, never let the hosts have their bodies back, so it didn't ultimately matter.

Natsu must find some meaning in his relationship with Nobu.

Another wolf poked its head from the grass and whined at the sight of its wounded comrade. After its eyes found Natsu, it froze.

Sasha squeezed the grip of his Glock and forced his mind to focus instead on the bits of the future that presented themselves. In some instances, the rest of the wolves arrived and ate him. In others, Madame got there first and ripped his heart from his chest. There were too many variables to get an accurate read on the future as it stood.

"He's going to feel that later." Natsu pulled his hand from the wolf's blood and slapped it against the side of the truck below the window. He swept his hand up in an arc to make a dome until the blood ran out. He stooped back over to the seemingly dead wolf to get some more along his fingers. "I haven't done this in a long while, Sokolov."

"I somehow doubt it puts you out too terribly."

Natsu smirked. "Broad brush, remember?"

The blood had been painted roughly into a circle. Inside, there were several marks that appeared random to the mind's eye, but ones Sasha knew to be anything but: a seal. Like the witches in Pennsylvania.

Natsu muttered something under his breath and slapped his hand on the door, right in the center of the seal. Dark light billowed from Natsu's palm into the lines of blood, rippling through it like water filling a trough. Once the seal pulsed with obsidian light, the loud thrum of magic vibrated against the metal of the truck and into the dirt.

The birds sitting along the power lines took to the air, flying in a coordinated swarm in the opposite direction.

The wolf on the opposite end of Sasha's Glock knelt and lay prone against the ground, resting its muzzle on top of its paws. Entirely complacent. After a measured breath, he dropped his weapon to his side.

"Bartholomew Armistead Evans!" Natsu announced to the sky. "I command you to come forth."

At first, nothing changed. Crickets chirped in the grass. The cowed wolf kept its eyes averted and nose down.

Then the ground moved.

The dirt, loose without the help of healthy roots, easily turned, swirling and funneling in a spiral, digging deep into the earth. Another wolf pressed through the brush, teeth bared. Then another followed. The sun was setting, and the wolves were ready. But whatever magic Natsu controlled, they must have recognized now that he summoned Bart.

Natsu kept his hand on the seal as the ground continued to contort under his magic. "If you wolves don't want to die, I suggest waiting on your Alpha."

One by one, the wolves appeared from the thicket and then paused at the sight of Natsu and his seal. From the ground, a head emerged. Then a torso. Then legs.

Bart.

Natsu had summoned him through the *ground*.

"Bartholomew Evans, I am going to need your cooperation." Natsu's gravelly voice echoed in the field. The wolves, frozen in fear, whined.

The Alpha, hands featuring elongated claws, shook at his sides. His teeth and face had already started to shift, and it didn't seem the man was terribly happy to see them.

"I knew there was something wrong with you at the airport," Bart growled and looked to the ground, eyes settling on the bleeding werewolf a few feet away. The words came out thick, like he'd already shifted so much that speaking was a chore. "I smelled something evil."

"As I'm about to make you an offer you can't refuse, I'd recommend keeping any unnecessary comments to yourself." Natsu smiled—all teeth.

"You look different from last time."

"Do you like my makeover?" Natsu waved his hand around, palm still coated in the wolf's blood. "I look much less scary in this body, I think."

Bart ignored Natsu and focused his green eyes on Sasha. "Diana is about to die. Her murder cast judgment. You summoned me out right before the fighting started."

Sasha closed his eyes and pulled in a steady stream of air, waiting for visions of Diana.

When they came, Sasha knew Bart was telling the truth.

Bart's face settled to something more human, and his nails began to recede. "What the hell do you want, Natsu? You disappeared for over a year, and now you summon me out of a fight right when I'm about to—"

"Kill Van Doren, I know." Natsu grinned when Bart's face paled. "Bartholomew Evans, I'm going to need you and your pack mates to forget Charles Van Doren and his family, along with any wrongs he might've inflicted on you and yours."

Bart snarled. His nails started to lengthen once more. He fought hard, but the wolf in him wanted out. "Why the hell would I do that?"

"Because I'm a going to give you a choice, Bartholomew Evans, and I'll only give you this choice if you scamper on home."

The wolf stilled. "What choice?"

Natsu turned to him and motioned to the house. "Go. I'll deal with these wolves and keep them out of the house. Save the crow, please. The kid's whining will be absolutely insufferable if she dies."

Since the werewolf situation was under control, Sasha removed his Sig from his other side and ran.

Sasha darted through the grass and passed a condemned house with a yard full of car parts and trash, but he only had eyes for Diana's home. He broke into the next yard and angled toward the partially collapsed porch, only casting the briefest of glances to his future before throwing open the front door.

He'd always kept a tight leash on his emotions. They'd done nothing but get him into trouble in his youth, and as his life became more dangerous with jobs for Madame, the only thing they were good for was impairing his judgment. However, seeing Diana squirm beneath the form of a man with his hands wrapped around her neck broke the dam he'd built, and the parts of him that longed to retreat to the comfort of reason vanished.

In the time it took for him to take a breath, Sasha raised his Glock and pulled the trigger.

THIRTY-EIGHT

DIANA

Even as a shower of blood dropped onto her face like summer rain, Diana couldn't find it in her to care about anything but the fire snaking down her throat.

She rolled onto her side and heaved a breath. Then another and another. She dropped the glass she'd been gripping, and blood leaked from the gashes it left behind.

Her blurred vision focused, first on the splintered floor and then on the people standing beyond. Her mother. Father. Lead Crow. The assembly. Olivia.

All of them, every single one of them, had been content to see her die. She expected it from most of them, but not Olivia. And the realization that her sister hadn't cared enough to even cry about Lead Crow's judgment hurt worse than her any physical injury could ever hope to.

It had happened so fast. Both of the males had descended upon her in a merciless sweep. She'd never seen crow shifters move that quick in their human form, but they had. Using Sasha's magic had given her the edge to stab one in the jugular with the broken glass, but she hadn't been fast enough to escape the wrath of the second.

"Diana."

She fixated on the voice she never thought she'd hear again. Heart pounding in her ears, she tracked the movement of the person walking in front of her and scanned up toward their face: Sasha.

He knelt down, setting one of his guns on the floor, and avoided her startled gaze to inspect her neck. He lightly touched her skin, and warmth rolled down her back as he pressed magic into her bruises. Diana focused on his hand moving along her flesh, healing as he passed over her carotid. It had been close. Much too close.

He continued pressing healing magic into her neck and winced. His other hand kept a firm grip on his other gun despite the pain of healing. "Are you all right?"

She shook her head and tried to ignore the lingering pain of the crow shifter's hand on her neck. While Sasha had lied to her, it would also be a lie to say she didn't feel relief at seeing him. She'd almost been killed, and no one else had moved to stop the man trying to squeeze the life from her throat. Just Sasha.

"Y-You killed him," a man of the assembly cried out, face pallid. "You killed him!"

"I did." Sasha kept his eyes on her and brushed through the hair stuck in the blood on her face. Softly. Carefully. If he felt any remorse over what he'd done to the crow shifter, no one would be able to tell by looking at him. Completely unrepentant.

He only had eyes for her, and for the first time, Diana noticed.

"How dare you!" The woman with an almost shaved head stepped forward, now with a blade in hand.

With the briefest turn of his head, Sasha lifted his weapon and pulled the trigger. The woman fell to the floor with a bullet hole in the center of her brow, and her knife clattered to the ground. Finished healing her face, Sasha brushed Diana's cheek with his thumb.

Her eyes brimmed with tears, but she didn't know why.

"I need you to sit up." Sasha moved his free hand to the small of her back. Diana clutched her dislocated arm as Sasha guided her up, the pain returning to her shoulder in spectacular form. He still hadn't looked away despite several threats lingering on the perimeter. Not that anyone dared to move.

Sasha leaned forward and placed his mouth beside her ear. "I am so sorry."

His breath, hot on the shell of her ear, sent a shiver down her back. She took all of him in, tracing his strong jaw and lower lip. His golden eyes wreathed in long lashes. Sasha brought a healing hand to the slope of her neck while his other continued to hold the room hostage with his gun. Numbness coated the nerves in her shoulder and coaxed her muscles to relax.

"Where's Nobu?" she asked, mouth dry.

Sasha searched her face for something, but she was unsure what. He grimaced again but kept pressing magic into her shoulder regardless. "Natsu is in control. He's taking care of the werewolves. No harm will come to the boy."

Diana licked her lips and looked where Bart had once stood, being greeted with a hole and splintered floorboards. She hadn't been given much time to process what happened to Bart. As the crows descended upon her, he'd been swallowed by a dense, black fog and yanked right into the ground.

"Who are you, and what are you doing here?" Lead Crow hadn't liked the interruption, and she figured he certainly didn't like that three members of the assembly had been killed instead of her. "You killed my colleagues."

"My name is Sasha Sokolov, and I am here for Diana." Sasha wrapped an arm under hers and guided her to her feet. Once she was standing, he kept a hand on her waist and held her firm against his side. Her heart swelled. "As for the death of your colleagues, I don't care."

A breath got stuck in her chest as she watched Lead Crow. The old ass had the murder's magic, sure, but how useful was that, really? He could teleport the murder away from danger should the need arise, but crows had never been intimidating physically. In her experience, the only things they killed were each other.

Wait—Lead Crow could teleport. Since she was technically the Lead Crow of her and Sasha's murder, could she do the same?

"If you move again, I will know, and I will kill you," Sasha announced and turned his back to the rest of the people in the house. He bent down, picked up the gun he left behind on the floor, and slipped it back into his holster. Apparently, he was confident that he could get them out of the house with only one weapon drawn.

No one said a word in response, but she had a feeling it had more to do with his remaining gun and eerie ability to shoot accurately without warning than being polite.

She could only imagine how she looked. Between busting her nose and being strangled, she knew it was bad. Yet the way Sasha watched her then, Diana wouldn't know it.

"I know a simple apology does not begin to make up for what I have done to you, but I hope it gives me a chance to fix it." He gripped the bicep of her dislocated arm, gaze flickering between it and her face. The muscles, still numb under the power of his magic, didn't feel his touch. "I want to fix it."

Her heart thundered in her chest as they stared at each other.

"Take a deep breath." Sasha's grip on her arm tightened.

She only started to inhale when he moved. After an excruciating pull and push, a wave of white pain flashed behind her eyelids. Diana screamed and fell forward into Sasha's chest. But instead of pulling away, she stayed there, hypnotized by the quickening beat of his heart and the fading pain in her shoulder being swallowed by his magic again.

"How are you using so much of your magic?" she asked.

Sasha snorted. "I'm borrowing some of yours. You don't feel it?"

"No," she spoke into his chest. If she'd told him about their bond in the first place, he could've been a more proficient healer. "But I feel terrible."

Loathe to break contact with him, Diana rolled her head against his chest and spared a glance to the rest of the room. The crows all stood in a silent stupor, as if they either couldn't believe the two of them defied the murder, or their lack of fear. Maybe both.

Without another word, he reached inside his jacket, and she rocked back on her heels. What would he do now? Maybe he'd kill the rest of the crows. Oddly enough, the thought didn't put her out too badly.

Instead, he pulled out a very familiar knife he'd secured to his holster. The metal of the blade glistened in the light of the setting sun streaming through the broken windowpanes, reminding her just how sharp and dangerous it was.

"You have three choices on what to do next, and you'll have to decide quickly." Sasha slipped the knife against her bloodied palm and pushed in a bit of healing magic into her skin as he did.

He was giving it to her? The knife was his freedom!

"Is that it?" Her father's voice broke through the quiet. "Is that Sheturath?"

Diana tightened her grip on the blade, still overcome with something she couldn't pin down. Maybe Sasha hadn't meant to hurt her at all. "Yes."

Her father took a few steps forward, hands outstretched. Even Lead Crow leaned closer, eyes sparkling.

Wearing a look of intense hope, her father moved closer. "Give it to me."

Sasha raised his gun once more, and the room tensed.

Diana clenched her jaw. "And why would I do that?"

"Because we're your family," Charles ground out.

Diana scoffed. "You're not my family."

"And he is?" Charles shouted, face red. He jabbed a finger at Sasha. "He is not crow."

"Yet he somehow remains my murder." Diana squeezed Sheturath and rubbed the bone handle with her thumb. A few other crows in the room gasped. "Can I ask you something?"

Her father said nothing. Not that she expected him to have anything worthwhile to say anyway.

"Earlier I accused you of not coming back for me when I fell from the nest." Diana looked between her parents. "And you didn't argue."

Charles kept his eyes on Sheturath. "That's hardly a question."

"Was I right?"

When her parents said nothing, Diana shook her head, disappointed but not surprised.

Sasha had said she had a choice with three options. The first choice she could take, presumably, was to hand over Sheturath to the murder, which she would not do. Not anymore.

What were her other choices?

She swallowed and looked up at Sasha, hoping to find her answer. He'd said he needed both her father and Sheturath to break his contract with Madame, yet he gave that chance away.

For her.

"Is Madame coming?" she asked, hands trembling as she stared at Sheturath.

"Yes." Sasha brushed a hand against her cheek and stole her attention from the blade. "So if you want to leave here with Sheturath, you must do it now."

THIRTY-NINE

SASHA

Sᴀsʜᴀ ʙᴇʜᴇʟᴅ Dɪᴀɴᴀ ᴛʜᴇʀᴇ, ʜᴀɴᴅ ɴᴇsᴛʟᴇᴅ ᴀɢᴀɪɴsᴛ ᴛʜᴇ sɪᴅᴇ of her face. She stared at him, mouth hanging open. The crows didn't dare move, and while he wouldn't earn his freedom without Sheturath, there was a smug satisfaction creeping inside his skull in turning the crows over. After what they'd done to Diana, a lifetime of servitude to Madame seemed appropriate.

"Why?" Diana glanced down at Sheturath. "Why would you do this?"

He smiled bitterly. "I'd hoped that was obvious."

"But this is your freedom!" She lifted the blade up a bit, eyes wide.

"I know." Sasha dropped his hand and motioned to the door. "Run. I will likely be tasked with tracking you down, but you can rest assured I will never catch you."

"But—"

"A life bound to my fruitless pursuit is better than living in fear, Diana." He put a hand on her lower back. "Please."

"No." Diana scowled. "A life living close enough to feel you but never getting to have you...that is not better."

Cold crept onto his skin. Madame's hideous sneer flashed in his mind, and his heart rate escalated. Diana would lose her chance. "You need—"

"I'm staying." Her voice wavered, and she looked to the door. "And we're going to free you."

Sasha's heart stuttered. Why, oh *why*, had he thought Diana would go along with his plans this time?

Diana stepped closer to him as dread swallowed the room, filled with Madame's magic. She kept hold of Sheturath and held the blade behind them, gaze tacked onto the door.

"You brought her here?" the oldest crow shifter in black robes bellowed. While he couldn't be sure, he'd bet that was Lead Crow. He motioned to the three remaining crows with him. "Come. We must go—"

"Perfectly executed, Sokolov." Madame's voice came out in a tight rasp as she crossed the threshold. She had on a different fur coat this time: mink. Black heels lightly tapped the floor as she stepped around the massive hole in the center of the living area. Her unfeeling eyes met his. "You were my finest achievement. Such a reliable servant."

The crow shifters froze and watched Lead Crow for instruction. He didn't know much about crow shifters, but Diana had mentioned that Lead Crow could use the murder's collective magic. If he were the betting sort, he'd guess that the abrupt end of three crows took a lot of magic from the old man's reserves. As deep as his connection with Diana was, he couldn't imagine losing three of those relationships all at once.

Sasha holstered his Glock. Diana's parents and the remaining members of the murder had frozen. Their eyes, wide and afraid, were tacked to the front door.

Madame adjusted her coat and pinned him with a cold stare. "Letting you go will likely be my greatest mistake."

Sasha willed his apprehension away from his face. "Yet you must."

Madame turned her attention to Diana. A snake. That's what Madame always reminded him of. A snake poised to attack, still and measured. Coiled and tense. Her hair had even been done up in tight pin curls.

"Indeed." Madame didn't move. Didn't blink. She turned from Diana. "I must."

The rest of the room had gone quiet. Charles Van Doren had taken a couple of steps back, mouth agape. Diana's mother didn't even bother to move away. Resigned. If they'd treated Diana with even the smallest amount of respect, he might feel sorry for them. Since they hadn't, he quite hoped Madame would snap their necks and drain them of their blood.

Diana likely wouldn't approve of his thoughts.

"However." Madame cocked her head over to look at Charles, and her neck cracked to an unnatural angle. Diana jumped beside him. "I have business to take care of before I sign anything."

The woman slinked over to Charles, ignoring the other shifters entirely. "Charles Van Doren."

Charles cleared his throat. "Madame."

"I paid you substantially for information regarding a werewolf pack I believed to be hiding out in Alabama." Madame ran her tongue over her fangs. "Would you like to know what I found in Alabama?"

All the color left Charles's face. His lip quivered. "The information I gave you was accurate."

"It was." Madame leaned forward. The smooth skin of her human visage started to peel away from her forehead like paper being eaten by a flame. "It was accurate. Except the wolves also paid you to warn them I was coming. And they left."

Charles swallowed, hands shaking at his sides.

Madame grinned and traced the side of the man's face with a red fingernail. The skin along her cheek sloughed off and revealed the gray leather of her true form beneath. "I caught them. They ratted you out to save their own skins."

The demon looked at the oldest crow shifter. Lead Crow pushed his shoulders back and held his chin high.

"You made a wise choice abandoning this one." Madame's skin

continued to fall from her face and hands. No one dared look at it collecting around her stilettos. "He's a liability of the worst sort."

Lead Crow said nothing.

"I'd recommend not moving an inch, crows. There is room for us to negotiate. Although, since you are all unrepentant cowards, I imagine you'd have stood there pissing yourselves regardless." Madame turned around farther and looked at Diana again. "Is that your daughter, Charles?"

"Diana helped make this possible." Sasha chose his words purposefully, not giving Charles an opportunity to answer.

Madame tossed back her head and laughed. "Your own family betrayed you? Oh, this is a beautiful day."

The demon cupped Charles's chin in her hand and held it firm, digging her nails into the skin along his jaw. Blood trickled from tiny cuts and ran alongside his carotid in a brilliant river. "I've waited a long time for this moment."

"M-Madame—"

"Shut your fucking mouth." Madame leaned in, mouth close to Charles's ear. "You'll ruin my moment with your words. You always have so many words."

She pulled back a little and tipped his chin up with her fingertips. "All you do is talk and talk...and lie."

"I don't—"

"Lie?" Madame reached forward and wrapped Charles's neck in the palm of her hand. A choked gasp cracked out of his mouth. He grabbed Madame's wrist, but the demon didn't budge, no matter how hard he yanked. "I've never met anyone with balls big enough to lie to me. Me! I am a general! I've commanded legions in Hell, and you lie right to my fucking face."

She squeezed tighter. Madame held him up in the air, expending little effort even as he bucked in her grip.

"You lied to a general of Hell. You made a fool of me." The last remaining bit of skin fell to the floor with a slap, leaving nothing but the worn, wrinkled gray flesh of an exiled demon in a fur coat. "And I don't like that."

Then Madame squeezed too hard and pierced Charles's neck with her nails.

Diana gasped as blood bubbled from the gashes on her father's neck, still holding Sheturath behind her back. Diana's mother, white as the moon's light, collapsed to her knees. A wail tore from her throat and shook the inside of the house like wind in a storm.

Sasha wrapped a hand around Diana's waist. Light. Comforting. He longed to properly hold her in his arms. To crush her to him and shield her eyes and whisper in her ear that she would heal from this. That he would be there if she needed him, and he would never let harm come to her again.

But too many uncertainties lie ahead. He couldn't make those sorts of promises when the future changed in seconds. When he saw her dead one minute and him the next, left to rot in a crumbling home to be torn apart by time and vultures and wild dogs.

So since Sasha could make no promises, he dropped his hand, allowing his fingers skim across her back before letting his hand fall to his side.

"Where are your lies now, Charles Van Doren?" Madame's grip on his throat increased. More blood ran from the gashes beneath the demon's nails. "Can't think of any?"

Blood bubbled from Charles's mouth and leaked from between his lips like a brilliant crimson waterfall. "P-Please—"

Madame snorted. "Please? If you insist."

The demon squeezed one last time.

In a matter of moments, half of Charles's throat had been summarily crushed beneath Madame's fingers. The skin and muscle and sinew, indistinguishable from each other beneath the sopping wet red, separated from his spine as Madame held him aloft with it tucked in her shaking fist. Blood ran down the top of her hand, to her wrist, and down her forearm, disappearing beneath the sleeve of her coat.

Diana turned into Sasha as blood splattered the floor.

Laughter tore from Madame's throat. A high-pitched cackle that scraped the exposed rafters above. She let Charles slide from her fingers and fall to her feet, spraying the front of her coat with red as she licked the blood from her fingers.

The rest of the house watched in silence.

FORTY

DIANA

Diana had loved her father once. But that had been before he'd abandoned her and dismantled her self-worth. After that, she'd tolerated him in hopes of getting what she wanted simply because she had nothing else. No one else. But now...

She swallowed and forced her gaze to the thing she'd been avoiding. Charles—bloody and dead. The very thing that got him in trouble was what killed him. So many lies came out of that throat.

Broken promises. Cons. Commands.

Goose bumps rolled along her arms as she took him in. His throat, a mangled mess of crushed flesh, reminded her exactly who she was dealing with. Madame lapped up the blood on her palm and cackled over her father's corpse.

Diana looked up at Sasha, surprised to find him staring at her too.

It hit her suddenly that Sasha had grown up like this. He'd grown up with Madame, watching as she ripped people to pieces and drank their remains. He'd lived under her demonic thumb for over twenty years, and he suffered that for the mother he couldn't make himself face out of shame.

Her throat swelled at the thought. Tiny, preteen Sasha holding a gun for the first time. Teenage Sasha standing over his first kill.

The hand holding Sheturath shook. Sasha's life had been stolen from him, and her only choice was to hand the blade over to the demon that had done it.

Madame swung her attention over to Amelia. Her mother, hunkered in a sobbing mass, had her face pressed against the floor. Dirt and grime had collected in the trails left behind by her tears, but even as she watched her sob, Diana couldn't find it in herself to feel pity.

"You must be Charles's wife." Madame snorted. "Sorry. I meant widow."

Amelia snarled. "You miserable bitch!"

"Read the room, my dear." The demon wiped her bloody hands along her mink coat. "I think it says something when your own children won't come to your defense."

Diana licked her lips and glanced at Olivia slumped against the wall, hand pressed to her mouth. How Madame knew about her sister was as much a mystery to her as what would happen next.

"However, you were not the one who swindled me." Madame held out a hand. "Sokolov—gun."

He looked to Diana, like he silently needed permission to hand it over. She flickered her gaze over to Madame and urged him to comply.

She wouldn't sacrifice for her parents. Not anymore.

Sasha reached into his jacket and pulled a gun from his holster. Madame strode over and swiped the weapon, leaving a smear of her father's blood along the back of Sasha's hand.

"You can either sign a contract to work for me, or you can remove yourself from the land of the living." Madame held out the gun by the barrel to her mother.

Amelia wiped her face with her hands and smeared dirt along her cheeks. Emotions unreadable, she sat on the back of her calves and stared at the gun a moment before taking it from Madame. Diana's heart beat inside her ears as she watched her mother marvel at the gun.

What would she choose? Like her father, Amelia Van Doren had always been a coward.

Amelia gripped the gun with two hands and fired.

Diana jumped at the deafening pop. Having been shot before, she knew with absolute certainty that getting hit with a bullet elicited some sort of physical response. Madame showed none.

One of the bullets tore through her torso and hit a member of the assembly, who clutched his bicep and cried out in agony.

It was unsettling to see Madame stand firm as bullets entered and exited her chest as her mother unloaded a magazine into it. The demon didn't flinch. Didn't blink.

Click. Click. Amelia stared at Madame, mouth agape. The gun hung limp in her hands a moment before sliding from her fingers and clattering to the ground. "Go to Hell!"

"I've been to Hell, Amelia Van Doren. I was born there. Bathed in its fires and rolled in the embers." Madame glanced down to her chest riddled with holes. "Did you truly think lead would be enough to stop me?"

"I will never work for you," Amelia bit out.

It was the bravest thing her mother had ever done.

Madame shrugged and spared a moment to primp her hair. Blood stained her fingertips. "Very well, Amelia Van Doren. Tell the Devil I said hello."

The demon moved fast—faster than even Jacques—and kicked her mother in the chest. Amelia slammed into the ground, and the back of her head smacked the floor with a sickening crack.

Madame walked over and pressed a heel to her mother's chest. "You've given my body several holes. I'd like to return the favor."

She held out a hand, and the nails along each of her fingers inched forward, growing into long, slender knives. Then Madame struck her mother like a snake, running her through with all five of them.

A scream pierced the heavy silence that had coated the abandoned house. Amelia squirmed against Madame's nails that sank into her skin like they would damp earth, the living blades sliding into her chest with ease until they hit the floor beneath her mother's back.

Diana looked away. The copper tang of blood and so much death collected on the back of her tongue.

Her parents were miserable crows. They only cared for themselves. Never her. They only cared what she could do for them. But that didn't mean she wanted to watch them get butchered.

"Sasha," she whispered, keeping her gaze tacked to the floor. "I can't do it."

She didn't delve into details, but she knew that Sasha would understand what she really meant. What she really couldn't find it in her to do.

She could not—would not—give Sheturath to Madame.

"Then don't." His voice came over her in a wave, and the wave brought calm. He might not know her plan, but whatever the plan was, he apparently trusted her to make it.

Diana rubbed the handle of Sheturath with her thumb and felt along the pores and ridges in the bone. Sasha had watched this sort of shit almost his entire life. Hell, he'd *done* this sort of shit almost his entire life. Madame was a monster.

Her mind drifted to Natsu. How could he be anything like this vile creature? Natsu gave up everything to save Nobu's life, and Madame was killing them for fun.

Diana inhaled. Exhaled.

Her mother had stopped screaming.

The only sounds left in the shack were of the crow shifter sobbing into his robe as he clutched his bleeding arm. None of the others moved to help him.

"Now that the pests have been dealt with, I can take care of our business, Sokolov." Madame walked over to them and licked Amelia's blood off her fingers. "Give me the blade."

"Not until I get a signature," Sasha said, voice firm.

Madame chuckled. Her skin started to grow back and creep up her jaw like a fungus. "Always so by the letter."

The demon reached into her coat and pulled out a rolled-up swatch of something. Leather? Diana's eyebrows knit together, and Madame unrolled it, revealing a block of words in old, sweeping calligraphy.

"Found yourself a girlfriend?" Madame asked, voice a little too sweet considering. Every muscle in Diana's back tightened.

"Perhaps." Sasha appeared to be completely unbothered by Madame's line of questioning. Diana knew better. Sasha was always, always thinking.

Madame smiled, all fang. "How delightful. Someone to enjoy your retirement with."

"Indeed." Sasha pulled his knife out of the holster beneath his jacket and held it out to Madame. "Your signature, please."

The demon took the blade and handed him the hide. "Is there any way I can convince you to remain in my employ?"

"No."

Madame snorted and sliced along her palm. Dark blood, almost black, pooled along her new skin. "That's fine. I'm about to sign the crows up. They won't be as useful, but I can certainly use them to spy on my...former colleagues."

Madame pressed a finger in the blood on her palm and signed along the dotted line on the bottom of the hide. When she lifted her finger, fire took the place of her name, burning along the lines left by her blood. The fire licked away at the leather, and suddenly the contract was a ball of fire in her hand.

Sasha didn't move. Didn't breathe.

Ash fell from Madame's hand and drifted to the floor. She turned her hand over, revealing her soot-covered palm mixed with bubbling blood. "Now, I'll be needing that knife."

FORTY-ONE

SASHA

Sasha had thought about the moment he'd be free from Madame every day since signing that damned contract. How would it feel to sever one's soul from a former general of Hell? He'd never known anyone to succeed, and the moments he'd dared to hope left him feeling so utterly helpless that he figured wasting time on such thoughts was foolish.

All he felt was calm. Quiet and ethereal calm.

"Sheturath. Give it to me." Madame's eyes bored into him. Red, scalding irises focused on him intently, and he wondered what she might be thinking. Did she see his loathing?

Sasha kept his gaze on Madame's extended hand. He'd left the fate of Sheturath to Diana. After her parents were summarily murdered, he had a feeling she'd never hand over the blade to Madame. While the more difficult path, he could sympathize with her.

Which meant the only way out of this house was to fight Madame, an exiled general of Hell with thousands of years of fighting experience and a fondness for violence.

He drummed his fingers along the sides of his thighs and fell into a swath of the future. His stomach clenched at the image of Madame's hand wrapped around his throat, fingers digging into it much like she had done to Charles.

Sasha didn't allow himself to watch Diana die. Their course of action was clear.

"Sokolov." Madame wiggled her fingers. "Surely you weren't stupid enough to come here without Sheturath? I've taught you better than that."

He shook his head but kept watching the future change in his mind's eye. Madame was unquestionably stronger than both of them. She was also uninhibited by emotion, which was almost more deadly. Madame had spent more time with him than his own mother, which meant she knew him. Taught him. Made him. Nothing he could do would surprise the general.

Diana was another matter entirely. The demon had no idea what the woman could do, and frankly, neither did he. Planning for Diana had proved to be a hopeless endeavor.

"Sheturath is here." Sasha forced his mind to let go of control. Trust her. *Trust her, Sasha.* He had given the blade to Diana. He had allowed her to make the choice. If he was right and her decision landed them in a brawl with Madame, he would fight until his last breath. "Diana has it."

He focused on settling his heart rate. If Diana chose to strike Madame instead of handing the blade over, then the element of surprise would be the only thing to save them. If they dragged out the fight, then they would die. Killing Madame quickly would be their only shot.

"Hand it over, Van Doren." Madame grinned. "Although, Sokolov, I feel I must warn you considering who her father is. You know that saying about apples and trees? I've been alive for a long time. That tends to be true."

Diana stiffened beside him as Madame held out her hand, waiting on the blade. The woman was a thief. A sneak. A wraith in the dark. There was no way of knowing how she'd respond to Madame now, but she was also stubborn. Clever.

He shouldn't have been surprised when Diana's fear morphed into a scowl. She spat on the ground. "Get fucked."

Diana jerked Sheturath out from behind her back and swung the blade through the air left to right. Madame, faster than any other being he knew, weaved away and swiped toward her face. Using what he imagined to be his magic, Diana dodged and swung the blade again.

It sliced through Madame's hand. The demon's appendage hit the floor with a *thunk*. Shock flickered on her face, but the moment was all too brief.

"You are just as insufferable as your parents!" Madame shrieked, her fresh skin peeling away once more as her blood seeped into the wood beneath her feet.

Diana, eyes wide in surprise that she'd lopped off Madame's right hand, still didn't see her left coming. The demon's nails raked across her right eye, and Diana hit the floor. Sheturath clattered to the ground.

"I'll grind your bones to season my dinner." Madame stomped forward, gripped the front of Diana's shirt, and hoisted her into the air with her remaining hand, lifting her feet from the ground with her enhanced strength. The demon glanced at her severed hand on the ground, panic blistering across her face. "It won't grow back. What have you done to me?"

Inhaling slowly to steady himself, Sasha bent down and wrapped his fingers around Sheturath.

He squeezed the handle, eyes on Madame's back.

"It won't come back!" Madame screeched and slammed Diana on the ground. Her body collided with the wood, floorboards bursting around her shoulders in a brilliant *crack*. "I'm going to kill all of you. You have damned all your kin, little crow."

"That's fine." Diana spat blood in Madame's face. "I don't care about them anyway."

And true to form, the crow shifters stood there, eyes wide and hands trembling. Even Lead Crow, the leader of the lot, did nothing but gape like a scared fool.

Then, before Madame could respond, Diana vanished.

Just...gone.

Sasha blinked, unsure what Diana had done. It shouldn't have surprised him that she had more tricks, yet there he stood, eyes wide in confusion. If they survived this, he made a mental note to get briefed on her abilities.

"Where is she?" Madame whipped her head around, her monstrous form free of all attempts at humanity. Her leathery, gray skin, hollowed cheeks, and crimson irises always featured in all his worst nightmares. She barred her sharp teeth, all of them sharp like needles.

The sound of something heavy hitting the ground behind him caught their attention. Diana, a heap on the wooden floor, took in greedy breaths as she rolled to her feet. One of the dead crow's blades, once abandoned on the floor, was now tucked in her palm.

"I thought only the Lead Crow could perform such a feat." Madame raised her remaining hand, and the nails grew out again into five blades.

"I *am* Lead Crow of my murder." Diana smirked.

He hoped that Lead Crow, still immobilized by fear, remembered using the very same power to leave Diana behind that fateful day in her youth. He hoped the old fool remembered his cowardice, and he hoped the man choked on it.

"And I will always protect my murder, which means you've gotta die."

Madame's red eyes flickered between them. "It's just as well. It'll make this fight more interesting."

Thanks to his new eyes, Sasha saw Madame move in time to block Sheturath with her nails. His arms shook against her superior strength, and he knew he needed to come up with a plan.

Not that Diana would comply.

"You insufferable boy!" Madame pushed harder and shoved Sheturath close to his chest. Seeing himself die once was enough to make his mind look for alternatives. Fighting this way was a losing battle.

The demon growled at him. "I made you, and this is how you repay my kindness?"

In a blink, Diana appeared behind Madame. She stabbed the demon in the back with the crow's blade, the tip of the knife sticking out of her stomach.

His visions changed.

The crow's blade did nothing but enrage her. Keeping her remaining hand pressed against Sheturath, Madame threw her other arm back and smacked Diana in the face with her elbow. Her nose crunched beneath the force, and she fell to the floor. Alive but bleeding.

Madame smirked.

Catching another vision, Sasha knew they'd won.

Her nails shifted against Sheturath with the impact, sliding down the blade enough to change her balance. Sasha stepped back, and Madame's arm jerked toward the floor as he knew it would. He spun to the left, eyes on her exposed back.

Without wasting another breath, Sasha drove Sheturath between Madame's shoulder blades.

An unearthly howl rattled against the rafters as she threw her shoulders back. Sasha jerked Sheturath free, the blade coming away easy.

"I free you...and this...this is how you repay me?" Madame's voice, heavy and labored, steeled his resolve. Dark blood spilled onto the ground.

"No." Sasha gripped the handle with both hands. "You took my life from me, and now I'm taking yours."

With twenty years of hate behind his swing, Sasha drove the blade through Madame's neck, cutting from one side to the other without pause. Clean swipe.

As he held Sheturath midair and Madame remained motionless, he doubted. Had he missed?

But then she bled. Black trickled out of a fine line separating Madame's head from her neck.

Heat shot through every nerve in his body, and the hand holding the blade began to shake. Frozen, he watched the demon for what felt like years, waiting. Was she dead, or was the legacy of Sheturath a lie? Could this blade truly kill a demon?

As if Fate herself answered him, Madame's head fell to the ground and rolled, striking the boot of Charles Van Doren and leaving a bloody trail behind it.

Then the rest of her body fell. Diana yelped when Madame's torso collided with her chest. She shoved the headless corpse off, her blood leaking into her eyes from the gouges left by Madame's nails. With adrenaline-powered movements, she crawled out of the splintered of wood around her, chest heaving.

Sasha couldn't get to Diana fast enough. He dropped Sheturath on the floor by his feet and pulled her into his arms, burying his face in her hair and placing a palm to her eye. He pushed magic into the cuts and ignored the burn in his chest.

He was free.

They were alive, and he was free.

"Sasha." Diana's voice shook, but she clung to him with the same vigor as he did to her. "Sasha, look."

He pulled his face from Diana's locks and turned to Madame's body. Black billowed out of Madame's exposed neck and hung along the ceiling like a dense fog. The hair on his arms stood on end, intimately familiar with the malevolence.

But the fog slowly dissipated. Sasha crushed Diana to his chest, afraid to let her go as the evil that was Madame disappeared into the night air. It wasn't until their heartbeats slowed that he looked away from the place the last of Madame had lingered, and longer still before he bothered to check on the remaining crow shifters in the room.

However, much like the threat of Madame, the crows were gone.

Diana slumped into him, her mouth close to his throat. She wound her fingers around the holsters on his sides and leaned into him.

"I will spend the rest of my life trying to repay you for this." Sasha pressed his lips to her forehead. "If you'll let me."

She shook her head. "No."

He froze. "Then I can leave—"

"Just shut up for a second." Still heaving deep, Diana pulled away and grabbed his hand. Dried blood caked her face, but she didn't seem to mind. She only focused on him. "You've spent your whole life living for someone else. After getting the shit kicked out of me the last twenty-four hours, I won't let you make that pledge again." She smiled, and his shoulders sagged in relief. "However, if you would like to live *alongside* me, you may."

Sasha stared at her, openmouthed.

"I don't want you to leave," Diana continued, watching him pointedly. He couldn't find the wherewithal to do anything but gape like a chastened teenager. "But you've got to be honest with me. I've lived with a liar my whole life, and I'm not doing that to myself again."

He nodded slowly, mouth dry and mind swimming in possibilities. Now that he was free, there were so many of them. "I understand."

"Good." Diana pointed to her nose. "Can you fix this?"

Sasha positioned his hands on either side of her nose, sending magic into it as he did. With a push of his thumbs, it cracked.

Diana cursed and leaned into his hands. "We need to go find Nobu."

"Indeed we do." Sasha pulled her to him again and fought against the discomfort of healing. It was a miracle—simply a miracle—that they both survived. He hoped he could do right by her forever. That he could enjoy her forever. That she'd never leave him, even though she deserved so much more than he could ever hope to be. "You want me to be honest."

Diana stilled and lifted her face out of his palms. Blood still dribbled out of her nostrils, but not much. "I do."

"Then I suppose now is a good time to mention that our possession of Sheturath will put us in the cross hairs of the three remaining generals." The corner of his mouth lifted at Diana's annoyed groan. "Which means we'll be running for the rest of our lives."

A pause. "Unless we kill them."

Sasha chuckled. "Unless we kill them."

He clung to her a moment more. There had been a time where

Sasha didn't know anything but brevity. Nothing stayed long. Nothing could because he wouldn't let it. If things stayed too long, he'd remember why he didn't deserve them. If happiness lingered on the edges of his mind even a moment, he'd lose himself in what a better life could be. In a life in service to a demon, those things were deadly. Soul crushing. Useless.

But now he was free, and he had an extraordinary woman in his arms. A woman who defied every plan he'd ever made. One he could cherish and savor, and even with the threat of endless running, Sasha intended to.

EPILOGUE

DIANA

It had been a week since Sasha had beheaded Madame in her old shithole of a house, and Diana couldn't believe the complete and utter joy that had infiltrated her life in that short a time. For the first time in twenty-eight years, she woke up looking forward to the days ahead, and even with the threat of the other generals looming, she wasn't terribly sorry for it.

The joy also seemed to be spreading.

"So everything's okay?" Diana smiled at the ultrasound image pinched between her fingers. In the mix of black and white, there was a blob. A white blob with an arrow pointing to it, denoting that the blob was, indeed, a baby.

Amir grinned and pointed at the little bean. "Yes. For the first time...yes. Heart rate over one hundred and sixty. The doctor says that means it's a girl."

Diana raised her eyebrows. While skeptical, she wasn't about to rain on Amir's baby parade. "Girls are pretty cool."

"I could not agree more." Amir laughed. "I wish you'd be here to meet her."

"It's too dangerous for us to stay anywhere long." Diana frowned at the thought of Sheturath nestled in Sasha's trunk. Given the circumstances, they were leaving the country. "If we happen to slaughter all the generals before we die, I'll happily return for a visit."

"You've already killed one, and the world is better for it. *I* am better for it, and I can never thank you enough." He nudged her with an elbow. "Now it is your turn to live."

"Technically, Sasha killed Madame. I just chopped off her hand." Diana smirked and motioned to Sasha's car parked on the curb with her thumb. Unlike their last meeting several weeks ago, she had a suitcase now. A suitcase filled with clothes—not stolen ones, either—and a counterfeit passport Sasha had purchased from one of his contacts. He'd even gotten one for Nobu. "And don't worry. I intend to live, travel, and be happy."

Amir nodded across the courtyard. Sasha and Nobu sat on the other side of the fountain at another table, a deck of cards between them. Sasha had forgone the jacket and tie and settled for a button-up and khakis. His version of vacation attire, she guessed. Nobu, hair still a ridiculous mess, leaned over the table, eyes narrowed at his opponent.

"Not exactly a murder of crows, are they?" Amir raised his eyebrows and snorted when Nobu dropped one of his cards on the pavement.

"No." Diana shook her head and smiled at the scene across from them. "They aren't crows. But they're mine."

In his pursuit of honesty, Sasha told Diana everything that happened after she forced them from the airport. He told her about Natsu's true identity as a former general of Hell, the demon's sacrifice for Nobu, and the fate of Bart's pack.

Apparently, while Sasha barged into the house and shot all the crows, Natsu had given Bart a choice. If he let his grudge with her father go, Natsu would destroy the contract binding Bart's pack to him. Or if he preferred, he'd keep Bart's pack on his payroll, which would keep them from being forced into a contract with another general. Regardless, he'd never call upon them again. The Alpha had chosen to remain Natsu's servant.

This bargain had only been made possible because Sasha and Natsu made a separate deal themselves before saving her life. The price Sasha had to pay for Natsu's help was a considerable pledge, one she knew both parties had to be completely certain of before signing the dotted line.

In exchange for Natsu's help, Sasha had promised to take care of Nobu forever. Sasha said it was the easiest deal he'd ever made.

Amir grinned and looked down at her. The werewolf had told her to find a new murder in what seemed to be a lifetime ago, but she doubted this was what he had in mind. "What are you going to do now?"

"Well, we're going to Russia first. Sasha hasn't seen his mom in a long time." Diana ran her palms along her biceps, chilled despite her jacket. She'd found the one Amir had gifted her in the house. It was the only thing she took from the shack before they left her parents and dead assembly members behind for the rats.

"After that?"

"I'm not sure. This is the first time we've been free to do anything. Kind of overwhelming." Diana pursed her lips. "What about you?"

"I am going to sleep soundly. I have not truly slept since becoming Madame's agent, and I'm tired." Amir smiled again and clapped his hands. "I'm free for the first time in years, and I wish to rest. Hold Farida. Live with the peace that comes with knowing your child won't be a demon's soldier."

"That sounds like a dream." Diana kept her eyes on Sasha, heart warming at the sight of him speaking easily with Nobu.

Amir made a face, nose scrunched. "You're really okay with the kid having a demon in him?"

"Yeah." Diana shook her head. "As bizarre as it is to say, Nobu's demon isn't that bad."

"Hm."

She rolled her eyes. "That's what Sasha said too."

"This Sasha." Amir sat up on the bench and searched her face. The old wolf had been the only pleasant person she'd had for years, and it hurt that she wouldn't see him again for a while. "I can trust him with you?"

Diana nodded and, for the first time in years, felt content. "Yes. We'll take care of each other."

———————

DIANA TALKED TO AMIR FOR CLOSE TO AN HOUR WHILE SASHA met with one of Bart's pack mates. Thankful for the interference that led to the freedom of his pack, Bart volunteered one of his subordinates to smuggle all Sasha's weapons to Russia on a cargo plane. Unwilling to entrust Sheturath to a commercial airline, Sasha was happy to accept the offer.

After one last hug good-bye, Diana joined her companions at their table by the fountain. Nobu glowered at Sasha as he stood and pushed in his chair.

"He's a cheat."

"I am not a cheat. You're just easy to read." Sasha looked her over. "Are you ready?"

Diana nodded. "Are you? You haven't seen your mom in a long time."

"I am." He reached down and grabbed her hand before walking toward the car. Nobu, still scowling, followed at her side. "I didn't expect to survive this endeavor, and I put some money in a safe box I intended for my mother to run away with. We can get that when we go visit her."

"Money, huh?" Diana leaned into him as they walked. "I guess now that all three of us are unemployed, we will need some cash."

"How much?" Nobu asked, hands tucked into the pockets of his jacket.

Sasha rubbed her hand with his thumb, which sent a wave of warmth through her being. "A little over one million American dollars locked away with a revolver, a case of silver rounds, and my mother's fraudulent passport."

Nobu's jaw dropped open, and Diana couldn't help but laugh.

"You put a million dollars in a safe box?" the boy sputtered, bangs swaying in his eyes. "Isn't that illegal?"

Diana rolled her eyes. Why was he so surprised? It wasn't like everything they'd done together in pursuit of Sheturath followed the letter of the law.

"It's not illegal. It's just not recommended." Sasha shrugged. "Besides, I didn't think I'd survive the past few weeks."

Nobu still shook his head when they reached the car, baffled. "Are you sure your mom would rather see *you* than that safe box, Sokolov?"

Sasha let go of her hand and opened the passenger door with a frown. "I am unsure which she would prefer."

Nobu climbed into the back seat and settled in, but Diana found herself unable to get in the car. They were about to go to the airport to see Sasha's mother. The mother he hadn't seen for years.

Diana thought back to the mangled bodies of Charles and Amelia Van Doren. She didn't have the best track records with parents.

"What if your mom doesn't like me?" Diana dropped her gaze to the sidewalk and pulled the sleeve of her sweater over her left hand. The hand with the missing finger. She knew she shouldn't be self-conscious, yet... "I know I'm probably not what she imagined for you—"

"She asked me to find someone who reminded me that I had a heart." Sasha moved his hand from the door to her waist. She leaned into him and rested her cheek against his chest, the faintest smile on her lips. "I did."

"I think with some work, it might even shine." Diana tapped his chest and looked up, unsurprised to find Sasha's face angled close to hers. His eyes glistened.

He leaned forward, lips a breath away. So close she could feel his smile. "Perhaps."

Thank you for reading! Did you enjoy? Please add your review because nothing helps an author more and encourages readers to take a chance on a book than a review.

Also be sure to sign up for the City Owl Press newsletter to receive notice of all book releases!

And don't miss more in the The Murder series coming soon! Until then read more from Gabrielle Ash with THE FAMILY CROSS. Turn the page for a sneak peek!

SNEAK PEEK OF THE FAMILY CROSS

On my seventh birthday, my father said I was a girl worth killing for. I didn't know what he meant at the time, but my mother had because she laughed. *Really* laughed. My brothers knew too because they rolled their eyes at him. Ashby-brown eyes. The ones we all had.

My father gave me my first pair of diamond earrings after the fact. Real diamonds. They were shaped into hearts and set in gold.

"Girls worth killing for wear diamonds," he said, "and Ashby women always wear diamonds."

My mother still wore them in her casket.

A girl worth killing for.

What did that even mean?

As I stared at the phone that buzzed in my hand, the weight of that conversation nineteen years ago rushed back in an unforgiving swell because my father hadn't really been talking about my worth then. Well, not the kind that fostered confidence or healthy self-esteem at any rate. After a long, slow breath, I answered the call.

"Matilda Jane, Richard will pick you up at seven." My father's voice echoed in the phone the second I put it to my ear. Great. Richard wasn't a terrible date, but he somehow managed to make dates feel like a trip to the DMV. "Edgar is speaking tonight, so dress appropriately."

Appropriately meant a white dress, not a black one, the one I would've preferred. But he didn't care about my preferences. "Of course."

"Don't be late." He hung up, leaving the *or else* unsaid.

The sun finally disappeared behind a cloud, but the heat had nothing to do with the sweat on my palms. Between my father and the irritating range of motion of my pencil skirt, I didn't have high hopes for the rest of the morning. I stepped into a crosswalk, a sea of skyscrapers stretching ahead, and weaved through a small cluster of teens with earbuds and lattes as my father's words bit at my ankles.

Dress appropriately...don't be late...

There were a million things I needed to do. I had a meeting at ten. Another at noon. Edgar needed the preliminary report for the month at two. My hair appointment was at five. The charity event tonight required a certain level of immaculate I couldn't achieve on my own, and my stylist could crank out a French twist in minutes, provided her kids weren't with her. I'd already laid out the white dress my father wanted on the bed. That would save time. I'd have maybe five minutes to myself for a snack. If I didn't eat then, I'd never get the chance. Then Richard would show up, I'd be bored out of my mind for a few hours, and the night would end with me watching Hallmark movies alone.

Maybe not a million things to do, but things that required attention, nevertheless.

But first—coffee.

Elle's Coffee Club was a modern take on an old idea, or at least that's what it said on their window. They had their own house blend that smacked you right in the nostrils when you walked inside, and their pastries were popular around the office. At least ten emails in the three months I'd worked at the Ashby Corporation had been about crumbs and ants, and all the leftover bits of pastry had come from here.

Since it was later in the morning, the line usually found in a Manhattan coffee shop had been halved. The tile, sparkling and white, shimmered in the summer sun that filtered in through the window. There were a mixture of booths and high-top tables with olive-green cushions, all featuring a tiny bonsai in the center with a plastic advertisement for the special of the month. As much as I wanted to sit down in the air conditioning, I simply didn't have the time.

"Hi, Miss Ashby." The barista smiled when I reached the counter.

Her name was Tracy, and she helped me most mornings. Her hair was green, and she had a hoop between her nostrils. If I ever showed up to work with green hair and a nose ring, my father would kill me. Well, he'd kill me after he bleached my hair. I wouldn't be allowed to have green hair at the funeral either.

"Hey, Tracy. I'd like a caramel macchiato."

"Is that all, Miss Ashby?"

"Just Matilda." I pulled my wallet out of my purse. "And I'd like to pay for the order behind me as well."

It wasn't the first time I asked to do it, and Tracy didn't look surprised.

"What for?" a man, presumably the one I'd be buying coffee for, asked.

Tracy's gaze moved over my shoulder and prompted me to turn around. Even then, it took a second before I realized whoever she was looking at hadn't sounded happy about me buying his breakfast.

The man was tall, over six feet, but that wasn't the reason he looked out of place. The thick coat he had on, a canvas jacket like electricians wore in the winter, did that for him. Why did he have that on in this miserable heat?

"You know...to pay it forward." I turned back around and passed Tracy my credit card. A pile of scones sat on a cake dish beside the register, and I spoke before my brain could protest. "Two of those, please."

When I looked at him, he had both eyebrows raised. A dark-purple bruise stretched across his light skin from his eye to his nose.

"You expect me to buy this asshole's coffee instead?" He threw a glance over his shoulder. The man standing behind him in a gray suit and loose tie pushed his shoulders back and puffed out his chest. "I ain't doing that."

"Um..." He was being ridiculous. "You can do whatever you like."

"What can I get you, sir?" Tracy asked with a tight smile. One of the fake ones reserved for annoying clients.

"Just a regular coffee," he said as I moved to the right of the counter. "None of that weird stuff in there."

Instead of worrying about Coat Guy anymore, I took my card from Tracy and put a few dollars in the tip jar on the counter. She glanced at Coat Guy again and pulled a disposable coffee cup from a towering stack beside the register. She'd probably never heard anyone complain about free coffee before.

Coat Guy, shoulders relaxed and hands tucked into his jacket pockets, had his eyes narrowed in a way I didn't like when he took his place beside me to wait. While it wasn't mean, it was off-putting. Like he didn't trust me or the coffee I bought him.

"You didn't have to do that."

"I know." I turned back to Tracy. She handed me a coffee cup with "pay it forward" scrawled along the side. Coat Guy continued looking me up and down even as I held out his drink.

A certain amount of contact was expected when passing something to someone, but it didn't make the urge to crawl in a hole go away when the rough pads of his fingers grazed the top of my thumb. I jerked my hand back a little, and my stomach flipped. It didn't help that my first thought was to compare the roughness of his hands to the silky skin of Richard's either.

Coat Guy wasn't terrible looking, but he did need a shower. His chestnut hair was slick with sweat, and I'd bet my left Louboutin he cut it himself. The ends were too uneven and blunt for any self-respecting cosmetologist to have done.

The corner of his mouth lifted, and he pulled his hand away with his coffee, leaving my fingers empty.

"It's the scissors."

A shot of warm air hit my face as someone pushed the door to the cafe open, but the momentary distraction didn't give me the insight I hoped for.

"Pardon?"

"I don't like people with sharp objects around my neck," he said as his eyes, a deep blue like the unseen depths of the ocean, turned up. "I cut it myself."

There weren't many instances in my twenty-six years of life I could remember standing in a stupor, unable to cobble together even the faintest semblance of logic to explain the actions of another human being. People were oftentimes pretty easy to figure out, especially if you stepped outside yourself and looked at them. I might have grown up in the Upper East Side, but I still possessed a pair of eyeballs and a brain.

However, eyeballs and a brain couldn't explain how the guy could have known I was thinking about his haircut, and that said nothing about his strange aversion to barbers.

I turned my gaze to the floor. Maybe I'd been staring at him too long. Or maybe I wasn't the first person to make a face at his obvious DIY job. What'd he use to make his hair look like that anyway? Safety scissors? Kitchen shears?

"Well, I'm scared of driving, so I don't drive," I eventually said. "So I guess avoiding things you don't like makes sense."

Tracy pulled my attention away again to the scones she held out, one in each hand. The scent of warm blueberry smashed against the paper bag made my mouth water. The perfect breakfast for a day spent beneath the immaculate loafer of my father.

I sat my coffee down on the counter and took the pair of scones.

"Here." I held out one to Coat Guy.

He frowned. "I can afford my own breakfast, Fancy Pants."

A puff of air passed my lips. It wasn't the first time someone assumed I picked them like a charity case. When your outfit cost more than most people's weekly take-home pay that tended to happen.

"My intention isn't to offend you. I just want to do something nice." I continued to hold out the scone.

"Why?"

"Why not?"

He stared at me for a moment, right through the core of me like a bullet through flesh. It was unnerving to say the least. The only other person who could make me feel completely transparent was my father, and I'd known him my entire life.

His gaze flickered down to the scone and back to my face again before he relaxed his shoulders. I waited for the feeling of rough skin when he reached over to grab his breakfast, but it never came.

Coat Guy held up the scone and nodded. His way of saying thanks, I guess.

The room got loud again, like I fell out of the cafe and into a silent dome for our interactions, only to get pulled back into the world now that they were over. People skirted around me to get to the counter filled with cream and sugar packets, and the heat that blistered under my eyes didn't make me feel a whole lot better about being in their way. I picked my coffee up.

"Have a good day then."

I turned on the tile, focused on putting one foot in front of the other to get out instead of my embarrassment. My good deed had caused too much trouble, and it would be a long time before I tried to pay it forward again.

As I wrapped my fingers around the cool metal handle of the door, I heard his voice.

"Fancy Pants."

I looked at him, hovering over the threshold with one foot on the sidewalk and the other in the cafe. He stalked over, coffee in one hand and scone in the other, and pushed the glass door open, yanking the handle out of my hand.

"Take a cab," he said, arm braced against the door. The sun's rays blasting against my skin again made it all the more curious he could stand to wear a thick coat in the late summer. "Don't walk."

"Maybe I need the exercise."

"A stiff wind could blow you across Times Square, so I doubt it."

The crowd bustling outside the door started to thin out, and if I pried myself away from him quick enough, I could merge right in.

"Take a cab," he said again, voice low. So much for being quick. "See that guy on the corner? Super douche with the popped collar?"

I took a deep breath and looked over my shoulder. There was a man perched on the street corner with his shirt collar standing on end, just as Coat Guy said. He had a phone pressed to his ear and a hand in his pocket. White, early thirties maybe. Blond hair with too much pomade.

"He's following you."

My throat turned bone-dry.

"I doubt that." The weakness of my voice did an excellent job contradicting my words.

"He is."

It was one of those nightmare scenarios I had been warned about growing up. *Don't go into stairwells alone. Always pay attention.* My mother always said as a woman I had to be careful. I had to take care of myself because rich boys with trust funds never went to court.

While Popped Collar wasn't likely a rich boy with a trust fund, at least by the looks of his shoes, the warning was still applicable.

"Take a cab," Coat Guy repeated a third time, and then he pulled away from the door.

As my back foot finished its journey across the threshold, I tightened my fingers around my cup. The lid popped off and fell onto the ground, and before I could pick it up, a breeze carried it into the street. The steady thump-thump of my heart, a beat that only increased as I weaved through the crowd and to the edge of the sidewalk, drowned out the chatter and peels of rubber against asphalt. At some point, my hand had shot into the air, and even as a cab slowed to a stop in front of me, I didn't remember raising it.

"Where are you headed, miss?" the cab driver asked as I opened the door. I didn't see what he looked like because my eyes weren't on him.

They were on the blond man on the corner. Cell phone and pomade and shirt collar on end. He was staring at me too.

When he noticed I saw him, he smiled.

———

Don't stop now. Keep reading with your copy of THE FAMILY CROSS

And find more from Gabrielle Ash at www.gabrielleashauthor.com

Want even more from Gabrielle Ash? Read THE FAMILY CROSS and be sure to sign-up to receive all the news and updates at www.gabrielleashauthor.com

---

Matilda Ashby has a pair of Ivy League degrees and a dream of unseating her brother as their billionaire father's favorite. But just as she inches close to her goal, Matilda's world is rocked by monsters roaming the Manhattan streets and the elusive enemy at her father's corporation who hired them to kill her.

With assassins on the heels of her Manalos, and the family business's reputation in danger of being destroyed, Matilda hires the mysterious Samson, a telepath with a shady past, to help her find out who wants her dead.

But when the would-be assassins can take the form of anyone in her life, Matilda doesn't know who she should fear most—the monsters hiding inside her family business or the ones coming for her head.

Please sign up for the City Owl Press newsletter for chances to win special subscriber-only contests and giveaways as well as receiving information on upcoming releases and special excerpts.

All reviews are **welcome** and **appreciated**. Please consider leaving one on your favorite social media and book buying sites.

Escape Your World. Get Lost in Ours! City Owl Press at www.cityowlpress.com.

ACKNOWLEDGMENTS

Every book is different, and every book has a different journey from inception to publication. Some journeys are easier than others. Some require a lot more emotional and mental fortitude. Some are linear, and others not so much.

This book was a *break me* book. At several points in its journey, I almost gave upon it. It is thanks to several people that I will forever be grateful to that this book made it to print.

Thank you, first and foremost, to my amazing agent, Julie Gwinn. This book and I could not have gotten through this process without you, and I'm so thankful for you. You're a rock star, and I could not ask for a better partner to navigate the publishing waters with.

Thank you to Danielle DeVor, Michele Moore, and the team at City Owl Press. Danielle, you saw *For the Murder* for what it was, and you gave it life, and I'll always be thankful to you for that.

Thank you to Shauna, for reading this book and giving me honest and solid feedback. You're a great friend, and I'm so excited to see where your writing (and crafting!) takes you!

Thank you to the #QuokkaCrew, for your feedback on my query, synopsis, and opening chapters during their multiple iterations. I could not handle this industry without your friendship and guidance, and I'm so, so thankful we met. I also love your gif game, and I am honored each and every time any of you use *Schitt's Creek* gifs in support of my crow shifters!

Thank you to the Owls, for supporting me and my books. I'm proud that my books sit next to yours on my City Owl Press bookshelf.

Thank you to my family, for being there.

Thank you to my kids, who unknowingly helped me through one of the most challenging times of my life.

Thank you to my husband, Caleb, who offered unwavering support despite being a thousand miles away. I am so proud of you, and I love you with every piece of my heart.

And thank you to Stacy, to whom this book is dedicated. This book would not exist without your constant, unwavering support. I would've given up on this book, really and truly, and I hope you know that the only reason it exists is because you never gave up on it (or me). Thank you for putting up with my crap (yet again!) and I can't wait to see *Bad Girls Drink Blood* and *For the Murder* sitting side by side on my shelf!

ABOUT THE AUTHOR

GABRIELLE ASH is a perpetually tired mom of four from the great state of Texas. Born into a family of mischievous storytellers, she grew up listening to tales of the chupacabra, ghosts, and other things that go bump in the night, never entirely confident that she wouldn't get eaten if she went out to the creek after sunset.

She attended the University of Texas at Arlington and received a Bachelor of Arts in English, which ultimately landed her in a high school classroom to teach writing and coach the debate team. Dismayed at her inability to wear sweatpants to work, she left the classroom and now dedicates her brain power to books and taking care of her family.

When not writing, she spends time with her husband, four daughters, and their dog.

www.gabrielleashauthor.com

facebook.com/gabrielleashauthor

twitter.com/GabrielleAsh4

instagram.com/gabrielleashauthor

ABOUT THE PUBLISHER

City Owl Press is a cutting edge indie publishing company, bringing the world of romance and speculative fiction to discerning readers.

Escape Your World. Get Lost in Ours!

www.cityowlpress.com

 facebook.com/YourCityOwlPress

 twitter.com/cityowlpress

 instagram.com/cityowlbooks

 pinterest.com/cityowlpress

Made in the USA
Coppell, TX
29 June 2022